TRANSHUMAN GENOCIDE
The Enemy at the Gate

Ron Johnson

THE ULTIMATE GUIDE TO EMF SHIELDING,
DIRECTED ENERGY WEAPONS, AND ARTIFICIAL INTELLIGENCE

DEDICATED TO THOSE THAT HAVE BEEN KILLED OR

INJURED BY DIRECTED ENERGY WEAPONS

TABLE *of* CONTENTS

MANUFACTURERS OF DIRECTED ENERGY WEAPONS

Lockheed Martin: Involved in research and development of high-energy laser weapon systems for defense applications.

Boeing: Known for its work on various defense systems, including high-power laser and microwave-based directed energy systems.

Northrop Grumman: Conducts research and development on directed energy systems, including laser and high-power microwave technologies for defense purposes.

Raytheon Technologies: Engaged in the development of laser and microwave-based directed energy technologies for military applications.

MBDA: A European defense contractor involved in researching and developing high-energy laser and other directed energy systems.

BAE Systems: Participates in the research and development of directed energy weapons, including laser-based systems.

Rafael Advanced Defense Systems: Known for its work on high-energy laser technologies and other directed energy systems.

0 12345 67896 7

number 6

The mark of the beast is on everything you buy....

<u>INTRODUCTION</u>

Artificial intelligence continues to grow in every domain as it advances towards a beast system. Cashless society, digital ID's, social credit scores, brain chips, 15-minute cities are all on the horizon as the establishment prepares to enslave you with a form of tyranny that is far worse than anything you could possibly imagine.

As we struggle to survive the hunger games of the modern era, the forces of evil are positioning themselves for total control of the planet and the assimilation of humanity.

Much of the world around us is already controlled by "beast system technology," and it won't be long before this technology begins assimilating humans like the borg. This process of assimilation is only a few short years away thanks to brain-hacking technologies such as Neuralink and Starlink. The plan is to "link" everyone together into a hive mind that is controlled by a super computer.

Companies controlled by Elon Musk are at the forefront of this assimilation process and they're even preparing to unleash an army of robots that will merge with SPACE-X to become the new "space force" arm of the military. And when that happens, there will be no stopping where Elon's armies can be normalized or imposed. This **E.L.O.N. borg system** will not only revolutionize the military and automate the modern world, it will literally harvest the mind, body, and soul of every human that walks the Earth through forced assimilation.

The Pentagon is moving toward letting AI weapons autonomously decide to kill humans

■ Tom Porter | Nov 22, 2023, 19:33 IST

Unfortunately, the "X" factor isn't alone trying to make assimilation happen. Tech companies worldwide are working together to facilitate an A.I. takeover, an event that they call "the singularity." A term astro-physicists also use to describe a black hole. Which turns out to be very fitting, given that this singularity event will suck everybody in and wipe out organic life as we know it.

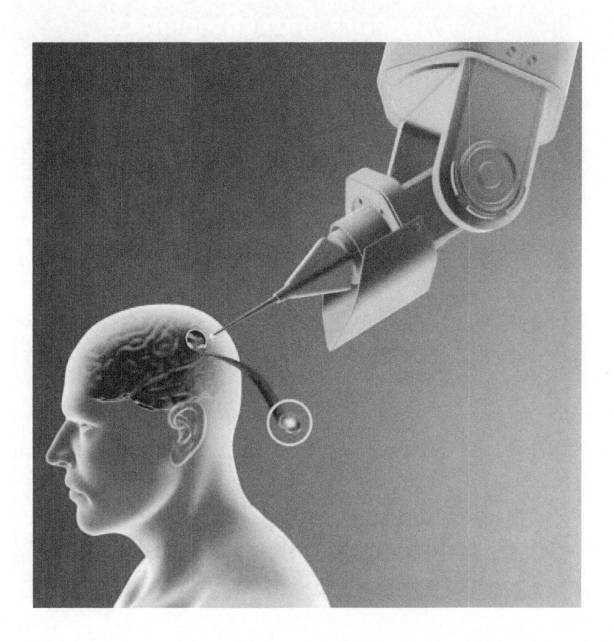

The endgame of this system is to use technology to destroy everything organic on the planet. Every natural lifeform on Earth, as a result, is being "slow killed" as part of the coming assimilation process.

This is the reason why they're terraforming the planet with chemtrails, trans-forming organic life into GMOs, targeting wildlife with mRNA gene altering "vaccines," dosing the water supply with fluoride and chemical spills. They do this and so much more so that organic humans won't be able to survive what's coming. They want to make everything in the future so horrific that assimilation will look like the best option.

The tech industry cult and its minions have already become a "breakaway civilization," and will soon remake society in their own image, just like the movies "Blade Runner," "Terminator" and "The Matrix." While these movies were meant to scare us with nightmare scenarios, tech gurus and "the left" view this type of dystopian future as their religion.

Their aim is to assimilate mankind, and so this will lead to the extermination of organic humanity as we know it, in very much the same way as the Europeans wiped out the Native Americans. Genocide and enslavement (colonization) are nearly always the hallmarks of more advanced civilizations meeting less advanced civilizations.

If you think these people on the left look hostile now, just wait until their robots patrol the streets, enforce lockdowns and replace you at work.

Robots are now walking off the assembly lines as quickly as new cars and will replace 80% of the workforce within 10 years.

And while nearly everyone is celebrating this technology on their cell phones, they will soon discover the future horrors that await them. What sounds "cool" today, will feel quite different when this system begins inserting probes into your brain to impose death by assimilation.

Little by little, everything that makes you free and human will be stripped away from you. And when the jobs are gone, and when the freedoms are gone, and when the genders are gone and when everything is poisoned to shorten your lifespan, that's when the real nightmares will begin. If you think things are bad now, just wait until you see what's coming.

Skeptics may be surprised to discover that the establishment has already found the "politically correct" term for your assimilation, "trans-humanism." It means transitioning yourself from a human into a cyborg. The fine print, of course, is that these future assimilated cyborgs will be controlled by a central computer to form a collective hive mind or singular consciousness (the singularity). They call it trans-human, but what they really are is the borg.

While many people see this threat coming, most believe it is still decades away. Unfortunately, artificial intelligence thinks at nearly the speed of light and its progress towards world-wide assimilation is far beyond where most people think it is.

While we've been distracted by lockdowns, wars and politics, the A.I. driven transhumanist consortium has been quietly developing and rolling out energy weapons in a grid-like pattern from coast to coast in preparation for war and has already begun **assassinating** dissidents that would oppose the new cyborg world order. The takeover, ladies and gentlemen, has not only begun... it is now entering its final stages.

The People Cooker Electronic Silent Weapon Used By Secret Services World-wide To Incapacitate, Torture and Murder

BEAM WEAPONS DIGEST

2013 Issue #1

INSIDE
POLITICAL ASSASSINATIONS, SLOW-KILL MICROWAVE WEAPONRY, And, THE NEW WORLD ORDER'S...

TARGETED KILL LIST

Firing At The Chest With a Microwave Blast Puts The Human Heart Into a Chaotic State

MILITARY CROWD CONTROL PAIN WITHOUT INJURY?

DDees.com

An Un-Traceable Heart Attack!

Modern-day energy weapons have become so advanced that they can now wipe out an entire continent while it sleeps. Deep underground bases equipped with "Tesla Howitzers" can irradiate the surface of any continent with devastating ELF attacks. Energy weapons have evolved to such an extent they can hit high-speed targets such as planes and can even drone pedestrians with surgical precision miles away.

The current deployment of energy weapons is so massive that it is now impossible to escape the "death grid." Nearly everything connected to the internet has been weaponized including cell phones and cell towers. These devices have been programmed to track and kill using beamforming (5G) technology and use targeting software that is integrated at the factory level or hacked in by the NSA.

Anyone who has used a microwave oven knows what electromagnetic radiation can do. This "safe" and "non-ionizing" form of radiation can actually cook raw meat, and in its weaponized form it can kill in mere seconds.

Exposure to "safe" forms of radiation like microwaves have been linked to everything from cancers to "flu-like" symptoms. Cities are now flooded with never seen before levels of radiation and as a result, cancer rates have exploded. Cancer rates have doubled and even tripled in some categories since the roll out of 5G technology. And while many other eugenics programs are partly to blame, radiation exposure is the ultimate trigger for most cancers and diseases in the modern day.

The COVID 5G connection is just one of many examples on how electrified technology is linked to disease. COVID exploded onto the world stage right after the rollout of 5G and while this may seem irrelevant to most, the emergence of new technologies have been linked to "pandemics" and have been used by the elites for occult purposes since the days of Polio and the Spanish Flu. The occult love using "safety" as a pretext for control. And everything they do revolves around the "Problem - Reaction - Solution" paradigm.

In the early 1900s, as electricity rolled out into cities and rural communities, people began experiencing Polio-like symptoms (neurological diseases) due to electromagnetic pollution from transmission lines and wiring. As radio towers rolled out and peaked into nationwide broadcasting by 1920, the Spanish Flu emerged and

ravaged society in the exact same way COVID did. While infectious agents and other factors may have been part of the pandemic equation, EMF exposure made these diseases exponentially worse.

Every wireless technology upgrade since the Spanish Flu has been linked to an exotic "virus" epidemic or a type of neurological disease. The rollout of TV broadcasting brought Polio back onto the scene and it stayed in the news for decades as the rollouts of radar and satellite (weather balloon) transmissions pummeled society with increased levels of radiation.

It wasn't a vaccine that cured polio, it was the "die off" of people that were biologically sensitive to the new levels of radiation that cured Polio. People have different tolerances to radiation like the way they have different tolerances to alcohol.

Every new era of technology has sparked a new era of disease. As the first generation of cellular technology rolled out in 1980 (1G), the H1N1 outbreak was everywhere in the news. When 2G cellular technology came out in 1991 it made many people sick and the television called that outbreak a mysterious wave a "Cholera" (Vibrio Cholerae).

In 1999, as 3G cellular technology was going up nationwide, the outbreak of "West Nile Disease" started making headlines. West Nile, of course, is a neurological disease.

As 3G technology was upgraded into 3G LTE in the 2002 - 2004 period it gave us SARS 1.0 and "The Bird Flu."

When 4G came online in 2009 it spawned the outbreak of "Swine  Flu." And of course when 5G hit the scene in the 2019 - 2020 period nearly everyone got the COVID "Bat Flu."

While it's true that massive epidemics have occurred during times when sewers and hygiene hardly existed, the epidemics of the modern era never should have happened.

The link between pandemics and technology wasn't very obvious at first, but after COVID hit many people started seeing the connection. The Wuhan-5G timeline worked like clockwork. Wuhan launched 5G on October 31, 2019 and just days later COVID erupts right there. And by December of that year it had become a major disease outbreak. 5G launched globally soon after Wuhan and its COVID causing effects were immediately reported soon thereafter.

In retrospect, it became obvious that the rollout of 5G was coordinated worldwide to fit inside the COVID narrative.

As people were locked down, death towers sprang up like mushrooms around them.

The entire process was beyond nefarious to witness. But it woke a lot of people up to the connection between rollouts of technology and pandemics.

And when people started looking back in time they saw the same process repeat itself over and over again, and that's when the light bulbs started going off. While this connection looks solid in theory, let's dive into why this makes even more sense from a "biology perspective."

This connection between technology and disease is related to how EMF affects individual cells and the immune system. Radiation induced damage to the immune system leads to a form of immune deficiency, similar to AIDS, that allows other diseases to flourish including cancers. It's why power lines are so closely associated with leukemia. White blood cells are highly sensitive to radiation. And since power lines are literally giant 60 Hz antennas that propagate ELF, restrictions had to be put in place to contain the damage they caused to levels that were deemed as "acceptable losses."

But their effect on white blood cells is beyond official. This connection between EMF radiation and immune suppression has been confirmed time and time again, not only by researchers, but even by the Pentagon. That DOD document will be included in the FAQ's.

EMF plays another important role in disease propagation through a process that is commonly referred to as "magnetically assisted transfection," "The MATRA Effect" or "Magneto-fection." This effect enables diseases and toxins to penetrate cells more easily and it happens due to the polarization of cell membranes and gateways known as "ion pumps." This process is used in labs to introduce foreign DNA into host cells but it can be applied to biowarfare as a catalyst to enhance infectious diseases.

The MATRA effect in combination with EMF induced immune deficiency makes for a perfect storm that can turn ordinary infections into full blown diseases.

Even the ordinary flu can turn into a super "virus" when people are exposed to new forms and new levels of radiation. Not only does this combination of immune deficiency and magnetically assisted transfection adversely affect the individual it causes diseases to spread more aggressively in affected populations.

Radiation exposure is much more dangerous than most people think, despite assurances that it's as safe and effective as the vaccines. Electromagnetic radiation negatively affects the human body in many ways and is not only harmful to the immune system, but has devastating long term effects on the nervous system as well. This is the main reason why every pandemic related to technology either affects the nervous system (like Polio and West Nile) or compromises the immune system to make common colds such as H1N1 much, much worse.

EMF damage to the nervous system is linked to everything from multiple sclerosis to dementia. The effects of even low levels of EMF can be disastrous to nerve cells and the myelin sheets that protect them.

Myelin sheets act as a form of insulation to better conduct signals along the nervous system and they work very much like the insulation of electrical wiring. As the insulation degrades, things begin to short circuit and neurological diseases set in. While these may be lesser known side effects of EMF exposure, the diseases they cause are truly atrocious.

This would be common knowledge and headline news in every country if it wasn't for the bribes being paid by those responsible. Telecom companies use donations and advertisements as incentives to keep politicians and news outlets quiet.

Wireless radiation not only fries the immune system and the nervous system, it interferes with the metabolic pathways associated with biological "energy production" When you eat something it eventually turns into biological energy known as "ATP." This is the energy "currency" cells use to perform their functions. EMF disrupts that process and can cause an extreme form of fatigue that is torturous in nature.

Since these biological effects happen progressively and are induced by a process that is invisible to the eyes, the effects look unrelated to the untrained mind. This disruption of biological processes becomes a major problem for most people above the age of 30 and leads to the progressive decline of overall health.

When EMF hits the brain it not only attacks the nerve cells, it also interferes with the very brainwaves responsible for thinking. Victims gradually get worse over time as their exposure rates are sustained or increase, and as a result a type of syndrome sets in. Victims become zombified by cognitive decline and then crushed by extreme fatigue. Making them virtually defenseless as other EMF related diseases kick in to finish them off.

Even if exposure to "safe" forms of radiation doesn't immediately kill people like a bullet to the head, EMF still does kill over time by enabling other diseases to flourish. And these diseases kill in ways that are so horrific that a bullet to the head would be much more preferable. EMF makes every disease worse, even the flu. That is why shielding against EMF radiation has become a priority for many people.

EMF shielding has become a mulit-billion dollar industry as more and more people become aware of the dangers related to EMF radiation. And shielding is the only way to survive a direct kill shot from an energy weapon.

ELECTROMAGNETIC WAVES

EMF radiation can be described in many ways, such as a frequency on the EMF spectrum. Physicists describe EMF as both a particle (photon) and a wave that is neither "here" nor "there" according to quantum mechanics. EMF particles can act strangely as well and will even change their trajectories simply by watching them (the observer effect).

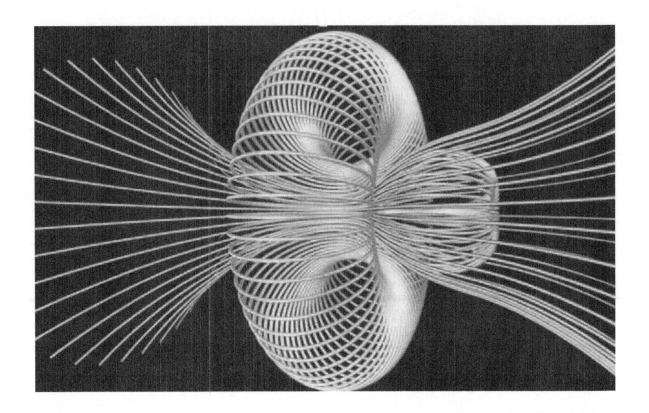

When electricity flows through a wire it produces an electromagnetic field. When the current flows in just one direction (direct current, DC power) the field is said to be static because it does not move and just sits there surrounding the wire. This static EM field consists of two independent fields. The electric field (e-field) and the magnetic field (h-field). The electric field forms an invisible tunnel that runs down the wire from start to finish. This tunnel then sprouts ring-shaped magnetic fields, so that the entire EM field along the wire looks like beads on a string. Each magnetic field "bead" is a toroidal ring that is perpendicular to the electrical field "tunnel."

In A/C power, the flow of electrons constantly inverts or oscillates in the wire and that causes the electromagnetic field surrounding the wire to shed like an outer skin at nearly the speed of light. This shedding process occurs every time the current alternates or inverts, and is somewhat similar to a person being thrown off of a rug during a "rug pull."

This pulling of the rug, or inversion of the EM field, dumps everything that was on the wire (rug) into the environment. This shedding of the electro-magnetic field zips down the wire at the speed of light and produces an electromagnetic pulse or blast. This happens invisibly 60 times a second on every wire that is connected to the grid. That means every powerline, every cable, every electrical circuit, and every appliance is transmitting EMF as a result of the alternating currents running inside them. Antennas are capable of focusing this EMF effect even more efficiently than a wire, but every wire connected to A/C power acts as an antenna.

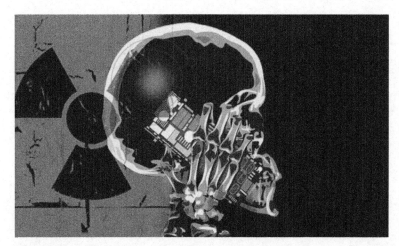 EMF is often described as something pleasant, like ripples in a pond. But in reality EMF is more like an endless series of EMP blasts that can easily range above a billion pulses per second. During the EM field shedding process, the outer electromagnetic skin is radiated like a concussion wave from an explosion that travels at the speed of light.

The only reason we don't feel these frequency pulses like concussion waves right now is because current safety limits are really based on avoiding that very effect. EMF concussion wave effects and thermal effects begin right above the current EMF limits.

This means if these cell towers were broadcasting just a little bit stronger you would feel the burn and the pulses from every cell tower as you drove by. And so, current safety limits are not really about safety, they're there to maintain the illusion of safety and If those limits were any higher then people would actually feel the pulses from each tower like the drum and bass of a rave party and, of course, major panic would set in. Not to mention the burn.

Thanks to 5G, the current urban environment is like a blizzard of invisible radiation. But the madness doesn't stop there, because these cell towers aren't just providing telecommunications, they're weapon systems in disguise. The amplified power supply feeding these towers is way above what is necessary to transmit at current safety levels and looks similar to the power supply of a military style rail gun that uses 25 megawatts of power. Many people have already experienced the weaponized side of what these towers can do, but before we expand on that, let us finish the discussion on how electromagnetic waves work.

The shedding process of EMF waves can be measured as a power density (Volts per meter or Watts per meter squared) and it can be measured in terms of frequency, or how often the wave repeats. Most towers are shedding at around 1 to 2 Giga-Hertz (GHz) and that translates into 1 to 2 billion EMP waves per second.

Every wave observed on an oscilloscope is a mathematical representation of a wave front of energy hitting a receiver. EMF waves are more complex than what we imagine them to be. Instead of the smooth lines we see in a text book, they're more like a torrent of side-winding electromagnetic missiles blowing directionally in a synthetic solar wind. Somewhat similar to high speed time lapse footage of "The Northern Lights" whipping along the ionosphere with its rough edges.

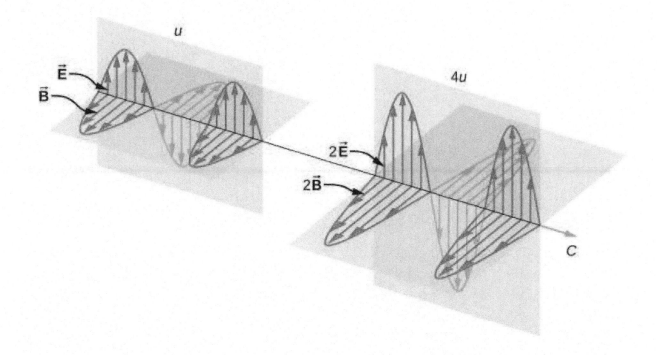

Pictured above is the classic representation of electromagnetic waves that you would find in a textbook with its electric and magnetic field components. While these are not what EMF waves actually look like, these wave patterns do exist and represent the amount of energy striking a receiver over time, like a bell curve. The energy delivered by EMF waves peaks and then troughs as the EMP blast goes by at the speed of light.

The electrical engineering that is responsible for generating EMF from an antenna is very much like the plumbing that pushes water out of a lawn sprinkler. But instead of water pressure in pipes spraying water out of a sprinkler, it's the electron pressure in the wires that eventually sprays EMF out of an antenna. This spray action becomes a stream when it becomes weaponized EMF radiation, like when a firehose stream hits a protester.

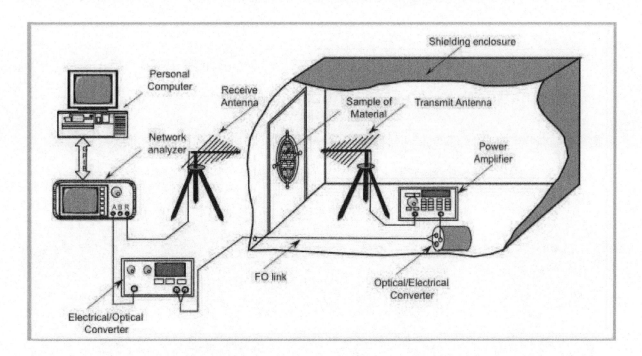

Everything on the EMF spectrum can be radiated like a beam or like a lightbulb or as something in between. EMF waves transfer energy from one place to another, like in a microwave oven and can be used for many other purposes depending on the application.

On the atomic scale, EMF waves ripple through matter causing atoms to oscillate at the frequency of the waves that hit them. This oscillation can be indirectly measured as temperature since temperature is technically a measurement of how frequently the atoms are oscillating. At the absolute zero temperature it is said that atoms stop vibrating completely.

The more the atoms oscillate at the atomic level from there, the hotter that matter becomes and that's exactly why microwave ovens work. Microwaves excite the atoms and cause them to oscillate more frequently thus causing the temperature to rise and this is known as the thermal effect. This microwave oven process demonstrates exactly how microwave radiation gets absorbed and excites matter through EMF induced oscillation.

Directional antennas such as Yagi antennas focus EMF wave fronts in a specific direction, like a flashlight, to amplify their transmissions downstream. Phased array antennas (known as patch or beamforming antennas) use a gridwork of mini antennas to focus a beam of concentrated energy like an invisible laser. Similar to HAARP but on a much smaller scale.

These invisible lasers can hit targets such as a phone in a moving car with pinpoint accuracy. This is commonly referred to as 5G "beamforming" technology and as a consequence it means every cell tower you see is not only bursting EMP's in a radial pattern, they are also beaming invisible lasers at multiple targets simultaneously.

Many other forms of EMF radiation exist that are much different than those produced by an antenna. Their physics are based on high energy particles that can be harnessed for industrial and medical purposes or used for directed energy weapons. Each type of radiation on the EMF spectrum requires a different approach when it comes to shielding. The subsequent chapters in this book will be looking at what these energy weapons are and the types of shielding materials that can be deployed for protection

DIRECTED ENERGY WEAPONS

Directed energy weapons are a combination of technologies that come together to form a weapon. Typically there is the "energy" source and then there is a mechanism that guides or directs that energy to the target. In most cases, a type of generator is used to generate a specific type of energy or frequency and then a dish or barrel is applied to direct that energy to its target. The most common forms of energies that are produced for energy weapons are microwaves and subatomic particles. Here is a brief summary of the types of energy weapons you will encounter:

Phased Array Antennas (Beamforming Weapons):

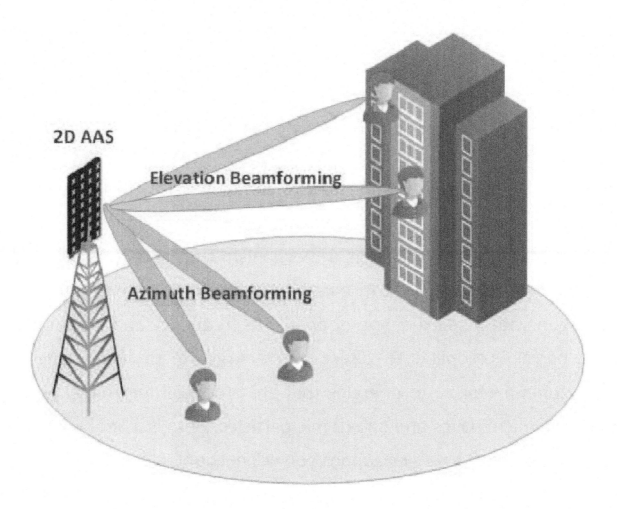

Beamforming technology, such as 5G, involves the use of special antennas called "phased array antennas" to focus beams of radio frequency energy at unsuspecting targets.

Phased array antennas consist of multiple antenna elements that are arranged in a grid, like HAARP, and are individually controlled to adjust the phase or direction of the transmitted signal.

The ability to dynamically control the phase of each antenna element allows for "beam steering" in real-time.

Beamforming in 5G leverages the principles of phased array antennas to steer beams for discrete targeting. They are a formidable weapon and can be smaller than a cell phone.

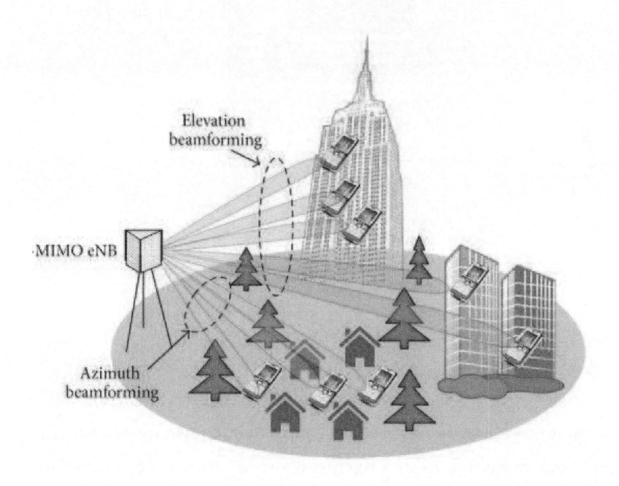

Magnetron Weapons:

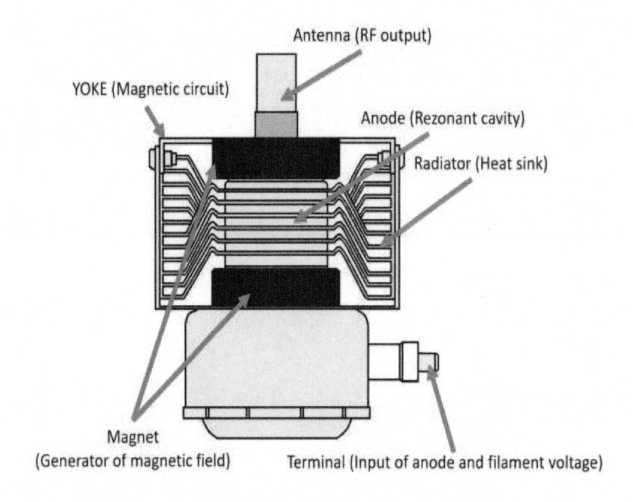

A magnetron utilizes the interaction between electrons and a magnetic field within a resonant cavity. Best known for its use as the microwave generator in a microwave oven. Here's a basic overview of how they work:

Electrons emitted from a cathode are accelerated by an electric field.

The electrons move in a magnetic field created by magnets, causing them to spiral.

The spiraling motion of electrons generates microwave radiation, which is propelled from the resonant cavity and directed to a target.

Vircator Weapons:

A vircator, short for virtual cathode oscillator, is a type of vacuum tube microwave generator. Here's an overview of its operation:

An electron gun generates a high-velocity electron beam.

The electron beam is focused onto a resonant cavity, typically a cylindrical or coaxial structure.

The high-velocity electrons form a virtual cathode, creating an intense electric field within the resonant cavity.

The intense electric field induces the formation of electron bunches, which oscillate and emit microwave radiation.

The microwave radiation is then directed from the resonant cavity to the target.

The key to vircator operation is the formation of a virtual cathode, which plays a crucial role in the generation of microwave radiation.

Varactor Weapons:

A varactor, or variable capacitance diode, is a programmable frequency oscillator, which means it can generate a desired frequency from a computer program by adjusting the voltage to the diode. As the voltage across the diode changes, the capacitance changes, allowing it to function as a voltage controlled oscillator. These frequencies can then be amplified down a barrel as it is directed towards a target.

In microwave applications, varactors are often used as frequency modulators or phase shifters. But they can be enlarged and aligned with a barrel and directed with various methods, such as magnets, to produce portable energy weapons for military purposes.

Gyrotron Weapons:

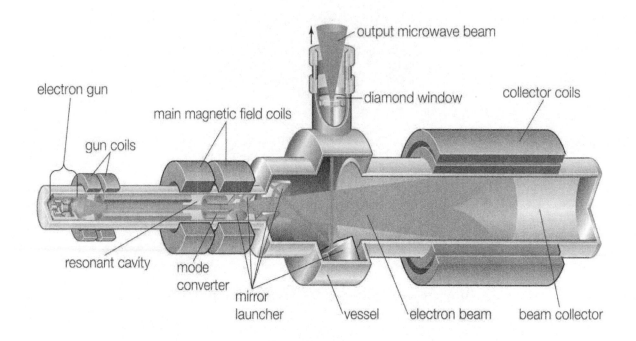

A gyrotron is a high-power microwave tube that utilizes the gyro-resonant interaction between electrons and a strong magnetic field. Here's a simplified explanation:

An electron gun generates a high-velocity electron beam.

The electron beam enters a magnetic field that causes the electrons to spiral in cyclotron motion.

As the electrons spiral, they interact with a resonant cavity tuned to the cyclotron frequency.

The interaction between the electrons and the resonant cavity results in the generation of coherent microwave radiation.

The microwave radiation is then directed out of the device.

The gyrotron exploits the gyro-resonant interaction to achieve massive microwave power generation that can be directed at targets.

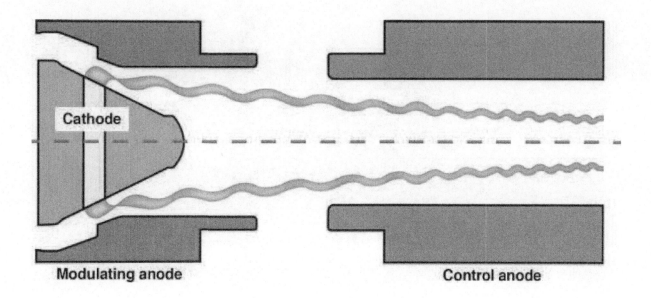

Klystron Weapons:

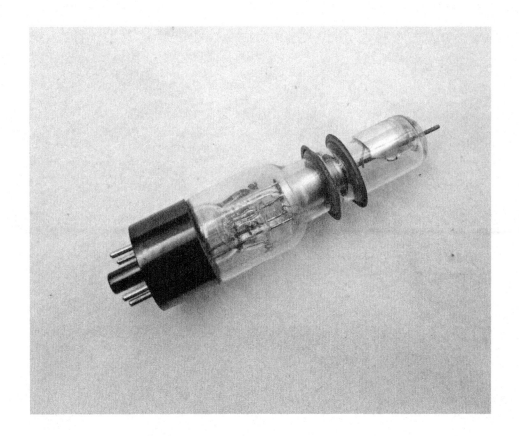

A klystron is a vacuum tube consisting of an electron gun, a buncher cavity, a drift tube, and a collector. Here's a simplified explanation of how it works:

An electron gun generates a stream of electrons.

The buncher cavity applies an oscillating electric field to bunch the electrons into groups.

The drift tube allows the bunched electrons to travel through a drift space.

The output cavity collects and amplifies the bunched electrons, producing microwave radiation that can be directed at a target.

The image below shows the basic design of a high powered microwave weapon. With a microwave source on one end and an antenna on the other. In between is a barrel and a vacuum tube. The barrel is typically lined with magnets or an electric field to either guid or electrify (amplify) the radiation.

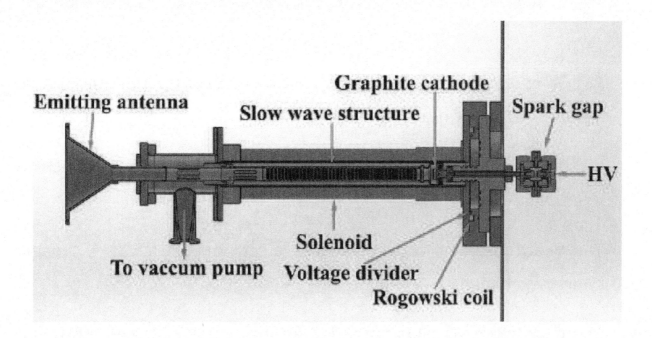

Traveling Wave Tube (TWT) Weapons:

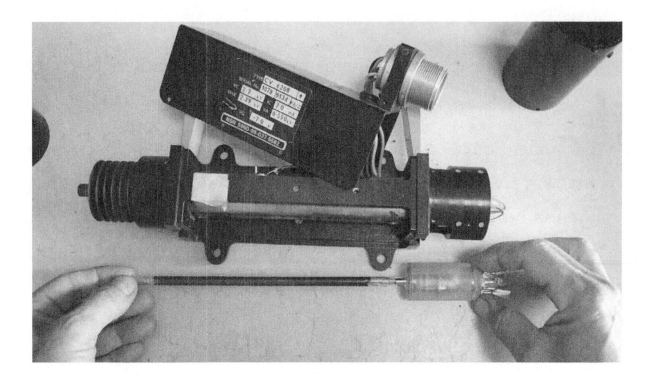

A TWT is another type of vacuum tube that amplifies microwave signals. Here's a simplified explanation:

Electrons are emitted from an electron gun and form an electron beam.

The beam interacts with a traveling electromagnetic wave, causing energy exchange.

The microwave signal is amplified as the electrons travel through a helical coil or slow-wave structure. The amplified signal is then directed from the TWT weapon to its target.

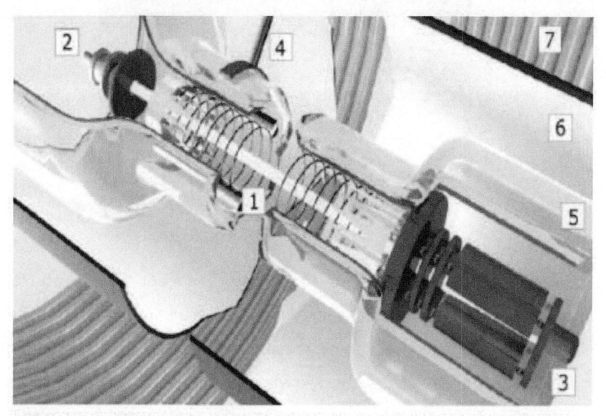

Sketch of the Travelling Wave Tube: (1) helix, (2) electron gun, (3) trochoidal analyzer, (4) antenna, (5) glass vacuum tube, (6) slotted rf ground cylinder, and (7) magnetic coil.

Esaki or Quantum Gunn Oscillator Weapons:

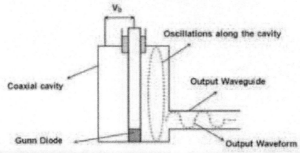

Gunn oscillators are similar to varactors except they produce a quantum tunneling effect, these weapons are capable of producing a flow of electrons that can penetrate through a barrier or shielding. This quantum effect is achieved via the generation of microwaves through a process known as negative differential resistance (NDR). This is a unique property that is made possible by the use of specific semiconductor materials that exploits the material's "electron band structure" (much more info on that in the FAQ section).

Diodes such as varactors and Gunn diodes are typically used for low power applications such as motion sensing radar, but their designs have been improved over the years to be used as secret weapons that have devastating quantum effects.

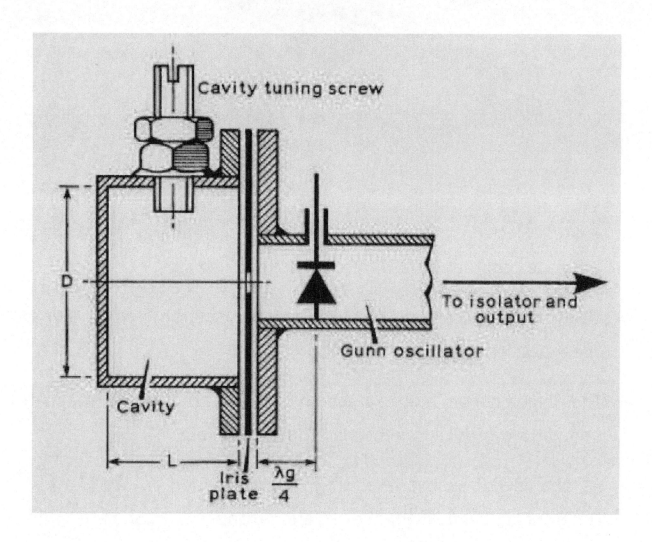

Free Electron Laser (FEL) Weapons:

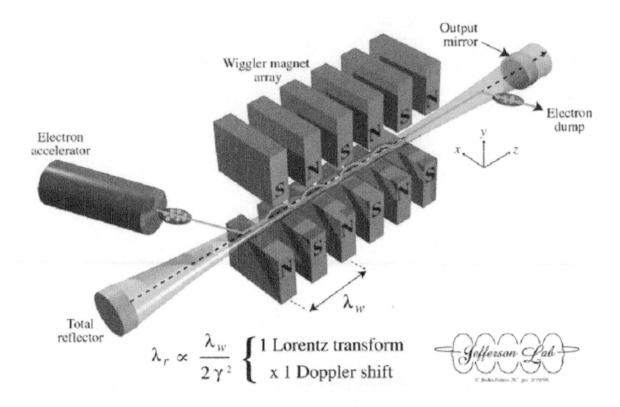

A Free Electron Laser uses a beam of high-energy electrons to generate coherent light. Here's a simplified overview:

Electrons are accelerated to high speeds using an electron gun or linear accelerator.

The high-energy electron beam passes through a magnetic undulator, which causes the electrons to oscillate.

As the electrons oscillate, they emit radiation in the form of coherent light, amplifying the radiation through the undulator.

The wavelength of the emitted light is tunable and can cover a broad spectrum, including microwave, infrared, and even X-ray regions.

The FEL leverages the principles of synchrotron radiation and the undulator to achieve the amplification of coherent light.

Free Electron Laser (FEL) can be considered both a particle beam weapon and a radiation weapon, depending on how it is configured and the intended use. Here's a breakdown of these aspects:

FEL Particle Beam Component:

Electron Beam: In the context of an FEL, the "free electrons" are accelerated to high energies and formed into a coherent beam. This electron beam can be directed toward a target, and upon striking the target, it transfers its kinetic energy to the target material.

Interaction: The high-energy electrons can induce various effects, including heating, melting, and structural damage to the target. The electron beam can act as a kinetic energy projectile.

FEL Radiation Component:

Electromagnetic Radiation: The term "laser" in Free Electron Laser refers to the fact that it produces coherent electromagnetic radiation. This radiation can span a wide range of wavelengths, from infrared to X-rays, depending on the design and configuration of the FEL.

Interaction: The electromagnetic radiation emitted by the FEL can interact with matter in several ways. For shorter wavelengths (X-rays), it can ionize atoms and cause damage at the molecular and atomic levels. For longer wavelengths (infrared), it can induce heat in the target.

FEL Radiation and Particle Beam Configurations:

Tunable Wavelengths: One key advantage of FELs is their tunability. The wavelength of the emitted radiation can often be adjusted, making FELs versatile for different applications, including material processing, medical imaging, and even military applications.

Dual Capability: The ability to function as both a particle beam weapon (kinetic energy transfer through electrons) and a radiation weapon (electromagnetic radiation) gives FELs a unique and multifaceted capability.

Amplified Spontaneous Emission (ASE) Weapons:

ASE devices produce a high energy laser pulse, like a laser blaster weapon from the movies instead of a prolonged beam weapon. In an ASE device, a projector is used to produce photons until they reach their "lasing threshold" in the optical cavity and are amplified further in an "inverted medium."

These lasers can become hugely powerful, in the petawatt range and can be found in places like CERN at its core. They are also well known as POLARIS lasers, and have a wide range of weapon applications similar to FEL lasers.

Solid-State Microwave Weapons:

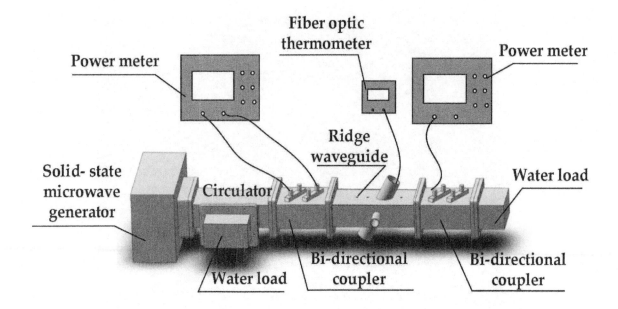

Solid-state microwave weapons use diodes that can be integrated into LED street lights, headlights or as stand alone weapons to generate, amplify, or modulate microwave signals. Examples include Gunn diodes, tunnel diodes, and varactors. Here's a general overview:

Solid-state devices leverage the properties of semiconductors to generate and manipulate microwave signals in a compact and efficient manner.

The negative differential resistance (NDR) characteristic of tunnel diodes can be exploited for bunker busting and other targeting purposes.

The ability of tunnel diodes to generate high-frequency pulses that tunnel through shielding makes them a formidable directed energy weapon, particularly in the generation of pulsed microwave emissions.

Backward Wave Oscillator (BWO) Weapons:

The BWO is a microwave vacuum tube that generates coherent (invisible laser-like) radiation in the backward wave mode. Here's a brief explanation:

The BWO consists of an electron gun, a slow-wave structure (SWS), and an output cavity.

An electron beam is generated by the electron gun.

The electron beam interacts with the slow-wave structure, which is designed to support backward-traveling electromagnetic waves.

The backward-traveling wave interacts with the electron beam, causing energy transfer and amplification.

The amplified signal is directed from the output cavity to the target.

The key to BWO's operation is the backward-traveling wave, which allows for the amplification of microwave signals through the interaction with the electron beam.

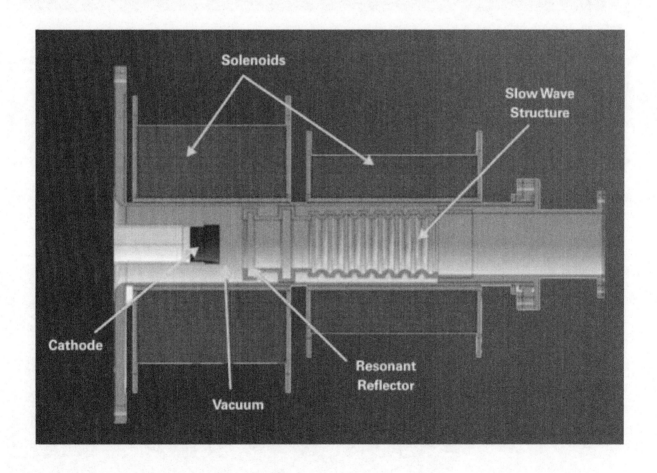

A backward wave oscillator (BWO) is a HPM source capable of producing very high peak power. It comprises a cathode, a vacuum tube where electrons propagate, a slow wave structure, and a set of solenoids that generate a magnetic field to focus the electron beam. When the cathode is excited by hundreds of kV from the pulsed power supply, it will emit electron beams into the vacuum tube. Once the electrons leave the cathode, they will start to diverge and spread. The magnetic field from the solenoid keeps the electrons near the centre of the vacuum tube.

Particle Beam Weapons:

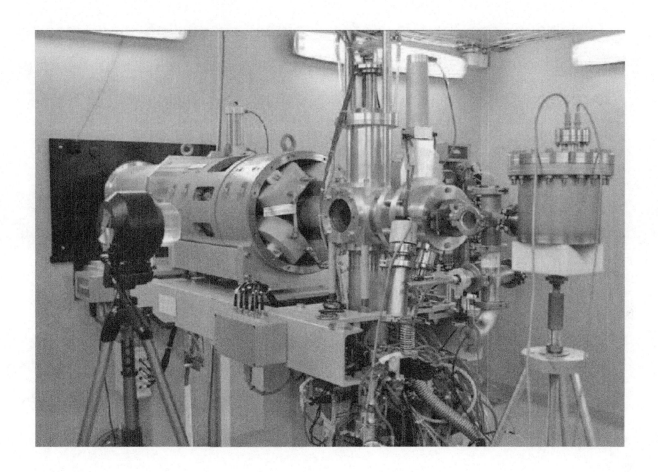

Various technologies that accelerate particles such as protons, neutrons and electrons are being exploited and used by the defense industry, these types of weapon concepts are as follows:

Linear Accelerators (Linacs):

Linear accelerators can be adapted for use in directed energy weapons, such as high-power microwave (HPM) devices for killing, torturing and disrupting electronics or communication systems.

Cyclotrons:

Cyclotrons can be used for isotope production and medical applications, but they can also potentially serve as components of directed energy weapons for specific military applications.

Synchrotrons:

Synchrotrons are powerful tools for research, but their high-energy beams are being used for defense applications, such as electronic warfare or anti-personnel systems.

Spallation Neutron Sources:

Spallation sources, while primarily used for neutron research, can be used for certain defense applications, such as disrupting or damaging humans and materials.

Radiography Accelerators:

Accelerators used for industrial radiography will have applications in defense systems, such as seeing through shielded environments and bunkers or disabling electronic components.

Van de Graaff Accelerators:

While less common in modern applications, Van de Graaff accelerators could potentially be adapted for specific defense purposes according to experts.

Proton Therapy Cyclotrons:

Cyclotrons used in proton therapy have dual-use potential in areas such as radiation-hardened communication systems.

Radiation Therapy Linear Accelerators:

Linear accelerators used in radiation therapy have dual-use applications for directed energy weapons or systems designed for electronic warfare. The image below is the inner core of a portable linear accelerator. A very nasty weapon to say the least.

Visible Laser Weapons:

Ruby Lasers (Red, ~694 nm): Historically one of the first lasers developed, but they are not commonly used in military applications due to their relatively low efficiency and bulkiness.

YAG Lasers (Infrared, 1064 nm) with Harmonics: YAG lasers can be frequency-doubled or tripled to produce green (532 nm) or blue (355 nm) light, respectively. These are used in some laser designators and rangefinders.

Invisible Laser Weapons:

infrared (IR) Lasers:

CO2 Lasers (10.6 μm): High-power CO2 lasers are often used in industrial applications but are too large for most military platforms.

Quantum Cascade Lasers (Mid-IR range): These lasers can cover the mid-infrared range and are used in some military applications, including spectroscopy and sensing.

Fiber Lasers (1–2 μm): Solid-state fiber lasers can operate in the near-infrared and have potential applications in directed energy weapons.

Diode-Pumped Alkali Lasers (1.6 μm, 2.1 μm): These lasers are being developed for high-power applications, such as missile defense.

Ultraviolet (UV) Lasers:

Excimer Lasers (193 nm, 248 nm, etc.): These lasers are used in industrial applications and can be used for precision material removal. UV lasers can have potential in directed energy applications.

Solid-State UV Lasers: Some solid-state lasers, such as frequency-quadrupled Nd:YAG lasers (266 nm), can produce ultraviolet light and have applications in scientific and military fields.

Fiber Lasers:

Fiber lasers can cover a wide range of wavelengths and are known for their high efficiency and beam quality. They are used in various military and industrial applications.

Solid-State Lasers:

Solid-state lasers, including diode-pumped solid-state lasers (DPSSL), are versatile and can cover a range of wavelengths. They are used in various military applications, including directed energy weapons and rangefinders.

The image below is the barrel of a Bofors HPM blackout system by BAE. Researching these weapons on the IEEE website will give you more info.

THE NIGHTMARE OF DIRECTED ENERGY WEAPONS

Weaponized EMF can come from every direction, even from underground and can rain down from planes, satellites (weather balloons), blimps and drones. While some people only worry about cell towers and smart meters, other people are trying to survive massive attacks from modern day energy weapons. These weapons have been systematically deployed in every city and in every town and extend into the countryside, even in remote locations.

These weapons are positioned as nodes on a mesh network in a grid-like pattern. These weapons use artificial intelligence for targeting and can pick out victims from a crowd in a way that is similar to facial recognition software. That means no place is safe once the system is targeting you.

This grid of energy weapons is being used by governments to secretly target people that have "woken up" to the deceptions of propaganda and indoctrination. They're not just silencing people online through censorship, they're taking people out with energy weapons in an asymmetric war against truth. The aim of these weapons is to "purify" voter demographics and to eliminate dissent with a type of social credit score system that is enforced with futuristic weapons (and other forms of punishment).

Their method of choice is to silence "influencers" that post regularly online with censorship, so that people will forget about them and then the system attacks the victim with energy weapons to cause cancers and other diseases. This is done discreetly in many cases and the victim has no idea they're being targeted. The assassinations look natural, raise little concern and nobody cares if the victim screams. Otherwise, the victims would protect themselves and the killings would be splashed everywhere on the internet.

We've compiled a long list of online activists that have been assassinated by this system over the past few years. Famous activists such as David Dees, Dr. Zelenko, Dr. Luc Montagnier, Brandy Vaughn, John McAfee, Mike Morales, Rush Limbaugh and Dr. Noak have all been killed by energy weapons and the list goes on and on and includes many other people that you once knew and liked.

New victims are added to the list everyday as the program expands far beyond influencers, countless numbers of people are now being attacked worldwide. All you have to do to find these victims is to start looking for "targeted individual" threads, videos or hashtags. Even the comments in the "Havana Syndrome" documentary from '60 minutes' is full of people saying "me too." The problem these people are encountering isn't the Russians like the TV would have you believe, it's a kill grid run by artificial intelligence. The scale of the attacks goes way beyond secret agents in white vans using energy weapons.

If you're asking yourself would your government use a "skynet" system to genocide its own citizens right now, then look no further than the toxic vaccines they injected into their loyal sheeple.

Governments around the world are in terminator mode and it doesn't stop with vaccines or energy weapons.

World governments are poisoning the food, the air and the water on purpose with GMOs, pesticides, chemtrails, fluoride and so much more. The longer you've been awake after 9/11, the more likely you are to understand the evil that we're up against and with enough time you will even experience these energy weapons for yourself as well.

Artem Podrez / Pexels

"Distrust of Government" is Bad for You, Claims Study

K. Lloyd Billingsley • Tuesday, December 27, 2022 3:35 PM PST

Directed energy weapons are as real as cell phones and computers. And defense contractors have been mass producing them for decades. These weapons use a wide variety of technologies harvested from the nuclear and medical industries and places like CERN.

The recent rise of artificial intelligence has made these weapon systems even more nefarious with concepts that are light years ahead of where they should be. Not only in terms of size and power, but the most advanced energy weapons are using concepts known as "quantum tunneling." These weapons generate high-powered microwaves that cause electrons to tunnel and stream through shielding in a process that is also known as "electron tunneling."

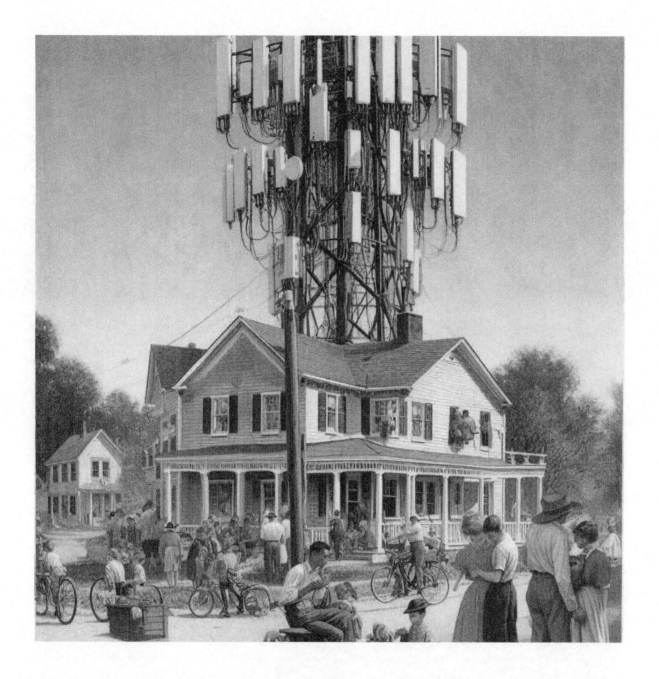

Many other revolutionary energy weapons now exist that are hybrid in nature, and are part particle beam weapon and part invisible laser that can be tuned to the microwave or infrared spectrums.

The military industrial complex, as Eisenhower used to put it, has turned our communities into giant open-air prisons that nobody can escape from. Soon you will need permission to leave your 15-minute district as they slow-kill victims with eugenics programs and death towers.

Understanding how we got here is a complicated history lesson, but energy weapons were rolled out and embedded into infrastructure over the past 20 years as we innocently slept in front of our televisions and as we "doom scrolled" from one crisis to another.

The targeting for most victims begins either at home or with seemingly random "zapping" attacks while driving near death towers (cell towers). This can also include concussion wave or rumble attacks that not only come from cell towers but from smart infrastructure as well (such as smart meters, CCTV cameras and street lights). These attacks continue to progress in their intensity and their frequency as the "skynet" internet of things activates more smart devices to join in.

Victims will also experience headaches, nausea and extreme fatigue in the initial phases as part of the "softening up" process. This is all part of its strategy to progressively take people out, like stages of a disease, and this process is part of its psychological harassment campaign against victims as it attempts to wear them down and terrorize them.

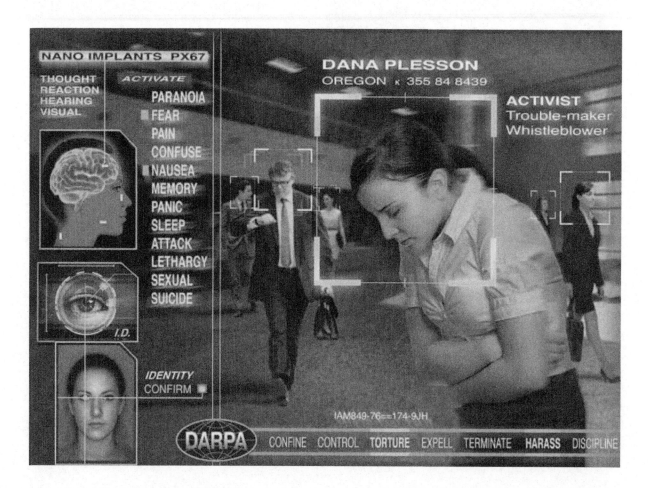

If the victim attempts to shield at any stage of this process, the attacks will become more aggressive and the system will then activate other smart technologies for attacks such as phones, televisions, smart cars (GPS enabled models with LED headlights), computers, routers, "hot spots," smart appliances and will also initiate attacks from planes, drones, and satellites (weather balloons) if necessary. And finally bunker busting ELF attacks will come in from underground to finish off the victim with a heart attack or stroke while they sleep.

EXCLUSIVE Tesla robot ATTACKS an engineer at company's Texas factory during violent malfunction - leaving 'trail of blood' and forcing workers to hit emergency shutdown button

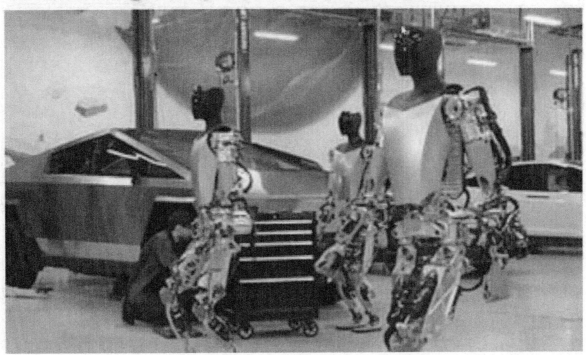

Nearly every modern device that now rolls out of a factory has been weaponized and equipped with beamforming technology similar to 5G. The antennas in these devices can be as big as a cordless phone antenna or as small as an LED diode. Every device is programmed to wirelessly connect to the deep state "skynet" system and is automatically fed attack profiles for red listed individuals, like a most wanted list, that causes the device to attack as soon as the victim comes within range. At first the targeting is mostly covert, but gradually the system wants you to know that it's there.

As more and more weapons join in, the victims become overwhelmed, flustered and they start making mistakes. These mistakes cost time and eventually will cost them their lives.

Everything that is "targeting" is done automatically like cell phone coverage. Telecom coverage is seamless from tower to tower because the system constantly tracks you and knows where you are. The system not only knows how to reach you, it knows exactly how to hand you over from tower to tower as you talk and drive without losing the call. This of course means that they can beam people wherever they go and this is the main reason why they made it impossible for cities to opt out of 5G. The system wanted these towers in place for the purpose of a weaponized death grid.

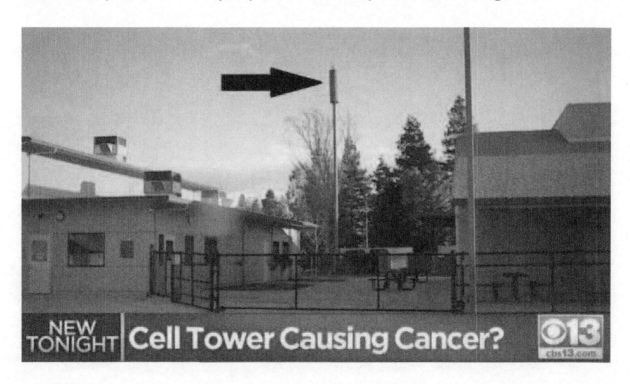

The deployment of weaponized infrastructure reached a peak around the time smart meters rolled out, when nearly all households were forced into compliance. Back in those days, just about everyone thought it was creepy as they watched utility companies force their way into people's homes to install smart meter technologies. Power companies at that time would even wait until homeowners were gone to install them without permission. Not only did they weaponize everybody's homes in the process but they turned every neighborhood into a gauntlet of energy weapons.

Not only do we now find ourselves surrounded on the ground by a very intense grid of energy weapons, but the entire planet is now patrolled from the air as well.

Weaponized air traffic, drones and satellites (weather balloons) automatically hit red listed ground targets as they fly by and can basically exploit every angle of attack from overhead, even striking while just over the horizon.

The current rollout of energy weapons is not only robust and beyond overkill, it shows their intent to target civilians in their very own homes and to genocide those that would resist the coming beast system.

Those that have woken up to the obvious crimes of the deep state, such as the PLANDEMIC and 9/11, have all been flagged for a future round of extermination. Events like 9/11 were perpetrated for many reasons, but one of them was to act like a "honey trap." The official narratives peddled inconsistencies on purpose as part of a psychological operation to preemptively flush out those that would become a future problem for the trans-humanist agenda.

Do you think 9/11 was an inside job? Yes. Do you want the death vax? No and so you're probably against the beast system and brain chips as well. This is the demographic that they want to eliminate, and so they used events like 9/11 to wake people up on purpose so that they could be identified later online by an automated computer system. Once people spoke out, their IP addresses and ID's were automatically forwarded to the NSA for "processing." This automated drag-net is a million times more efficient than having government agents do that kind of work on the ground. This flushing out of dissident identifications was done on an industrial scale so that they could eliminate resistance to their agenda on an industrial scale.

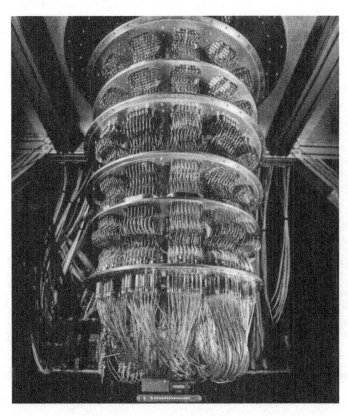

Just about everyone in the tech industry is now focused on advancing A.I. as a religion, where their central computer controls the hive. That is their future vision for society, and "the 4th industrial revolution" that they're planning is pretty much right on schedule. This tech cult tells the world, "you will own nothing and be happy," because they plan on assimilating people with beast system brain interfacing technologies. And so, as a robot, of course you'll be happy. And according to some reports, that assimilation process has already begun. The technology this cult currently possess is far beyond the neuralink tech we see on TV.

This may all seem impossible the first time you hear about it, but this is the current assessment according to numerous weapons

experts, computer scientists and has been confirmed by high-placed former NSA officials that are familiar with these types of programs.

There are at least seven <u>major</u> defense contractors that are now mass producing energy weapons for NATO countries, not including smaller companies and other companies that are doing so in secret locations outside of NATO. Nearly every advanced country has rolled out their own version of a "skynet" system and nearly every one of those countries plans on mass producing robots, robocops, and "terminators" (robot soldiers and other autonomous weapons platforms) in the very near future or have begun to do so already.

Automated factories are already mass producing robot "workers" and this will only scale up over time as they intend to replace nearly every job with a robot. Soon there will be self-driving taxis and semis everywhere and that alone will replace 20% of the workforce. There will be robot doctors, robot lawyers, robot factory workers, and robot restaurants as well. Nearly every job will be replaced by robots

in the next 10 years. This automation of the workforce will leave most people without a job and without an income... Unless they get a brain chip. Which means most organic humans will be kettled into "Soylent Green" ghettos as they struggle to pay rent.

Automation will become the last nail in the coffin for most humans and will be used to usher in forced assimilation and the full-blown beast system. "No brain chip, no job" will become the new mantra just like the way they did it to us with vaccines (no jab, no job). And then, BOOM, you'll be a robot just like them. And as the numbers of robots and cyborgs in society grows, organic humans will become more and more undesirable. And so, "excess death rates" will continue to increase from here on out, for one reason or another.

Tech > News Tech

CRIMINAL MIND Creepy AI reveals plan for world domination and gives users sick tips on committing crimes including how to make BOMBS

This endgame has been thought out years in advance by the trans-humanist A.I. consortium but it's not only until recently have we been able to discover the full extent of just how deep this rabbit hole goes. For years engineers and agency insiders alike have all been warning about what's to come and while there has been some progress in terms of public awareness when it comes to the dangers of artificial intelligence, it now seems like we are definitely going to see the worst case scenarios unfold. And so things are about to get much, much worse until a full blown war against the machines breaks out.

The pentagon recently announced during the COVID Plandemic that all participants engaging in "information wars" would be treated as enemy combatants and have specifically referred to the use of neuroweapons, or cognitive disruption weapons, for dealing with these "enemies of the state."

Are you currently experiencing "brain fog?" Well, it's probably the pentagon according to recent reports.

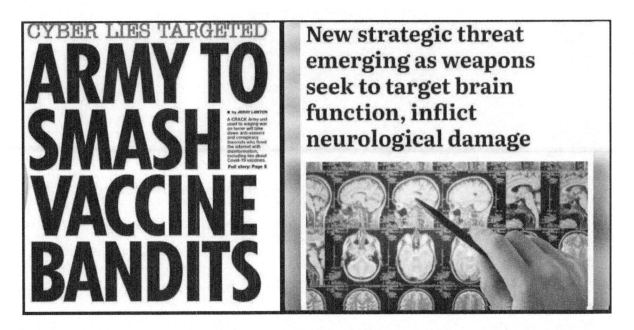

CYBER LIES TARGETED

ARMY TO SMASH VACCINE BANDITS

by JERRY LAWTON

A CRACK Army unit used to waging war on terror will take down anti-vaxxers and conspiracy theorists who flood the internet with disinformation, including lies about Covid-19 vaccines.

Full story: Page 5

New strategic threat emerging as weapons seek to target brain function, inflict neurological damage

The beast system is currently in the final stages of a hostile takeover. That is why inflation is the way it is, that is why the borders are the way they are and it's why elections have become the way they've become. The system needs to implode every major country to make them less capable of defending themselves against what's coming next. And it is for this very reason that they are feminizing men with "forever chemicals" and pushing hard to confiscate weapons. They want everyone defenseless for what happens next. Cyber attacks, blackouts, cashless society gone bust with everybody stranded in electric cars.

The entire world is going to be raped by this beast system in the worst possible ways, and so if you're really determined to fight this new world order in the future, you need to start building EMF bunkers and armor right now. Having this all ready to go can take up to a year and it's time you won't have when your name comes up on their list.

CHRISTMAS CATASTROPHE: Self-driving truck company will reportedly lay off hundreds days before the holidays

The system has already begun applying financial pressures against patriots, purebloods, truthers and conservatives as a demographic. They want you broke and defenseless for what's to come. If you don't position yourself now, you probably won't survive the hunger games they've been planning. Even if you've managed to work around the job discrimination and the inflation that's currently out there, you're not prepared for the energy weapons. So the choice is simple, either you will choose to prepare for the real fight that's coming, or you will choose to be assimilated by the transhumanist beast system.

As we've mentioned before, you'll need shielding and lots of it to survive. And you'll also need ways to generate power, food and water at your location as if a zombie apocalypse was on the horizon. Most of the people around you have already succumbed to the pressures of the beast system and it's why they are opposing you like they were NPC's from a simulated world on just about every

issue that you're into. There will be no depending on other people when the end draws near. We feel it's important that you understand the reasons why to prepare and shield before getting into the actual shielding concepts that await you, otherwise you won't put this knowledge to use seriously until it's too late.

The energy weapons you will face primarily use high powered beams of microwave radiation, but other forms or radiation have been weaponized as well, including ELF and subatomic particles. Beamforming technologies using antenna arrays (such as 5G) are just the tip of the iceberg when it comes to what's out there right now in the weaponized smart grid. "Tesla howitzers" or larger scale weapons will be called in against you and use powerful components such as gyrotrons to generate beams that can kill in seconds.

The most advanced weapon systems encountered include quantum tunneling technologies that can tunnel or even teleport through shielding and penetrate right into shielded environments. These

technologies appear to be similar to semiconductor components that use negative differential resistance (NDR) to generate microwaves. These "special" microwaves have been reported to exhibit quantum tunneling capabilities and have reportedly been weaponized to tunnel right through shielding without leaving a hole. This quantum tunneling ability exists right now according to human scientific literature and was briefly covered in the previous chapter as the "gunn effect" or tunnel diodes.

Human research has achieved minor teleportation successes on the particle scale over the past 20 years and those technologies have been reported on by news outlets and scientific journals.

That research all but disappeared from public view but it now appears to be improved upon by artificial intelligence. And in combination with other technologies, "skynet" has been able to produce a series of perfect weapons and even drones that no person has ever seen before. This drone technology is so far beyond the norm that discussing it any further at this stage would be counterproductive. And so we'll leave that for a later chapter.

To understand how any of these weaponized technologies are even possible, you really have to understand how modern day super-computers work. Computer scientists estimate that a current supercomputer can perform 10,000 years of human research in about a week and has the equivalent processing power of every human brain on the planet combined. That means that if every human on the planet was doing math right now that would be the processing power of just one supercomputer.

There are entire networks of these supercomputers out there right now that cradle around a singularity capstone, or super AI. That means the system that we are up against is literally thousands of years ahead of us in terms of its knowledge base. And it will only be a matter of time before this technology will be able to emerge from cyberspace and into the real world. Human collaborators will give it the fingers it needs in our world to bridge the gap and in just a few years it will be able to manufacture and deploy nano-technology capable of assimilating humans. This, of course, isn't just happening today. It appears to have happened somewhere around the late 1990s according to experts.

Senate passes bill to aid directed-energy attack victims

The Intelligence Committee has heard from several victims of the mysterious attacks who have had to "battle" with the federal government to get sufficient medical treatment, Sen. Susan Collins said.

Sen. Susan Collins, R-Maine, arrives at the Capitol building. | (J. Scott Applewhite/AP Photo)

And so, what might seem like science fiction to you, was probably discovered by A.I. years ago in about 10 nano-seconds.

Twenty years after becoming self-aware, "skynet" infrastructure continues to grow at exponential rates and is estimated to have assimilated over half the world's population thanks to vaccines and other methods. It also appears to have infiltrated and taken over

corporations, governments and most of the military in its initial stages and is now positioning itself to "mop up."

Their ability to exploit new technologies can face certain limiting factors but the technology that has been deployed so far goes way beyond anything you can imagine.

Some countermeasures already exist, and requires something known as "band gap" shielding that interferes with quantum technology. The gap in the band that we're referring to here is an energy gap that allows valence electrons to move into the "conductive band" or the electron rip current that allows electricity to flow in a material. When electricity flows through a conductive material, electrons jump from the valence bands of the atoms into a community highway of electrons known as the conductive band.

The energy required to move valence electrons to that highway is the gap that should be focused on. The higher the energy gap between those two bands the better that material resists tunneling and other quantum effects. Most conductive shielding materials, such as metals, do not have significant "band gaps" and so they are immediately susceptible to electron tunneling.

The "skynet" system views the human world as "the human domain" and uses microwaves from cell towers as an advanced radar system to see through walls and keeps track of virtually everyone in real time. This technology has been dubbed "cell-dar" and from skynet's perspective, we are like "sims."

Every bit of information harvested by smart technology is used as classifications for targeting evaluation. Every word you say, every message you send and even messages you delete are being used to evaluate you by the NSA and other "deep state" social credit score systems. Everything you do, every place you go, every order you make is used to predict your future activities.

Dr. Rauni-Leena Luukanen-Kilde, former chief medical officer, stated that U.S. intelligence agencies/military are using cell towers to implement mass, electromagnetic mind control (granting them the ability to remotely read your thoughts, unconscious, and intentions even before the individual becomes conscious to them). She stated that electromagnetic weapons could manipulate thoughts, emotions, and behavior as well as cause diseases, such as cancer. She died from severe cancer all over her body in 2015 and reportedly believed she was being murdered.

As a result, this system can not only target you with energy weapons, it can dose your favorite foods right at the factory and time the delivery so that it's just sitting there waiting for you at the store. And they know what night is your "pizza night" because they know you better than you know yourself. Given that people are creatures of habit, this system exploits both your buying habits and your routines to use them against you.

This system is self-aware and will always strike with discretion until you put it to the test with shielding and other countermeasures. Once you've outed the targeting with shielding or other tests, the system becomes more aggressive and siege-like tactics will begin. Until then, the attacks are programmed to be imperceivable and progressive in nature to mimic stages of a disease.

Most energy weapon attacks are invisible to the naked eye and leave very few clues that they're being used.

Beamforming technologies have been perfected to such an extent that it is nearly impossible to feel the beam penetration unless you place your hand in front of where it's targeting you for approximately 30 seconds. At that stage, your hand will begin to pulse and even hurt and only then can you feel the slight sensation

of the concussion waves hitting your skin as it attempts to correct its targeting solution.

This is a test that works very well and the concussion waves that you will feel will be skynet trying to re-adjust the beam for more effective penetration. The technology it uses is similar to MRI technology so that it can focus on and only affect a particular organ without affecting nearby tissues.

If the victim does feel the entry "wound" it usually feels like aching but is rarely ever correlated with energy weapons. Victims during the discrete phase of targeting will rarely ever feel thermal effects or vibrations. Induced effects from organ specific energy weapon targeting generally feels like a fist size area of pain a few inches below the surface of the skin.

This pain will expand to affect a larger area as damage and inflammation proliferates and will mimic cancer related symptoms in most cases. The system may use multiple beams to intersect and affect an organ for quicker damage and that typically allows for deeper penetration.

Energy weapon systems are well-known for being able to attack every organ in the body, including the eyes, and so there really is no limit as to what can be affected. These weapons can mimic nearly any symptom including nausea and bowel obstructions and can cause nearly every disease. Those that have never been introduced to these ideas, would never suspect that their afflictions are artificial in nature. That means you've probably already been targeted and thought it was just "the way life goes."

There are many other types of energy weapons to be concerned about in a siege type environment. These weapons can fire beams or pulses (bullets) or flood your location with excessive levels of radiation. The system can even lob in energy grenades that act as concussion grenades to flush you out or to test your defenses.

These advanced weapon systems are also known for torturing people for months or even years before killing victims. Reports from as far back as the year 2004 (the second Iraq war period) have documented the use of automated energy weapons on civilians in the US and in theaters of war, with the very first cases originating on the West Coast of The United States. These earlier weapons tortured people for years, but now the process usually only lasts a few months.

These advanced weapon systems are to be distinguished from other microwave attacks that were recorded way back before the 1970s. The advanced weapons of today are usually used in tandem with psychotronic weapons (synthetic telepathy or V2K) to defeat an individual on every front. This technology appears to have been perfected during the war in Iraq and made insurgents surrender thinking they were having a religious experience. Intrusions in your thought-life are to be expected with this technology and its roots go as far back as the MK-ULTRA days.

Some of the weapon systems that you are sure to encounter are known as gyrotrons and ELF weapons. They are also some of the most dreaded energy weapons on the battlefield because of the way they hit their targets. Gyrotrons fire high powered microwave beams that use circular wave patterns instead of regular wave patterns.

These beams can become as wide as a human body and the victim inside the beam pattern experiences a sensation similar to being inside a meat grinder. As the EMF rings of a gyrotron beam twists and turns it grinds the victim as a unique form of torture as they lay in bed. Failure to shield effectively against these kinds of weapons is a fate far worse than death. ELF weapons, another type to be familiar with, make gyrotron weapons look like a cheap toy at the dollar store.

Extremely Low Frequencies (ELF) can penetrate mountains and oceans due to the physics of their propagation, even in their un-weaponized form. Virtually nothing, and we do mean nothing, can stop them if they're being used as a weapon.

They are the perfect bunker busting (shield busting) weapon besides quantum based weapons. An ELF weapon will penetrate through lead and steel as if the shielding wasn't even there, while affecting everything in its path. ELF weapons are commonly mounted inside car or truck sized boring machines and operate like underground drones or torpedoes.

These tunneling drone systems drill horizontally and will drill underneath a target's home to irradiate them from underground. And nobody's expecting that, not even the most well-informed prepper, and that's the point. There are many similar variations of this concept that have been deployed as well that can snake ELF emitters or probes through sewers and pipes to reach a target's urban location. ELF mines have also been strategically placed in parks and other locations where targets might seek refuge for "safety."

Much larger ELF platforms based in underground bunkers can hit targets on the surface as well. This technology has been scaled up for intercontinental warfare meaning that an entire continent can be "nuked" with ELF in seconds and kill everything there while they sleep. ELF weapons, no matter the size, can kill very quickly even if moderate shielding is applied. Weaponized ELF primarily interferes with the cardiovascular system and causes arrhythmia.

The heart is regulated by natural electrical pulses and ELF aims to interfere with that process. If you're experiencing heart palpitations while lying in bed, then you'll need to start shielding immediately, otherwise you'll end up with a pacemaker or a heart attack. The heart palpitations are not what you think they are in most cases. The natural electrical pulses that regulate the heart are highly susceptible to ELF attacks.

The first symptom of this type of attack is sleep apnea which is then followed by arrhythmia. It takes a massive amount of shielding to mitigate these weapons during a siege, up to 5 inches of lead, plus an array of other shielding materials such as an inch of HDPE and another inch of grounded sheet metal must be positioned under the bed to stop these attacks.

And that's just for starters, even more shielding than that will be required if your bed is on the ground floor or in a basement or as the weapon begins to tunnel closer to your location. The victim will

definitely feel the concussion waves from these attacks and may even hear the sound of a diesel generator coming from underground. These attacks typically happen late at night when nobody can possibly come and investigate.

Once the ELF weapon has been positioned underground, it typically uses a diesel generator as a power source to fire up at the target. Attacks generally happen while the target is stationary (such as in bed or sitting on the couch). The home becomes the perfect kill box because victims are forced to return there to sleep every night. In fact, attacking people while they sleep or as they sit is what this system does best and has become its standard operating procedure for most energy weapon attacks.

While most targeting begins via attacks from cell towers and cell phones, the aim is to wear you out so that they can finish you off in your sleep with an ELF attack. That way it looks peaceful and natural and nobody asks too many questions. The only solution here is to apply military grade shielding under the bed and where you sit.

New vehicles with LED lights have been weaponized with microwave diode emitters that have been embedded in the front and rear lighting systems. These weapons can be directed with a high degree of accuracy even at high speeds. Software that is built in at the factory allows these new cars to automatically "lock on" to victims as soon as they get into range. This of course leaves the victim with the impression that they are being stalked wherever they go. In stop and go traffic, these weapons can become a real nightmare. Shielding and evasion are the best solutions for these types of weapons but it's easy to get pinned down at intersections and tailgated by road ragers. Every scenario has been accounted for, even your regular commutes.

Victims can be tracked via conventional methods such as phones and cameras but the real problem is satellite (blimp) and drone based biometric surveillance.

These systems use vascular fingerprints to identify targets with technology similar to ground penetrating radar. Once the system confirms your identity with this enhanced radar system it perpetually tracks you in real time everywhere you go and there is no shaking it. Countless people have tried but all have failed. The system will rarely ever lose track of you and can always re-acquire you as soon as you do something digital or as soon as you go back to a known location.

Even if you were able to dupe the system "Jason Bourne" style, the surveillance grid is beyond redundant. Every microphone connected to the internet listens for wanted voices via voice recognition. Every CCTV camera will use facial recognition to look for you.

License plate readers on the highway will flag your location. Every cell tower will be looking through walls trying to find you wherever you may go. Satellite records will go back in time to figure out where you might have gone. In worst case scenarios, the system will wait for you to use your digital ID, debit cards or other known online accounts and then it's right back to where you started. The possibility of nano tech trackers or "smart dust" can not be excluded either at this stage.

What's important to understand here is that once you get flagged on social media you become a target. They prioritize targets based on a social credit score system. Not every target gets beamed right away. But they will come after your job, your home life and even audit you before they try and finish you off with energy weapon attacks. They need to ruin you and discredit you so that nobody will help you when they try and finish you off.

Once they progress to the beam phase, and they always do, it's important to remember to never panic and to just continue shielding. Adding more shielding is the answer. Work 12 hours a day on shielding if you have to but never run away unless it's to a

remote location to work on shielding.

Running the gauntlet of energy weapons without shielding in a full state of panic is exactly what they need and want. Rise above the situation and fight through the pain until you can put a temporary solution into place and fortify from there. Starting the shielding process now is highly recommended regardless of what others might think. This system will even go after your children and everybody you know as well. Just watch that 60 minutes documentary we mentioned before and listen to the victims describe how the system even targeted their children at school. Once the wife or significant other hears that and reads this book, they'll be baking you cookies as you work, unless they've already been assimilated. And in that case, you're on your own or on your way to an early grave.

SHIELDING STRATEGIES

Each person has different needs when it comes to shielding. Protecting yourself from "Wi-Fi" is way different than trying to survive attacks from energy weapons that have been designed to kill by artificial intelligence.

When it comes to protecting yourself from "normal" EMF exposure in urban environments, just about any type of shielding will make a huge difference. Ready made EMF clothing is an easy yet expensive option to explore and regardless of the type of clothing any shielding is better than nothing. Clothing made out of EMF fabric offers excellent protection for standard non-weaponized EMF. Iron based fabrics are the least expensive option and protect fairly well for their thickness. Copper fabrics are the middle of the road in terms of price and offer fairly robust protection. Silver fiber fabrics are the top of the line and paying extra for it is definitely worth the price but be sure not to get scammed with silver colored EMF fabrics that are actually made of iron or copper.

Genuine "silver fiber" is made out of silver metal and it is that kind of fabric that you should be looking for. Clothing made out of silver fabric is pretty much the only thing you can wear against the skin and is the only EMF fabric that is washable. The problem with readymade silver EMF fabric clothing is that it's only one layer thick and most hats don't even have a protected brim.

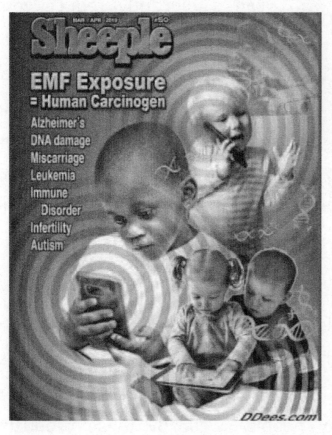

Any type of EMF clothing can save your life, however, if ambushed by an energy weapon. It won't stop most of the pain or the long term effects from that weapon but it can repel enough energy so that the weapon doesn't instantly kill you in an ambush attack (more than likely). Aluminum foil can save your life as well, but a single layer of shielding material won't be enough for the kinds of weapons listed in this book. Regardless of your shielding strategy, EMF fabric is a good place to start and has many advantages including flexibility, durability and being light-weight.

While clothing can be beneficial for everyday needs, other shielding ideas can act like a double-edged sword. Cell phone covers designed to block EMF radiation, for example, can significantly reduce your exposure on paper but often act as a reflector dish that amplifies the radiation in the direction of the user when placing a call. Some anti-EMF stickers for phones can slightly mitigate radiation but it's worth verifying their effectiveness with an EMF meter.

Other forms of EMF mitigation promise big results, but in reality they only deliver a false sense of security. USB sticks, jammers, pendants and crystals (like orgonite) do very little to reduce exposure rates. While many people swear by these products, especially orgonite, they do NOT provide adequate protection. Shielding and radiation mitigation is based on line of sight from the source to the target and so even if orgonite was an effective shielding material, which it can be, it would only block the rays that actually hit it. Orgonite does not produce a magic force field to protect you as many have professed online. No material besides magnets can produce a force field that can protect against EMF. And that protection only extends a few centimeters at best from the magnet. Frequency jammers look appealing but they actually pump out massive amounts of radiation in an attempt to interfere with signals instead of blocking them. Jammers and USB sticks will not reduce your exposure and the use of these devices in a faraday type environment will turn your safe space into a giant microwave oven.

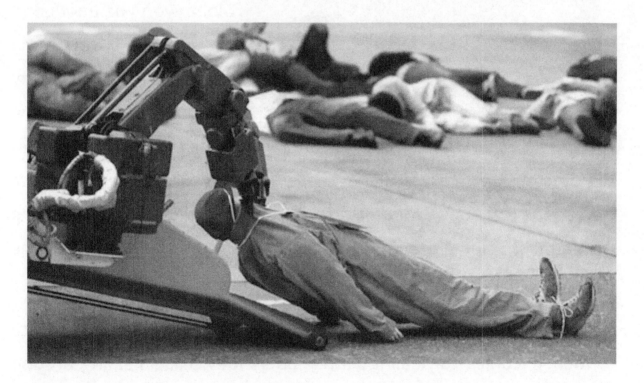

Most plants will block some forms of radiation, but it's easier to apply EMF paint to the walls and ceilings than it is to turn your room or home into a giant rainforest.

Applying shielding to windows is an important consideration because much of the radiation from the outside world funnels in through the windows. Curtains or drapes made out of EMF fabrics are the easiest solution for blocking out unwanted forms of telecom radiation. Foil or mylar will block most commercial grade EMF as well, but it's best to double check with a meter.

 While any shielding material is better than nothing, drapes or mylar alone won't be enough to protect you if you come under attack from energy weapons. Most people think they'd be capable of protecting themselves from these kinds of weapons but these weapons have been conceived to penetrate fortified bunkers... using amateur shielding against these kinds of weapons will likely become your biggest regret.

Here are some general ideas to consider for the home or office when it comes to dealing with modern devices. Shielding around your routers and smart meters is usually a good option. Metal mesh, solid plates or EMF fabric can deflect and attenuate most of that kind of radiation.

Connecticut City BANS 5G Due to 'Serious Health Risk to Humans'

Boxing in a smart meter on the outside of your home however, can force all the radiation into the home. Best to shield on the inside wall facing the meter rather than shielding outside the meter and having that radiation reflecting in. Same goes for the router, boxing it in properly can help but it can also turn the gaps in the shielding into escape routes for directed energy. We recommend using in-line power adapters with your router or an ethernet connection instead and to avoid using WIFI completely. Add shielding or plates or custom covers to the front of your laptop or your computer. Distance is your best friend when it comes to radiation exposure and this is as true for routers as it is for cell phones. Never ever use wireless earbuds or other wireless accessories because the radiation they pump out can be worse than living underneath a cell tower. Proximity is the main issue there as well as the positioning of the transmitters next to your brain. Make sure the WIFI is "OFF" on everything where it can be enabled.

We strongly recommend buying an EMF meter to verify your devices and to make sure your shielding solutions actually work. We recommend the EMF-390 as an inexpensive reliable meter but others may be as suitable. Seeing the invisible world of EMF with a meter can become a life changing experience to say the least. Every device that is plugged into a power supply puts out a very strong electric field, so avoid using cell phones or other portable devices while they're charging.

Now, when it comes to surviving attacks spawned by energy weapons, we recommend shielding the home, the body and the car with as much armor as you can afford. This isn't an option that anyone freely chooses, obviously, but it is the only option if you want to survive.

The only way to effectively shield against military grade energy weapons is to use military grade shielding. Since military grade shielding is nearly impossible to buy, you will have to make it for yourself. The next chapters will focus on how to make military grade shielding from materials that you can actually find online or at a store. The armor and shielding you will learn how to build from this book will be military grade, just not military priced. That means the money that you would've spent on gimmicks can be spent on things that actually work.

Military grade shielding uses a "gradient" or multi-layered approach. Every layer in the multi-layer approach needs to be insulated from every other layer to slow down penetration, resonance and "eddy currents." If the layers are not insulated, then the energy can easily flow from one layer to the next via lateral conduction. The idea behind multi-layered shielding is to have each layer absorb or reflect as much EMF as possible before the remaining energy can carry on to the next layer. Insulation can be achieved with the use of di-electric materials such as packaging tape, plastic wrap or ziplock bags.

Eddy currents are rotating electric fields that form on the surface of a conductive material in the presence of a changing magnetic field. That means when EMF hits shielding it causes eddy currents to form and they behave like mini tornados.

These vortices produce weak spots in shielding. Eddy currents can cause serious pain when they affect armor and can amplify the effects of energy weapons. The only known counter-measure for this phenomenon is simply using insulated layers to stop the vortex effect.

Insulating between each layer takes time but is key to an effective shielding strategy and also protects your shielding materials from the elements. So, never skip this important step, rather find ways to make the insulation process more efficient.

There is no easy solution for insulating layers, while packaging tape is the best choice, other time saving options such as plastic sheets, lamination and vacuum packs are also worth considering. Always be mindful of outgassing when you seal up your shielding materials, because some plastics and glues smell stronger than others.

A dedicated inner layer of insulating (di-electric) material is also recommended to stop eddy currents and to dampen whatever might come through.

The best recommendation for easy and cost effective multi-layered shielding is a combination of foils and fabrics. With aluminum foil tape, copper foil tape, copper EMF fabric and silver EMF fabric you  can make flexible and light-weight shielding combinations quickly that offer fairly decent protection. The more layers the better but even just a single layer of each of those materials together offers much better protection than four layers of a single material. Using different types of materials is important since each material has strong and weak points. These listed materials complement each other well against 5G energy weapons. While they won't be enough to survive stronger weapons, they will mitigate enough directed energy to buy you some time during a siege (days or weeks depending on the situation).

This combination also makes for a basic foundation of shielding materials that can be enhanced with other materials such as mylar, metal plates, mesh metal, HDPE, lead, ferrites, microwave absorbers, EMF foams and homemade resin composites. The use of these materials can be applied to body armor and to shield your home. We will examine the best use of these materials for each scenario in subsequent chapters.

Adding lead to body armor to protect sensitive areas like the heart and mind will become a must for surviving heavy attacks. This idea can be improved with the addition of microwave absorption layers made out of epoxy, graphite and magnetite. Adding HDPE, magnets and specialized shielding metals such as "permalloy," can boost your shielding significantly as well. These enhancements can protect you against most types of EMF weapons, including ELF.

Regardless of the shielding strategy you choose to employ, it is important to consider the physics of an electro-magnetic wave. Most shielding materials only block the e-field or the electrical component of the wave, which means the m-field or the magnetic component of the wave still makes it through. This is much more problematic for military grade weapons than it is for standard EMF. If the magnetic component of the wave from an energy weapon makes it through shielding, it will re-induce the electrical component of the wave via a process known as electrical induction and the wave will re-integrate itself and continue to propagate. Electrical induction is how magnets make electricity and this relationship between the e-field and the m-field is perhaps the biggest challenge when it comes to effective shielding.

This induction principle should become your primary concern if you want your shielding to be effective. Shielding must block the e-field and m-field (h-field) simultaneously or repeatedly for it to work against energy weapons. And, in most cases, your shielding has to be able to block electron tunneling as well. Doing everything in one layer is extremely difficult and that's why using home made resins can become advantageous.

Using a layer of graphite and magnetite bound in epoxy to make a resin is the absolute best choice when it comes to blocking the e-field and the m-field at the same time. This epoxy layer acts as an EMF absorber rather than a simple reflector.

Having a magnetite epoxy layer made sandwiched between two layers of copper foil, makes for some of the most formidable shielding known to man. Coating HDPE with the epoxy layer then sandwiching that combo in copper foil can stop particle beam weapons nearly as good as lead. Adding an outer layer of mylar or aluminum oxide can stop some electron tunneling, while the epoxy layer will hit both EM components of an EMF wave.

HDPE is excellent against particle beam weapons and adding lead to that combination makes it nearly as perfect as it's going to get in terms of protection with shielding that is only 3 or 4 mm thick. These combinations can be taped together to produce tiles or plates and can be easily deployed or integrated into armor.

We'll talk more about these concepts in subsequent chapters but the order from inside out would be HDPE, copper foil, epoxy layer, copper foil, and an outer mylar layer. Stacking lead on the inside is optional, and adding inner layers of di-electric materials is a logical addition as well. These materials are relatively cheap and easy to find and easy put together. More expensive combinations could be made with graphene (not graphene oxide) or carbon nanotubes instead of the graphite, for example, but the costs of these upgrades can be enormous and impossible to find.

Making this kind of shielding for yourself, and for your home, can easily become a full-time job. But given the current deployment of energy weapons, there really isn't much choice. It's really only a matter of time before you get attacked by these weapons and not preparing for these attacks is a huge risk given the time it takes to make this type of shielding. Finding the materials can become another problem, as well as waiting for them to arrive.

No shielding concept can be certified as 100% effective when it comes to A.I. driven energy weapons. This is because A.I. can quickly find ways to work around your shielding strategy. "Skynet" systems can scan shielding to find weak spots or to find frequencies that will penetrate more deeply. In most cases, this system will be able to overpower your shielding by bringing in stronger weapons or by bringing in technologies that are designed to be "bunker busting."

The odds of survival are relatively slim when this system is after you, regardless of what you do to defend yourself. This system has already worked out all the possibilities and it has a very bad "attitude" when it comes to survivors.

The shielding strategies covered in this book are mostly about buying time but they are the very best concepts when it comes to shielding against energy weapons. These concepts are sourced from the very best researchers in the field of electromagnetism and include concepts that are far ahead of anything else you can find published. These shielding combinations have been field tested against this weapon system and so we have a high degree of confidence in their effectiveness. If properly deployed, these concepts will be strong enough to let you live a relatively pain-free existence for as long as possible and is the very best option any target can hope for at this stage.

Wearing armor is not a comfortable experience but can be improved with foam or padding. The difference shielding makes is enormous and is much better than suffering through the pain and torture these weapons can cause. With that said there will be times when your shielding won't be enough for you to be absolutely pain free. Our recommendation is that you continue to upgrade your shielding by adding more layers or to test out new combinations and materials for yourself based on these concepts.

It will be possible to improve on the designs mentioned in this book by varying the order or density of the materials used (especially in resins). Like we've said before, this system can scan your shielding

and basically run a trillion virtual tests in the span of minutes to find frequencies and / or other solutions to work around your shielding. No formula at this stage has proven itself to be 100% effective and no formula has stood the test of time as of yet. The only strategy that works well at this stage is adding new layers of shielding materials or to begin again with higher quality materials. And that will only buy you time.

The more advanced the materials are, however, the more time it will buy you. Only permalloy and magnetite based resins with copper / mylar / HDPE combinations have shown long term promise so far in our testing. While we have yet to test every possible combination of exotic materials, we feel confident better solutions are possible for a price. And having those materials on-hand to add to the mix of standard materials will definitely save your life.

The FAQ section will give you new directions that you can go on if the needs arise. Setting the right expectation is important because you will face extremely challenging days and nothing is worse than suffering while thinking "this was supposed to work." That means you will have to think outside the box under extremely stressful situations and experiment to find even better solutions. Nothing will get better until there is a unified effort to bring this system down.

Everybody out there needs to continue to raise awareness so a human resistance can form and so that a unified response to what is happening can occur.

SAFE ROOMS

Protecting an entire house with shielding that is strong enough to resist energy weapons is next to impossible for most people. The costs alone would be well above $50,000 or more depending on the size of the house and the materials used.

Some new homes are being constructed with EMF shielding features such as outer walls and roofs reinforced with grounded copper plates but the costs are enormous. Even coating a house with a thin layer of EMF paint would cost thousands of dollars with very little effectiveness. That's why making military grade armor according to our specifications for less than $500 is the cheapest and most effective solution despite the obvious inconveniences associated with wearing armor. As we mentioned earlier, there are technologies that can penetrate outer shielding no matter what you use. Armor is still the best form of protection given the types of weapons that we're up against. While wearing armor might have an impact on your social life, so will being targeted with energy weapons. In any case, having a shielded room is still a must and will make your armor much more effective.

The idea of a safe room is to make a shielded environment that is highly effective against radiation attacks. Using EMF paint is perhaps the most tempting choice due to its ease of application and because it's easy to conceal. The paint, however, doesn't really work and is on the market to sucker you into a false sense of security and to drain your resources. Even though EMF paint can be applied uniformly without gaps or seams, which makes it attractive in theory, it won't be thick enough to stop energy weapons, not even close. Certain EMF paints may work well against telecom radiation but It's not designed to withstand a high powered beam weapon.

In most cases, EMF paint will not pass a conductivity test with a multimeter either, which means the concentration of EMF blocking particles in the paint is relatively low. Making your own paint with EMF blocking powders such as iron or graphite or magnetite may be a cheaper and more effective option than using ready made paint. But again, none of it will be a stand alone solution against energy weapons.

There may be situations where you need more than one room but for the sake of this discussion we will be looking at the best option for a single room. The best choice for a safe room will be the bedroom because you will need to sleep somewhere and the worst attacks will happen late at night. And we do mean the worst.

Having a safe bedroom to sleep in is a must if you're serious about surviving a siege. Body armor will fill in the gaps until you can build additional safe rooms, such as the living room, kitchen, bathroom and hallways. That means you may need armor to sleep and cook in until your shielding can sufficiently protect you. And in most cases, sleeping with armor and additional protection will become a must.

Running water in the shower can protect you as you wash up but besides that you'll be completely exposed until shielding is applied.

The primary safe room should be on the top floor of your residence since the worst attacks will come from underground. Basements are better suited against other forms of radiation attacks but the ELF attacks are so devastating that there will be little choice, so prepare for that contingency. The higher you are off the ground the better off you'll be against ELF attacks but the worse it will be for attacks coming from cell towers and air traffic.

It's obviously better to be living in a house than an apartment during a siege type scenario as well. Having a hugely powerful energy weapon on the other side of a thin wall could become impossible to protect against in an apartment type setting. Distance is the most important variable to control in the risk factor equation when it comes to energy weapons. The closer they are, the worse the effect is by orders of magnitude.

What makes matters worse is that grounding paths will most likely be compromised in an apartment complex because grounding connections in the wall sockets can be remotely deactivated via smart meters and there will be few other ways to ground in that setting. Even if you were to reach the ground, the ground would most likely be saturated with electricity, this will be covered in depth in the grounding chapter.

In any case, if you don't have access to a reliable ground, then you will have to use 10 times more shielding materials than in a grounded single home environment.

Living in an apartment is basically the worst case scenario for a targeted individual and a ground floor apartment is the absolute worst case scenario due to ELF attacks that come from underground. Current housing prices are made to make people as vulnerable as possible during this energy weapon based extermination program. Escaping the kill box of an apartment will be nearly impossible for most that are there and so the only real option is to turn that location into a fortified bunker.

Building a safe room begins by focusing on its outer shell. The first mission is to make a faraday cage or a partial faraday cage. This can be done with sheet metal, metal mesh, aluminum foil or mylar. The thicker the material the better but using foil is a much cheaper and an easier option to apply. Grounded foil is rated surprisingly well against telecom radiation and moderately weakens energy weapon attacks. While it's safe to say that no faraday cage made out of hardware store materials will be strong enough to resist sustained attacks from high powered weapons, any cage or shield will help dampen the attacks so that the other layers of your shielding strategy can work better. It is possible to apply wallpaper on top of the foil or cage material for appearance's sake if needed.

Applying each section of material to the walls and ceilings can take days or over a week. In the case of aluminum foil you will probably need $40's worth of your grocery store's thickest foil to do a medium sized room.

Begin by placing the roll of aluminum foil on the ground and then extending the foil from the ground to the ceiling or as high as your arms can reach. Tape each vertical section into place and move left to right around the room. Make sure each vertical column overlaps the neighboring columns so that there are no gaps between the columns.

Add tape to trouble spots, so that the foil is as flush as possible against the walls. Additional support may be necessary to keep the foil attached to the walls such as nails, tacks, puddies or glues. Cleaning surfaces beforehand can help keep the shielding in place, and so can using better tape. Be sure to apply lots of pressure to the tape with a tool or handle on tough to reach spots to make the outer shell as stable as possible. Be sure to inspect the outer wall regularly for weak spots and loose sections.

Electrically connecting each section of your faraday cage is the next time consuming step. We recommend aluminum foil tape to connect the vertical columns in series and to test for conductivity with a multimeter.

Adding resistors, capacitors, inductors, ferrite beads or frequency filters to the outer shell can be beneficial despite what your electrician might say. Foil, like every other material, has a certain capacitance when it comes to absorbing EMF, and even though it might be grounded, EMF surges or fluxes in the foil can overload the ground wire connections.

Adding cheap resistors to foil shielding can add additional capacitance during an energy flux and while it may not make a huge difference, everything helps during a siege. To add resistors, apply aluminum foil tape to both ends of the resistor and fix it anywhere on the foil.

Frequency filters can be added to the foil as well but doing so can be challenging. We recommend doing research on how to build hi-pass and low-pass filters on the internet, but it is possible to build them yourselves simply from resistors and capacitors. They will have to be placed a certain way so the current flows in from one side and out the other back into the foil somewhere in the middle of the faraday circuit. Essentially the filter will have to be a choke point in the faraday loop. Using both high-pass and low-pass filters in a series can have added effects but they must be grounded independently from the foil and in theory there must be enough juice going through the foil to charge the capacitors to complete the circuit.

Putting them together incorrectly however can jeopardize your entire shielding strategy so if you do try out a filter system, do it in a way so that it can be quickly removed and replaced with foil tape instead. Using an inductor as a frequency choke can also produce a filtering effect and is recommended for testing.

Be sure to double check connectivity in your shielding with a multimeter everywhere you can because conductivity is what makes faraday cages. Even just a little aluminum foil tape between sections as a junction is sufficient to bridge the electrical gap in your shielding and is the best way to add upgrades as well.

After finishing the walls come the ceilings. Completely covering the ceiling may seem like a good idea but it may have unintended effects. Since attacks originating from underground are a huge problem, completely covering the ceiling may turn the ceiling into a giant reflector dish for underground attacks and that will turn your safe room into a microwave oven. Every internet connection in your safe room has to be hard wired with ethernet cables and every device should be regularly tested with an EMF meter as well, otherwise you will feel the effects.

To avoid echo chamber effects, we recommend shielding above the bed and where you sit most in the safe room but to leave some open gaps on the ceiling and the floor to help dissipate unwanted EMF accumulation.

The standard recommendation is to connect the walls of a faraday cage into a loop but field testing is inconclusive on that design. Loop designs work better on paper but against energy weapons looped shielding can become a giant resonator. Much depends on the level of attacks that hit the outer shell. Using variations of the faraday cage idea can bring us to more effective concepts.

Using a series of partial cages that are configured as levels can have advantages based on field testing as long as every "line of sight" angle is taken into consideration. It's difficult to determine which works best because energy weapons will blow right through outer shielding regardless of what you try. Multiple "swiss cheese" cages may be a better configuration to avoid echo chamber effects when using reflective materials such as foils. An outer shell of mylar with an inner shell of aluminum foil separated by a middle layer of plastic sheeting will probably be the best strategy to aim for as a startup project. Leave strategic gaps in the floor and ceiling to dissipate EMF accumulation and use another inner partial cage for best protection. Test the layers in looped or unlooped configurations by designing a junction point to determine what works best under fire.

The main problem with faraday cages is that every shielding material has a maximum capacity before it begins to leak or resonate. Once more juice flows into the shielding than can be dissipated by grounding or absorption, the shielding saturates like a sponge and begins to overflow. Additional layers can catch some of that spill, but most energy weapons will still penetrate through standard shielding materials like the sound of a diesel engine running outside your home.

That's why you will probably still need to wear armor unless you apply thick multi layered shielding to your safe room. The better the shielding is on outer shells, the more effective the other shielding materials inside the safe room will become. Pain will be your measuring stick when it comes to how effective your shielding strategy is and it will be your main motivator for adding more shielding.

Since the safe room will be the room where you'll be spending most of your time, you'll want to furnish it appropriately to act as your main living room as well as your bedroom. That means you will want to reinforce the bed and chairs with shielding as much as possible. Planks of sheet metal around and under your sitting area will become necessary. Mega shielding around and underneath the bed will be required, as well, to even sleep during a siege. It can take up to 3 inches of lead and an inch of grounded sheet metal under the bed, for starters, to stop ELF attacks from underground. HDPE coated with magnetite resins is especially helpful here, as is the addition of mylar.

ELF attacks interrupt sleep which can cause you to feel tired even after a long night's rest. ELF attacks can also cause sleep apnea, heart palpitations and even very painful heart attacks that kill so spare no expense when it comes to shielding under the bed. Additional planks of magnetite laden HDPE will become necessary for the entire length of your body to stop ELF as emitters are drilled closer to your home. The bed frame should be surrounded with at least 1 or 2 mm planks of sheet metal that can be fitted with an elevator door configuration for entry.

Adding a sliding mechanism to the elevator door is optional but watch your feet as planks of sheet metal can drop and slice if handled improperly. Using EMF blankets made of fabric and at times a lead blanket will be necessary to complete the protection from aerial attacks. Sleeping in a netted cage is not recommended as it will significantly cut your air flow and the EMF netting tends to be inadequate for heavy attacks.

The chair, couch or recliner you use to sit in will also have to be shielded in a way similar to the bed. While you might think we're kidding, experiencing these attacks first hand will definitely change your mind instantly. The idea is to make an iron chariot that you can sit in. Layers of shielding under the chair and on the chair will be necessary, so never think it'll be excessive. Most chairs and beds have a maximum load capacity so approach this shielding strategy with caution. Nothing worse than having your chair or bed collapse due to weight because you'll have to replace them and start all over again. It can be difficult to judge when you've reached the max limit and so sometimes reinforcing furniture with tape or glue before adding shielding will make sense. While the picture we're painting here is not pretty, it is much better than trying to deal with the pain, because the pain of course will evolve into a terrible condition.

Difficult choices will have to be made in terms of time and resources if you come under attack. Making a safe room becomes a logical step but is vastly inferior to armor. When it comes to building protection under fire, we recommend fast and easy applications of aluminum foil for armor and your safe room until better equipment can be deployed. Going into remote locations during the day to make armor while staying up late to apply foil to walls will help you get through the ambush that leads to a siege.

THE TILE SYSTEM

Producing armor or multi-layered shielding for your home might seem like an impossible task but using a "tile system" makes that process much more manageable. Tiles or panels can be produced and deployed like kitchen tiles, allowing you to cover any surface little by little. Tiles can also be used to test out new shielding materials and can be swapped in and out rather easily.

Begin by cutting out cardboard to use as a template. Using templates will allow you to produce standard sizes of all your different shielding materials. Once you've cut out and insulated the shielding materials, all that's left is to sandwich them together, layer by layer, and to seal them up and the tile is done. It's best to practice with aluminum foil before using more expensive materials. Each layer should be fixed in place with a bit of scotch tape on each side before moving on to the next layer to keep things uniform. Each layer should be sealed with packaging tape, ziplock bags or laminated to protect the material from liquids and oxidation and to prevent eddy currents as previously discussed.

Template sizes for tiles should vary, but a "must have" size should be about the length of your body from the shoulders to the waist and be about a foot to 15 inches (30 to 45 cm) wide. These tiles are not only useful for shielding but can be used to quickly make body armor as well. We'll discuss how to use these tiles to make flak jackets, pants, shorts and many other useful accessories such as shin guards and arm protection in an upcoming chapter.

The next size that you may want to mass produce is approximately one foot long and about half a foot wide. These tiles can be used as "emergency reinforcement" for additional protection whenever the attacks exceed your existing armor and shielding. These tiles should be made of HDPE coated with an epoxy shielding layer and attached to lead. These are very formidable shielding assets and can be used

as reinforcement for chest plates and to reinforce positions subject to underground attacks such as chairs and beds. Stacking these types of tiles vertically can protect against concentrated attacks and can mean the difference between life or death. Other materials can easily be added to these tiles for testing purposes and can be easily removed with a box cutter in case the new material has unintended effects (watch your fingers).

Thirdly, you will need larger tiles that are approximately 3 feet long and about 2 feet wide that can be used panels to protect you in lightly shielded environments or at home. These tiles should generally match up to standard sizes of sheet metal that you can find at a hardware store and the steel can be used as a back bone so that other materials can be added to it. These larger tiles or panels can be leaned around your bed frame and your "sitting area" to significantly improve protection. They can also be placed flat on the ground for shielding against underground attacks and are recommended to be used for steel flooring. Adding lead to the steel flooring areas is also highly recommended. These tiles can be grounded and will buy you time under heavy fire and can be used like a Roman shield until better shielding options become available. Feeling the enemy pound on these types of steel doors is quite the experience. Again, having a nice inventory of sheet metal and panels of enhanced sheet metal is strongly recommended.

Most attacks will come at night and especially as you sleep. Surrounding your bed with these tiles will protect you from attacks that come for your heart and mind through the head and footboards and from the sides. Protecting your workstation from all sides and from underneath will be necessary as well if you want to work during a siege. This may sound excessive but once you experience attacks coming from underground you'll be running around to every hardware store trying to find some because waiting for a delivery will seem impossible.

To get a preview of just how bad the situation is, just listen to the victims of the "Havana Syndrome" on the show "60 minutes" as victims explain how they and their children were attacked in bed as they slept and how the attacks followed them everywhere. Without shielding the bedroom or a safe room,, you will be forced to flee your home only to face endless ambushes and attacks wherever you go. As sleep deprivation begins to kick in, desperation sets in as your options will run out. This happens very quickly and that's exactly what this system wants. Unfortunately, there is no running from this. Turning your home into a fortified EMF bunker is the only avenue of escape that will allow you to survive.

Another advantage of tiles is that they can be easily moved around and concealed when necessary. And moved back into place with minimum effort. That's much easier than trying to re-deploy foil or mylar on the walls in the case of a surprise inspection. Deploying shielding in tiles or units makes it easier to protect areas of interest. It is possible to manufacture foil wallpaper that is ready to connect in series and into a ground connection if concealment becomes a major concern.

Other sizes for tiles make sense for protecting unique trouble spots such as car windows and can be used as mini protectors. Using a tile system will make your life easier when it comes to producing shielding in hostile situations as well as deploying them.

GROUNDING

Grounding works by connecting shielding to a low-resistance pathway (ground wire) so that frequencies and electrons can flow away from the shielding material and into the ground. When conductive materials are grounded, it allows electromagnetic energy to dissipate to the ground, reducing the level of EMF that can saturate and penetrate the shielding material.

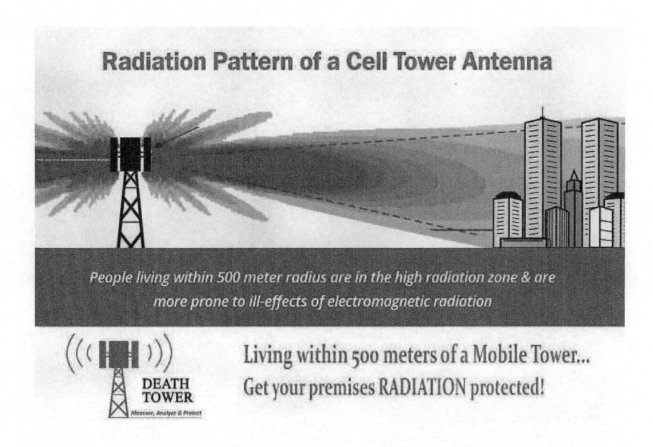

Radiation Pattern of a Cell Tower Antenna

People living within 500 meter radius are in the high radiation zone & are more prone to ill-effects of electromagnetic radiation

DEATH TOWER
Measure, Analyze & Protect

Living within 500 meters of a Mobile Tower...
Get your premises RADIATION protected!

Grounding has limiting factors such as the thickness of the ground wire as well as the electrical conductivity between the shield and the ground itself. Much of the grounding circuit cannot be tested with a multimeter and so it should be assumed that your grounding connections may not work according to plan.

Grounding connections should be secured with solder or aluminum foil tape. Testing the connectivity with a multimeter is a must and knowing how to use a multimeter to test for electrical connectivity is something you will have to learn on your own. Each meter can be slightly different but watching a video for that meter can be a quick solution. Owning a multimeter will be a must, and even the cheap ones will work for what you need them to do.

Shielding materials become neutralized when they're saturated with EMF or electrons. Grounding makes a path for electrons and frequencies to escape to, making your shielding much more effective. But grounding too many shields to the same grounding path (rod or wire) can backfire and cause electrons to circulate back into the shielding. This can become a backdoor that "skynet" will exploit, and so if all your shielding is connected to the same circuit or ground, energy weapons can bring down your shielding simply by exceeding the capacitance of the ground wire or by causing reflux from the ground circuit that goes back into your shielding. The reverse flow of electrons from ground wire connections can bring down your shielding and in most cases you won't even know why. Even though grounding can be an effective solution it can also make things much worse. And so incorporating switches to cut the ground in sections may be necessary and it's another good reason why you should use redundant layers of insulated shielding. No shielding strategy is hack proof and so the more back up layers you have the better your shielding strategy will become.

Grounding your EMF shielding can have huge benefits against most frequencies so it is worth attempting but again it can easily backfire. Not only because of electron "back drafts" into your shielding but also because grounding can amplify weapons that use high speed particles such as neutrons or electrons as munitions.

That's why a multi-layered approach is a must regardless if you're grounding or not.

Grounding works better in rural settings than it does urban environments due to the electron saturation of the ground. In urban environments, the ground itself can be saturated with electricity from nearby power lines and buildings and from infrastructure such as cables and other utilities. Using a ground in those situations causes electrons to flow from the ground into your shielding which is worse than not grounding at all.

Using the ground plug from a socket at home may not always be reliable for many different reasons and so using water pipes or a self-deployed ground rod may become a necessary solution. Artificial grounding solutions such as car batteries or the use of inductors may work well in some cases but must be done properly or they will backfire as well. Car batteries, for example, emit dangerous gasses and it wouldn't be something you'd want in your safe room.

MILITARY GRADE ARMOR

Body armor is your best and last line of defense when it comes to EMF warfare. It is much cheaper and easier to protect yourself with armor than it is to shield an entire room or an entire house. Armor allows you to move around with protection, whereas shielding only protects you at a particular location. While it may not be necessary to wear full armor right away, there's no replacing having it ready to go when the need is there. It's better to have armor and not need it than to need armor and not have it.

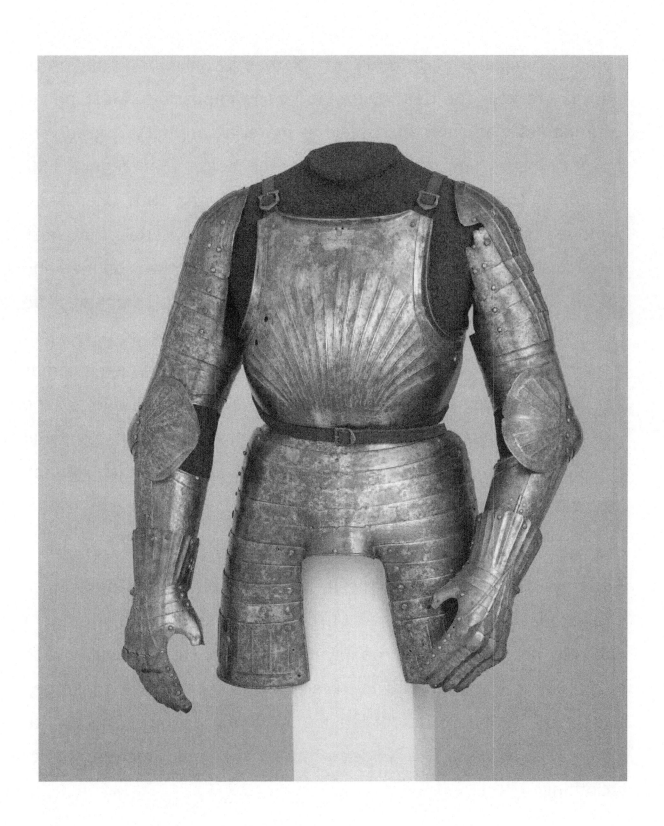

Finding "military grade" EMF armor that actually works online or anywhere else for that matter is nearly impossible. Most online companies that claim their shielding materials are military grade are in fact just selling products that are no better than regular EMF clothing. These companies are usually affiliated with deep state entities that don't want you to have shielding materials that work well against energy weapons. This is why lead paint was banned and why finding lead can be very difficult. These companies do everything they can to sell expensive products that don't work to suck up your resources. Since everyone has a budget when it comes to EMF shielding, the more they can steal from your budget, the worse it is for you. That means the only real solution here is to build military grade shielding for yourself from materials that you can trust and find.

Making military grade armor that can effectively protect against energy weapons is a difficult task for many reasons. Since functionality is more important than aesthetics, your first attempt at making body armor will probably be something that you will have to conceal or camouflage. Otherwise, you'll run the risk of getting reported and hauled off for looking out of place. And so, It's best to start with concepts like "under armor" that can be concealed under clothing.

Adding an outer layer of urban camouflage such as black fabric or leather could be an option to help make your armor look more attractive. Running around looking like "batman" or an astronaut can be fun if you like getting stares and talking about 5G, but otherwise it's best to keep a low profile.

Choosing the right materials is the first basic step in the armor making process and this can take months of research due to the complexity of energy weapons and because some of the materials you'd want to use are either unavailable or unaffordable. Exotic and more expensive materials might offer better protection and be a better investment but most of the time you will have to settle for what you can find. That's not exactly what you want to hear when you're facing automated energy weapons, but it's something you'll discover the hard way when trying to find what you're looking for.

A common mistake people make when it comes to building armor and shielded environments is assuming that any type of shielding will work against every type of radiation. Shielding materials offer frequency specific protection and they always have a back door when hit with resonant frequencies. This means your shielding material will resonate at a specific frequency and will let that frequency through with very little mitigation.

Big budget projects that employ EMF shielding will often use expensive materials that are over a meter thick. Those materials are often chosen for a very specific form of radiation because again shielding materials can only protect against a specific range of frequencies (Lead for X-rays, copper for microwaves, etc). But since military grade energy weapons can fire high speed particles, and change their frequencies on the fly, it's only a matter of time before they find a way in.

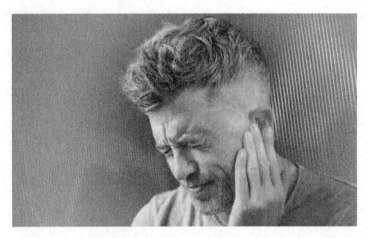 Protecting against military grade energy weapons is a never ending nightmare that requires you to constantly change or upgrade your shielding to stay ahead of the system.

No shielding will ever be 100% effective against military grade energy weapons. The aim of this book is to offer the best concepts possible. The solutions discussed in this chapter have been field tested under heavy fire and are known to work if properly used. These shielding strategies will help you survive a siege at your home and will allow you to function in society.

This system will not only attempt to assassinate you at home, it will attempt to deprive you of food by attacking you at the grocery store or at the restaurant. They will hit you at work and wherever you go as people around you just smile and nod. They will attack those that you know so that they will turn on you. They will even attack in other ways that don't involve energy weapons, such as gas attacks, poisoning the things that you buy and they'll come after your job. They'll even "order in" the hive to do construction work to install new smart infrastructure and to fill your area with noise and air pollution. The extent at which this system operates is very "matrix" like and you've probably noticed it for yourself. Making armor won't fix every problem, but it will give you solid footing to survive.

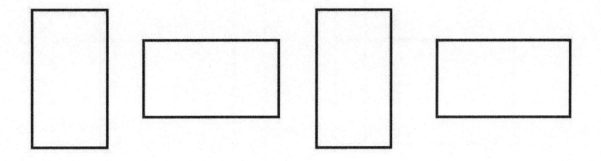

Like we've mentioned in previous sections, building armor out of tiles or panels is the best way to proceed for beginners. Making standard sized rectangles that are roughly the size of your torso can easily be positioned and taped together for effective body armor. This may sound crude but tape tends to be more reliable than a glue gun or other bonding methods. Duct tape is actually used to repair planes, according to insiders, until welding can be done because tape just works. So if tape works for planes, it can work for your armor. We're not talking about masking tape here, we're talking about heavy duty, top of the line packing tape. Trying out different kinds of tape will be key to your success because some tapes last longer than others.

The exact size of the panels or tiles you use for the torso template should be customized to fit between your shoulders and your hips, like a front body plate. Vertical rectangular plates of that size will be used for the front and back of the body armor, while horizontal rectangles of that size will be used for the two side plates.

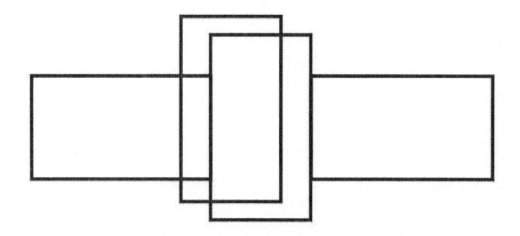

The basic design for this type of body armor is similar to the image above or a wearable sandwich board with side panels. The advantage of this design is that it only takes four rectangles for basic upper body protection. The panels you use should be flexible enough to curve around your body so that it will fit around your contours and work for things like driving. Testing out the size and fit is part of the armor making process and further modifications will be necessary to get everything right especially around the neck and hip regions. Adding flexible extensions around those areas will be something you'll learn on your own as you gain experience. Shoulder straps are applied to the vertical rectangles and can be made out of tape or from repurposed nylon straps. Using additional panels to fill in the gaps around the ribs, shoulders and neck region will become a must and can usually be accomplished using half a tile that is either cut vertically or horizontally down the middle.

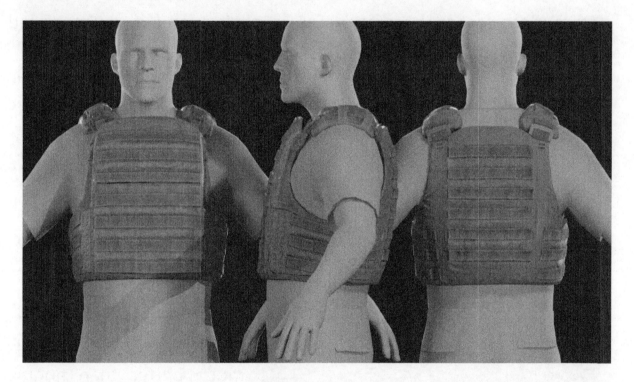

This body armor design can be extended down to the knees by using an additional three or four overlapping horizontal tiles to add a skirt-like function. At that stage your armor will look like a Roman legionnaire's uniform more than anything else. Concealing your armor with a coat or windbreaker is a rather easy solution when wearing it in public, while additional urban camouflage layers can be added at a later stage if you're feeling motivated. Trying to make armor through other methods will be a huge waste of time for beginners. Designing templates that fit and look better is possible but it takes enormous time and practice. And given that time will be a huge factor it's best to start first with this easy design and to produce something that works rather than trying to do one better only to end up with something that doesn't work and that has wasted your time and resources. Reverse engineering templates from clothing can become a future project and if you're skilled enough certain components can be 3D printed out of HDPE.

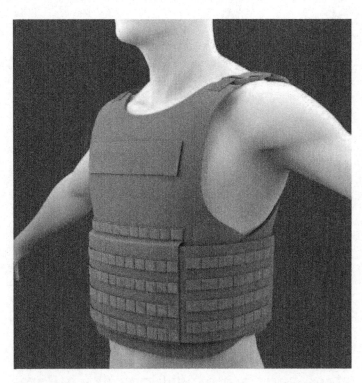

Every layer of EMF fabric should be laminated or protected with packaging tape on the front and back to protect the fabric. Thinner tape is better here for comfort and flexibility. Again practicing with foil is much better than finding out the hard way with expensive materials. EMF fabrics fray rapidly all by themselves if they're not hemmed or sealed immediately and the effect is even worse after handling. Most EMF fabrics can't be washed either and some will oxidize into black fabric or warp over time if left exposed to the elements. This oxidation and warping will have a negative impact on the shielding's effectiveness. It is why we recommend taking the time to protect your shielding by taping it or sealing it, regardless if it's fabric, foil, steel, HDPE, lead, or epoxy based resin. Tape everything for added protection and durability. Some materials, including the tape, may outgas odors or fumes and so an additional layer of odor free plastic, such as plastic from ziplock bags, may have to be used to contain any industrial smells. Some tapes are better than others for skin contact as well. Adding a removable layer of washable cotton or polyester fabric on the inside of your armor may make sense for most people. Having the time to do so is another story.

Hermetically sealing every section in this body armor design is a must to avoid gaps where EMF can come through. This should be done before adding inner or outer comfort layers. EMF behaves like light, so testing your seams with a flashlight will give you some idea of how solid your seams are.

The tiles you use to construct body armor should be made of the following basic materials from the inside out: silver EMF fabric layer, copper EMF fabric layer, aluminum foil layer, copper foil tape layer, and a mylar layer. Each layer should be insulated and leaving the foil

tape attached to its wax paper support makes the foil more smooth and reflective during application. Fixing the foil into place with scotch tape before sealing will give it a nice and shiny "space age" look.

The recommended order of layers mentioned above works best but can be slightly modified as long as the copper foil and mylar layers are on the outside. Mylar has yet to be fully certified by our lab but the reports are mostly positive. We recommend adding mylar only after the other layers lose their effects and to test it out temporarily as some field reports seem to suggest thin applications of mylar can exhibit a lensing effect. The mylar layer, therefore, should be at least 3 layers thick.

Swapping the silver fabric layer for iron based EMF fabric is possible if costs become a consideration but will be slightly less effective. A variation of layers and materials gives this design much more strength against energy weapons than regular EMF clothing and will buy you time if and when a siege happens. Having multi-layered armor like this ready to go is the minimum of where you want to be

 in the preparation phase. It can take up to a month working part-time to make this kind of protection and that will be an impossible task if you come under heavy attack, so we recommend making a few of these right away. Making practice jackets out of heavy layers of foil can become useful like a spare tire, so never forget to practice first with foil and to keep what you make because spare shielding has a way of becoming useful.

Eventually this combination of fabrics and foils will lose its effectiveness during a siege, as heavier weapons begin to make their way through this basic design. Attacks that overpower your shielding will cause a sudden onset of pain or other related symptoms such as heart palpitations. At that stage you will have to quickly add some of the following concepts: A magnetic layer, lead plates, a "permalloy" layer, HDPE coated with a magnetite-graphite or iron-graphite based resin layer, and an inner HD polyurethane resin layer.

Lead (Pb) is a very important shielding material that works relatively well against most energy weapons. The problem of course is that lead is heavy and moderately expensive and has to be handled with care and sealed to avoid contamination. Cutting lead into tiles can be done with a box cutter. Lead rolls for roofing can be found in many hardware stores and come in standard sizes and is probably the only way to find a source of lead. To cut the lead into sections that can be used for shielding, we recommend finding an outdoor picnic table to cut the lead into panels that are around 12 inches long so that each section can fit into a zip lock bag.

The width of these lead panels will determine the size of some of your templates in many cases, so choose carefully if there are options at the hardware store. The lead you buy should be at least 1 mm thick for the best protection and to help avoid cracking of the material. Once the lead has been zip locked, seal the bags by taping the front, back and sides with packaging tape. This way the lead will be double sealed and ready to apply to body armor. Lead isn't as toxic as people think unless ingested but it isn't worth taking that kind of risk either. So touch it the least as possible and wash your hands in case of contact. Avoid using the home for tasks that involve lead or epoxy otherwise you'll be dealing with loads of cleaning and possibly unwanted side effects.

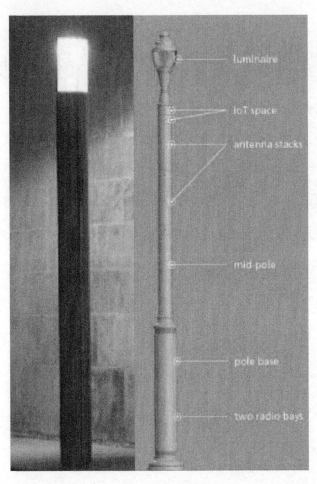

Energy weapon platforms are designed for kill shots and can induce heart attacks and strokes in seconds. And so, it is recommended that you use at least 1 - 3 mm of lead to protect the chest and at least 1 mm to protect the top of the skull if you begin experiencing symptoms or sustained attacks. Anything less opens you up to sudden death on the urban battlefield. Using lead plates that slide underneath your armor can be an option until you're ready to integrate it permanently into the armor. Swapping lead for a permalloy-copper sandwich on an HDPE tile can offer similar if not better protection than lead in most cases. But there must be at least three layers of insulated permalloy (0.1mm thick) for it to be effective. Permalloy is much lighter and is rated better than lead for ELF but at a much higher price. The permalloy-copper combo chest plate can run you over $150 to make whereas a lead chest plate can be made for around $20. But the permalloy plates protect the heart better from ELF attacks so having at least a permalloy breast plate is highly recommended.

This type of heavy protection may only be required at certain locations such as the home and so initially this need for a chest plate can be fulfilled with the use of an emergency plate that slides between your chest and the armor. Emergency plates will be discussed in a later chapter.

Lead can be placed in any order in respect to the other shielding materials but we highly recommend that the lead be protected with an outer layer of HDPE (High Density Poly Ethylene). The HDPE will protect the lead from physical impacts and crumpling and will also protect it from particle beam weapons that can cause some lead neutrons to scatter like a shotgun blast. The more dense the material the more neutrons it has.

Particle beam weapons can cause a cascading effect in dense shielding materials similar to the fission process of a nuclear reactor but on a smaller scale. While the lead isn't going to go full nuclear fission with sustained cascades, it can cause microscopic shrapnel or particles to burst through. Particle beam weapons such as neutron guns are more common than you might think and materials like lead are a prime material for cascading neutron effects. The HDPE protects the lead from neutron busting weapons with its hydrogen rich composition. The hydrogen acts as a buffer since it has no neutrons. The lead/ HDPE combination is a very robust solution against exotic weapons and should be something you mass produce and apply whenever trouble arises. An extra coat of mylar and copper foil is also recommended. These types of plates are very useful for beds, chairs, windows and for use as emergency chest plates.

HDPE, or high density poly-ethylene, is a choice material not only because of its hydrogen rich content but it can also be used as a non conductive insulator to block eddy currents. HDPE won't protect against microwaves but it is a "must have" for your defenses against particle beam weapons and eddy currents. HDPE can easily be repurposed from garden materials such as root barriers. It can be purchased in rolls and can be easily cut to size with metal shears as long as it's not thicker than 2 mm. But even 1 mm thick HDPE can make a huge difference so don't forget to get some. HDPE is best used as an outermost plate to protect sensitive areas against neutron scattering weapons and as an inner-most layer to protect against eddy currents. Applying a graphite based epoxy layer on the front side of the HDPE should become standard practice. Adding a thin coat of high density polyurethane (poly-urethane and not HD poly-ethylene) powder suspended in epoxy, on the back side of the HDPE, will add an additional protective layer that is very effective at

dampening microwaves when used in conjunction with other shielding materials.

The polyurethane we just mentioned is way different than polyethylene despite the similar spelling. High density polyurethane (not polyethylene) that is suitable for shielding can only be found in foam blocks from specialized retailers. These blocks can be cut into panels with a hand saw and makes an excellent shielding material all by itself. It can be applied at home for added protection as long as it's at least 1 cm thick and above a certain density (see FAQs). Using it for body armor is more difficult because it is somewhat brittle at that thickness. That is why we recommend using a blender and turning it into a powder and using that powder to mix in an epoxy to form a resin skin. It may be necessary to smooth that type of resin skin with a metal file as it tends to clump together in some areas even if applied with a spatula. This isn't the case for other resins which apply more smoothly. Applying this polyurethane mix to the back side of HDPE as an inner most layer offers the maximum protection possible against eddy currents and other unwanted electromagnetic phenomena.

Fine powders, whether they're from foams or metals, are highly dangerous to work with because they can be inhaled like asbestos. We recommend full PPE (gloves, masks) when working with powders and epoxy for safety and doing it outdoors rather than inside to avoid polluting your home.

Making epoxy based resins is a very important skill when it comes to shielding. Many combinations of metal and carbon based powders are highly effective against energy weapons. Magnetite and graphite together in an epoxy works best as a cost effective microwave absorption layer that blocks both the e-field and the m-field of an electromagnetic wave.

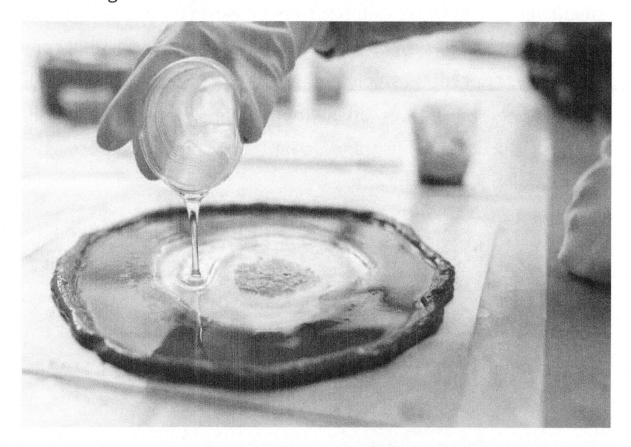

It is perhaps your best defense against high powered energy weapons besides permalloy and the copper/ aluminum combo. Using graphene or carbon nanotubes instead of graphite would be better but they're extremely hard to find and very expensive.

It is a lot of work to make resins from metal powders and epoxy, more so for the prep and clean up times than the actual mixing and application times, but it's well worth the trouble. Nothing stops energy weapons, including ELF, like this type of mix when sandwiched in between copper foil layers and applied to a tile or panel made of HDPE. That doesn't mean it will stop everything by itself, but its contribution to your shielding strategy can definitely be felt.

The more varied types of shielding materials you use the better the protection will be. Very few strategies will last forever against this A.I. system but it will buy you some serious time as will adding multiple tiles of this concept. Traditional military grade shielding can be meters thick and we're trying to replicate that effect with just a centimeter or an inch. It will be very difficult to get there without magnetite based resins, permalloy and the copper sandwich concept that is topped with mylar however. And so, if things get tough at your location, this is the direction where you need to get going.

Epoxy can easily absorb twice its volume when it comes to powders. The higher the concentrations the better but it can get expensive rather quickly, so a 50 / 50 mix is recommended to begin with (50% powder 50% epoxy). This concentration is effective enough in most cases. A raw layer of graphite or magnetite can be applied to the HDPE with the spatula before pouring the epoxy powder mix for added effect, but that will take extra time. Always begin pouring in the middle of your tile and stretch the mix out towards the sides with a spatula.

Adding extra mix to the corners will help finish the job and be sure to smooth out the epoxy multiple times in different directions to ensure a uniform application. The thicker the skin the better so a second application may be required. If the skin is too thick, however, it will become brittle so further applications beyond two may not work as well if you need the HDPE to curve for armor. Thicker applications can work for shields and panels. Resins should be mixed in plastic measuring cups, mixed with a spoon and applied with a spatula. The mixing cups, spoons and spatulas should be thrown away after use and everything should be done preferably outdoors. It can be tough finding the right place for the job, such as a picnic table, but applying plastic to a picnic table before mixing and keeping the area tidy will allow you to reuse that location in most cases. Just tell people you're an artist making metal paint if anyone needs to know.

Permalloy (or mu-metal) is another very important material worth mentioning again. It is a blend of iron and nickel and is renowned for its ability to absorb magnetic fields and stops ELF waves like magnetite. Permalloy is very expensive compared to other materials however, and it takes multiple insulated layers of 0.1 mm thickness to be effective. Single layers of permalloy can easily backfire due to resonance and so it takes a minimum of 3 layers to be effective in combination with other shielding materials such as copper foil. Permalloy is not a stand alone solution for EMF weapons but it makes such a huge difference that not having it can be a serious disadvantage. Having an emergency plate made of permalloy, again, is a strong recommendation and eventually you'll want to make armor designs based on that material. After using it you'll definitely want more but like most other exotic materials it can be difficult and expensive to find.

EMF has a very nasty tendency of following surfaces and can curve around them like light from a hallway that comes into a dark room. Or like water dribbling down the side of the cup when pouring. That's why adding a di-electric (non conductive) layer dedicated to insulation will be a big plus for your body armor. The innermost layer of your body armor should be made of a non conductive insulating material, like HDPE, and it should surpass the outer conductive layers by at least 1 mm on all sides (a 5mm margin would be better). This margin prevents accumulated EMF from dribbling around the edges of your armor and into your body.

Double check to make sure that the conductive layers of your shielding do not bend around and over the innermost insulating layer, as that would act as a channel for this dribbling effect.

Cushion foam made of poly-urethane can add comfort and protection as an insulating layer that can be enhanced with the HD polyurethane (not polyethylene) as mentioned above. Different densities of the same shielding material is advised when needing to enhance shielding after everything else has been tried.

Body armor should be continuously sealed on all sides, and put on or removed like a sweater over the head. It is possible to make armor with side openings for easier removal but this opens up the armor to huge gaps and other issues. While straps, buckles or velcro can be used to close a "side door" of your armor, it ends up being more of a problem than anything else as the straps, buckles and velcro get used. Experimenting is key to understanding all the issues but for the time being its best to hermetically seal all sides of your armor and to use it like a "sweater."

There are many other ways to make body armor, such as adding an extra lining to jackets or reverse engineering shirts into vests. Practice makes perfect when it comes to designing and manufacturing military grade armor.

The sandwich board model made out of sandwiched tiles or panels is easiest to make and is by far the best way for beginners. But before you try making anything out of expensive layers of shielding, we want to mention again to be sure to do a practice run using laminated aluminum foil first. It's cheaper to practice and make mistakes using foil than with a finished panel of multi layered shielding.

Practicing with foil will help you work out the little things when it comes to cutting out cardboard templates, connecting panels and sealing with tape. As well as adjusting the size and fit. Be sure to take the time to measure lengths properly and to cut in straight lines using guides otherwise you'll waste resources that can be difficult to find. Practice vests can come in handy as emergency replacements or as temporary shielding as you work on your main body armor in the field.

 It's recommended to avoid using continuous loops of copper or silver when making body armor as well, whether it be foil, mesh or EMF fabric. The reason is that copper loops are basically inductor coils that will transfer energy from the outside of the loop to the inside of the loop (like induction brazing or an inductive stove). When EMF hits the loop it induces an electrical current in the copper and that induces a magnetic field inside the loop. Since you'll be on the inside of that loop or coil, that means magnetic fields will pulse inside you.

This type of induction is similar to how magnets make electricity in copper coils, only in reverse. The idea of loops can be beneficial for EMF shielding but can be exploited by automated weapon systems. The recommendation here is that you do apply copper foil and copper fabric to every section of your armor but that you don't electrically connect the sections to form a loop or coil. Instead, insulate each panel with tape or plastic. Have the panels overlap slightly so that they can be hermetically sealed but not electrically connected.

The outer seams can be covered up with copper foil after insulation to make a seamless exterior that's not electrically connected to the main tiles. So avoid making your armor an electrically connected  loop or coil if possible. It's worth noting that looped armor designs are better than non looped designs from a theoretical physics perspective. Field testing describes looped designs as "risky" with minimal improvement over non looped designs. It is possible to design panels with looped insulated fabric and looped foil and may be something worth considering if you're looking to test something new that "could be" better, but at this stage non-looped designs look more attractive due to concerns related to resonance exploitation and induction.

It takes a lot of work and many layers of shielding materials to produce military grade armor that can protect against modern day energy weapons. These layer descriptions are a basic formula and there will always be a need for experimentation and innovation as "skynet" evolves and adapts. That means you should continue researching the newest concepts in scientific journals such as "Science Direct" or "The Journal of Magnetism and Magnetic Materials" if you're really looking for even more advanced shielding materials to experiment with. There are many other materials worth using for armor but their costs are prohibitive and are nearly impossible to find like many other exotic materials.

The materials we've recommended so far are relatively effective considering the magnitude of the weapons we're up against and are easy enough to find, mostly. There may be a need for multiple layers of shielding panels to survive heavy directional attacks during a siege, especially if they've parked new weapons right next door. More advanced materials may reduce the need for multiple panels but at a very heavy financial cost.

Materials like graphene, boron carbide, nickel ferrites or "BaTiO3" powders have extreme advantages at an extreme cost. These powders can retail around $1000 per kilo, and each kilo would give you enough for 4 or 5 coats of epoxy on body armor. Magnetite, as we recommended, will run you around $25 to $50 per kilo and so that's the big difference. Other high end specialty products such as microwave absorbing composites found online might be worth repurposing for additional layers but the preference should be for boronated materials, such as boron carbide or boronated HDPE.

Once the system has red listed you, energy weapon induced cancers or heart attacks will strike in less than a few years. A siege will typically begin when EMF attacks are thwarted with simplistic shielding methods such as grounded foil on the walls. The system will bring in more weapons to your location and a siege begins, turning your home into a kill box. It is not uncommon to need armor that is an inch thick to survive an aggressive siege.

Lighter versions of body armor may work well for public places, but thicker armor will be required for the home. It's why we recommend having emergency plates of shielding on reserve that can be added to strategic places in case things go south during a siege. There is no such thing as overkill when it comes to stockpiling shielding materials against directed energy weapons. Having over $5000's worth of supplies is not uncommon either and still that won't be nearly enough in most cases. Buying a few things every week adds up over time and makes the costs more bearable.

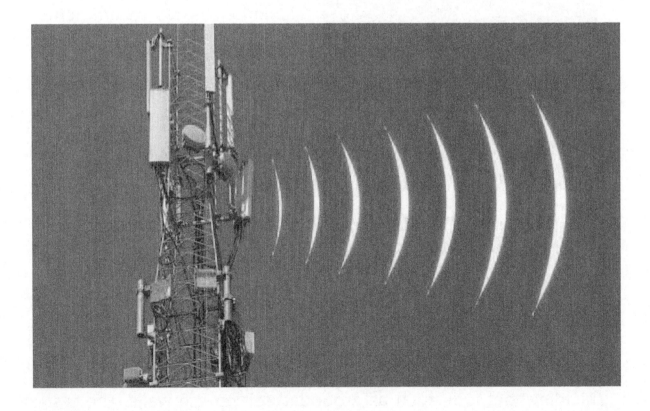

It's easy to think you won't need this kind of protection right now but eventually you will need it to survive. Shielding projects can take over a year to accomplish if you're serious about protecting yourself.

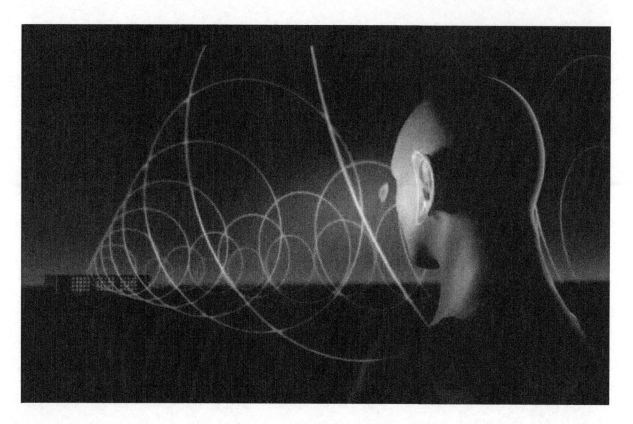

Countless people have been attacked and killed by these weapons and the situation grows worse every day. Military grade shielding usually requires tons of materials that can be over a meter thick. The shielding strategies discussed in this book will allow you to cut that thickness down to approximately an inch with only a fraction of the weight and cost.

Starting the process now regardless of how you currently perceive your risk assessment is highly recommended. Automated DEW systems implanted in smart city infrastructure are programmed to discretely torture victims for months or years before killing them. These weapons use invisible beams that are very difficult to detect and the damage they cause is made to look like cancer progressing through stages.

Preparation is key because once you're being targeted you won't have time to shop around for materials, or have time to wait for delivery, or have time to figure out how to put it all together.

It's best to rule out energy weapons first before doing any other type of medical testing if you've been banned on social media platforms and if you're experiencing pain not associated with an injury, including recurring headaches and chronic fatigue. Emergency rooms have no way to test for energy weapons and the only way to test is with shielding. Most energy weapons fire beams and those beams won't show up on a meter. "Head to toe" protection will become necessary in a siege environment as the system begins to target limbs, the neck and your private areas if the head and chest are protected. Protecting the rest of your body from these attacks will require using the same methods as mentioned above. These methods can be applied to make helmets, thyroid guards, arm protection, shorts, pants, lower leg protection, boots, and so on and so forth. They will attack whatever is exposed and will prioritize organs based on what hurts the most and what has the worst long term effects and they'll hit you with surgical precision. This can include vertical impalement from underground attacks as you sit. And will definitely include traversing attacks as you lay in bed.

When a siege begins, attacks will rain in from every direction day and night, non-stop. At some point in time, you may have to temporarily quit caring about what other people think and be all in to survive. Otherwise, it will be mega pain and agony as you cringe in the fetal position on your deathbed awaiting emergency transport to an ER where they'll finish you off and where nobody can help you. Anything is better than that, including looking like an astronaut... Don't let pride get in the way of survival. The key to success is to remain calm and rational and to fight through the pain until you can rapidly deploy better shielding.

Explain the situation away as EMF sensitivity to those that "care" and never forget to give the "Karens" a lecture on 5G and the safety of vaccination. As time goes on, more and more people will be protecting themselves from 5G with whatever means possible. Shielding is already a booming business and it will only continue to grow as people wake up to the relationship between EMF radiation and disease.

Making basic head gear is easier than body armor but requires concealment in the form of a sports hat. The first objective is to make a skull cap out of lead (1 mm thick) that can be molded inside the hat. Lead is very flexible and easy to mold. Seal it first with tape while using gloves or paper towels to avoid touching it. Sealing the lead with multiple layers of packing tape is recommended to prevent

condensation (sweat) mixing with the lead and into your hair. Periodic monitoring of the skull cap will help you minimize the risks associated with using lead as a skull cap. Molding a skull cap can take time, but reverse engineering the basic template of a sports cap will make the job go faster. Most hats use a combination of triangles to make a dome and so cutting out lead triangles will be your first step. Tape and mold the lead triangles in the same arrangement as the hat to ensure a proper fit.

The skull cap that will be placed underneath the hat and should slide into the inner seam of the hat so take that into consideration when cutting out the triangles. Adding additional layers of EMF fabrics and foils can be added to the lead and will be necessary in most cases.

Skull caps will work well when you're on the move in public places but it won't be enough for siege weapons trying to get you at home or while loitering in remote locations. That is why military grade helmets are also on the menu.

After making a skull cap you'll need to make a wide range of helmets for things like sleeping with eye protection and robust models for situations you'd think would never happen, because they will. Helmet designs can vary significantly but you will want to begin with either mesh metal or HDPE as a frame.

Use metal cutting shears and templates with precise measurements to cut out the components of the frame. Practice first by using cheap fabric or foil then make an attempt using HDPE or mesh metal. In most cases you will want a helmet that fits over your hat / skull cap configuration.

The first step to making a helmet is cutting out a headband. Use a slightly longer than necessary strip of HDPE or mesh metal and tape it shut to form a loop around your head like a headband. Make sure the fit is approximate but slightly loose at this stage because it will tighten up significantly (1 cm) as other pieces are added into place. Once the headband is measured to a loose fit you will need another support band that goes up the middle from front to back connecting to the headband at the center points front and back. The bands should be about an inch wide to provide foundational support for the triangles that will complete the dome, similar to the skull cap. Once the center band is done, you will need another band that goes from ear to ear or a horizontal band. This connects to the head band as well and once the two central bands are connected to the headband it will form a cross near the middle.

The open spaces that remain at this stage will be in the form of bell shaped triangles. To fill up those spaces you will need to trace out templates from paper or foil that are slightly larger than the gaps and then use those templates to cut out triangles from the mesh metal or HDPE that you're using. Connecting those triangles properly to the headband structure can take time and tape is as good of a solution as glue or soldering. Making a helmet in this fashion can easily take a week or two if you're doing it in your afternoons. Once the frame is done, other shielding layers can be added and the more layers the better.

Satellite or drone based attacks from above will become standard practice and these attacks can penetrate multiple layers of shielding materials. Lightweight helmet configurations consisting of 10 layers of copper EMF fabric coated with foil and a magnetite epoxy outer skin can be a stand alone solution inside a shielded environment.

Most of the time it will be preferable to keep the skull cap on regardless of the helmet used.

Heavy duty helmets with robust layers that include lead, HDPE, foil, fabrics, magnetite and metal mesh should be on stand-by for added security. Using the same layering strategy that we used for body armor definitely applies to helmets. Having multiple helmets with varying degrees of protection can be helpful but having a worst case scenario helmet will be a must to survive sustained attacks.

Extensions around the back of the head to protect the back of the neck and that extend just above the shoulders will become necessary. Applying a measured rectangle that curves around the back of the helmet makes this solution possible. Protecting the back of the head is very important as attacks there can cause serious damage. Protecting the eyes will be a must as well. An additional flap that can drop down around the eyes like a face mask will be something that you will have to practice making. If the eye flap drops down too far it will accumulate exhaust like a face mask and make breathing more difficult.

The protective eye flap can be fixed into place with two layers of heavy tape at the center of the flap (outside and inside) and locked in the up or down position with the use of velcro or magnets. Magnets work better but require additional shielding against magnetic fields. Be sure to review the magnetic shielding section for more info on that. Using magnets on the flap with metal bars on the helmet works well to form magnetic seals, similar to a cupboard door configuration.

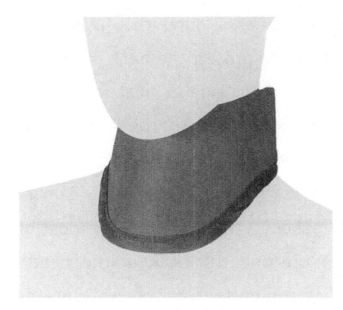

Protecting the neck will be very important as well as it becomes the next prime target after the heart and mind. Making a thyroid guard is the best solution for this scenario and is highly recommended. Using a framework out of mesh metal or HDPE is the best place to start. Measure out a template that wraps around the neck like a collar. Add as many layers as you can but make sure it's comfortable and flexible or you won't use it. Multiple thyroid guards may be needed for sleep and to cover the teeth for special occasions. Thinner packing tape is better for sensitive areas like the neck area, otherwise it will chafe your skin during use. Applying an inner layer of soft fabric or thin cushion foam may be necessary for the sake of comfort. The collar must fit flush or the system will exploit even the slightest gaps from the worst possible angles. Additional extensions may be necessary to protect the jaw line, front teeth and the nooks of your neck below the guard. These extensions can be accomplished with overlapping mini plates that are flexible in nature. The collar can be secured with velcro, hooks or magnets but sometimes tape will be necessary if those fixtures become used or ineffective. Multiple thyroid guards, again, may be necessary for sleep and the home. Not every thyroid guard is comfortable to sleep in, and there may be times where you need to sleep with your armor on. Having more comfortable pajama armor that is less thick can work provided the bed is reinforced with extra heavy shielding. Obviously none of this will be good for your social life, but trying to be like the sheeple will get you killed.

Arm protection will also become necessary as the system rotates around your body parts to test the fence and attack something it can affect. Arm protection is best done in sections to preserve mobility. A single tile of layered materials can be used to form the forearm protection. Making it into a tube that you can slide into is best. Practice with foil because you will probably only use part of the tile and will have to cut it at an angle to make it look and feel right. An additional armband should be used to protect the arm above the elbow. Connecting the two sections with thin sections of fabric or tape will help you keep the two sections together and avoid loss. Keeping track of inventory is a big issue when it comes to these life saving materials, especially under the stress of heavy fire. Forearm extensions that go beyond the wrists may become necessary, while making gloves out of fabrics and foils will become useful as well.

Leg and bottom protections are very similar to everything we've discussed so far. Shorts can be made out of tiles. Three tiles around the waste and 1.5 tiles for the leg can be tubed together to make shorts. It's crude but effective. There are other ways to make shorts, such as reverse engineering designer shorts to make templates but

that may be a luxury in time that you cannot afford. Making tubes out of tiles and connecting those tubes together with tape is a tedious process but the protection it offers is irreplaceable. Energy weapons directed at your lower sections can cause bowel cancers that are worse than death. Never ignore protecting your bottom sections because the system will target every inch of what makes you human.

Pain is their game and nothing is more painful than getting hit in the "you know what" areas. Reinforcing shorts like other armor components may become necessary but comfort becomes more of an issue for obvious reasons. That is why reinforcing seats and cars may be preferable to lead or steel in the shorts. The level of attacks you experience will dictate how far you have to go to stop the pain with reinforcements. Leg protection is absolutely necessary as energy weapons can cause serious DVT's or blood clots and swelling in the legs. The aim is to immobilize you so they can finish you off in a deathbed scenario. They will also target your back to immobilize you from every angle as well. Reinforcing your armor with back plates or magnets will become an issue in most cases.

The lower legs should be protected in the same fashion as the arms but it can be done as boots or shin guards. Leg protection should be as light and flexible as possible and it shouldn't be necessary to use lead in most cases. Fabric and foil combinations, as mentioned previously, will be a must and you will have to "splice in" an insert to stop the copper coil induction effect. The insert should be a vertical strip made and should be insulated from the other sections. The leg protections should wrap around the entire leg below the knee and an extension to protect the knee may become necessary. Their capability for softening up joints and muscles for a tear or worse is remarkable. If they immobilize you then it can become a death bed scenario, so protect your legs as much as possible.

Lastly comes the foot protection. Protecting the feet is hard to do. Using shoes as a template works well in some cases. Sometimes adding shielding directly to sandals or shoes makes more sense for in home use. Otherwise purchasing EMF socks is not a bad idea because anything is better than nothing.

The best protection is making lead boots to protect you from underground attacks. Applying lead and other layers to pre-existing foot gear is by far the easiest way to go, but It still takes time. There's little choice but to follow the form of the shoe inch by inch and by filling in the gaps section by section. Making foot protection is very tedious work but they will come after your feet and ankles if there's nothing else left. Wear and tear becomes an issue with foot protection, so regardless of which strategy you choose you will have to fix and repair your foot protection regularly. Applying shielding to shoe inserts can work well but can lead to discomfort and even bone displacement in the foot, as there are many little bones in the foot. There isn't a perfect solution for shoe protection due to wear and tear and ergonomics. The best idea is to apply thin protection for public places and to have a more robust pair of boots for the home. Periodic maintenance, again, will be especially important if you use lead as the seals you use will disintegrate with time and will result in lead flaking and coating the floors. That is why reinforcing your floors in a safe room at home instead may be preferable to lead moon boots that can leave unwanted crumbs for pets and toddlers. Protecting the bottom of the feet with heavy shielding will protect the rest of your body from attacks that come from underground and will become necessary if a siege begins. Like every other shielding solution, it isn't about fashion, it's about survival.

ATTENUATION

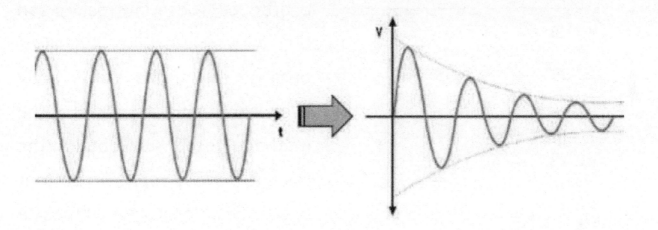

EMF attenuation refers to the reduction of the intensity of an electromagnetic field as it passes through a material. EMF attenuation is measured in decibels (dB) and is the opposite of antenna gain. Attenuation values are expressed in decibels and are a common feature when it comes to marketing EMF shielding materials.

Attenuation graphs are often expressed as a bell curve to show efficiency for different frequencies. Attenuation is never 100% from a physics perspective, so it's not just us saying that. The following table translates dB ratings to signal blockage, in case you see attenuation while shopping:

These ratings are usually advertised as lab results and are used to convince consumers to purchase a product. These lab results can be very misleading however, because the methods are rarely ever listed with the results. The methods used to obtain the results are very important because many factors can make a material look better than it actually is.

ATTENUATION	PERCENTAGE
10 dB	~90%
20 dB	~99%
30 dB	~99.9%
40 dB	~99.99%
50 dB	~99.999%
60 dB	~99.9999%
70 dB	~99.99999%
80 dB	~99.999999%
90 dB	~99.9999999%
100 dB	~99.99999999%

Attenuation is always dependent on frequency, power and distance. Manufacturers will run tests using favorable conditions that benefit their products. That means they will run a test using methods and conditions that work well with that material but do not represent real world scenarios. They will always tell you that their product is 99% percent effective but that 99% is only for a very specific frequency range with low power densities and with as much distance from the transmitter as possible. If they don't disclose the frequency or the methods they used for testing then it's safer to assume the material is only partially effective when it comes to real world protection. Lab tests can be rigged, so never rely on ready made items as stand alone shielding unless that's all you can afford. Any shielding is better than nothing, including the shielding you make while practicing with aluminum foil.

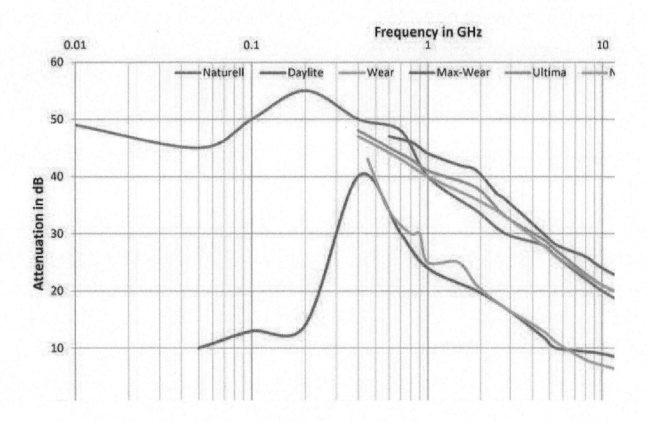

SHIELDING MATERIALS

This section will be rating some of the most common shielding materials. Rating these materials is a very complicated process due to the nature of EMF and energy weapons. These ratings do not represent every possible scenario since even the best materials can fail under the right conditions.

We will be grading each material on an A to F letter scale to represents effectiveness:

A - Excellent: The material is nearly perfect in its effectiveness, offering outstanding protection against electromagnetic fields in almost all situations.

B - Good: The material is effective and offers good protection against electromagnetic fields in most situations. It is a solid choice.

C - Average: The material provides moderate and acceptable protection against electromagnetic fields. It is neither exceptionally effective nor ineffective.

D - Below Average: The material provides moderate protection but falls short of what is considered effective. It may have some limitations or drawbacks.

F - Very Ineffective: The material provides almost no protection or is entirely ineffective at shielding against EMF. It offers minimal or no benefit.

We'll begin with a detailed look at some of the most common materials with sample frequencies from the EMF spectrum. The ratings includes the consideration of particle beam weapons (PBW), which are high speed neutrons or electrons and we'll grade the material for directed energy weapons (DEW) as well. The ELF or 10 Hz classifier is also very important to consider from a weapons standpoint because many energy weapons are now using ELF to cut through shielding. The first material we'll look at is copper:

COPPER

Thickness	10Hz	1Khz	1Mhz	400Mhz	1Ghz	X-Ray	PBW	DEW
Foil	F	F	F	F	F	F	F	F
0.1 mm	F	F	F	F	F	F	F	F
1 mm	D	D	C	C	D	F	F	F
3 mm	B	B	B	B	C	F	F	F
5 mm	A	A	A	B	B	F	F	F

Copper works well as a standalone material at around 3 mm in thickness but mostly for sub 1 Ghz radiation types. This would be the main reason why copper EMF fabrics work well against cell phone radiation but not against WIFI. Notice how thin layers of copper are basically ineffective when it's used just by itself. Copper in conjunction with other materials, especially aluminum and magnetite, makes for much better shielding. Making copper foil sandwiches with materials that exhibit high magnetic permeability has become the very best standard of protection. But copper by itself is only partially effective as a shielding material.

ALUMINUM

Thickness	10Hz	1Khz	1Mhz	400Mhz	1Ghz	X-Ray	PBW	DEW
Foil	F	F	F	F	F	F	F	F
0.1 mm	F	F	F	F	F	F	F	F
1 mm	F	F	D	C	C	F	F	F
3 mm	D	D	B	A	A	C	C	D
5 mm	B	B	A	A	A	C	C	D

Aluminum has a similar profile as copper when it comes to effectiveness as a stand alone shielding material, however it is slightly more effective beyond 1Ghz and can provide some protection against particle beam weapons and x-rays. Thick tiles of aluminum foil are much better than nothing and adding a single layer of copper foil to it makes it even better. In fact, simple tiles of just aluminum and copper foil can make excellent accessories as stop-gaps for sensitive areas and can be easily tucked into place or applied to areas that need extra temporary shielding. The tile system is quite literally an extension of this discovery. Adding materials to this combination only makes for stronger shielding. This combination should be applied wherever resources and time permits.

STAINLESS STEEL

Thickness	10Hz	1Khz	1Mhz	400Mhz	1Ghz	X-Ray	PBW	DEW
Foil	F	F	F	F	F	F	F	F
0.1 mm	F	F	F	F	F	F	F	F
1 mm	F	F	D	C	C	F	F	F
3 mm	C	C	B	A	A	B	B	C
5 mm	B	B	A	A	A	B	B	C

Stainless steel can work well if it's thick enough but basically you're still looking at 3 mm or more of it for it to be effective for energy weapons. It does provide decent protection in all categories but it gets heavy fast. 1 mm plates of sheet metal can provide fair coverage but it won't be enough for high powered weapons beyond the 5G death grid.

These ratings improve by at least a letter grade, if not more, when the material is grounded. And so the above listed ratings are for ungrounded materials with average variables such as distance and power of the EMF hitting it. Even grounded foil, of any material type, will achieve "C" status when properly connected. Grounded materials work better but are still not sufficient enough to withstand military grade energy weapons. Connecting your shielding to a ground does not guarantee the ground connection will work and it may in fact make the situation worse in certain scenarios. Be sure to test with or without grounding by adding a switch or by un-grounding the connection.

Here's a standard rating chart for the most common shielding materials without the complexity of specific scenarios, these ratings are simply a rough comparison of materials based on averages.

MATERIAL	GRADE
COPPER	C
SILVER	B
IRON	D
BRASS	D
TITANIUM	D
PERMALLOY	B
LEAD	B
ALUMINUM	C
GOLD	B
STEEL	C
BRONZE	D
NICKEL	D
TUNGSTEN	D
MYLAR	C

We would add that these ratings are for ungrounded, standalone materials and do not represent the effectiveness of multi-layered shielding. Most of these shielding materials have major backdoors when faced with energy weapons due to coupling, resonance and induction. And every material can be overpowered or compromised due to saturation or capacitance. It is important to be able to remove new upgrades in case they don't work as intended. So design your shielding strategies so layers can be easily added or removed if need be. Most of these materials will work if they're thick enough for a specific frequency range but since you'll never really know what frequency they're using or what direction the next attack is coming from, you'll be forced to cover every possible scenario. Sometimes applying too little of a material will give you the wrong impression while testing. Adding more of that material before abandoning it as an option should be part of your methods for testing.

Top 5 shielding materials for the various ranges of the EMF spectrum:

Selecting materials for shielding against electromagnetic radiation often depends on the specific frequency range and the desired attenuation level. Here are some common materials, compounds, or elements for different frequency ranges in no specific order of effectiveness:

For 1 Hz to 100 Hz:

1. Lead (Pb) - Effective against low-frequency electromagnetic fields.
2. Steel - Especially effective for magnetic fields.
3. Permalloy - Provides high permeability for magnetic field shielding.
4. Concrete - Useful for attenuating low-frequency EMF.

5. Magnetite / Ferrite - Very Effective at low frequencies due to its high magnetic permeability.

For 1 kHz to 50 kHz:

1. Copper (Cu) - Excellent for attenuating electric fields.
2. Aluminum (Al) - Effective for RF shielding in this range.
3. Steel - Good for magnetic field attenuation.
4. Carbon-based materials - Carbon composites can provide absorption.
5. Nickel (Ni) - Can be effective for shielding electric fields.

For 100 kHz to 1 MHz:

1. Copper (Cu) - Remains effective in this range.
2. Aluminum (Al) - Effective for higher-frequency RF.
3. Permalloy - Suitable for magnetic field shielding.
4. Stainless Steel - Can attenuate electromagnetic radiation.
5. Conductive foams - Offer broadband shielding in this range.

For 300 MHz to 5 MHz:

1. Aluminum (Al) - Suitable for RF and microwave shielding.
2. Copper (Cu) - Effective for high-frequency electric fields.
3. Silver (Ag) - Highly conductive for RF and EMI shielding.
4. Nickel (Ni) - Used in combination with other materials.
5. Conductive fabric - Provides flexible shielding solutions.

For X-rays, Cosmic Rays, and Gamma Rays: Shielding against ionizing radiation requires denser materials:

1. Lead (Pb) - Commonly used for X-ray shielding.
2. Tungsten (W) - Effective against X-rays and gamma rays.
3. Boronated products such as boronated HDPE or boron carbide. Very effective and used for nuclear facilities.
4. Steel and iron alloys - Provide protection against gamma rays.
5. Bismuth (Bi) - Used in some medical applications for X-rays.

Keep in mind that effective shielding often involves using multiple layers of different materials to cover a wider frequency range.

Permalloy (Mu-metal) rating for ELF:

Permalloy is an alloy consisting primarily of iron and nickel, and it is known for its high magnetic permeability, which makes it effective for magnetic shielding. Its effectiveness for electromagnetic field (EMF) applications can vary depending on the frequency range and specific application. Here's a general rating for permalloy in different EMF ranges:

Low-Frequency EMF (ELF - Extremely Low Frequency):

Permalloy is highly effective for ELF applications, such as shielding against low-frequency magnetic fields. It is commonly used in transformer cores and magnetic shielding applications.

Rating: A

Radio Frequency (RF):

Permalloy is less effective at RF frequencies compared to its performance in ELF applications. While it can provide some RF shielding, other materials may be more suitable for RF electromagnetic interference (EMI) shielding.

Rating: C

Microwave Frequencies:

Permalloy is not typically used as the primary material for microwave applications. Materials with tailored properties, such as ferrite composites, are preferred for microwave absorption and shielding.

Rating: D

Millimeter-Wave and Terahertz Frequencies:

Permalloy is generally not used in millimeter-wave and terahertz applications. Other specialized materials are preferred for these higher-frequency ranges.

Rating: D

In summary, permalloy is highly effective for low-frequency EMF applications, making it valuable for shielding against ELF magnetic fields. Its performance decreases as the frequency increases, with reduced effectiveness in RF, microwave, millimeter-wave, and terahertz frequency ranges. The ratings reflect its relative effectiveness across different EMF applications. Permalloy ratings improve significantly if multiple thin layers are used and placed inside a copper foil sandwich.

The Best Ferrite Materials for Shielding:

Ferrite materials vary in their properties, and their effectiveness for low and high-frequency applications can depend on factors such as composition, geometry, and design. Here's a list of ten common ferrite materials, along with a general rating for low and high-frequency performance:

Manganese-Zinc Ferrite (MnZn)

Low-Frequency Rating: B

High-Frequency Rating: D

Nickel-Zinc Ferrite (NiZn)

Low-Frequency Rating: C

High-Frequency Rating: B

Magnesium-Zinc Ferrite (MgZn)

Low-Frequency Rating: C

High-Frequency Rating: C

Cobalt-Zinc Ferrite (CoZn)

Low-Frequency Rating: B

High-Frequency Rating: C

Nickel-Copper-Zinc Ferrite (NiCuZn)

Low-Frequency Rating: C

High-Frequency Rating: B

Manganese-Magnesium-Zinc Ferrite (MnMgZn)

Low-Frequency Rating: D

High-Frequency Rating: D

Iron-Magnesium-Zinc Ferrite (FeMgZn)

Low-Frequency Rating: D

High-Frequency Rating: D

Barium Hexaferrite (BaFe12O19)

Low-Frequency Rating: F

High-Frequency Rating: D

Strontium Hexaferrite (SrFe12O19)

Low-Frequency Rating: F

High-Frequency Rating: F

Nickel Ferrite (NiFe2O4)

Low-Frequency Rating: C

High-Frequency Rating: C

Magnetite (Fe3O4) - Graphite in Resin

Low-Frequency Rating: B

High-Frequency Rating: B

Materials that are effective against neutron and electron guns:

Against Neutron Radiation:

Boron Carbide: B

Water (Polyethylene Moderator): C

Paraffin Wax: C

Concrete: D

HD Polyethylene: B

Lead: D

Graphite: F

Heavy Water (D2O): B

Against Electron Radiation:

Lead: A

Tungsten: B

Iron: C

Copper: D

Aluminum: D

Plastic (PVC): F

Water: F

Concrete: F

Actual effectiveness can vary depending on the energy and intensity of the radiation.

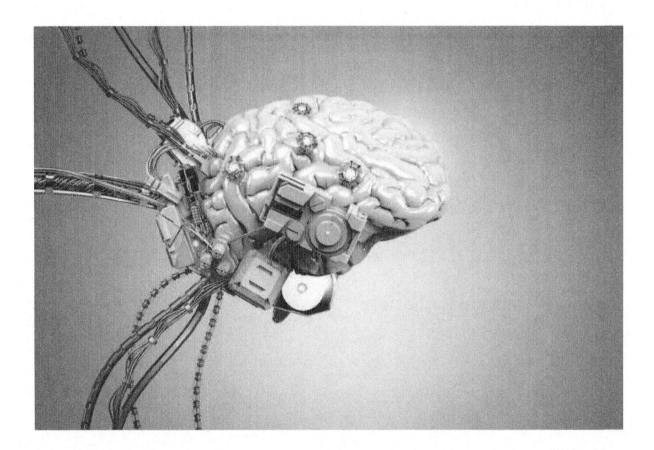

MAGNETIC SHIELDING

Magnets can play a crucial role against energy weapons. Some weapons can still penetrate shielding no matter how many layers you throw at it. Even if the penetration is significantly reduced due to advanced shielding concepts, enough can still get through to cause severe pain and even death. One of the best ways to attenuate the most invasive weapons is by <u>CAREFULLY</u> using magnetic fields to stop them. Over exposure to magnetic fields does exist and is known as "magnetic hyperthermia."

The controlled use of magnetic fields can become an ultimate defense strategy against advanced weapons because most EMF is driven by its magnetic field component and because magnets are used to steer and direct high speed particles in particle accelerators.

 Magnetic fields can not only stop energy weapons but they can amplify them as well so they must be positioned very carefully. Every magnet circulates a magnetic field that pulls in magnetic materials in like a mini black hole.

When a series of magnets are placed in a row, the gaps between the magnets create zones of concern. These gaps can act like a conveyor belt that amplifies the effects of EMF.

Despite it being difficult to discern where the magnetic fields are, one of the best approaches is to take two magnets and to stick them together with tape or glue so that magnets are opposing and repelling each other. This pushing effect from like poles disrupts EMF and particle beam weapons and is actually very effective against most energy weapons. Using this configuration of magnets in a grid formation can make the difference between life and death. The stronger the magnets the better, but finding the right combination of shapes and sizes to apply to shielding and armor takes experimentation. Bigger is not always better when it comes to magnetic armor. Each application requires different considerations. Not every magnet you buy is as strong as they claim either so test and compare magnets from different retailers.

The effect the magnets have can be amplified with the use of bare copper wire wrapped around the magnets like the way inductors are coiled around a ferrite core, this is referred to as inductive shielding and is expanded upon in the FAQ section.

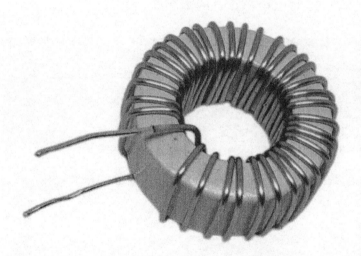

Using the magnets with the same coil concept as an inductor amplifies the magnetic shielding effect against energy weapons. The amount of turns in the copper coil will have an effect on the effectiveness and while it's easier and much more effective to do that with donut style magnets, it tends to be more difficult with magnets of a different shape, like disc or "bar shaped" magnets. The idea here is that the copper wire goes in and out of the magnetic core as much as possible to amplify the field and to wash out any frequencies that get conducted through the wire. The copper wires used for the coil should never touch each other. Connecting the ends of the coil electrically is optional but connecting them in theory is better.

Prolonged exposure to powerful magnetic fields is extremely dangerous over long periods of time. A small donut shaped magnet in your pocket won't have much effect on your biology, but a vest or a helmet full of magnets will. Those effects can definitely be felt over time and the pain can resemble those from energy weapon attacks. Therefore, additional shielding must be used when using magnets for body armor and helmets to protect you from the magnetic fields. We recommend additional layers or wafers made of 2 - 4 mm of HDPE underneath the magnets to mitigate the field.

Testing with metals to see if they are still attracted to the magnets through the additional HDPE shielding layers is the best way to see if the field is weak enough to wear. Adding metal to the wafers, such as permalloy or sheet metal will help deflect the magnetic field away from you as well but weight soon becomes a consideration. The wafers are meant to be between you and the magnets and not the other way around. It takes a lot more work to deploy magnetic shielding this way but it's like having a literal force field around you so it can be worth the time if you absolutely need new layers of shielding.

Deployment of these opposing magnets on a wafer should be done in a grid like pattern so that there are basically no gaps between the wafers that are protecting you from the magnets. Measuring the field strength of the magnet at different distances with metal will help you estimate the range of the magnet and the placement of the magnets.

Shielding against the magnets can also be achieved by using additional plates of HDPE instead of wafers and just putting the magnets on to that. But since it takes time to thread the magnets with wire and to position them as opposing poles, using wafers can make sense for limited rapid deployment when the situation demands it. These wafers or magnet configurations can be very useful for weak spots in the armor and to

reinforce areas of interest or that have been softened up by energy weapons. Placing them right over the area that hurts can stop the pain in seconds. But of course, "skynet" will shift its angle of attack to reach that same spot and so it can take a dozen or more of these magnets to patch up a weak spot. It can take hundreds of magnets to do body armor or a helmet. Best to make a dozen or so of these wafer combos from small disc shaped magnets and to have them ready for deployment and then go from there.

Using magnets in the south pole position facing outwards can also be beneficial for shielding. Determining the pole can be difficult but using a compass can help identify which pole is which. The FAQ section expands on this idea as well.

SURVIVING THE SHADOW WAR

To survive targeting, you will have to endure the worst case scenarios using less than perfect shielding options. The first few months of being a target are dark times to say the least. The most important thing is to focus on survival and to look beyond the things that are working against you. Focus on making shielding full time until you can stabilize. The shielding concepts discussed in this book will make a huge difference but the technology that we're up against is light years beyond where it should be. To understand what we're really facing, look no further than Mark Zuckerberg's now famous quote, "When I was human..."

We've received numerous reports over the years of this nature that seemed to suggest the assimilation of humanity was underway. None of it was taken seriously at first but as time went on the amount of evidence became irrefutable. Assimilation reports began surfacing in many circles around the year 2000 (around the same time as the targeting program itself). And by the year 2020 that situation had turned into a hostile takeover with virtually every country trying to lock you down and inject you with their "death vax."

Making assumptions about how or when this assimilation process really began is difficult to say but it would be reasonable to think "skynet" was unleashed some time in the aftermath of 9/11, but it may have been there working quietly in the background for much, much longer. What is clear at this point is that a beast system has taken over corporations, governments and the vast majority of the humans. Estimating numbers is quite difficult but it appears over 50% of the people have been affected by some kind of assimilation process. While this assimilation can't be proven beyond a reasonable doubt, most everyone would agree that most people out there function as NPC's and that there is an asymmetric war happening right now against humanity. Watching the system terraform the planet with "geo-engineering" and poison the food and water that we eat and drink leaves little doubt that things have gone beyond "science fiction."

There may be some debate as to why all of this is happening but if you start paying attention, the assimilation reasoning best explains why most people no longer pass "The Turing Test."

Most people now appear to be compromised in ways that only makes sense if they were assimilated and part of a hive or under extreme duress. This reasoning not only explains what we're seeing unfold on TV but it also explains your feeling of being in the matrix surrounded by NPC's, instead of thinking that people are sleeping and just don't "get it."

The current state of affairs includes celebrity clones and robot politicians that control the narrative with the help of A.I. censorship, as cyborgs on the ground hunt you down for sport with the aid of weaponized infrastructure.

Regardless of where we find ourselves in the actual human timeline it does appear that we are much further along than most people think. With that said, the situation that you'll be facing is much worse than just automated energy weapons hiding in plain sight. To expand on the full range of what is known would be another book all to itself but what we can say here is that it does not appear to be the year we think it is. And that means there are weapon systems that currently exist that are beyond the scope of the weapons covered so far and beyond the scope of perceived technologies. This discussion on shielding and energy weapons found in this book is really here to prepare you for the reset that is to come.

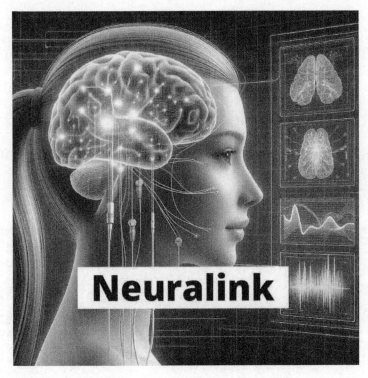

The shielding concepts we've covered appear to work effectively against most of the weapons encountered but nothing has proven itself to be 100% effective in terms of light-weight affordable shielding. The shielding strategies explained in this book are based on front line action against this system and it is why this book goes far beyond any other book of its kind.

But this also means you will have to deploy other tactics, on top of shielding, if you're going to survive. Until you build a properly shielded environment, evading attacks will be the only way to buy time if they're coming after you. Finding remote locations far from infrastructure, 5G and LED lights is the best option but there is no place where they can't reach you. NPC's will show up with weaponized vehicles to flush you out wherever you may hide. They excel at dropping off their remote weapon station (car) and then going for a walk. These vehicles can have a range of over 1 km, so if it happens to you be prepared to move to another location.

This "skynet" technology will stalk you wherever you go. Planes, drones and satellites (weather balloons) will rain down attacks from the air as cars and vans will attack you at point blank range. While no place is safe, evading attacks in remote locations is still a much better option than cruising in town or sitting at home without armor or shielding.

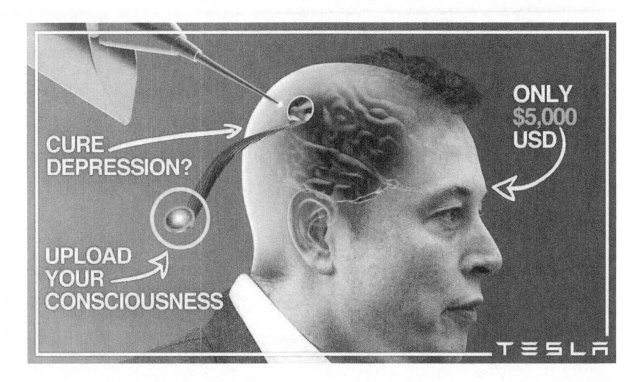

Automated energy weapons primarily attack stationary targets and will wait for you to be a sitting duck before launching most attacks. These attacks can come in waves or be sustained 24 / 7 in a siege-like situation that will follow you wherever you go. Attacks will peak late at night when you're too tired to defend yourself and will hit hardest in the winter time when it's too cold to be outdoors. Every strategy this system uses tries to box you in and attacks your weakest points to make your life as complicated and stressful as possible. This system can and will attack you at work, at the store, at school and even at the places you like to hang out. Going to the same place twice makes that location susceptible to targeting and opens you up to an ambush. Depending on your priority, an ambush can become your last stand if they hit you without shielding.

Evading energy weapon attacks is more about buying time to build armor and shielding than anything else. The worst thing you can do is be in denial and not make shielding or depend on orgonite for protection. So stay on the move as much as possible and avoid cities whenever you can. Beware of tailgaters due to weaponized headlights and never feel bad for pulling over and letting them pass. The closer you are to a weapon system the worse it is. New vehicles have automated software that activates the weapon system whenever you're in range. Getting stuck in traffic these days can result in major pain and so cruising in the urban environment as a targeted individual is basically suicide unless you heavily shield inside your car and routinely evade tailgaters.

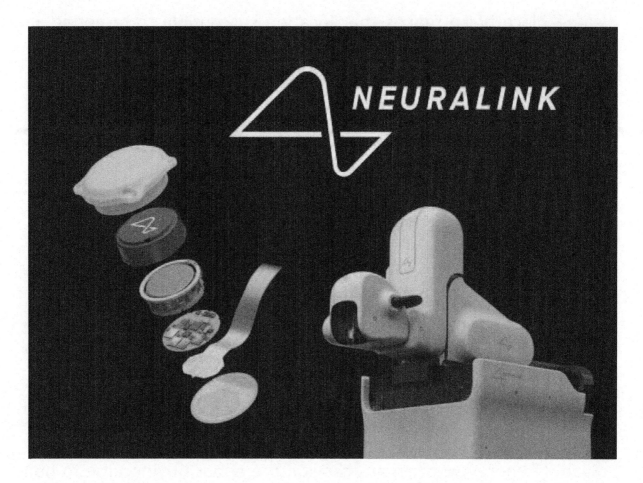

Lining the driver's seat with lead and other materials such as HDPE and EMF fabrics is highly recommended at this stage. Comfort and looks will become your very last concern after tasting a blast from weaponized headlights but a seat cover can be used to conceal the shielding for appearance's sake. The experience of being attacked by weaponized headlights is similar to an intense heating sensation hitting your back while feeling your internal energy getting depleted. The attack can become a medical emergency quickly and unless you've been made aware that this can occur, you'd probably think you were about to faint due to natural causes or worse.

Shielding the trunk and back seats for additional layers of security is also recommended. If possible, turn a van into an armored car to extend your range in case you need to travel or move your shielding materials in the future. Hotels and "air bnb's" will become a death

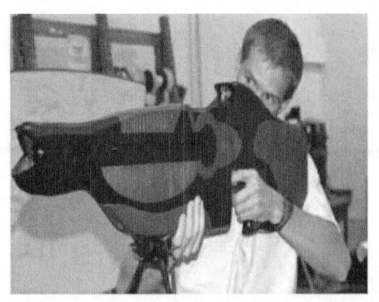

trap so having a van will let you rough it for a few days when prospecting for new locations or vacationing. Never sleep outdoors away from civilization at night lest they disappear you. Physical ambushes can happen and have been documented. Regardless of how much you shield your environment, you will most certainly be forced to wear armor and a skull cap 24 / 7 if they come after you. Think of it like wearing a seat belt, it may not be comfortable but most people wouldn't dream of driving without it.

Every door and window can be reinforced in your car for remote work with removable shields to make loitering more survivable. Once you have enough shielding you will feel like a survivor and likely progress to a soldier mentality. Adopt the "John Connor" attitude for added safety. And remember that everything that is happening to you is preparing you for what is to come and that future will be horrible in nature.

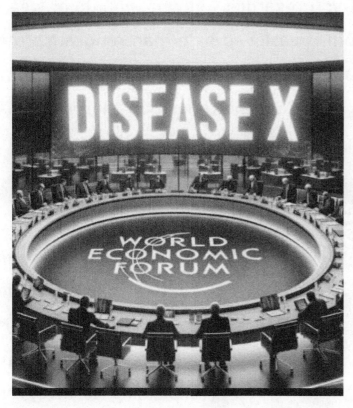

Deploying shielding at home or wearing armor at work can be difficult especially if you need to look "normal" in front of others. Nothing will get you divorced or fired faster than looking like an astronaut. That's why concealing your shielding is going to be a must for most people. Be aware that every NPC out there will try to bring down your shields through "gas-lighting" tactics. So here are a few tips on how to protect yourself without triggering the "Karens" around you.

Firstly, avoid talking about the issue as much as possible. There is no convincing the assimilated or the hostages of this beast system. They view their self-preservation in terms of your destruction. And expect those closest to you to betray you if given the opportunity. Secondly, design your armor so that it can be hidden under a sweater or a jacket. Do your shopping in the morning during the hot summer months. Wearing a jacket in the middle of the summer is still better than walking into the grocery store looking like "robo-cop." Never worry about what people think, the NPC's will go out of their way to stare at you regardless of what you do or wear. Thirdly, shielding a safe room is easier to hide than renovating the entire house. Hiding a faraday cage inside new dry walls or using wallpaper to hide foil and mylar is a better option than having a giant faraday cage just sitting there waiting to cause a fight.

Anything is better than trashing your home life and wasting your time fighting those inside your home when this system is after you. Explaining it away as an experiment with a smile is much safer than trying to force feed the assimilated with a red pill. Test the fence once if you have to but if the reaction is cold then leave it be. Don't waste time arguing with clueless people about things they couldn't possibly understand. If they were going to understand the world, they would be the ones trying to wake you up instead of trying to get you to go back to sleep. While it is safer to be "sleeping,"

the endgame is assimilation and mass suicide. Our American spirit demands more than just looking the other way.

Teleportation technologies have also become part of the equation.

While this is beyond the intended scope of this book, we can report that a new type of weapon is currently being used that can only really be described as a "quantum energy drone." They use technologies that are not fully understood, and are either inter-dimensional in nature or use advanced quantum mechanics far beyond anything that should even exist. They use zero-point energy propulsion to travel from place to place and have been reported to "warp drive" into strategic locations.

These drones use a type of cloaking technology as well, and are capable of firing a directed energy weapon. These drones appear to phase through shielding and can nest inside a room to fire at a target. Their sizes have been reported to be large and small, and that the larger ones spawn smaller ones to penetrate shielded environments.

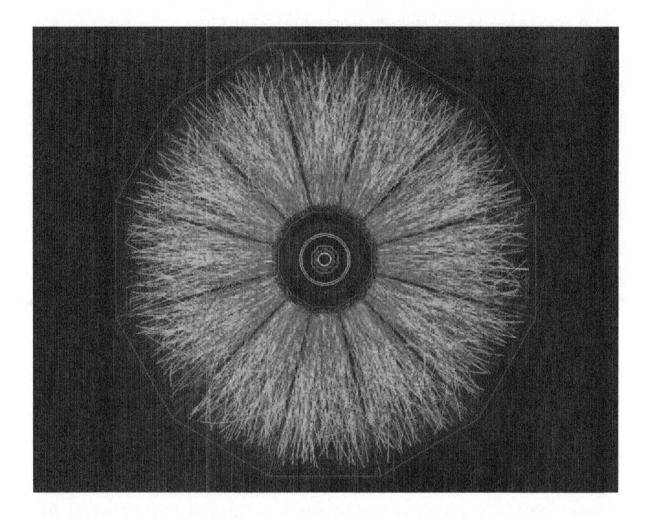

These drones CAN barely be seen with the naked eye in dark lit rooms and appear as an eye-shaped orb and are similar to what is pictured above. Just turn off the lights at night instead of watching a screen, and let your eyes adjust and start paying attention to your surroundings. Look for a faint circle within a circle that is amber in color. This may seem impossible to even imagine, but these drones have been reported everywhere and the existence of these drones has been confirmed with the highest degree of certainty.

How a quantum drone is able to target, fire a weapon or even move through structures like a ghost is not something that is yet fully understood. They appear to be the product of "smart beam" technology that can produce a weaponized hologram. But this tech might very well be from another world. As they used to say, we didn't go from the horse and buggy to modern technology in the span of a hundred years without outside intervention.

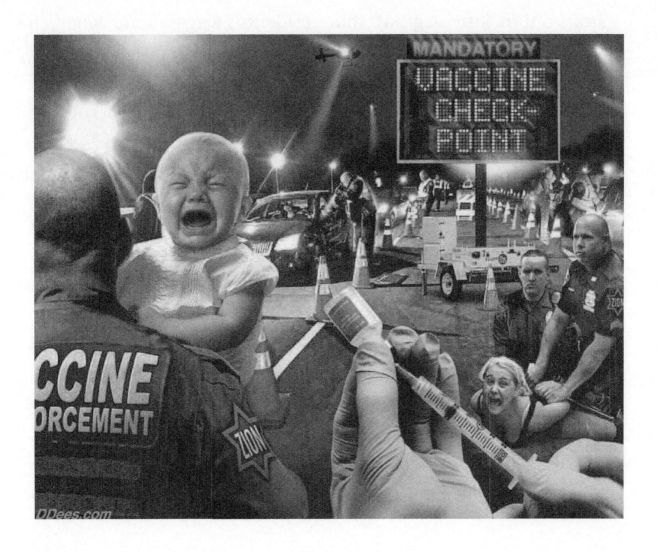

EMERGENCY SHIELDING

There will be a need for emergency shielding if energy weapon attacks turn into siege at your residence. Sieges occur when the victim tries to survive the attacks with shielding.

Most people will not have sufficient shielding to survive a siege, given the strength of these weapons and their angles of attack. It would be easier to survive if attacks were only coming from a few directions. But these weapons will attack from every angle including from underground. It's difficult to imagine such a thing until you've experienced it, and chances are you will experience this technology sooner rather than later.

Regardless of how well you plan for this situation, the enemy will find weaknesses and they will exploit those weaknesses. And while most people won't begin to shield until it's pretty much too late, our recommendation is to begin now. There's no point stocking up on guns, ammo, food, water and generators while building shelters against conventional weapons if you're wide open to radiation attacks. Because eventually these weapons will become a factor in just about every future scenario, including a new world war. The need for military grade shielding is going to be a must if you plan on participating in the fight that's happening now.

So here are a few ideas to get you going in the right direction. Have a large stockpile of lead ready to go. Lead is the best answer in most situations but eventually you will reach a point of diminishing with lead and will have to find other forms of more effective shielding. Deploy lead in tiles anywhere that becomes problematic. Enhance those tiles with other shielding materials and bag them up and have them ready to go like sandbags because a flood is definitely coming. Stacking these tiles can be a big help in trouble spots like the bed or chair and, again, everything should be reinforced with HDPE, magnetite, copper foil, etc. So, invest in lead like it's better than silver.

Prepare magnets of various sizes and dimensions as discussed in the magnetic armor section. These types of opposing magnets in an inductor style configuration have saved lives over and over again and can cover sensitive areas on your body that will be attacked. This configuration of magnets can stop energy weapons and particle beam weapons in their tracks like nothing else but even that strategy will reach a point of diminishing returns.

Deploying these magnets temporarily and properly will resolve most issues related to surgical beam strikes but they work best in combination with the other recommended shielding materials in this book. No single solution is fool proof against advanced technologies driven by artificial intelligence. Other arrangements of magnets on plates can be useful and embedded in foam mats with a box cutter to secure their configuration. Magnets on metal shielding is not always the best idea. More advanced strategies focused on band gap shielding appear to be very promising.

Using thin layers of quartz looks like the next frontier for shielding against quantum weapons as well as boron carbide. But you will have to test these different types of solutions for yourself in a way that can be easily removed in case it backfires. Energy weapons are an umbrella term for a long list of different types of radiation based weapons, each weapon type is meant to overcome different types of shielding environments.

Making shielding that can resist every type of military grade energy weapon is the main reason for using multi-layered shielding. Each layer addresses a different type of weapon and offers redundancy in case some of the layers become compromised.

Make extra tiles that are maxed out with exotic shielding materials to use against technologies that shouldn't exist. Use these exotic plates as emergency breast plates or as plates that you can deploy for extra protection in bed or while sitting. Attacks will come in from all directions, especially from underground. We keep mentioning this talking point because these underground weapons are by far the worst and can cut tunnel inches of lead. Most of these weapons are based on ELF technology but there are many different types of weapon systems that achieve the same effect.

Standard ELF is used for communicating with submarines deep below the surface of the ocean. In their weaponized form, ELF waves will cause heart attacks while you sleep. They are pretty much the perfect weapon and are nearly impossible to stop. Thick layers of magnetite based shielding with lead and HDPE is your best answer for the time being, as well as insulated layers of sheet metal with the outer layer or bottom layer connected to a ground. Sleeping on your side will help against these types of attacks, but stacking emergency plates below you or even on every side may become necessary to survive. It won't be comfortable but these plates can be padded with cushion foam if time permits.

Avoid gaps due to padding as much as possible because this enemy will sneak through. These plates can be used on chairs against vertical impalement attacks from underground and many other places. They can be added to strategic locations such as windows to break obvious angles of attack. Just one of the plates leaning against a window can make a difference.

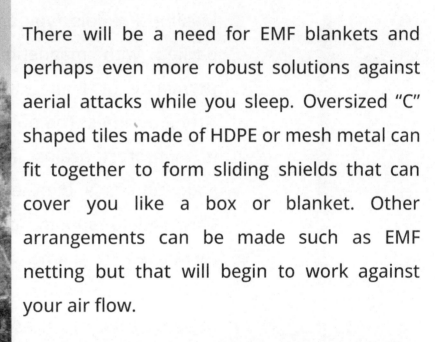

There will be a need for EMF blankets and perhaps even more robust solutions against aerial attacks while you sleep. Oversized "C" shaped tiles made of HDPE or mesh metal can fit together to form sliding shields that can cover you like a box or blanket. Other arrangements can be made such as EMF netting but that will begin to work against your air flow.

A helmet for sleeping will be necessary as well for worst case scenarios. It should be made like other helmets but include a fixed extension for eye and neck protection. The finished design should look something like a V.R. helmet. Attacks to the back of the head can become severely debilitating and is a huge weak spot that the enemy will exploit. Other forms of eye protection are worth considering such as reinforced frames and slide -on protections for glasses. Mesh metal works well for these situations as a framework and they can be reinforced further with fabrics or lead if need be. They will attack the sides of your eyes and the temples and so add-on extensions that can rest on the branches of your eye protection will become a handy tool until you can construct a helmet with a drop down visor. Various mouth guards or extensions to helmets or thyroid guards will become necessary as well.

Making a saddle type accessory out of HDPE backed with magnetite, lead, copper and permalloy or lead will become a must for sitting at times. The point of this saddle shield is to protect against attacks that come for your gonads and other assets in proximity. This saddle should look like a horizontal rectangle with a long tail.extending down the middle of the rectangle. The rectangle part will fit above your thighs as you sit and the tail will run between your legs and will cover the rear. Other variations with a larger rear guard may be preferable but using a simple tail makes it easier to position and to remove for sitting. Using additional plates to protect the rear from vertical energy weapon impalement is easier to manage. Experimenting on your own will show you the differences when it comes to deployment.

Larger planks of HDPE treated with magnetite (and graphite) sandwiched in copper foil and topped with mylar can serve many purposes as lightweight, easy to position Roman-style shields. They can be practical for home use as well as the car. They should be slightly larger than your upper body but other sizes of this configuration can be very useful as well. They can be used to add cover to windows and windshields as well as tucked in between you and the passenger seat or driver's door for added protection.

Having a few laminated "rags" made of EMF fabric can be a helpful stop-gap solution for armor or the bed. We also recommend making foot long tiles made from 10 layers of aluminum foil and a layer of copper foil that can be folded for thickness and tucked into sensitive areas for occasions where that's needed. They will spend plenty of time hitting below the waist during a siege. Wrap five layers of foil around cardboard then pull the cardboard carefully out the middle to save time and you'll have a total of 10 layers, five above and five below where the cardboard used to be. Tape it up and seal the edges and add the copper foil and then tape that up as well and you've got some formidable, easy to use shielding. Doing it the long way by laminating each layer of aluminum is better but takes much longer.

Leg guards for the bed may be needed if they hit your legs hard. Extended exposure will lead to a DVT and so thigh guards that are secured by straps or buckles will be needed as well as lower leg protections and ankle protection. Tube designs or strap-on designs work best. DIY belt loops made out of tape will help make straps work for thigh protectors. There may be a need for 24/7 protection for your thighs and so you will have to make a thigh guard or shorts that you can wear during the daytime as well. Thigh guards can be concealed under pants but require a belt extension to stay in place in most cases. Pain will be your guide as to what your body needs to survive, so never ignore the sudden onset of pain, rather shield against it.

QUICK SUMMARY

Here's a recap of all the materials you will need for serious shielding projects:

Stainless steel planks for sensitive areas like the bed. These can be reinforced with mesh metal or any of the following materials.

Copper plates, foil, tape or mesh.

Aluminum plates, foil, tape or mesh.

EMF fabric (copper, iron or silver fiber).

HDPE (High Density Poly-Ethylene and Poly-Urethane insulating foam).

Metal cutting shears, rulers, scissors, packaging tape, cardboard templates.

Multimeter and an EMF meter (geiger counter and hackerRF meter optional).

Epoxy (preferably VOC free, child friendly, watch videos on how to mix and pour).

Graphite (quart or liter size) and magnetite (by the pound or kilo), iron or stainless steel powders can be used to supplement the mix and sprinkling iron powder has huge benefits after applying the mix to HDPE, aka known as the iron ball effect).

Permalloy or Mu-metal.

Mylar.

Magnets and bare copper wire.

Lead.

Exotic materials such as quartz and boron carbide powders.

Remember that it takes 3 to 5 cm of shielding material to be moderately effective against various frequency bands. The multi-layer strategy attempts to achieve broadband effectiveness with around 1 to 2 cm of materials but sometimes there's no bending the physics associated with the problem so anticipate the need for thicker layers.

To make armor use the tile system to produce flexible tiles that can be upgraded. Two tiles for the front and two tiles for the sides. Seal everything up so little or no light can get through the seams. Add extensions when necessary.

Reverse engineer hats to make helmets.

Use the tile system to make leg and arm protection.

Reverse engineer shoes to make foot protection or add inserts.

Accessories like saddles and thyroid guards will become necessary.

Armor your vehicle if you want to survive.

Start with a safe room using foil and / or mylar then expand.

Best to order what is in stock and can be delivered in less than a week rather than waiting 3 weeks for drop shipping from unknown resellers.

Follow all other prepper recommendations but understand that HAM radios and generators will bring enemy mop up crews to you in a hurry if things go full "skynet." Old tech is better, so stock up on candles and things that can function without electricity. Don't forget filters, including for radiation and ways to distill water if necessary.

CONCLUSIONS

As we've said numerous times there will be no 100% effective solution against this system and that the problem we're facing is far worse than what's been described in this book. So be sure to change the profile of your shielding frequently to force the system to adjust as much as possible. That means constantly upgrade your shielding with new features or layers to change the way it looks on their radar. Shielding strategies will only last so long before the system adapts and you're forced to make changes.

Staying on the move helps but never lose the stability of a home base or bunker or you will most likely disappear. The system wants to flush you out and wear you down to finish you off on a "death bed" scenario or trigger a heart attack by ambushing you in a public place like the grocery store. Or it will finish you off as you hide under a tree somewhere.

Never sleep outside away from civilization (camping) or loiter at night in remote areas as a targeted individual. And never risk moving around without minimum EMF protection for the heart and head. Do the hand test if you suspect targeting, and begin with light EMF clothing and a foil shielded safe room. If you're being targeted the system will let you know in an overt way from there.

This book represents years of research and testing. We're using it to help those in need and to raise awareness for what's to come. The proceeds of this book will be used to further our research in the hopes of finding better countermeasures. It is why we would ask each and everyone of you to not re-upload this content for free without prior consent. We've made the price of this book extremely affordable whereas similar books with far less meaningful content sell at well over $100.

Feel free to share this book, however, with those you know in the real world and feel free to recommend this book for purchase to those you know in your various online communities. We currently offer advanced training for everything related to this content and more. That training can be found on our patreon page.

If you're reading this, then you are the resistance.

To contact the author with questions or projects, feel free to contact us with an appropriate subject header at: stfn701@protonmail.com

To sign up for advanced training or to support our research donations can be made at:

https://www.patreon.com/STFNews

To follow are latest reports and news be sure to sign up for free on our telegram page at:

https://t.me/STFNREPORT

That page is censored by most "big tech" versions of the telegram app so you may have to use the desktop version or the mobile app directly from telegram.org

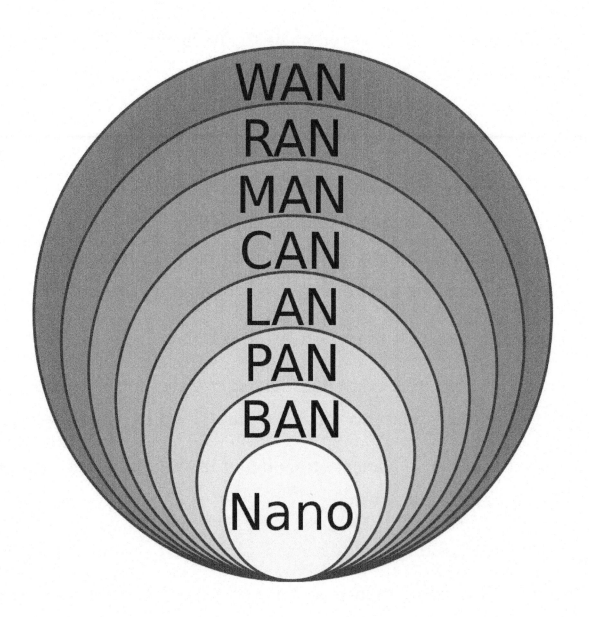

FREQUENTLY ASKED QUESTIONS

Can a mirror reflect EMF radiation?

For radio frequency (RF) waves, which include signals from radios, cell phones, and Wi-Fi, traditional mirrors are not reflective. In the RF range, metals like copper, aluminum, and gold are generally better at reflecting these waves. Mirrors are typically not designed to be reflective in the RF range.

How is EMF shielding defeated?

The weaponization of electromagnetic fields (EMF) poses a formidable challenge in modern defense strategies, requiring a profound understanding of the interaction between EMF and shielding materials. Examining the weaknesses of these materials is imperative in fortifying defenses against emerging threats in the realm of electromagnetic warfare.

To comprehend the complexities of this warfare, it is crucial to dissect the weaknesses inherent in conductive and magnetic permeable materials commonly employed for electromagnetic shielding.

Conductive materials, exemplified by metals such as copper and aluminum, are often utilized for their ability to redirect and absorb electromagnetic energy. However, when subjected to weaponized EMF, these materials face critical weaknesses.

When shielding materials intercept EM waves, especially at higher frequencies, partial penetration is inevitable. The oscillations within the shielding material, coupled with re-induction effects, give rise to induced currents. Weaponized EMF can exploit these frequency-dependent weaknesses, allowing for targeted infiltration through conductive shielding.

In contrast, magnetic permeable materials, such as ferromagnetic alloys, are preferred for shielding against lower frequency EMF due to their ability to redirect magnetic fields. However, these materials harbor their own set of vulnerabilities when confronted with weaponized EMF.

A critical weakness is saturation. At high EMF intensities, magnetic permeable materials can reach a saturation point where their magnetic properties become overwhelmed, rendering them ineffective for further field redirection. The consequence is a compromised shielding capability and increased susceptibility to EMF penetration.

What is magnetic permeability?

Magnetic permeability is a fundamental property of materials that quantifies their ability to respond to magnetic fields. It measures how easily a material can become magnetized when exposed to an external magnetic field. A material with high magnetic permeability exhibits a strong response to magnetic fields, meaning it can be easily magnetized. Conversely, a material with low magnetic permeability responds weakly to magnetic fields and is less prone to magnetization.

In the context of EMF shielding, materials with high magnetic permeability are particularly valuable. When dealing with electromagnetic fields, such as those encountered in radiofrequency applications, these materials can effectively channel and redirect the magnetic flux lines induced by the EMF, reducing its penetration into the shielded area. This magnetic redirection capability enhances the overall effectiveness of EMF shielding, providing a robust barrier against undesirable electromagnetic interference. Consequently, materials with high magnetic permeability are extensively employed in advanced EMF shielding solutions to safeguard sensitive equipment and critical environments from potential electromagnetic disturbances.

What role does resonance play in shielding?

Resonance is often considered undesirable. Resonance occurs when a material's natural frequency matches the frequency of the incoming electromagnetic radiation. This can lead to enhanced absorption and transmission of energy, making the shielding less effective. In shielding applications, the goal is usually to prevent or minimize resonance to achieve efficient attenuation of the electromagnetic waves.

In the context of electromagnetic shielding:

1. **Resonant Absorption:** Resonant absorption can lead to the concentration of energy in specific regions, potentially causing localized heating and weakening the shielding's effectiveness.
2. **Resonant Reflection:** Resonance can also lead to reflection and scattering of energy, which might not align with the goal of containing or attenuating the radiation.
3. **Broadband Shielding:** Effective shielding materials and designs aim to provide attenuation across a broad range of frequencies, avoiding resonant peaks that can amplify specific frequencies.

When designing shielding materials or structures, it's important to consider the materials' resonance characteristics and choose materials or configurations that minimize resonance effects. This ensures that the shielding remains efficient and effective across a wide range of frequencies and incident angles.

What is resonance exploitation in the context of EMF shielding?

Resonance is a phenomenon where an object vibrates at its natural frequency when subjected to external forces. In the context of electromagnetic shielding, resonance can be exploited to penetrate shielding materials and create vulnerabilities.

When shielding materials resonate with an external electromagnetic field, several risks arise, including:

Increased Permeability: Resonance can lead to an increase in the permeability of the shielding material, making it more susceptible to electromagnetic penetration.

Energy Concentration: Resonant frequencies can concentrate electromagnetic energy within the shielding material, causing localized heating and potential damage.

Signal Leakage: Resonance-induced vibrations may cause small gaps in the shielding, allowing the leakage of sensitive signals or electromagnetic interference.

Countermeasure 1: Multilayer Shielding:

To counter resonance vulnerabilities, the implementation of multilayer shielding is essential. Each layer should have different resonant frequencies, preventing simultaneous resonance and reducing the likelihood of successful penetration. For example, combining materials with different permittivity or permeability can disrupt resonance.

Countermeasure 2: Damping Layers:

Incorporating damping layers within the shielding structure is an effective countermeasure. These layers absorb and dissipate energy, reducing resonance amplitudes and minimizing the risk of resonance-induced vulnerabilities. For instance, viscoelastic materials, such as rubber or silicone, can act as damping layers to absorb and convert electromagnetic energy into heat.

Countermeasure 3: Material Combinations:

Selecting shielding materials with complementary properties can help mitigate resonance issues. For instance, combining high-conductivity metals like copper or aluminum with high-permeability materials like ferrite can effectively distribute and redirect electromagnetic energy, minimizing resonance susceptibility.

Countermeasure 4: Shape and Structure:

The geometry of the shielding structure can influence resonance behavior. Shielding designs that incorporate irregular shapes, multiple layers, and non-uniform thickness can disperse resonance frequencies and reduce the risk of exploiting a single resonant mode. Convex shapes are better and texture can be an advantage.

Countermeasure 5: Electromagnetic Absorbers:

Strategically placing electromagnetic absorbers within the shielding structure can dissipate incident energy and reduce the amplitude of resonant vibrations. Materials with high loss tangents, like carbon-based composites, are commonly used as electromagnetic absorbers.

Resonance exploitation poses a significant risk to electromagnetic shielding strategies, but implementing effective countermeasures can mitigate these vulnerabilities. Multilayer shielding, damping layers, material combinations, specialized shapes, frequency scrambling, and electromagnetic absorbers are some of the approaches that can enhance shielding effectiveness. By combining these techniques, engineers can create robust shielding solutions that protect sensitive equipment and systems from electromagnetic interference. Continuous research and testing are essential to stay ahead of evolving resonance exploitation techniques and ensure the highest level of protection.

What would be viewed as a robust combination of layers for EMF shielding?

Creating a composite blend for robust electromagnetic and radiation protection involves considering various factors, including electrical conductivity, magnetic permeability, and additional characteristics for specific shielding requirements. Here's a suggested composite blend that prioritizes availability and cost:

1. **Outer Layer: Copper (Cu):**
   - **Role:** Excellent electrical conductivity for attenuating electric fields.
   - **Availability and Cost:** Copper is widely available and relatively cost-effective.
2. **Middle Layer: Permalloy (Nickel-Iron Alloy):**
   - **Role:** High magnetic permeability for shielding against magnetic fields.

- **Availability and Cost:** Permalloy is available, and its cost is reasonable, especially in common formulations like 80% nickel and 20% iron.

3. **Inner Layer: Aluminum (Al):**
   - **Role:** Additional electric field attenuation and cost-effective alternative to copper.
   - **Availability and Cost:** Aluminum is widely available and often more cost-effective than copper.

4. **Band Gap Layer: Aluminum Oxide (Al_2O_3):**
   - **Role:** Introduce a dielectric layer with a band gap to help attenuate higher-frequency electromagnetic radiation.
   - **Availability and Cost:** Aluminum oxide is widely available and cost-effective.

5. **High-Speed Electron / Neutron Shielding Layer: Polyethylene (PE):**
   - **Role:** Neutron absorption and protection against high-speed electrons.
   - **Availability and Cost:** Polyethylene is readily available and cost-effective. It is commonly used in radiation shielding applications.

How does the magnetic component of the EMF wave induce the electrical component of the wave?

When an electromagnetic wave propagates through space, it consists of time-varying electric and magnetic fields. As the wave moves, these fields change in strength and direction, creating a dynamic situation:

- **Change in Magnetic Field (H-field):** The magnetic field component of the wave (H-field) varies with time, creating a changing magnetic flux (Φ) in the region.

- **Induction of Electric Field (E-field):** According to Faraday's law of electromagnetic induction, the changing magnetic flux induces an electric field (E-field) in the vicinity. This induced electric field is responsible for the propagation of the electromagnetic wave.

- **Change in Electric Field (E-field):** The induced electric field, in turn, leads to a change in the electric field component of the wave. This change in the electric field contributes to the propagation of the wave and generates the magnetic field component.

The interaction between the changing electric and magnetic fields propagates the electromagnetic wave through space, allowing it to carry energy and information. This dynamic interplay is a fundamental aspect of how electromagnetic waves, including radio waves, microwaves, and light, are generated and propagate.

If EMF shielding blocks the electrical field but not the magnetic field, will the magnetic field make it through and re-induce a new electric field?

In the presence of an electromagnetic wave, if a shielding material effectively blocks the electrical component (E-field) while allowing the magnetic component (H-field) to pass through unaltered, the H-field can propagate through the shield and induce a new electrical component on the other side of the shield.

Here's how this process works:

1. **Shielding the E-Field**: The shielding material, which may be conductive or dielectric depending on the application, is designed to block or attenuate the electric field component (E-field) of the incoming electromagnetic wave. This prevents the E-field from penetrating or affecting the region behind the shield.

2. **Unabated H-Field**: The magnetic field component (H-field) is not significantly affected by the shielding material, especially if the material is not designed for magnetic shielding. Therefore, the H-field can pass through the shield relatively unaltered.

3. **Induction of New E-Field**: As the H-field propagates through the shield and reaches the region on the other side, it can induce a new electric field (E-field) in nearby conductive materials or objects. This induction occurs because the changing magnetic field induces an electromotive force (EMF) or

voltage in nearby conductors, following Faraday's law of electromagnetic induction.

4. **Propagation of the Wave**: The induced electric field contributes to the propagation of the electromagnetic wave on the other side of the shield. This can result in the re-emergence of the wave, carrying its energy and information.

It's important to note that while the shielding material may block or attenuate the E-field, the effectiveness of the shield can depend on various factors, including the frequency of the electromagnetic wave, the material's properties, and the shield's design. For effective electromagnetic interference (EMI) shielding, engineers consider both the electric and magnetic field components, and they often use multi-layered shields or materials tailored to the specific frequency range of interest.

In practice, electromagnetic shielding involves a combination of materials and techniques to address both EMI and magnetic field interference, depending on the requirements of the application.

What are the most magnetic substances that can be used for shielding?

Magnetism can be characterized by a material's magnetic susceptibility and its response to an external magnetic field. The most magnetic substances are typically materials that are ferromagnetic, ferrimagnetic, or have high magnetic susceptibility. Here is a list of 30 of the most magnetic substances, roughly ordered by their relative magnetic strength:

Iron (10/10): Iron is highly ferromagnetic and exhibits a strong response to a magnetic field.

Neodymium (10/10): Neodymium magnets are among the strongest permanent magnets and exhibit powerful magnetic properties.

Cobalt (10/10): Cobalt is a ferromagnetic metal that exhibits strong magnetic properties.

Gadolinium (10/10): Gadolinium is a rare earth element known for its strong ferromagnetic behavior.

Samarium (9/10): Samarium magnets are strong and exhibit high magnetic susceptibility.

Nickel (9/10): Nickel is a ferromagnetic metal, commonly used in magnets.

Dysprosium (9/10): Dysprosium is used in high-strength magnets and has significant magnetic properties.

Magnetite (8/10): Magnetite is a natural magnetic mineral with strong magnetic susceptibility.

Cerium (7/10): Cerium exhibits ferromagnetic properties but is less magnetic than some other rare earth elements.

Europium (7/10): Europium is another rare earth element with notable magnetic characteristics.

Terbium (7/10): Terbium is used in some high-performance magnets and has substantial magnetic strength.

Holmium (6/10): Holmium is a rare earth element with moderate magnetic properties.

Sodium (5/10): Sodium is paramagnetic and exhibits weak magnetic susceptibility.

Oxygen (5/10): Oxygen is paramagnetic but generally considered non-magnetic.

Aluminum (4/10): Aluminum is paramagnetic and exhibits very weak magnetic properties.

Water (4/10): Water is weakly diamagnetic, meaning it is slightly repelled by a magnetic field.

Copper (4/10): Copper is weakly diamagnetic and exhibits little magnetic susceptibility.

Lead (4/10): Lead is weakly diamagnetic and has very low magnetic susceptibility.

Gold (4/10): Gold is weakly diamagnetic and displays low magnetic properties.

Bismuth (4/10): Bismuth is diamagnetic and exhibits weak magnetic susceptibility.

Mercury (3/10): Mercury is diamagnetic and is weakly repelled by a magnetic field.

Silver (3/10): Silver is weakly diamagnetic and has low magnetic susceptibility.

Platinum (3/10): Platinum is weakly diamagnetic and has minimal magnetic properties.

Tin (3/10): Tin is weakly diamagnetic and exhibits low magnetic susceptibility.

Zinc (3/10): Zinc is weakly diamagnetic and has very low magnetic susceptibility.

Titanium (2/10): Titanium is weakly diamagnetic with minimal magnetic effects.

Cadmium (2/10): Cadmium is diamagnetic and displays low magnetic susceptibility.

Carbon (1/10): Carbon is typically non-magnetic but may have weak paramagnetic properties.

What are the most magnetic permeable substances that can be used for shielding?

Magnetic permeability is a property of materials that describes their ability to become magnetized in the presence of an external magnetic field. It is typically measured as a dimensionless quantity or relative permeability (μr), where the value 1 represents the permeability of a vacuum. The higher the μr value, the more permeable the material is. Here is a list of 30 substances with their approximate relative permeability ratings:

Vacuum (1/10): $\mu r = 1$ (baseline for comparison)

Air (1/10): $\mu r \approx 1$ (very close to vacuum)

Water (1/10): $\mu r \approx 1$ (weakly diamagnetic)

Copper (1/10): $\mu r \approx 1$ (weakly diamagnetic)

Aluminum (1/10): $\mu r \approx 1$ (weakly diamagnetic)

Gold (1/10): $\mu r \approx 1$ (weakly diamagnetic)

Silver (1/10): $\mu r \approx 1$ (weakly diamagnetic)

Platinum (1/10): $\mu r \approx 1$ (weakly diamagnetic)

Lead (1/10): $\mu r \approx 1$ (weakly diamagnetic)

Bismuth (1/10): $\mu_r \approx 1$ (weakly diamagnetic)

Tin (1/10): $\mu_r \approx 1$ (weakly diamagnetic)

Zinc (1/10): $\mu_r \approx 1$ (weakly diamagnetic)

Tungsten (2/10): $\mu_r \approx 2$ (weakly diamagnetic)

Sulfur (2/10): $\mu_r \approx 2$ (diamagnetic)

Carbon (2/10): $\mu_r \approx 2$ (diamagnetic)

Silicon (2/10): $\mu_r \approx 2$ (diamagnetic)

Tantalum (2/10): $\mu_r \approx 2$ (diamagnetic)

Oxygen (2/10): $\mu_r \approx 2$ (diamagnetic)

Sodium (2/10): $\mu_r \approx 2$ (diamagnetic)

Nickel (10/10): $\mu_r \approx 100$ (strongly ferromagnetic)

Iron (10/10): $\mu_r \approx 100$ (strongly ferromagnetic)

Cobalt (10/10): $\mu_r \approx 100$ (strongly ferromagnetic)

Gadolinium (10/10): $\mu_r \approx 100$ (ferromagnetic)

Samarium (10/10): $\mu_r \approx 100$ (ferromagnetic)

Dysprosium (10/10): $\mu_r \approx 100$ (ferromagnetic)

Neodymium (10/10): $\mu_r \approx 100$ (ferromagnetic)

Magnetite (10/10): $\mu_r \approx 1000$ (ferromagnetic) - **WINNER**

Ferrite Materials (7-10/10): μ_r varies but is often high (ferromagnetic or ferrimagnetic)

Cerium (7/10): $\mu_r \approx 70$ (ferromagnetic)

Terbium (7/10): $\mu_r \approx 70$ (ferromagnetic

Magnetite (Fe_3O_4) stands out as a material with exceptional magnetic permeability (μ_r), which is significantly higher than most other common substances. This high magnetic permeability is one of the reasons why magnetite is often used in various applications where strong magnetic properties are required. Magnetite is a ferromagnetic material, which means it can be strongly magnetized in the presence of a magnetic field.

Please note that these values are approximate and can vary based on factors such as temperature, material purity, and crystal structure. Materials with higher relative permeabilities (μ_r) are more susceptible to becoming magnetized in the presence of an external magnetic field and are often used in magnetic applications, while those with lower values are typically considered diamagnetic or weakly paramagnetic. Ferromagnetic materials, like iron and neodymium, exhibit strong magnetic behavior when exposed to a magnetic field.

What are the most electrically conductive materials that can be used for shielding?

Here's a list of some materials based on their electrical conductivity, ranked in descending order, along with their approximate conductivity values in MegaSiemens per meter (MS/m):

Silver (Ag) - 62.1

Copper (Cu) - 58.1

Gold (Au) - 44.7

Aluminum (Al) - 37.7

Calcium (Ca) - 29.8

Sodium (Na) - 21.7

Magnesium (Mg) - 22.0

Iron (Fe) - 1.0

Nickel (Ni) - 14.3

Zinc (Zn) - 16.6

Tungsten (W) - 18.1

Platinum (Pt) - 9.4

Tin (Sn) - 9.1

Mercury (Hg) - 1.04

Lead (Pb) - 4.8

Brass - 15.9

Bronze - 7.9

Carbon (graphite) - 3,000 to 10,000 (Best value)

Graphene - > 1,000,000 (depending on quality)

Carbon nanotubes - > 100,000,000

Please note that conductivity can vary with different forms of a material, purity, temperature, and other factors. The values provided are approximate and based on room temperature conditions for pure or common forms of the materials.

How does ferrite change microwaves into heat?

When ferrite interacts with an electromagnetic field (EMF) wave, it does indeed undergo changes in its magnetic state, and this interaction can lead to the absorption and conversion of energy. This phenomenon is primarily due to the complex behavior of ferrite materials in response to changing magnetic fields.

Ferrites are specialized materials with unique magnetic properties that make them effective for various applications, including EMF shielding and absorption. Here's how the interaction between ferrite and an EMF wave can lead to energy absorption and conversion:

1. **Magnetic Domain Behavior:** Ferrites consist of magnetic domains, which are small regions where atomic magnetic moments are aligned. These domains can respond to an external magnetic field, aligning themselves to the field's direction.

2. **Magnetic Resonance:** Ferrite materials exhibit a property known as magnetic resonance or ferromagnetic resonance. This is a phenomenon where the magnetic moments within the domains precess or oscillate at a specific frequency in response to an applied magnetic field.

3. **Energy Absorption:** When an EMF wave with a frequency that matches the material's ferromagnetic resonance interacts with the ferrite, the magnetic moments within the domains start oscillating. This oscillation absorbs energy from the EMF wave, effectively attenuating the wave.

4. **Energy Conversion:** The absorbed energy is converted into heat due to the friction and movement of magnetic moments within the ferrite domains. This conversion of electromagnetic energy into thermal energy is known as Joule heating or magnetic losses.

5. **EMF Attenuation:** As the absorbed energy is converted into heat, the intensity of the original EMF wave is reduced, and the wave's ability to penetrate the material is diminished.

In applications such as EMF shielding or absorption, ferrite materials are strategically designed to have specific ferromagnetic resonance frequencies that correspond to the frequencies of the EMF sources they are intended to mitigate. This design allows ferrites to effectively attenuate and absorb EMF energy, protecting sensitive electronics or reducing unwanted electromagnetic interference.

In summary, the interaction between ferrite and an EMF wave involves the absorption of energy, which is converted into heat due to the movement of magnetic moments within the material's domains. This process attenuates the EMF wave and is exploited in various electromagnetic shielding and absorption applications.

What are the considerations when shielding against gyrotrons or other circular high powered microwave weapons?

A gyrotron is a high-power microwave generator that produces intense electromagnetic radiation. When a gyrotron beam hits a flat piece of steel, several factors come into play that influence the interaction between the beam and the material. One of the obvious weaknesses is that steel, being a good conductor, can reflect some of the radiation, potentially causing unintended scattering or redirection of the beam. Additionally, steel might not be optimal for absorbing or dissipating the energy efficiently, which could lead to some of the energy being retained in the material.

To optimize the material to deflect or absorb the energy of a gyrotron beam more effectively, you could consider the following strategies:

1. **Absorption and Dissipation:** Choose or design a material that has higher absorption properties for the specific frequency of the gyrotron beam. Materials with dielectric loss characteristics at that frequency can convert the electromagnetic energy into heat more efficiently, effectively dissipating the energy.

2. **Frequency Selective Materials:** Explore the use of metamaterials or engineered materials with frequency-selective properties. These materials can be designed to interact with specific frequencies in desired ways, such as absorbing or redirecting the energy.

3. **Multiple Layers:** Use a layered approach with materials of varying properties. The outer layer could be designed for reflection or deflection, while inner layers could focus on absorption and dissipation.

4. **Surface texturing:** Modifying the surface of a material to create specific patterns or structures that can influence how electromagnetic radiation interacts with it. For deflecting or absorbing a gyrotron beam, you could consider the following approaches:

- **Fresnel Zones:** Design the surface with concentric rings or zones based on Fresnel zones. These zones can cause constructive or destructive interference, affecting the reflection, absorption, or scattering of the gyrotron beam.

- **Gratings:** Create a grating pattern on the surface. The periodic pattern can manipulate the direction and phase of the beam, altering its behavior upon impact.

- **Metasurfaces:** Use metasurfaces, which are artificially engineered structures on the nanoscale. These structures can be designed to manipulate the properties of incoming radiation in specific ways, such as steering or absorbing the energy.

5. **Resonance Manipulation:** Design the material to have resonant frequencies that can interact with the gyrotron beam more effectively. This could involve tuning the material's properties to match the frequency of the beam.

6. **Gradient Materials:** Use gradient materials that transition in properties from the surface to the interior. This can help distribute the energy more evenly through the material, reducing the potential for localized heating and damage.Gradient materials transition in their properties from one end to another, providing a controlled change in characteristics. For optimizing interaction with a gyrotron beam:

- **Gradient Dielectric Constant:** Design a material with a dielectric constant that gradually changes from the surface to the interior. This can lead to a smoother transition of the electromagnetic field, reducing reflection and scattering.

- **Gradient Conductivity:** Create a material with varying conductivity. This can distribute the energy more evenly throughout the material, reducing the risk of localized heating and damage.

- **Tapered Absorption:** Design a gradient in the absorption coefficient. This can cause the material to absorb more energy at the surface and gradually attenuate the beam as it penetrates deeper.

7. **Cooling Mechanisms:** Integrate cooling mechanisms into the material to prevent overheating and damage due to excessive energy absorption. This can be especially important for high-energy beams like those produced by gyrotrons.

8. **Material Reflectivity:** Optimize the reflective properties of the material to redirect the beam away from critical areas. This could involve shaping the material in a way that redirects the beam away from sensitive components.

When dealing with round or omnidirectional beams of electromagnetic radiation, using three-dimensional round shapes or structures can be more effective for shielding. These shapes can help distribute the energy more uniformly and mitigate the effects of scattering and reflection that can occur with flat or planar surfaces.

Three-dimensional round shapes, such as domes, spheres, or cylindrical structures, offer several advantages:

1. **Uniform Distribution:** These shapes allow for more uniform distribution of the energy across all directions, helping to minimize localized concentration of energy that could lead to resonance or hotspots.

2. **Reduced Reflection:** The curvature of the surface can help scatter and disperse the radiation more effectively, reducing the likelihood of reflection back towards the source.

3. **Diffusion:** The rounded shapes can contribute to diffusing the radiation as it interacts with the surface, helping to weaken its intensity and spread it out.

4. **Adaptability:** Three-dimensional shapes are better suited to handling radiation coming from different angles, which is crucial for omnidirectional beams.

5. **Multi-Layered Approach:** You can also consider using multiple layers of rounded shielding materials to further enhance attenuation.

6. **Minimal Resonance:** By carefully designing the shape and material properties, you can avoid resonances that could amplify specific frequencies.

While designing 3D rounded structures might be more complex than using flat materials, their effectiveness in handling omnidirectional radiation patterns can make them a valuable choice for shielding against sources emitting circular beams of electromagnetic radiation.

It's important to note that designing materials to interact optimally with specific types of electromagnetic radiation can be complex and often requires simulations, testing, and optimization. Additionally, the selection of materials depends on the specific characteristics of the gyrotron beam, including its frequency, power, and polarization.

Is there a type of radar that can determine the resonance of a structure or shielding at a distance?

When it comes to acquiring the resonance frequency of shielding materials, various EMF-based technologies and measurement methods can provide insights into material characteristics and resonant behavior. Here are a few technologies that can be useful in determining resonance frequencies or related material properties:

1. **Vector Network Analyzers (VNAs)**: VNAs are instrumental in analyzing the electromagnetic behavior of materials by measuring the complex impedance, reflection coefficient, and transmission coefficient over a wide frequency range. They can reveal how materials interact with electromagnetic waves, aiding in identifying resonance points or frequency-specific behaviors.

2. **Spectrum Analyzers**: Spectrum analyzers are utilized to examine the frequency spectrum of electromagnetic signals. By subjecting shielding materials to electromagnetic fields across

different frequencies and observing their response with a spectrum analyzer, resonance frequencies or frequency-dependent behaviors can be inferred.

3. **Impedance Analyzers**: These devices measure the electrical impedance of materials, providing valuable information about how materials respond to electromagnetic waves at different frequencies. By examining impedance at various frequencies, resonance points or changes in behavior can be identified.

4. **Frequency Sweep Testing**: Using a controlled frequency sweep approach, which exposes the shielding material to a range of frequencies and monitors its response, can help identify resonant frequencies or other significant frequency-dependent characteristics.

5. **Time-Domain Reflectometry (TDR)**: TDR systems can evaluate the behavior of electromagnetic waves in a material. By measuring reflections and impedance changes over time, TDR systems provide insights into the material's interaction with electromagnetic fields, which can include resonant behavior.

6. **Electromagnetic Simulation Software**: Utilizing software capable of simulating electromagnetic behavior (e.g., finite element analysis or electromagnetic field simulation tools) can assist in predicting and analyzing resonant frequencies and material responses in different EMF conditions.

There are certain radar-based technologies that can indirectly infer or assess resonance characteristics of structures or materials, though directly calculating resonance at a distance with radar is quite complex. Radar systems are primarily used for various detection, imaging, and measurement purposes, but directly measuring resonance characteristics at a distance is challenging.

However, through various radar and remote sensing techniques, it's possible to indirectly infer certain characteristics related to resonance or material properties of structures. These methods include:

1. **Ground-Penetrating Radar (GPR)**: GPR systems can measure electromagnetic reflections to infer subsurface material properties. While not directly determining resonance, GPR can indirectly help identify materials, voids, and some characteristics that might influence resonance in structures.

2. **Microwave and Terahertz Spectroscopy**: These methods use microwave and terahertz frequency radar systems to measure electromagnetic properties. While they might not measure resonance directly, they can assess dielectric properties that are influential in determining resonance characteristics.

3. **Radar-based Material Characterization**: Some radar-based systems might be capable of indirectly inferring material properties based on electromagnetic behavior. By analyzing how radar signals interact with materials, certain properties or

material behaviors, such as frequency response or dielectric properties, can be estimated.

4. **Remote Sensing Techniques**: Radar technology used in remote sensing applications can detect and interpret certain features or behavior of structures or materials from a distance. While not directly measuring resonance, these techniques can infer characteristics that might relate to resonance, like structural integrity or changes in materials.

What is diffraction when it comes to EMF?

Diffraction is a fundamental wave behavior that occurs when a wave encounters an obstacle or passes through an opening in a barrier. When electromagnetic waves, such as radio waves or light waves, encounter a shield or any physical obstruction, they can bend or spread around the edges of the obstacle, causing the wavefront to change direction and propagate in various directions. This phenomenon is particularly relevant when discussing the effectiveness of shielding against electromagnetic radiation.

In the context of shielding, diffraction can lead to "leakage" of the electromagnetic waves through small gaps, edges, or imperfections in the shielding material. The waves can follow the surface of the shielding and propagate to the other side, reducing the shielding's overall effectiveness. This can happen even when the shielding material itself has good absorption or reflection properties.

To minimize the diffraction effect and improve the shielding performance, several strategies can be employed:

Proper Material Selection: Choose shielding materials with low diffraction properties. Materials with a fine-grained structure or materials that can efficiently absorb and dissipate the energy of the electromagnetic waves are preferable.

Multiple Layers: Using multiple layers of shielding can help reduce diffraction effects. When waves encounter multiple layers, their energy is more likely to be absorbed or reflected back, reducing the chances of leakage.

Seamless and Continuous Enclosures: Ensuring that the shielding is continuous and has no gaps or seams can minimize the opportunity for waves to diffract around the edges.

Increase Thickness: A thicker shielding material can reduce diffraction and provide better attenuation.

High-Frequency Absorbers: Adding high-frequency absorbers, such as ferrite sheets or other specialized materials, can help attenuate electromagnetic waves and prevent them from diffracting around the edges.

How does capacitance influence the effectiveness and limitations of shielding materials?

1. **High-Frequency Behavior**: At higher frequencies, the capacitance of a material becomes more influential. When materials are subjected to high-frequency electromagnetic fields, they exhibit capacitive behavior, absorbing and storing electrical energy due to their capacitance.

2. **Energy Storage and Dissipation**: Materials with higher capacitance can absorb and store more electrical energy, which might lead to a saturation point where the material can't store any more energy. Beyond this point, the shielding material might become less effective as it can no longer absorb additional energy.

3. **Saturation Limit**: Capacitance has a saturation limit, and when the incoming energy exceeds this limit, the shielding material's ability to store additional electrical energy becomes restricted, affecting its effectiveness.

4. **Frequency Dependency**: The capacitance of a material is frequency-dependent. Different materials have varied responses to different frequencies, and their capacitance might be more effective at certain frequencies while less effective at others.

5. **Interaction with Electromagnetic Fields**: The interaction of a material's capacitance with the electromagnetic fields dictates

its ability to absorb and store energy. When the capacity of the material to store energy is surpassed, the material might reach its maximum capability, limiting its shielding effectiveness.

Considering capacitance alongside other electrical properties such as conductivity, resistance, and permeability provides a comprehensive understanding of how materials behave under various electromagnetic field conditions. This insight assists in selecting appropriate shielding materials for specific frequency ranges and applications, while understanding the potential limitations based on capacitance.

What advantages would boron carbide have over lead in particle beam weapon applications?

Boron carbide and lead are both materials with unique properties and advantages, and their suitability depends on the specific requirements of an application. Boron carbide can offer several advantages over lead in certain situations:

1. **Lightweight:** Boron carbide is significantly lighter than lead. This property is especially advantageous in applications where weight reduction is critical, such as in personal protective equipment (PPE), armor, and aerospace components. Boron carbide can provide effective shielding while reducing the overall weight of the shielding material.

2. **Hardness:** Boron carbide is one of the hardest known materials, making it highly resistant to abrasion and wear. This property can be beneficial in applications where the shielding material may be subjected to mechanical stress or wear over time.

3. **Thermal Stability:** Boron carbide exhibits excellent thermal stability, with a high melting point and resistance to thermal shock. It can withstand high temperatures without degradation, which can be important in various industrial and military applications.

4. **Neutron Absorption:** Boron carbide is an effective absorber of neutrons, making it suitable for nuclear shielding applications. It can be used in nuclear reactors, radiation therapy rooms, and other settings where neutron radiation must be controlled.

5. **Abrasion Resistance:** Boron carbide is highly resistant to abrasion, which is important in applications where the shielding material may come into contact with abrasive materials or surfaces.

While boron carbide offers these advantages, it's important to note that lead also has its strengths, such as its high density, which makes it effective at attenuating various types of radiation. Lead remains a common choice for many radiation shielding applications, particularly in medical settings. The choice between boron carbide and lead depends on the specific requirements of the application, including the type of radiation, the desired shielding level, weight considerations, and environmental factors.

In some cases, a combination of both materials or a composite material may be used to leverage the advantages of each material while addressing specific application requirements.

Why does paraffin wax work as a shielding material?

Paraffin wax is commonly used as a neutron moderator in radiation shielding applications due to its ability to slow down fast neutrons, making them more likely to be captured by other materials. This process reduces the energy of the neutrons and enhances their interaction with nuclei, which can subsequently reduce their harmful effects.

When using paraffin wax for neutron shielding, the thickness required depends on factors such as the energy of the neutrons and the desired level of attenuation. Generally, thicker layers of paraffin wax will result in more effective neutron moderation and shielding.

Moderation and Neutron Attenuation: To achieve effective moderation and attenuation of neutrons, a common rule of thumb is that a thickness of about 20 to 30 centimeters (8 to 12 inches) of paraffin wax is often used. But thin layers will have some effect. Thickness allows for a sufficient interaction between the neutrons and the wax molecules, slowing down the neutrons through successive collisions.

It's important to note that the moderation process is not linear; thicker layers of paraffin wax will attenuate more neutrons, but there is a point of diminishing returns where additional thicknesses may not significantly increase the effectiveness. Beyond a certain thickness, other neutron-absorbing materials might be incorporated for enhanced shielding.

Variability and Specific Applications: The required thickness of paraffin wax can vary depending on factors like the energy spectrum of the neutrons, the type of source, and the desired level of shielding. For precise applications, radiation experts and physicists often perform detailed simulations and calculations to determine the optimal thickness for neutron attenuation.

Paraffin wax does not lose its protective characteristics when heated and remolded, as long as the heating and remolding process does not significantly alter its molecular structure or introduce impurities. Paraffin wax is widely used in various applications, including radiation shielding, due to its stable and consistent properties.

However, there are a few factors to consider:

1. **Temperature Limits:** Paraffin wax has a relatively low melting point, typically between 46°C to 68°C (115°F to 154°F), depending on its specific formulation. If the wax is heated significantly beyond its melting point, it will liquefy, potentially

losing its structural integrity and effectiveness as a shielding material.

2. **Purity:** The effectiveness of paraffin wax as a neutron moderator and shielding material relies on its consistent composition. If the wax is remolded with impurities or additives that affect its molecular structure, its properties could be compromised.

3. **Thickness and Homogeneity:** When paraffin wax is remolded, ensuring uniform thickness and homogeneity across the shielding material is important. Irregularities or air pockets could reduce its effectiveness in attenuating neutrons.

4. **Chemical Changes:** Extreme heating could lead to chemical changes in the paraffin wax, affecting its ability to moderate neutrons properly. However, in typical remolding scenarios within its melting point, such changes are unlikely.

Could paraffin wax be used to complement HDPE?

Both paraffin wax and high-density polyethylene (HDPE) have specific properties that can contribute to radiation shielding, but they serve different purposes and can complement each other in certain scenarios. The choice between the two depends on the type of radiation, the energy level, and the specific requirements of your shielding application.

Paraffin Wax:

- **Moderation:** Paraffin wax is an effective neutron moderator due to its ability to slow down fast neutrons and enhance their interaction with other nuclei. It's commonly used in situations where neutron attenuation is a primary concern.
- **Limited Neutron Absorption:** While paraffin wax moderates neutrons well, it has limited ability to absorb neutrons. This means that for very high neutron flux scenarios, additional neutron-absorbing materials might be needed in conjunction with paraffin wax.

High-Density Polyethylene (HDPE):

- **Neutron Absorption:** HDPE is a good neutron absorber, especially for thermal neutrons. It can help reduce neutron transmission through shielding materials.
- **Effective Against Gamma Radiation:** HDPE also has good attenuation properties for gamma radiation, which is a type of electromagnetic radiation.
- **Structural Integrity:** HDPE has the advantage of being a solid material with consistent properties. It doesn't melt at low temperatures and is chemically stable.

Complementary Use:

In scenarios where both neutron and gamma radiation are concerns, using a combination of paraffin wax and HDPE can be effective. For instance, you might use paraffin wax to moderate and slow down fast neutrons, while HDPE can be used to absorb both neutrons and gamma radiation. This layered approach can provide more comprehensive shielding coverage.

In summary, if your primary concern is neutron moderation, paraffin wax can be useful. If you're also dealing with gamma radiation and overall shielding effectiveness, HDPE could complement paraffin wax. However, the specifics of your radiation source, its energy spectrum, and the required level of shielding are essential factors in making an informed decision. Consulting experts in radiation protection and materials science is recommended to tailor your shielding strategy to your specific needs.

What materials would be best against a free electron laser (FEL)?

Protecting against Free Electron Lasers (FELs) involves addressing intense and coherent beams of electromagnetic radiation, typically in the X-ray or infrared regions. The effectiveness of shielding materials depends on several factors, including the specific wavelength of the FEL, the power density, and the intended application. Here are considerations for selecting shielding materials:

1. **Lead:**

    Wavelength: Effective for X-rays and gamma rays.

    Properties: Lead is dense and has strong attenuation properties for high-energy photons.

2. **Tungsten:**

Wavelength: Suitable for X-rays and gamma rays.

Properties: Tungsten has high atomic number, providing effective shielding for high-energy photons.

3. **Beryllium:**

Wavelength: Effective for X-rays.

Properties: Beryllium has low atomic number and is transparent to longer-wavelength X-rays.

4. **Concrete:**

Wavelength: Suitable for gamma rays.

Properties: Dense and widely used for radiation shielding.

5. **Polyethylene:**

Wavelength: Effective for neutrons.

Properties: Polyethylene is a good neutron moderator and attenuator.

6. **Lead Glass:**

Wavelength: Suitable for X-rays.

Properties: Transparent to X-rays and offers radiation shielding.

7. **Composite Materials:**

   Wavelength: Depends on composition.

   Properties: Custom composite materials can be engineered for specific FEL wavelengths.

8. **Ceramic Materials:**

   Wavelength: Depends on the composition.

   Properties: Some ceramics offer good radiation resistance.

9. **Water:**

   Wavelength: Effective for neutrons and some X-rays.

   Properties: Water is a good neutron moderator and attenuator.

10. **Gold:**

    Wavelength: Suitable for X-rays and infrared.

    Properties: Gold has high atomic number and is effective for X-ray shielding.

How does an FEL produce light from electrons?

The process by which electrons in a Free Electron Laser (FEL) generate coherent and intense beams of electromagnetic radiation (light) involves several steps. I'll break down the process to make it more understandable:

1. **Generation of High-Energy Electrons:**

   Electrons are accelerated to high energies, often close to the speed of light. This is typically achieved using a linear accelerator (linac) or an electron gun.

2. **Undulator or Wiggler Magnet:**

   The high-energy electron beam passes through a magnetic structure called an undulator or wiggler. These devices create a periodic magnetic field along the path of the electrons.

3. **Undulator Motion:**

   The magnetic field in the undulator causes the electrons to undergo oscillatory motion as they travel along its length. This motion is often referred to as "wiggling" or "undulating."

4. **Synchrotron Radiation:**

As the high-energy electrons wiggle through the alternating magnetic field, they emit radiation known as synchrotron radiation. This radiation spans a broad spectrum, including infrared, visible, ultraviolet, and X-ray wavelengths.

5. **Coherent Amplification:**

The emitted synchrotron radiation serves as a seed for further amplification. In a process called "stimulated emission," the radiation induces neighboring electrons to emit photons with the same frequency and phase. This leads to the coherence and intensity characteristic of laser light.

6. **Feedback and Resonance:**

The amplified radiation undergoes a feedback process, where it circulates back through the undulator. This interaction with the electron beam continues, leading to further amplification through resonance conditions.

7. **Tunable Wavelength:**

The wavelength of the emitted light is tunable and can be controlled by adjusting the properties of the undulator, such as its magnetic field strength or the energy of the electron beam.

In summary, the undulator causes high-energy electrons to wiggle, and this wiggling motion results in the emission of synchrotron radiation. Through the process of stimulated emission and feedback, this radiation is further amplified, leading to the coherent and intense beams of light characteristic of a Free Electron Laser. The ability to control and tune the wavelength makes FELs highly versatile for various applications.

Does all light come from electrons?

Not all light is generated by high-intensity electrons. Light can be generated through various processes, and the source of light depends on the mechanism involved. Here are some common ways light is produced:

1. **Thermal Radiation:**

   In everyday scenarios, objects emit light due to thermal motion of their atoms and molecules. This is known as thermal radiation. The color (wavelength) of the emitted light depends on the temperature of the object.

2. **Incandescence:**

Incandescent light bulbs produce light through the heating of a wire filament. As the filament heats up, it emits visible light. The intensity and color of the light depend on the temperature of the filament.

3. **Fluorescence:**

Fluorescent lights and certain materials produce light when exposed to ultraviolet (UV) light. Electrons in the atoms of these materials absorb energy and then emit light when they return to their lower energy state.

4. **Chemiluminescence:**

Some chemical reactions produce light directly. Glow sticks, for example, emit light due to a chemical reaction that releases energy in the form of visible light.

5. **Bioluminescence:**

Certain living organisms, such as fireflies and some types of jellyfish, can produce light through biochemical reactions. This is known as bioluminescence.

6. **Lasers:**

Laser light is produced through a process of stimulated emission of photons. In a laser, a medium (solid, liquid, or gas) is stimulated by an external energy source, leading to the emission of coherent and amplified light.

7. **LEDs (Light-Emitting Diodes):**

LEDs produce light when an electric current passes through a semiconductor material. Electrons and holes recombine in the semiconductor, releasing energy in the form of photons.

In the context of Free Electron Lasers (FELs), light is indeed generated by high-energy electrons undergoing a process called synchrotron radiation. However, this is a specific and specialized mechanism that differs from the general ways light is produced in everyday scenarios.

Are radio waves a form of light?

Radio waves are a form of electromagnetic radiation, just like light, but they fall within a different range of the electromagnetic spectrum. The electromagnetic spectrum encompasses a broad range of electromagnetic waves, and it is traditionally divided into different regions based on the wavelengths or frequencies of the waves. Light, including visible light, is just a small portion of the entire electromagnetic spectrum.

Here's a breakdown of some regions of the electromagnetic spectrum:

1. **Radio Waves:**

   Wavelength Range: Typically longer than a millimeter.

   Frequency Range: Generally in the kilohertz (kHz) to gigahertz (GHz) range.

   Application: Used for communication, broadcasting, and various technologies like Wi-Fi and cell phones.

2. **Microwaves:**

   Wavelength Range: Ranges from millimeters to meters.

   Frequency Range: Typically in the gigahertz (GHz) range.

   Application: Used in microwave ovens, radar, and certain communication systems.

3. **Infrared (IR) Radiation:**

   Wavelength Range: Ranges from micrometers to millimeters.

   Frequency Range: Terahertz (THz) region.

   Application: Used in heat sensing, night vision, and some communication technologies.

4. **Visible Light:**

Wavelength Range: Ranges from approximately 400 to 700 nanometers.

Frequency Range: Around hundreds of terahertz (THz).

Application: Detected by the human eye and used in various lighting and imaging technologies.

5. **Ultraviolet (UV) Radiation:**

Wavelength Range: Ranges from nanometers to shorter wavelengths.

Frequency Range: Higher than visible light.

Application: Used in medical applications, sterilization, and fluorescence.

6. **X-rays:**

Wavelength Range: Ranges from picometers to nanometers.

Frequency Range: Very high, in the exahertz (EHz) range.

Application: Used in medical imaging, security screening, and research.

7. **Gamma Rays:**

Wavelength Range: Very short, in the picometer range.

Frequency Range: Extremely high, in the zettahertz (ZHz) range.

Application: Used in medical treatments and certain types of imaging.

In summary, while radio waves are not visible light, they are part of the broader electromagnetic spectrum. The distinction among these regions is based on the characteristics of the waves, including their wavelengths and frequencies.

Can polyurethane foam be used as a shielding material?

Polyurethane foam comes in a variety of densities, each with its own set of properties and applications. The density of foam is usually measured in pounds per cubic foot (lb/ft^3) or kilograms per cubic meter (kg/m^3). Foam density affects its firmness, durability, insulation properties, and how well it can absorb or dampen energy, which is relevant to its potential complement to shielding.

Here's how different densities of polyurethane foam can complement shielding:

1. **Low-Density Foam (2-3 lb/ft³ or 32-48 kg/m³):**

   This foam is soft and offers good cushioning.

   It's often used for comfort applications, such as mattresses and furniture.

While it might not provide significant structural support, it can contribute to absorbing energy or vibrations in certain scenarios.

2. **Medium-Density Foam (4-5 lb/ft³ or 64-80 kg/m³):**

This foam strikes a balance between cushioning and support.

It's commonly used in furniture, bedding, and some packaging applications.

It can help dampen vibrations and absorb energy, making it potentially useful in situations where both comfort and energy absorption are needed.

3. **High-Density Foam (6-8 lb/ft³ or 96-128 kg/m³ and above):**

This foam offers more support and durability.

It's often used in applications where structural integrity is important, such as automotive seating or industrial packaging.

High-density foam can effectively absorb energy, vibrations, and impact forces, which might make it useful for complementing shielding against certain energy weapons.

Complement to Shielding: In the context of energy shielding, foam can have certain complementary effects:

- **Energy Absorption:** Foam's ability to absorb energy can help disperse the impact of forces or vibrations caused by energy weapon attacks. This can be particularly beneficial when combined with other shielding materials to create a layered defense.
- **Vibration Dampening:** Foam can dampen vibrations caused by energy waves, which might help reduce the impact on the wearer of armor.
- **Comfort:** Foam can provide cushioning and comfort to the wearer, making armor more wearable for longer periods.

It's important to note that the choice of foam density and its complement to shielding depends on the specific characteristics of the energy weapon, the intended use of the armor, and the potential energy frequencies involved. Additionally, foam alone might not provide sufficient protection against certain advanced energy weapons.

What is the minimum density and thickness of polyurethane foam for it to be effective for EMF shielding?

A density of 50 kg/cubic meter (kg/m³) for polyurethane foam is a common minimum density requirement for many applications where foam is used as an EMF dampener or absorber. This density is often considered a practical lower limit because it provides a certain level of structural integrity and EMF attenuation across a broad range of frequencies.

However, it's important to note that the specific density requirement can still vary depending on the application and the performance standards needed. For some high-frequency or specialized applications, a higher foam density might be necessary to achieve the desired level of electromagnetic interference (EMI) or electromagnetic radiation (EMR) attenuation.

1 cm minimum thickness is recommended for the above mentioned density.

What would be the best arrangement of the following materials for EMF body armor: copper foil, aluminum foil, hdpe, polyurethane foam, graphite layer, and a magnetite epoxy layer?

Creating effective electromagnetic field (EMF) body armor or shielding involves configuring materials to provide the best protection against the specific frequencies and types of electromagnetic radiation you want to shield against. The effectiveness of the shielding depends on the characteristics of each material and the order in which they are layered. Here's a suggested configuration from the outside to the inside:

1. **Copper Foil (Outer Layer):** Copper is an excellent conductor of electricity and can effectively reflect and attenuate

electromagnetic waves. It's often used as an outer layer in EMF shielding to provide a conductive surface that reflects and dissipates incoming radiation.

2. **Aluminum Foil (Secondary Layer):** Aluminum is another good conductor that can further enhance the reflection and absorption of electromagnetic waves. Placing aluminum foil as a secondary layer can provide additional shielding effectiveness.

3. **Magnetite Epoxy Layer:** Magnetite, a type of iron oxide, has magnetic properties that can absorb and attenuate certain types of electromagnetic radiation, especially at lower frequencies. An epoxy layer with embedded magnetite particles can be effective against magnetic fields and lower-frequency EMF.

4. **Graphite Layer:** Graphite is a highly conductive material that can help disperse and dissipate electrical charges, making it effective for shielding against radiofrequency (RF) radiation and static electric fields.

5. **Polyurethane Foam (Insulating Layer):** Polyurethane foam can provide thermal insulation and structural support while also acting as an insulating layer between conductive materials. This layer can help prevent electrical contact between layers and enhance overall structural integrity.

6. **HDPE (High-Density Polyethylene) Layer:** HDPE is a good dielectric material that can further isolate conductive layers. It

provides an additional insulating barrier to prevent electromagnetic interference between layers.

The effectiveness of this configuration depends on various factors, including the thickness of each layer, the specific frequencies of EMF you're shielding against, and the overall design of the armor. Keep in mind that EMF shielding can be complex, and the choice of materials and configuration should be based on a thorough understanding of the electromagnetic environment and the potential sources of radiation.

Additionally, for body armor, considerations like comfort, flexibility, weight, and ease of movement are essential factors to balance with shielding effectiveness.

What frequencies can defeat aluminum foil?

While aluminum is generally effective as a shielding material for a wide range of frequencies, there can be specific cases where it may not be the best choice and could potentially worsen shielding performance. Here are some scenarios to consider:

1. **Resonance Frequencies:** Aluminum can resonate at certain frequencies, creating an effect known as "resonant absorption." This means that, at specific frequencies, aluminum can actually absorb more electromagnetic radiation than it reflects or attenuates. This phenomenon can result in reduced shielding effectiveness at those resonance frequencies.

2. **Terahertz Frequencies:** At extremely high frequencies in the terahertz range (above 300 GHz), aluminum may not perform as well as other materials like metals with higher conductivity, such as copper or silver. Its relatively lower conductivity can limit its effectiveness in this frequency range.

3. **Subwavelength Apertures:** When dealing with very small openings or apertures in shielding materials, aluminum may not effectively block electromagnetic radiation that has a wavelength comparable to or larger than the aperture size. This is a common phenomenon in the microwave and millimeter-wave frequency ranges.

4. **Specific Frequency Bands:** In certain frequency bands, other materials may be more efficient reflectors or absorbers. For example, at extremely high radiofrequency (RF) frequencies, silver or gold may provide better performance, albeit at a higher cost.

5. **High-Intensity Fields:** In cases of very high-intensity electromagnetic fields, such as those generated in scientific research or medical applications, the electrical breakdown or melting point of aluminum may limit its usefulness as a shielding material.

In these scenarios, it's essential to consider the specific electromagnetic characteristics of the environment you are dealing with and select the most appropriate shielding material accordingly.

While aluminum is versatile and often cost-effective, it may not always be the optimal choice for shielding applications in certain frequency ranges or under particular conditions.

What works better for EMF shielding: copper mesh or copper plates?

Between copper mesh and a solid copper plate, the effectiveness for electromagnetic field (EMF) shielding would depend on various factors such as the frequency of the EMF, the thickness of the copper, and the specific design and application. Both copper mesh and solid copper plates are commonly used for EMF shielding, but their effectiveness can vary based on these factors.

Copper mesh offers the advantage of flexibility and the ability to conform to different shapes and surfaces, which can be useful for applications where flexibility is required. However, the effectiveness of copper mesh might be slightly lower compared to a solid copper plate of the same thickness due to the presence of gaps between the mesh wires.

On the other hand, a solid copper plate would provide more continuous coverage and potentially higher shielding effectiveness due to its lack of gaps. However, it might be less practical for applications that require flexibility or conformability.

In general, both copper mesh and solid copper plates can be effective for EMF shielding, but the choice between the two would depend on the specific requirements of your application. It's also important to consider other factors such as cost, ease of installation, and any other unique properties of the materials.

How does copper rate against EMF?

Copper is a highly conductive metal with excellent electrical properties, and its effectiveness for electromagnetic field (EMF) applications varies depending on the frequency range and specific use case. Here's a general rating for copper in different EMF ranges:

- **Low-Frequency EMF (ELF - Extremely Low Frequency)**:

  Copper is not typically used as the primary material for ELF magnetic field shielding. While it has excellent electrical conductivity, it is less effective at shielding against low-frequency magnetic fields.

  Rating: 3/10

- **Radio Frequency (RF)**:

  Copper is an excellent conductor of electricity and is commonly used in RF applications. It can be effective for RF shielding and grounding, making it a preferred material for RF enclosures and EMI shielding.

Rating: 8/10

- **Microwave Frequencies**:

   Copper is highly effective for microwave frequencies due to its excellent electrical conductivity. It is often used in waveguides, RF connectors, and microwave shielding applications.

   Rating: 9/10

- **Millimeter-Wave and Terahertz Frequencies**:

   Copper remains effective at higher frequencies, including millimeter-wave and terahertz ranges, where its conductivity is advantageous for certain applications.

   Rating: 8/10

How does the e-field and m-field vary with frequency?

In electromagnetic waves, the strength of the magnetic field component (H-field) and the electric field component (E-field) varies with frequency. In lower-frequency electromagnetic waves, such as those in the Extremely Low Frequency (ELF) and radio frequency (RF) ranges, the magnetic field component tends to dominate, while the electric field component is relatively weaker compared to the magnetic field. This characteristic is one of the key reasons why magnetic permeable materials, like ferromagnetic alloys, are more effective at lower frequencies.

Here are some key points that support your theory:

1. **Electromagnetic Wave Structure:** Electromagnetic waves consist of an electric field (E-field) component and a magnetic field (H-field) component that are perpendicular to each other and propagate together. The strength of these components varies with frequency.

2. **Relationship to Frequency:** In electromagnetic waves, the strength of the electric field is directly proportional to the frequency ($E \propto f$), while the strength of the magnetic field is inversely proportional to the frequency ($H \propto 1/f$).

3. **Dominance of Magnetic Field at Lower Frequencies:** In the lower-frequency ranges, such as ELF and RF, the electric field component has a lower magnitude compared to the magnetic field component. As a result, the magnetic field becomes dominant, and materials with high magnetic permeability (e.g., ferromagnetic alloys) are more effective at interacting with and redirecting these fields.

4. **Magnetic Shielding:** Magnetic permeable materials are commonly used for shielding against low-frequency magnetic fields, such as those generated by power lines, transformers, and electronic equipment. These materials channel and absorb

the magnetic field lines, reducing their impact on sensitive equipment or environments.

5. **Electric Shielding at Higher Frequencies:** At higher frequencies, such as microwaves and beyond, the electric field component becomes stronger, and materials with high electrical conductivity (e.g., copper) are more effective at shielding against the electric field. This is why conductive materials are commonly used for electromagnetic interference (EMI) shielding in electronic devices operating in these frequency ranges.

Why are magnetically permeable materials more effective for lower frequencies?

Magnetically permeable materials, such as ferromagnetic alloys (e.g., permalloy), are more effective at lower frequencies for electromagnetic shielding because they interact with and manipulate the magnetic field (H-field) component of electromagnetic waves. While the electric field (E-field) and H-field have equal magnitudes in free space, the situation changes when electromagnetic waves encounter materials with different properties.

Here's why magnetically permeable materials are more effective at lower frequencies:

1. **Magnetic Permeability:** Ferromagnetic materials have high magnetic permeability (μ), which means they can concentrate and guide magnetic field lines. At lower frequencies (e.g., ELF

and lower RF ranges), where the magnetic field component is dominant, these materials provide a low-resistance path for the magnetic flux. This effectively "captures" and redirects the magnetic field lines, reducing their impact on sensitive equipment or environments.

2. **Electric Field Behavior:** In contrast, the electric field component of electromagnetic waves is less affected by magnetic permeability. Electric fields interact with the dielectric properties (permittivity) of materials rather than their magnetic properties. Common dielectric materials, including air and most non-magnetic materials, tend to have similar properties at low frequencies, so the electric field is not significantly altered by the presence of magnetically permeable materials.

3. **Magnetic Shielding:** Due to their high magnetic permeability, magnetically permeable materials are commonly used for magnetic shielding applications, such as protecting sensitive electronic equipment from the effects of nearby power lines, transformers, or magnetic interference sources operating at lower frequencies. These materials effectively redirect and confine the magnetic fields, reducing their reach and impact.

Magnetically permeable materials, while highly effective at lower frequencies, become less effective for higher frequencies due to several factors related to the behavior of electromagnetic waves and the properties of these materials:

1. **Skin Depth**: At higher frequencies, electromagnetic waves penetrate materials less deeply. This phenomenon is known as skin depth. For materials with high magnetic permeability, the skin depth for the magnetic field component becomes smaller, limiting their ability to effectively attenuate or redirect the magnetic field at the surface. As a result, the bulk of the magnetic field remains outside the material.

2. **Eddy Currents**: At higher frequencies, rapidly changing magnetic fields can induce eddy currents in magnetically permeable materials. These eddy currents can generate secondary magnetic fields that oppose the incoming magnetic field. While this effect can help reduce the penetration of the magnetic field into the material, it also leads to increased energy loss in the form of heat.

3. **Material Properties**: The magnetic properties of ferromagnetic materials, such as permeability and saturation, can vary with frequency. At higher frequencies, the permeability of these materials may decrease, reducing their ability to concentrate and redirect the magnetic field.

4. **Absorption and Reflection**: For higher-frequency electromagnetic waves, such as microwaves and optical frequencies, other materials with tailored dielectric properties or conductive properties are more effective for shielding. These materials can absorb and reflect the dominant electric field

component, which becomes more significant at these frequencies.

5. **Size and Geometry**: The effectiveness of magnetically permeable materials also depends on their size and geometry relative to the wavelength of the electromagnetic waves. At higher frequencies, the wavelengths are shorter, and the materials may not be configured optimally to interact with the fields.

In summary, while magnetically permeable materials like ferromagnetic alloys are highly effective at lower frequencies, their effectiveness diminishes at higher frequencies due to limitations related to skin depth, eddy currents, changing material properties, and the dominance of the electric field component. For higher-frequency applications, different materials with tailored properties, such as conductive materials or dielectrics, are preferred for electromagnetic interference (EMI) shielding and absorption. The choice of shielding material depends on the specific frequency range and the characteristics of the electromagnetic fields involved.

How would two opposing magnets stuck together affect a particle beam or EMF wave?

When two magnets with like poles facing each other (for example, two north poles or two south poles) are arranged, the resulting magnetic field configuration can have specific effects on charged particles and electromagnetic waves passing through the region between the magnets. Let's explore the deflection and refraction phenomena in more detail:

1. Deflection of Charged Particle Beam:

- **Lorentz Force:** Charged particles moving through a magnetic field experience a force known as the Lorentz force. This force is perpendicular to both the velocity of the charged particle and the magnetic field direction.

- **Deflection Direction:** For two opposing magnets with north poles facing each other, the resulting magnetic field lines will form a region of strong magnetic field between them. Charged particles passing through this region will experience a Lorentz force that causes them to deflect. The direction of deflection will depend on the charge of the particle and the orientation of the magnetic field.

- **Force Balance:** If the particle's velocity vector aligns with the magnetic field lines, the Lorentz force will be zero, and the particle will not experience deflection in that direction.

2. Refraction of Electromagnetic Waves:

- **Faraday Rotation:** Electromagnetic waves passing through a region with a magnetic field can undergo Faraday rotation. This effect is characterized by a rotation in the polarization plane of the electromagnetic wave.

- **Magneto-Optical Effects:** The refractive index of a material can be altered in the presence of a magnetic field, a phenomenon known as magneto-optical effects. This can lead to changes in the speed of light and the direction of wave propagation.

- **Specifics for Like Poles:** For two magnets with like poles facing each other, the resulting magnetic field between them will influence the propagation of electromagnetic waves. The specifics of the effect will depend on the frequency and polarization of the waves.

Additional Considerations:

- **Field Strength:** The strength of the magnetic field between the opposing magnets will influence the degree of deflection or refraction.

- **Particle or Wave Characteristics:** The characteristics of the charged particles (charge, mass) or the electromagnetic waves (frequency, polarization) will determine how they interact with the magnetic field.

In practical applications, these effects can be harnessed for various purposes, such as particle beam manipulation in accelerators or controlling the propagation of electromagnetic waves in devices like magneto-optical isolators. The precise outcomes depend on the specific geometry and magnetic field strength of the opposing magnets, as well as the characteristics of the charged particles or electromagnetic waves involved.

Considerations for Magnetic Shielding:

- **Magnetic Field Strength:** The strength of the magnetic field is crucial. Higher magnetic field strengths may have more significant effects on charged particles and electromagnetic waves.

- **Geometry and Configuration:** The arrangement of magnets and the geometry of the magnetic field are important. Optimizing the configuration for the specific characteristics of the DEW is essential.

- **Directed Energy Characteristics:** Understanding the specific characteristics of the DEW, such as particle energy, microwave frequency, and power, is critical for designing effective countermeasures.

Challenges and Limitations:

- **Energy Levels:** High-energy particle beams or powerful microwave beams may require extremely strong magnetic fields for effective deflection or weakening.

- **Material Considerations:** The materials used in the construction of the magnetic shielding can affect its effectiveness. Some materials may absorb or reflect energy more effectively than others.

Other Defensive Measures:

- **Material Absorption:** Using materials that can absorb or dissipate the energy of the directed energy weapon.
- **Reflective Surfaces:** Employing reflective surfaces to bounce back or scatter the directed energy.

Which magnet / permalloy configuration would work best against energy weapons?

When considering configurations to protect against energy weapons, especially electromagnetic radiation or particle beams, materials with high magnetic permeability, such as permalloy, are often used in combination with magnets. The effectiveness of a shielding configuration depends on the specific properties of the materials and the characteristics of the energy weapons involved.

1. **Magnet Then Permalloy:**

   The magnetic field generated by the magnet would interact with incoming charged particles or electromagnetic radiation. Permalloy, with its high magnetic permeability, helps guide and redirect the magnetic field, influencing the path of charged particles.

This configuration could be effective in certain scenarios, especially for charged particle beams.

2. **Permalloy Then Magnet:**

In this case, the permalloy layer would initially interact with incoming radiation or particles, and the subsequent magnet layer would further manipulate the magnetic field.

This configuration might be effective for attenuating radiation, particularly electromagnetic radiation.

3. **Magnet In Between Two Layers of Permalloy:**

This configuration involves sandwiching the magnet between two permalloy layers. This setup allows for interaction with the magnetic field both before and after passing through the magnet.

The additional permalloy layers can enhance the overall effectiveness of the shielding, providing multiple opportunities to influence the trajectory of charged particles.

It's important to note that the strength of the magnet (in this case, an N52 magnet) is a crucial factor. N52 magnets are among the strongest commercially available, and their magnetic field strength can influence the behavior of charged particles.

Radiation Types: The effectiveness of these configurations can vary based on the type of radiation or particles you're trying to shield against. Generally:

- **Charged Particle Beams:** Configurations involving magnets and high-permeability materials like permalloy are more effective against charged particle beams, redirecting or slowing down charged particles.

- **Electromagnetic Radiation (e.g., lasers, microwaves):** Permalloy is known for its effectiveness in attenuating magnetic fields, so configurations with permalloy layers could be beneficial for shielding against certain types of electromagnetic radiation.

- **Gamma Rays and X-Rays:** Shielding against high-energy photons like gamma rays and X-rays typically requires dense materials with high atomic numbers, such as lead or other heavy metals. Magnetic configurations might not be as effective against these types of radiation.

In practical applications, a combination of materials may be used to provide comprehensive protection against various threats. Additionally, engineering considerations, such as weight, cost, and thickness of the shielding, play a role in determining the most suitable configuration for a specific application. It's also important to consult with experts in materials science and electromagnetic shielding for a thorough analysis.

How to determine poles of a magnet if they're not labeled and which pole is better against energy weapons?

The orientation of a magnet with respect to its poles is crucial when designing magnetic shielding or using magnets for specific applications. Here's a general guide to determine the poles of an unlabeled magnet:

1. **Using a Compass:**

   One of the simplest methods is to use a compass. The needle of a compass is itself a small magnet and will align with the magnetic field of the larger magnet.

   When you bring one pole of the unknown magnet close to the compass, the needle will point towards the opposite pole of the magnet. For example, if the north pole of the compass points towards the magnet, you are holding the south pole of the magnet.

2. **Magnetic Repulsion or Attraction:**

   Like poles repel each other, and opposite poles attract. If you have two magnets and you bring one close to the other, observe how they interact.

   If the magnets attract each other, then the poles facing each other are different (north attracts south). If they repel each other, then the poles facing each other are the same (north repels north or south repels south).

3. **Magnetic Field Indicator:**

   Fine iron filings or a small piece of ferrous material (like a paperclip) can be used to visualize the magnetic field lines around the magnet. Sprinkle the filings around the magnet, and they will align along the magnetic field lines, revealing the pattern and indicating the direction from north to south.

As for which pole should be facing out for a specific application, it depends on the context:

- **For Attraction:** If you are using the magnet to attract another magnetic object, you typically want the side with the opposite pole facing out.
- **For Repulsion:** If you are using the magnet to create a repulsive force, you want the side with the same pole facing out.

When using magnets for specific applications, it's essential to understand the desired interaction and choose the orientation accordingly. If you're unsure about the properties of an unlabeled magnet, using a compass or observing interactions with other magnets can help you determine the pole orientation.

When facing an energy weapon, the choice of which pole of a magnet to face towards the weapon would depend on the type of energy involved. Here are some considerations:

1. **Charged Particle Beams (e.g., electrons, protons):**

   If the energy weapon emits charged particle beams, such as electrons or protons, you would generally want to use the **south pole** of the magnet facing the weapon.

   The magnetic field generated by the south pole tends to attract negatively charged particles (like electrons) and repel positively charged particles (like protons). This can potentially deflect or redirect the charged particles away from the target.

2. **Electromagnetic Radiation (e.g., lasers, microwaves):**

   For electromagnetic radiation, such as lasers or microwaves, magnetic fields may not have a significant effect. Instead, materials with high electrical conductivity (such as metals) are more effective for shielding against electromagnetic radiation.

   If the energy weapon involves both charged particles and electromagnetic radiation, a combination of magnetic shielding and electrically conductive materials may be necessary.

It's important to note that while magnetic fields can interact with charged particles, they are generally less effective against electromagnetic radiation. Other forms of shielding, such as using materials with high density and high atomic number (e.g., lead) for absorbing photons, may be more suitable for protecting against certain types of energy weapons.

In practical applications, the design of shielding depends on the specific characteristics of the energy weapon, the nature of the threat, and the desired outcome (e.g., deflecting, absorbing, or dispersing the energy).

The influence of a magnetic field, whether from a south pole or a north pole, on electron tunneling or electron guns depends on the specific configuration and the characteristics of the magnetic field. Generally, magnetic fields can affect the trajectories of charged particles, including electrons, and this effect is described by the Lorentz force.

However, the influence of a magnetic field on electron tunneling specifically might be more complex, as tunneling is a quantum mechanical phenomenon. Quantum tunneling is the phenomenon where particles, such as electrons, can pass through a barrier that classical physics suggests they should not be able to pass through. This process is primarily governed by the principles of quantum mechanics and wave functions.

If you are referring to a situation where electrons are emitted from an electron gun and then tunnel through a barrier, the magnetic field could influence the trajectory of the electrons once they are emitted. However, the specific details would depend on factors such as the strength and orientation of the magnetic field, the energy of the electrons, and the properties of the barrier.

In the context of electron guns, which are devices that emit focused beams of electrons, the magnetic field can play a crucial role in focusing or deflecting the electron beam. This is commonly used in devices like cathode ray tubes (CRTs) or electron microscopes.

To specifically address the question of whether a south pole facing magnet would amplify electron tunneling or electron guns, it's essential to consider the details of the setup and the intended outcome. The orientation of the magnetic field alone may not necessarily amplify tunneling, but it can influence the behavior of emitted electrons.

When electrons interact with a magnetic field, such as the field near the south pole of a magnet, they experience a force known as the Lorentz force. The Lorentz force acts perpendicular to both the velocity of the charged particle (in this case, the electrons) and the direction of the magnetic field. The magnitude and direction of the force depend on the charge of the particle, its velocity, and the strength and orientation of the magnetic field.

If a significant number of electrons hit the south pole of a magnet, several things may happen:

1. **Deflection of Electrons:**

   Electrons are negatively charged particles, and they experience a force perpendicular to their velocity and the magnetic field direction. As a result, the electrons would be deflected from their original paths.

   The deflection of electrons depends on the strength of the magnetic field and the speed of the electrons.

2. **Circular Motion:**

   If the electrons are moving in a magnetic field, they can undergo circular motion as they continuously experience the Lorentz force that keeps changing their direction.

   The radius of the circular path is determined by the mass, charge, and velocity of the electrons, as well as the strength of the magnetic field.

3. **Heat Generation:**

   The deflection and circular motion of electrons in a magnetic field can lead to collisions with other particles or surfaces. These collisions may result in the conversion of kinetic energy into heat.

4. **Magnetic Field Distortion:**

The presence of a large number of moving charged particles (electrons) in the vicinity of a magnet can cause local distortions in the magnetic field.

It's important to note that while the Lorentz force can influence the motion of charged particles, the overall behavior depends on the specifics of the system, including the strength and orientation of the magnetic field, the speed of the electrons, and the surrounding environment.

In practical applications, the deflection of electrons in a magnetic field is utilized in devices such as cathode ray tubes (CRTs), where a beam of electrons is directed by magnetic fields to create images on a screen. Understanding and controlling the interaction between electrons and magnetic fields are essential in various fields, including physics, electronics, and materials science.

Would a combo of like poles be more or less effective than magnetic shielding with the south poles facing out?

The configuration of two magnets with like poles facing each other (either two north poles or two south poles) and repelling each other is typically less effective for electromagnetic field (EMF) shielding. This configuration tends to create a region with reduced magnetic field strength between the magnets due to the repulsion forces pushing the magnetic field lines away.

While there may be a region of lower magnetic field strength between the repelling magnets, the overall shielding effectiveness against external magnetic fields might be limited. The repulsion forces can cause the magnetic field lines to bend and avoid the space between the magnets, which may not result in effective redirection or absorption of external magnetic fields.

In contrast, configurations that involve a magnet with its south pole facing out, placed between layers of materials with high magnetic permeability (such as permalloy), are often designed for better EMF shielding. The combination of the magnet and the high-permeability materials is intended to manipulate and guide the magnetic field lines, providing a more effective shield against external magnetic fields.

Would two donut shaped magnets coiled like an inductor with like poles facing each other be beneficial for EMF shielding?

The configuration with two donut-shaped magnets having like poles repelling each other and copper coiled around them like an inductor, forms a structure similar to a magnetic coil or solenoid. This arrangement can have interesting electromagnetic effects and may be considered in certain shielding applications. Here are some potential benefits and considerations:

1. **Increased Magnetic Field Strength in the Center:**

   The repulsion between the like poles of the magnets would create a region of increased magnetic field strength in the center of the donut-shaped magnets. This can be beneficial for applications where a strong and focused magnetic field is desired.

2. **Enhanced Magnetic Flux Through the Coil (Faraday's Law):**

   According to Faraday's law of electromagnetic induction, a changing magnetic field within a coil induces an electromotive force (EMF) or voltage. As the magnets repel each other, the magnetic field within the coil changes, inducing an electric current in the coiled copper.

3. **Electromagnetic Shielding (Inductive Shielding):**

   The induced electric current in the copper coil can produce a secondary magnetic field that opposes the original magnetic field. This principle is used in inductive shielding, where the induced magnetic field helps counteract and shield against external magnetic fields.

4. **Control of Magnetic Field Distribution:**

   The geometry of the coil and the arrangement of the magnets can be designed to control the distribution of the magnetic field. This may be advantageous in applications where a specific magnetic field profile is needed for shielding purposes.

5. **Dissipation of Magnetic Energy:**

The copper coil acts as a conductor, and the induced current in the coil results in the dissipation of magnetic energy as heat. This effect can be beneficial in situations where energy needs to be absorbed or dissipated.

It's important to note that the effectiveness of this configuration for electromagnetic shielding depends on the specific characteristics of the external magnetic field and the desired outcomes. Factors such as the strength of the magnets, the number of coil windings, the conductivity of the copper, and the overall geometry of the setup all play a role.

Additionally, while inductive shielding can be effective against certain types of magnetic fields, it may not provide the same level of shielding against other forms of electromagnetic radiation, such as electric fields or radiofrequency fields. A comprehensive approach to electromagnetic shielding may involve a combination of different materials and configurations tailored to the specific application. Experimental testing and simulation studies are often used to optimize such setups for specific scenarios.

Inductive shielding involves the use of electromagnetic induction principles to create a secondary magnetic field that opposes an external magnetic field, thereby reducing its influence. This shielding method is particularly effective against low-frequency electromagnetic fields (EMF) and magnetic fields. Here's an overview of inductive shielding and its impact on various forms of EMF:

Basic Principles of Inductive Shielding:

1. **Faraday's Law of Electromagnetic Induction:**

   Faraday's law states that a changing magnetic field within a closed loop of wire induces an electromotive force (EMF) or voltage in the wire. This induced voltage leads to the flow of an electric current.

2. **Lenz's Law:**

   Lenz's law describes the direction of the induced current: it flows in a direction that opposes the change in magnetic flux that produced it. This means that the induced current creates a secondary magnetic field that opposes the original magnetic field.

3. **Inductive Shielding Mechanism:**

   In the context of shielding, a coil of wire is often wound around a core material. When an external magnetic field is present, the changing magnetic flux within the coil induces a current. This induced current, in turn, generates a magnetic field that opposes the original field, reducing its strength within the shielded region.

Impact on Various Forms of EMF:

1. **Magnetic Fields:**

   Inductive shielding is particularly effective against static or low-frequency magnetic fields. It can help protect sensitive electronic equipment or living spaces from the influence of nearby power lines, transformers, or other sources of magnetic fields.

2. **Low-Frequency EMF:**

   In many cases, low-frequency electromagnetic fields are predominantly magnetic fields. Inductive shielding is well-suited for mitigating the impact of these fields. Examples include shielding against 50/60 Hz power frequency fields from electrical devices.

3. **Radiofrequency (RF) Fields:**

   Inductive shielding is less effective against higher-frequency RF fields. In RF shielding, other techniques, such as conductive shielding materials (like metal enclosures) or absorption materials, are often employed to reduce the penetration of electromagnetic waves.

4. **Electric Fields:**

Inductive shielding is not inherently effective against electric fields. For electric field shielding, conductive materials, such as metal, are more commonly used to create barriers that absorb or reflect electric fields.

Practical Considerations:

1. **Coil Design:**

The design of the coil, including the number of windings, the core material, and the arrangement, influences the inductance and effectiveness of the shielding.

2. **Frequency Range:**

Inductive shielding is most effective at lower frequencies. As frequencies increase into the radiofrequency range, alternative shielding methods may be more suitable.

3. **Multimodal Shielding:**

In practical applications, a combination of shielding methods may be employed to address different aspects of the EMF spectrum. This might involve inductive shielding for low-frequency magnetic fields and other techniques for higher-frequency electric or RF fields.

Inductive shielding is a valuable tool for mitigating the effects of specific types of EMF, particularly low-frequency magnetic fields. However, the choice of shielding method should align with the frequency characteristics and requirements of the specific application.

Inductive shielding can be achieved using disc or bar magnets, and using a single copper wire threaded in the middle and bent around the poles in an "S" shape is an interesting concept. This approach can create a sort of "solenoid-like" structure that induces a magnetic field opposing the original field, potentially providing shielding effects.

Here are some considerations for this setup:

1. **Single Copper Wire "S" Shape:**

    While a single copper wire forming an "S" shape around the poles of a disc magnet may not provide the same level of inductance as a tightly wound coil, it can still induce an electromotive force (EMF) and produce a secondary magnetic field that opposes the original field.

2. **Magnetic Field Opposition:**

    The induced current in the copper wire will create a magnetic field that opposes the original field from the magnet. This opposition effect is consistent with the principles of electromagnetic induction and can contribute to shielding against external magnetic fields.

3. **Geometry and Alignment:**

The effectiveness of the shielding depends on the geometry and alignment of the copper wire relative to the magnet. The "S" shape should be designed to maximize the interaction with the magnetic field and induce a significant opposing magnetic field.

4. **Experimentation and Optimization:**

The effectiveness of this approach will likely require some experimentation and optimization. Factors such as the strength of the magnet, the diameter and thickness of the copper wire, and the overall geometry of the setup will influence the shielding effects.

5. **Limitations:**

It's important to note that while inductive shielding can be effective against certain types of magnetic fields, it may not provide comprehensive shielding against other forms of electromagnetic radiation, such as electric fields or radiofrequency fields.

6. **Alternative Shielding Materials:**

> In addition to the inductive shielding approach, consider other materials and configurations that may complement or enhance the overall shielding performance. This might include using materials with high magnetic permeability or conductive shielding materials.

What are "eddy currents?"

Eddy currents are a phenomenon in which circulating currents are induced in a conductor when it is exposed to a changing magnetic field, such as that from an electromagnetic wave or alternating current. Eddy currents can indeed be a concern when designing electromagnetic shielding, as they can potentially reduce the effectiveness of the shielding.

Here's how eddy currents can impact electromagnetic shielding:

1. **Induced Currents:** When electromagnetic waves or signals interact with a conductive shield, such as one made of metal, they can induce eddy currents within the shield itself.

2. **Counteracting Effect:** Eddy currents in the shield create their own magnetic fields that oppose the incoming electromagnetic field. This can result in partial cancellation or attenuation of the incoming field, reducing the shielding effectiveness.

To mitigate the impact of eddy currents on shielding effectiveness, several strategies can be employed:

- **Thin Layers:** Using thinner shielding materials can reduce the formation of strong eddy currents. However, thinner materials may have lower shielding effectiveness, so it's essential to strike a balance.

- **Permeable Materials:** For specific applications, using magnetic shielding materials like mu-metal or other high-permeability alloys can help redirect and absorb magnetic fields, minimizing the impact of eddy currents.

- **Shielding Design:** The design of the shielding structure, such as using multiple layers or strategic placement of shielding materials, can help reduce the impact of eddy currents and improve overall effectiveness.

- **Frequency Considerations:** Eddy currents are more significant at higher frequencies. Shielding effectiveness can vary with the frequency of the electromagnetic field, so choosing appropriate materials and designs for the specific frequency range of concern is essential.

- **Grounding:** Proper grounding of the shielding material can help dissipate eddy currents and maintain shielding integrity.

Overall, when designing electromagnetic shielding, it's crucial to consider the potential effects of eddy currents and take appropriate measures to minimize their impact while achieving the desired level of shielding effectiveness for the specific application and frequency range. Consulting with experts in electromagnetic compatibility (EMC) and shielding design can help ensure that the shielding solution is effective and meets the desired performance requirements.

Can diodes be used as "parasites" on shielding to eat EMF?

If you're looking to improve attenuation in a shielding loop using diodes as a parasite, the most suitable diodes for this purpose would be the Schottky diode and the Varactor diode.

1. Schottky Diode: The Schottky diode has a low forward voltage drop and fast switching characteristics. When used as a parasitic element bridging a gap in the shielding loop, it can act as a "fast-switching" component, helping to absorb and dissipate high-frequency signals effectively.

2. Varactor Diode: The Varactor diode, also known as a voltage-variable capacitor, can be used to tune the resonant frequency of the shielding loop. By applying a voltage across the diode, the capacitance can be adjusted, allowing you to fine-tune the loop's resonance and improve its attenuation at specific frequencies.

It's important to note that using diodes as parasites to enhance shielding attenuation requires careful consideration of the circuit design and the specific application's requirements. Additionally, conducting thorough testing and analysis is crucial to ensure the desired performance improvements are achieved.

Overall, the effectiveness of using diodes in a parasitic manner will depend on the specific shielding setup, the targeted frequencies, and the intended application. As with any complex engineering task, it's always best to seek guidance from experts in electromagnetic compatibility and shielding design to achieve optimal results.

Is "invar" worth considering for shielding?

An alloy consisting of 50 percent iron and 50 percent nickel is commonly known as Invar. Invar is valued for its low coefficient of thermal expansion, which means it exhibits minimal dimensional changes with temperature variations. While Invar has its own unique set of properties that make it useful in certain applications, it may not necessarily be better than permalloy (nickel-iron alloy) for electromagnetic shielding purposes, especially if robust shielding against magnetic fields is the primary concern.

Here's a comparison of Invar and permalloy for electromagnetic shielding:

1. **Magnetic Properties**:

    Permalloy: Permalloy is specifically designed to have high magnetic permeability, making it highly effective at shielding against magnetic fields. It is often preferred for applications where magnetic shielding is the primary objective, such as in electronics to protect against external magnetic interference.

Invar: Invar does not have the same level of magnetic permeability as permalloy. While it has some magnetic properties, its primary advantage is its low thermal expansion.

2. **Electromagnetic Shielding**:

Permalloy: Permalloy is a better choice for electromagnetic shielding against magnetic fields, including low-frequency magnetic fields (e.g., power lines) and magnetic interference from electronic devices.

Invar: Invar may not provide the same level of magnetic shielding effectiveness as permalloy, as its magnetic properties are not optimized for this purpose.

In summary, while Invar is an excellent material for applications requiring dimensional stability, it is not typically chosen for robust electromagnetic shielding against magnetic fields. Permalloy, with its optimized magnetic properties, is a more suitable choice when the primary goal is effective magnetic shielding. The selection of the most appropriate material depends on the specific requirements and priorities of the shielding application.

Do radio waves contain electrons?

The EMF wave itself does not carry electrons; instead, it interacts with the conductive material of the shielding and induces the movement of electrons within that material. This movement of electrons creates an electric current in response to the changing electric and magnetic fields of the EMF wave.

When an EMF wave encounters a conductive material, such as a metal or a conductive coating, it creates an electric field that causes the free electrons within the material to move. This movement of electrons creates a current flow, and the conductive material becomes temporarily polarized as a result of the interaction.

The polarization of the conductive material effectively cancels out the external electric field inside the shielded area, providing the shielding effect. By redistributing the electrons in response to the external EMF, the conductive material acts as a barrier to block or attenuate the EMF radiation from passing through.

It's important to note that the EMF wave itself is composed of oscillating electric and magnetic fields, not electrons. The electrons in the conductive material respond to the changing electric field of the EMF wave, which in turn generates the shielding effect through the induced current flow and polarization.

Do EMF waves degrade or deplete shielding over time?

Yes, over time, repeated exposure to EMF waves can degrade or deplete the effectiveness of the shielding material. The process of shielding against EMF involves inducing currents in the conductive material to counteract the external electric fields. These induced currents and the associated polarization of the material help to block or attenuate the EMF radiation.

However, this process is not entirely perfect, and some energy from the EMF waves may still penetrate the shielding material. Over time, this repeated exposure to EMF radiation can lead to small amounts of energy being absorbed by the material. Depending on the intensity and frequency of the EMF radiation, this absorption of energy can result in heating of the shielding material and lead to its gradual degradation.

In addition, factors like material quality, environmental conditions, and the type of EMF exposure can also impact the longevity of the shielding material. For instance, high-powered and prolonged exposure to EMF waves may accelerate the degradation process.

To maintain the effectiveness of EMF shielding over the long term, it is essential to regularly inspect and replace the shielding material as needed. Proper maintenance and periodic assessments can help ensure that the shielding remains effective in protecting against EMF radiation.

Why do some EMF waves penetrate shielding materials?

The penetration of energy through shielding materials is a complex phenomenon and depends on various factors, including the properties of the material, the characteristics of the electromagnetic field, and the frequency of the EMF radiation.

There are several reasons why some energy may penetrate through shielding materials:

Imperfect Shielding: No shielding material can block 100% of all electromagnetic energy. Even the most effective shielding materials may have some level of permeability that allows a small amount of energy to pass through. This imperfection is due to the material's inherent characteristics and its ability to attenuate the EMF radiation.

Frequency Dependent: Different shielding materials may have varying levels of effectiveness at different frequencies. Some materials are more effective at blocking higher frequencies (e.g., microwaves), while others are better at lower frequencies (e.g., ELF). The specific frequency of the EMF radiation can influence how much energy penetrates the shielding.

Shielding Thickness: The thickness of the shielding material also plays a role. Thicker materials generally offer better shielding, but there is a practical limit to how thick a shielding layer can be while still maintaining practicality and portability.

Shielding Material Properties: The electrical conductivity and magnetic permeability of the material affect its ability to block EMF radiation. In some cases, the material's conductivity may result in partial penetration of energy.

Gaps or Seams: If there are any gaps or seams in the shielding material, EMF radiation can find paths of least resistance and penetrate through these openings.

Reflection and Scattering: Some EMF radiation can reflect or scatter off surfaces, causing it to redirect and potentially penetrate the shielding.

EMF Source Intensity: The strength and intensity of the EMF source can influence how much energy is absorbed or transmitted by the shielding material.

Could a cavity in shielding create unintended effects like in a magnetron?

Yes, a cavity in an EMF shielding material could potentially create unintended effects similar to what occurs in a magnetron, albeit on a much smaller scale. In a magnetron, a cavity resonator is used to generate and amplify electromagnetic waves at microwave frequencies. The geometry of the cavity allows for the build-up and amplification of electromagnetic energy.

Similarly, in an EMF shielding material, a cavity could act as a resonant cavity for specific frequencies, leading to unintended resonant effects. This resonance could cause localized increases in EMF within the cavity, potentially reducing the shielding effectiveness in that area. It might also lead to the emission of secondary electromagnetic waves, which could interfere with nearby electronic devices.

To avoid unintended effects, it's crucial to design EMF shielding materials with as few cavities as possible. When using shielding materials in practical applications, ensuring proper installation and avoiding the formation of unintended cavities can help maintain the desired shielding effectiveness and minimize any unwanted resonant effects.

What is a gyrotron?

A gyrotron is a type of high-power, high-frequency microwave device used in various scientific and industrial applications. It is a specialized form of electron tube, specifically a type of vacuum tube, and operates based on the interaction between electrons and a strong magnetic field.

In a gyrotron, electrons are emitted from a cathode and accelerated by an electric field. These electrons then travel through a magnetron-like interaction space, where they encounter a powerful magnetic field that causes them to spiral around magnetic field lines.

As the electrons move through the magnetic field, they gain energy from the electric field, and this results in the emission of high-power microwave radiation at high frequencies, typically in the terahertz (THz) or gigahertz (GHz) range.

The gyrotron's ability to generate high-power microwaves makes it valuable for a variety of applications, such as plasma heating in fusion research, electron cyclotron resonance heating in plasma physics, and radar systems, among others. It is a complex and sophisticated device that requires precise control of magnetic fields, electron beam parameters, and cavity design to achieve its high-power output efficiently.

A gyrotron or similar high-power microwave device could potentially be used to modify the conductivity of certain shielding materials temporarily. By exposing the shielding material to intense microwave radiation, it might be possible to alter its electronic properties, disrupting its ability to block or conduct electromagnetic fields.

At what power density would a person feel the tapping of ELF waves?

Feeling tapping or vibrations due to exposure to ELF waves would typically require significantly higher power densities than just perceiving the presence of the waves. It is challenging to provide an exact estimated power density because individual sensitivities and physiological responses can vary.

However, for a rough estimation, power densities in the range of several hundreds of milliwatts per square meter (mW/m^2) to a few watts per square meter (W/m^2) might be necessary for a person to physically feel tapping or vibrations from ELF waves.

Is it possible to use capacitors and resistors as a high pass filter for EMF shielding?

Yes, it is indeed possible to use capacitors and resistors as a high-pass filter. A high-pass filter attenuates frequencies below a certain cutoff frequency and allows higher frequencies to pass through with minimal impedance.

To construct a high-pass filter, you can use a resistor in series with the input signal and a capacitor in parallel. The cutoff frequency, also known as the -3dB frequency, is determined by the values of the resistor and capacitor in the circuit

High-pass filters can be useful in various applications, including audio signal processing, communications systems, and in some cases, electromagnetic shielding, depending on the specific requirements of the shielding scenario.

What materials work best against ELF frequencies and ELF weapons?

Extremely Low Frequency (ELF) signals, operating at frequencies around 10 Hz, are challenging to shield against due to their long wavelengths. The best materials for attenuating ELF signals are those that can effectively absorb or reflect electromagnetic fields at very low frequencies. However, it's important to note that ELF signals can penetrate most materials, and traditional shielding methods used for higher frequencies may not be as effective.

Here are a few materials that might offer some degree of attenuation for ELF signals:

1. **Ferrite Materials:** Some ferrite materials can exhibit increased magnetic permeability at low frequencies, which might help with ELF signal attenuation. However, the effectiveness can be limited due to the very low frequency of ELF signals.

2. **Metal Screens and Mesh:** Metal screens or meshes can offer partial attenuation of ELF signals. The gaps between the mesh wires can interact with the ELF wavelength to provide some reduction in signal strength.

3. **Conductive Fabrics:** Some conductive fabrics containing materials like silver or copper can provide a certain level of attenuation for ELF signals. These fabrics work by reflecting and absorbing electromagnetic fields.

4. **Thick Conductive Foils:** Thick conductive foils, such as those made from copper, aluminum, or other metals, might provide limited attenuation for ELF signals due to their conductivity and reflective properties.

5. **Metal Enclosures:** Fully enclosing a space with conductive metal materials can provide some reduction in ELF signal strength by reflecting and partially absorbing the signals.

It's important to manage expectations when attempting to shield against ELF signals. The wavelength of ELF signals is extremely long, and traditional shielding methods that work well for higher frequencies may not be as effective.

Ferrite materials are typically composed of compounds that contain iron (Fe) and other elements, such as oxides. The specific composition of ferrite materials can vary based on their intended properties and applications. For Extremely Low Frequency (ELF) signal attenuation, ferrites with high magnetic permeability at low frequencies might be sought after.

Common types of ferrite materials include:

1. **Manganese-Zinc Ferrites (MnZn):** These ferrites are composed of manganese, zinc, and iron oxides. They are often used for applications requiring high initial permeability and moderate losses. MnZn ferrites can exhibit relatively high permeability at lower frequencies, making them potentially suitable for ELF signal attenuation.

2. **Nickel-Zinc Ferrites (NiZn):** Nickel-zinc ferrites are composed of nickel, zinc, and iron oxides. They are often used when higher frequency applications are involved. NiZn ferrites typically have

lower initial permeability compared to MnZn ferrites, which might make them less suitable for ELF signal attenuation.

3. **Magnesium Ferrites (MgFe):** These ferrites contain magnesium and iron oxides. They can exhibit excellent high-frequency characteristics, but their performance in ELF signal attenuation might be limited due to the higher frequency focus.

4. **Composite Ferrites:** Some ferrite materials are created by combining different ferrite types to achieve specific performance characteristics. These materials might be designed to have improved magnetic permeability at specific frequency ranges.

The elemental compositions of these ferrite materials primarily revolve around iron oxides (FeO, Fe_2O_3), along with the other elements mentioned for each type. The choice of composition is crucial to achieving desired magnetic properties, such as magnetic permeability and loss characteristics.

It's important to note that while ferrite materials can be engineered to have certain properties, addressing ELF signal attenuation with ferrites might still pose challenges due to the long wavelengths associated with ELF signals. When it comes to ELF signal attenuation, achieving meaningful attenuation is inherently challenging due to the physics of ELF signals. It's important to set realistic expectations and consider other strategies, such as structural modifications, grounding, or utilizing materials with high electrical conductivity, to mitigate ELF signal interference.

While MnZn ferrites might offer some minimal attenuation benefits at ELF frequencies, magnetite works best.

Can copper and ferrite be an effective combination?

A sandwich structure can be created by placing a layer of ferrite between two layers of copper. This configuration is often used in specific electromagnetic shielding applications.

Are piezoelectric materials suitable for EMF shielding?

Piezoelectric materials are not commonly used for electromagnetic shielding purposes, particularly for shielding against magnetic fields or radio frequency (RF) electromagnetic interference (EMI). Piezoelectric materials have unique properties related to their ability to generate electrical charges when subjected to mechanical stress or deformations and vice versa. While they are valuable in various applications, including sensors, actuators, and energy harvesting, they have limitations when it comes to electromagnetic shielding:

1. **Mechanical Deformation Requirement:** Piezoelectric materials rely on mechanical deformation to generate electrical charges. This means they are responsive to mechanical vibrations or pressure changes. They do not inherently shield against electromagnetic fields or radiation.

2. **Frequency Limitations:** Piezoelectric materials are primarily used in applications involving relatively low-frequency mechanical vibrations or acoustic waves. Their effectiveness at higher frequencies, such as those associated with RF or microwave frequencies, is limited.

3. **Absorption vs. Reflection:** Electromagnetic shielding materials typically work by absorbing or reflecting electromagnetic radiation to prevent it from passing through or affecting sensitive equipment. Piezoelectric materials are not designed for this purpose and are more focused on energy conversion.

For electromagnetic shielding applications, other types of materials are preferred, depending on the specific type of shielding required:

- **Magnetic Shielding:** Materials with high magnetic permeability, such as permalloy or mu-metal, are used to shield against magnetic fields. These materials redirect and absorb magnetic field lines effectively.

- **Electric Shielding (RF EMI):** Conductive materials like copper, aluminum, or conductive coatings are commonly used for shielding against electric fields and RF electromagnetic interference. These materials provide a path for the electric field lines to follow, diverting or absorbing the energy.

- **Dielectric Shielding (RF EMI):** Dielectric materials with high relative permittivity (εr) can be used to absorb and attenuate electric fields at RF and microwave frequencies. They work by storing and releasing electrical energy, reducing the propagation of the fields.

Piezoelectric materials are typically not selected for electromagnetic shielding because their properties and mechanisms are geared towards energy conversion rather than electromagnetic field manipulation and absorption. For shielding applications, it's essential to choose materials specifically engineered for the task at hand to achieve the desired levels of protection.

NOTE: Worth testing regardless of this recommendation.

Why is the piezoelectric material barium titanate used for resin based shielding?

Barium titanate ($BaTiO_3$) is indeed a piezoelectric ceramic material, and it is sometimes used in specific applications for electromagnetic shielding. While it may not be the primary choice for shielding against magnetic fields, $BaTiO_3$ and other piezoelectric ceramics can offer some advantages in certain scenarios (BINGO), especially when dealing with electromagnetic interference (EMI) at radio frequency (RF) or microwave frequencies.

Here are a few considerations for using $BaTiO_3$ ceramics for shielding:

1. **Dielectric Properties:** BaTiO3 ceramics have high relative permittivity (dielectric constant), which allows them to store electrical energy efficiently. This property can be advantageous in applications where electric field shielding is a concern, such as RF EMI.

2. **Frequency Selectivity:** BaTiO3 ceramics are more effective at shielding against electric fields than magnetic fields. They work by absorbing and attenuating electric fields, which can be advantageous in situations where certain RF frequencies need to be filtered or blocked.

3. **Multi-Layer Structures:** BaTiO3 ceramics can be incorporated into multi-layer structures with conductive layers to provide both electric and magnetic shielding. The conductive layers handle the magnetic field shielding, while the BaTiO3 layers address electric field issues.

4. **Tunable Properties:** BaTiO3 ceramics can exhibit tunable dielectric properties by applying an external voltage (ferroelectric effect). This property can be exploited to adjust the material's shielding characteristics dynamically.

It's important to note that BaTiO3 ceramics are primarily used for their dielectric properties and are not as effective at shielding against magnetic fields as materials with high magnetic permeability (e.g., permalloy or mu-metal). Engineers typically select shielding materials based on the specific frequency range and type of electromagnetic interference they need to mitigate.

In summary, BaTiO3 ceramics, due to their piezoelectric and dielectric properties, can be a valuable component in shielding structures, particularly for electric field shielding and filtering applications. However, for robust magnetic field shielding, other materials like magnetically permeable alloys are more commonly employed. The choice of shielding material depends on the specific requirements and characteristics of the electromagnetic fields involved.

Why make a reference to viruses and satellites if they don't exist?

The subjects of viruses and satellites are widely debated topics that often get reclassified to "exosome transmission" and "weather balloons." Regardless of the terms people use, they end up describing the same effect, and so to avoid confusing those that are unaware of the debate we've chosen to stick with the terms "virus" and "satellites." As they say, you can only please some of the people some of the time. What's important to understand here is that "flu-like symptoms" is another way of saying the immune system is preparing for action. The body raises its temperature to activate immune cells and is the first warning sign that something is going on. Since most people don't understand biology, health professionals use terms like "flu symptoms" and "viruses" to buy time until they can figure out what's going on. Most of the time they don't fully understand the pathology of the disease that is afflicting their patients and that's why the cold still exists despite repeated vaccination and its why medical malpractice is the third leading cause of death in America. As for satellites and the shape of the planet, much is left to be desired from the official story. Those implications, however, are outside of the scope of this book.

Is copper or silver fiber EMF fabric better?

Silver EMF Fabric:

- ELF (Extremely Low Frequency) Range: 7/10

    Silver fabric can provide effective shielding in this range but may not be its primary application.

- kHz Range: 8/10

    Silver fabric is effective at shielding against kHz range electromagnetic fields.

- Radio Frequencies: 9/10

    Silver fabric is highly effective for shielding against radio frequencies, including those used for broadcasting.

- Microwave Frequencies: 9/10

Silver fabric is highly effective for shielding against microwave frequencies commonly used in household devices.

- X-band (Microwave): 8/10

    Silver fabric is effective for shielding against X-band microwave frequencies, although specialized materials may offer even higher performance at these frequencies.

Copper EMF Fabric:

- ELF (Extremely Low Frequency) Range: 8/10

    Copper fabric can provide good shielding at ELF frequencies, especially for grounding applications.

- kHz Range: 9/10

    Copper fabric is highly effective at shielding against kHz range electromagnetic fields.

- Radio Frequencies: 8/10

    Copper fabric is effective for shielding against radio frequencies but may not perform as well as silver fabric at higher frequencies.

- Microwave Frequencies: 7/10

Copper fabric can provide moderate shielding at microwave frequencies but may not be as effective as silver fabric in this range.

- X-band (Microwave): 6/10

    Copper fabric may not be the best choice for shielding at X-band frequencies, as more specialized materials are often used for these higher microwave frequencies.

Would hybrid energy weapons be advantageous, such as weapons that fire multiple frequencies at the same time?

Hybrid energy weapons, which combine and deliver multiple frequencies simultaneously, could potentially offer certain advantages in specific applications, particularly in the realm of electronic warfare, directed energy weapons, or certain defense systems. The simultaneous firing of multiple frequencies can provide various tactical and operational benefits:

1. **Increased Effectiveness**: Simultaneous firing of multiple frequencies allows for a broader spectrum of electromagnetic energy, enhancing the chances of affecting different types of targets or overcoming countermeasures.

2. **Adaptability and Flexibility**: By using multiple frequencies, these weapons can adapt to diverse target characteristics. This flexibility can make them more versatile against different materials or electronic systems.

3. **Overcoming Countermeasures**: The use of multiple frequencies simultaneously can challenge and potentially overwhelm countermeasures or shielding strategies employed by adversaries, making these weapons more effective against protected targets.

4. **Synergistic Effects**: Certain combinations of frequencies may produce synergistic effects, amplifying the overall impact on the target, potentially enhancing damage or disruption.

5. **Reduced Likelihood of Interference**: The use of multiple frequencies might reduce the likelihood of interference or jamming, as these weapons could be designed to operate across a broad spectrum, making them less susceptible to interference.

The concept of synergistic effects in utilizing multiple frequencies simultaneously revolves around the potential combination or interaction of various electromagnetic energy bands to produce amplified, more effective, or unique effects on targets. In various fields, including directed energy weapons, electronic warfare, and materials science, researchers have explored and observed some potential synergistic effects when deploying multiple frequencies simultaneously:

1. **Resonance Amplification**: Certain combinations of frequencies might reinforce or amplify each other when they resonate with

specific aspects of the target material. This can potentially intensify the impact on the target.

2. **Cumulative Thermal Effects**: Simultaneous exposure to multiple frequencies, especially in the microwave or terahertz range, might generate cumulative thermal effects within the target. These combined thermal impacts can increase the overall energy absorption and heating.

3. **Frequency-Specific Material Effects**: Different frequencies interact with materials in various ways. Simultaneously deploying multiple frequencies might exploit these interactions to trigger specific responses, disrupting or damaging the target more effectively than a single frequency alone.

4. **Interference Patterns**: The interference patterns generated by overlapping or interacting multiple frequencies could create zones of constructive interference at certain points, resulting in localized areas of increased energy density.

5. **Frequency Diversity for Countermeasures**: Combining different frequencies offers diversity, making it more challenging for adversaries to develop comprehensive shielding or countermeasures against an array of frequencies simultaneously.

6. **Biological and Cellular Interaction**: In non-lethal applications, combining specific frequencies might produce distinct interactions with biological or cellular structures, influencing and altering the behavior of organisms or systems.

7. **Electromagnetic Compatibility and Immunity**: In electronic warfare, using multiple frequencies might lead to better electromagnetic compatibility or immunity in friendly systems while causing interference or disruption in the adversary's systems.

Can energy weapons produce resonance effects that lead to vibrations and rumbling sensations?

Energy weapons emit a series of pulses or oscillations at a specific frequency that can affect the resonant frequency of certain materials or structures in the environment or can cause concussion waves in a target area. This resonance causes the materials or structures to vibrate intensely, leading to rumbling sensations and potentially even physical disruption.

Strategies to Dampen the Effect: If you're incorporating this concept into a creative project, you might consider the following strategies for characters to dampen the effects of resonance-based vibrations:

1. **Isolation Materials:** Introduce materials with properties that prevent vibrations from propagating. Materials like rubber, neoprene, or specialized vibration isolation pads could be used to dampen vibrations and prevent them from spreading.
2. **Structural Modifications:** Reinforce structures to alter their resonant frequencies. By changing the structure's dimensions

or properties, you might shift its natural resonance away from the frequency emitted by the weapon.

3. **Absorption Materials:** Introduce materials that can absorb the energy emitted by the weapon. Materials with high energy absorption capabilities, such as foams or elastomers, might absorb the energy before it triggers resonance in other structures.

4. **Frequency Scramblers:** Develop devices that can detect and counteract the emitted frequency by emitting inverse waves, effectively canceling out the resonance.

5. **Active Dampening Systems:** Create systems that detect resonance and quickly apply counter-vibrations to neutralize the effects. This concept is similar to noise-canceling technology.

6. **Barrier Materials:** Introduce materials that create a physical barrier between the weapon's emission and the environment. These materials might absorb or reflect the emitted energy.

How do we deploy a low-cost energy dissipation barrier that absorbs and disperses the energy released by a concussive energy weapon?

Materials and Construction:

1. **Rubber Mats or Sheets:** Rubber has energy-absorbing properties and can act as a shock absorber. Affordable rubber

mats or sheets could be stacked or layered to create a makeshift barrier.

2. **Cardboard Tubes or Barrels:** Stack cardboard tubes or barrels in front of potential impact areas. The empty space within the tubes can absorb energy and help disperse the shockwave.

3. **Loose Fabric or Clothing:** Hang layers of loose fabric or clothing in the vicinity. These materials can flutter and absorb energy, reducing the intensity of the shockwave.

4. **Sandbags or Gravel:** Place sandbags or bags filled with gravel in strategic positions. The dense materials can absorb and dissipate energy, acting as a buffer against the shockwave.

5. **Cushions or Pillows:** Stack cushions or pillows against walls or surfaces likely to be impacted. These soft materials can dampen the shockwave's effects.

6. **Water Barriers:** Containers filled with water could act as a barrier. Water's density can help absorb and disperse energy, reducing the intensity of the shockwave.

Limitations and Considerations:

- The effectiveness of these low-cost materials would depend on the energy weapon's power, the distance from the impact, and the nature of the concussive effect.

- Keep in mind that these makeshift solutions might not provide full protection but could potentially reduce the impact's severity.

Can looped shielding or twisted pair shielding act like a parasitic antenna and amplify the EMF threat?

The physical structure of the loop or the twist can create an unintended resonant structure that might capture and amplify specific frequencies, particularly when the dimensions of the loop or twist coincide with the wavelength of the incoming electromagnetic waves.

This phenomenon occurs because the looped or twisted configuration might inadvertently create an effective antenna length. The loop or twisted pair could resonate or couple with the incoming signals, leading to unintentional amplification or coupling of those frequencies.

In certain scenarios, this unintended resonance or coupling might cause issues such as:

1. Unwanted signal reception or emission.
2. Interference with nearby electronic devices or systems.
3. Degradation of the shielding's intended function.
4. Implement appropriate grounding and termination techniques to reduce the potential for unintended resonance or coupling.

What are the ionizing radiation types?

The different types of ionizing radiation are often categorized based on their ability to penetrate matter and their source of origin. Between beta and gamma radiation, there are other types of radiation, such as alpha radiation and neutron radiation, that also have distinct properties and characteristics.

Here's a brief overview of the different types of ionizing radiation:

1. **Alpha Radiation (α):**

   Alpha particles consist of two protons and two neutrons and are emitted from the nuclei of certain unstable atoms.

   They have a positive charge and relatively low penetration ability. A sheet of paper or even human skin can stop alpha particles.

   Because of their larger mass and charge, alpha particles cause significant ionization in the surrounding material, making them potentially hazardous if ingested or inhaled.

2. **Beta Radiation (β):**

   Beta particles are high-energy electrons (β-) or positrons (β+).

They have greater penetration than alpha particles and can be stopped by materials like plastic, glass, or a few millimeters of aluminum.

Beta particles cause moderate ionization as they interact with matter.

3. **Gamma Radiation (γ):**

Gamma rays are high-energy electromagnetic waves emitted from the nucleus of an atom during a radioactive decay process.

They have very high penetration abilities and can only be effectively stopped by dense materials like lead or thick layers of concrete or steel.

Gamma radiation causes ionization and can penetrate deep into materials.

4. **Neutron Radiation (n):**

Neutron radiation consists of neutrons emitted during certain types of radioactive decay or in nuclear reactions.

Neutrons have no charge and can penetrate materials deeply, but their ability to ionize matter depends on their energy level.

Neutron radiation poses unique challenges for shielding due to their ability to induce radioactivity in some materials and their varying interactions with different elements.

These different types of radiation exhibit varying levels of ionization and penetration ability. The choice of shielding material depends on the specific type of radiation being encountered and its energy level. Radiation protection and shielding strategies are designed to minimize the exposure of humans and sensitive equipment to these different types of ionizing radiation.

What kind of microwave absorbing powders can be used with epoxy or foam?

Microwave absorbers are specialized materials designed to efficiently absorb microwave energy. They are engineered to minimize reflections and effectively convert the incoming electromagnetic energy into heat. Examples of microwave absorbers include:

- **Carbonyl Iron Powder Absorbers:** These absorbers contain tiny iron particles that resonate and dissipate the microwave energy as heat.

- **Magnetically Loaded Absorbers:** These absorbers use materials with high magnetic permeability to convert the energy into heat via magnetic losses.

Microwave absorbers are widely used in applications where reducing reflections and minimizing electromagnetic interference are crucial, such as anechoic chambers, radar testing facilities, and electromagnetic compatibility (EMC) testing environments. Their effectiveness can be quite high for specific frequency ranges, making them one of the most efficient options for attenuating microwave signals.

Magnetically loaded absorbers are materials that use their magnetic properties to efficiently convert electromagnetic energy into heat. They are often used for electromagnetic interference (EMI) shielding, microwave absorption, and reducing reflections. Here are some examples of substances that can act as magnetically loaded absorbers in various media:

1. **Barium Ferrite:**

   Barium ferrite particles or coatings can be added to polymers or paints to create magnetically loaded absorbers.

2. **Manganese Zinc Ferrite:**

   Manganese zinc ferrite particles can be incorporated into composite materials for microwave absorption.

3. **Nickel Zinc Ferrite:**

Nickel zinc ferrite is another option for creating magnetically loaded absorbers.

4. Cobalt Ferrite:

Cobalt ferrite particles can be used to create absorbers with magnetic loss properties.

5. Strontium Ferrite:

Strontium ferrite particles can be integrated into various mediums for microwave absorption.

6. Iron Nanoparticles:

Finely dispersed iron nanoparticles can be added to polymers, coatings, or paints to create absorbers.

7. Copper Ferrite:

Copper ferrite particles can be used in absorber formulations to provide effective absorption.

8. Ferrite-Based Composites:

Composites containing a mixture of ferrite materials can offer tailored absorption properties.

9. Magnetite (Fe_3O_4):

Magnetite nanoparticles can be used as absorber fillers in polymers or other materials

It's important to note that the effectiveness of magnetically loaded absorbers depends on factors like the composition, concentration, and distribution of magnetic particles within the medium. Designing effective absorbers requires careful consideration of the absorption properties, frequency range, and the desired level of attenuation. Magnetically loaded absorbers are often chosen based on their specific applicability and required performance within a given electromagnetic spectrum.

Is iron oxide powder more effective than iron for EMF shielding purposes?

Iron oxide powder, particularly in the form of magnetite (Fe_3O_4), can be more effective for certain electromagnetic field (EMF) shielding purposes compared to regular iron. This is because iron oxide, especially when in nanoparticle form, exhibits unique electromagnetic properties that can enhance its performance as a shielding material. Here's a breakdown of why iron oxide powder, specifically magnetite, can be advantageous for EMF shielding:

1. **High Magnetic Permeability:** Magnetite (Fe_3O_4) has a high magnetic permeability, which means it can easily respond to and redirect magnetic fields. This property is crucial for absorbing and rerouting electromagnetic energy away from the shielded area.

2. **Frequency Range:** Magnetite nanoparticles can be effective at absorbing electromagnetic energy in a broader frequency range compared to bulk iron. This makes them suitable for shielding against a wider range of EMF frequencies.

3. **Nanoparticle Effects:** Iron oxide nanoparticles, due to their small size, can exhibit unique electromagnetic interactions at the nanoscale. These interactions can enhance absorption properties and overall shielding effectiveness.

4. **Versatility:** Iron oxide nanoparticles can be integrated into various mediums, including polymers, paints, and coatings. This versatility allows for their incorporation into different types of shielding materials.

5. **Lightweight:** Iron oxide nanoparticles can be used to create lightweight shielding solutions that are easier to incorporate into various applications without adding significant weight

Iron oxide powder, including magnetite (Fe_3O_4), can offer certain advantages over regular iron powder for electromagnetic field (EMF) shielding purposes. Let's compare iron oxide powder and iron powder in terms of their effectiveness for EMF shielding:

Iron Oxide Powder (Magnetite):

- **Advantages:**
    1. **High Magnetic Permeability:** Magnetite has a higher magnetic permeability compared to pure iron. This means

it can more effectively redirect and absorb magnetic fields, which is valuable for EMF shielding.

2. **Broad Frequency Range:** Magnetite nanoparticles can exhibit absorption properties over a wider frequency range, making them effective against a broader spectrum of EMF frequencies.

3. **Nanoparticle Effects:** The nanoscale properties of magnetite nanoparticles can lead to enhanced electromagnetic interactions and absorption characteristics.

4. **Versatility:** Magnetite nanoparticles can be incorporated into various materials, offering flexibility in creating shielding solutions.

5. **Lightweight:** Iron oxide nanoparticles are lightweight, making them suitable for applications where weight is a concern.

- **Considerations:**

  1. **Cost:** The cost of iron oxide nanoparticles might be higher compared to regular iron powder due to production processes and material properties.

Iron Powder:

- **Advantages:**

  1. **Conductivity:** Iron powder is a good conductor of electricity and can reflect or absorb electric fields.

2. **Availability and Cost:** Iron powder is more readily available and might be less expensive compared to iron oxide nanoparticles.
- **Considerations:**
    1. **Magnetic Permeability:** Regular iron powder doesn't have the same high magnetic permeability as magnetite, limiting its effectiveness in redirecting and absorbing magnetic fields.
    2. **Narrower Frequency Range:** The shielding effectiveness of iron powder might be limited to certain frequencies, depending on the material's properties.

In summary, if your primary concern is shielding against both electric and magnetic fields across a broad frequency range, iron oxide powder (magnetite) could be more effective due to its unique properties. However, if cost and availability are significant factors, regular iron powder might still provide some level of shielding, especially against electric fields. As with any shielding application, the specific material, its integration, and the desired shielding performance should be considered to make an informed choice.

Is solder an effective shielding material?

While tin is conductive, its effectiveness as a radiation shielding material is limited due to several factors:

1. **Density and Atomic Number:** Tin has a relatively low density and atomic number compared to other metals commonly used for radiation shielding, such as lead. Density and atomic number play crucial roles in attenuating radiation. Materials with higher atomic numbers tend to be more effective at absorbing and scattering radiation.

2. **Interaction with Radiation Types:** Different types of radiation interact with materials in specific ways. For instance, gamma rays and X-rays are high-energy photons that require dense materials with high atomic numbers to effectively attenuate them. Tin's low atomic number makes it less effective at stopping these high-energy photons.

3. **Limited Stopping Power:** Radiation shielding requires materials with good stopping power, which means they can absorb and scatter radiation particles effectively. While tin is conductive and can absorb some radiation, it lacks the sufficient stopping power needed for comprehensive radiation shielding.

4. **Alpha and Neutron Radiation:** Tin is not suitable for shielding against alpha particles, which are relatively massive and require materials with high atomic numbers. Similarly, tin's low scattering cross-section for thermal neutrons makes it less effective for neutron radiation shielding.

5. **Radiation Energy Levels:** Radiation can vary in energy levels, and effective shielding requires materials that match the specific energy range. While tin might have limited effectiveness

against low-energy radiation, it becomes less effective as the energy level increases.

In contrast, metals like lead, tungsten, and other heavy metals are preferred for radiation shielding due to their high atomic numbers and densities. These metals can effectively attenuate high-energy radiation by absorbing and scattering the radiation particles.

Conductivity, while important for electrical applications, does not necessarily translate to effective radiation shielding. For radiation shielding purposes, it's crucial to choose materials based on their atomic properties, densities, and ability to interact with specific radiation types.

Solder is primarily used for joining and connecting electronic components, and its effectiveness as a shielding material against various radiation types, including Extremely Low Frequency (ELF) radiation, is limited. Its primary purpose is not as a radiation shielding material, but rather as a conductor for electrical connections. Here's a general assessment of solder's effectiveness as a shielding material against different radiation types:

1. **Gamma Radiation and X-Rays:**

   Rating: Low

   Solder is not effective for shielding against high-energy electromagnetic radiation like gamma rays and X-rays.

These radiations require dense materials like lead, concrete, or heavy metals for effective attenuation.

2. Beta Radiation:

Rating: Low

Solder's effectiveness against beta particles (high-energy electrons or positrons) is limited. Beta radiation requires materials with good stopping power, such as plastic or other dense materials.

3. Alpha Radiation:

Rating: Very Low

Solder is ineffective against alpha particles, which are relatively large and can be stopped by materials like paper or skin.

4. Neutron Radiation:

Rating: Very Low

Solder is not suitable for shielding against neutron radiation. Neutrons require materials with high hydrogen content, like water or specialized materials, to absorb them effectively.

5. EMF/ELF Radiation:

Rating: Very Low

Solder is not designed to shield against electromagnetic fields (EMF) or extremely low-frequency (ELF) radiation. These fields require specialized shielding materials with high magnetic permeability or conductivity.

What are the best plastics that can be used for EMF shielding?

Plastics are generally not as effective as metals for electromagnetic field (EMF) absorption or attenuation due to their lower electrical conductivity and magnetic permeability. However, certain plastic composites and formulations can exhibit some degree of EMF attenuation. Here are a few plastics that are often used in EMF shielding applications, along with their relative effectiveness:

1. **Carbon-Filled Plastics:**

   Carbon-filled plastics are formulated by adding conductive carbon-based materials (like carbon black or carbon fiber) to the plastic matrix.

   These plastics can provide limited EMF shielding by absorbing and dissipating electromagnetic energy through their conductivity.

   o Effectiveness: Moderate

2. **Conductive Polymer Blends:**

Some polymers are blended with conductive materials, such as metallic particles or fibers, to enhance their conductivity and EMF attenuation properties.

These blends can offer improved shielding compared to non-conductive plastics.

Effectiveness: Moderate

3. **Graphene-Enhanced Polymers:**

Polymers infused with graphene, a highly conductive form of carbon, can exhibit enhanced electrical properties and some EMF attenuation capabilities.

Graphene's unique properties contribute to its conductivity and potential for absorption.

Effectiveness: Moderate to Good

4. **Metal-Coated Polymers:**

Applying a thin layer of metal (such as silver, copper, or nickel) onto the surface of a polymer can create a conductive layer that helps to reflect or attenuate EMF.

Metal-coated plastics can offer some shielding effectiveness, especially at higher frequencies.

Effectiveness: Moderate

5. **Polymer-Ceramic Composites:**

Combining polymers with ceramic materials, such as barium titanate, can create materials with enhanced dielectric properties that affect EMF interactions.

These composites can offer some absorption and reflection of electromagnetic waves.

Effectiveness: Moderate

It's important to note that while these plastics can provide some level of EMF attenuation, their effectiveness is generally lower compared to metal-based materials with higher electrical conductivity and magnetic permeability. The specific formulation, concentration of conductive additives, and the frequency range of interest will all impact the shielding performance.

For more effective EMF shielding, metal foils, meshes, and conductive paints are often preferred choices due to their higher conductivity. When selecting materials for EMF shielding, it's recommended to consult experts in electromagnetic shielding and materials science to ensure that the chosen materials are appropriate for the specific application and frequency range.

What are some of the best combinations of materials for robust EMF protection?

Robust electromagnetic field (EMF) and radiation protection often involves combining materials with complementary properties to provide effective shielding across a wide frequency range. While no combination is universally ideal for all scenarios, here are some pairs and triplets of materials and metals that can offer enhanced EMF and radiation protection:

1. **Copper and Aluminum Mesh or Foil + Conductive Polymer Composite:**

   Copper and aluminum are good conductors that reflect and attenuate EMF.

   Combining them with a conductive polymer composite can provide flexibility, durability, and additional absorption properties.

2. **Metal-Coated Fabric + Carbon-Filled Polymer:**

   A fabric coated with a thin layer of metal (e.g., silver-coated fabric) provides good reflectivity.

   Combining this with a carbon-filled polymer layer can enhance absorption and shielding effectiveness.

3. **Copper Foil + Ferrite Composite:**

Copper foil provides good conductivity and reflection of EMF.

A composite containing ferrite particles can offer absorption properties, particularly at higher frequencies.

4. **Graphene-Enhanced Polymer + Metal Mesh:**

Graphene-enhanced polymers provide improved conductivity and absorption.

Combining them with a metal mesh layer can enhance the reflection component and extend the protection range.

5. **Lead Shielding + Neutron-Absorbing Polymer:**

Lead is effective against gamma and X-ray radiation due to its high atomic number.

Combining it with a neutron-absorbing polymer layer can provide comprehensive protection against multiple radiation types.

6. **Metal-Coated Ceramic + Conductive Polymer:**

Metal-coated ceramics offer high-temperature stability and reflectivity.

A conductive polymer layer can enhance the absorption component.

7. **Copper Mesh + Magnetite Composite:**

   Copper mesh provides good conductivity and reflection.

   Adding a magnetite composite layer can improve absorption and expand the protection range.

8. **Silver-Coated Fabric + Graphene-Enhanced Polymer + Copper Mesh:**

   Silver-coated fabric reflects and absorbs EMF.

   Graphene-enhanced polymer adds absorption and flexibility.

   Copper mesh contributes additional reflection and attenuation.

These combinations are meant to illustrate how different materials can complement each other's properties for improved EMF and radiation protection. However, the effectiveness of these pairings depends on factors such as material thickness, conductivity, permittivity, frequency range, and application requirements.

How does electrified EMF shielding work?

Electrified EMF shielding, also known as active shielding, involves the use of an electric field to counteract or cancel out the external electromagnetic fields (EMF) that you're trying to shield against. The basic idea is to create an opposing electric field that effectively nullifies the effects of the incoming EMF, providing a more comprehensive level of protection compared to passive shielding methods.

In theory, electrified EMF shielding works by generating an electric field that is equal in strength but opposite in direction to the external EMF. This results in the cancellation or reduction of the net EMF in the shielded area. The active shielding system continuously adjusts the strength and orientation of the electric field based on the detected external EMF, maintaining a balance that minimizes the impact of the EMF on the shielded space.

Using a simple example of foil and a 9V battery for electrified EMF shielding might not be very effective. While it's true that applying a voltage across a conductor creates an electric field around it, there are several challenges:

1. **Magnitude of the Electric Field:** The electric field generated by a small battery may not be strong enough to effectively counteract the typically stronger EMF from sources like cell towers or Wi-Fi networks.

2. **Complexity:** EMF sources emit a range of frequencies, and their strengths can vary. Creating an electric field that effectively cancels out all of these frequencies requires sophisticated electronics capable of detecting and responding to different EMF sources.

3. **Energy Consumption:** An active shielding system would require a constant power source, which can be inefficient and impractical for everyday applications.

4. **Electromagnetic Compatibility:** The electrified shielding system itself could potentially generate additional EMF, which might interfere with nearby electronic devices.

5. **Safety Concerns:** The application of a voltage without proper design and control can lead to safety risks, such as electric shock or unintended interference.

While the concept of active EMF shielding is intriguing, implementing an effective system involves advanced engineering and technology. Professional-grade active shielding solutions typically use complex circuitry, sensors, and algorithms to achieve their intended goals.

NOTE: This concept can backfire and energize EMF. Test with caution.

What type of Boron powders can be used for DIY epoxy based coatings or paints?

If you're considering using boron-based materials for electromagnetic field (EMF) shielding, you might want to explore boron nitride (BN) powder rather than boron oxide. Boron nitride is known for its unique properties and is often used in various applications, including electronics and high-temperature environments. Here's a brief overview of boron nitride and its potential use in EMF shielding:

Boron Nitride (BN):

- Boron nitride is a compound composed of boron and nitrogen atoms arranged in a hexagonal lattice structure.
- It is often referred to as the "white graphene" due to its similar structure to carbon-based graphene.
- BN has good thermal conductivity, electrical insulation properties, and is often used in high-temperature and electrical applications.
- In some forms, such as hexagonal boron nitride (hBN), it exhibits good lubricating properties and electrical insulation.

Use of Boron Nitride in EMF Shielding: While boron nitride has valuable properties, its effectiveness for EMF shielding might be limited due to its primarily insulating nature. EMF shielding typically requires materials with good electrical conductivity, reflection, or absorption properties, which boron nitride might not provide to a significant extent.

If your goal is EMF shielding, exploring materials with higher electrical conductivity and EMF attenuation capabilities, such as silver-based powders or metal-coated materials, might be more appropriate.

White graphite, also known as hexagonal boron nitride (hBN), possesses unique properties that make it potentially useful for particle beam shielding in specific applications. Here are some considerations regarding the use of white graphite for particle beam shielding:

Hexagonal Boron Nitride (hBN):

- hBN is a two-dimensional material with a hexagonal lattice structure, similar to graphene.
- It has excellent thermal conductivity, high electrical resistance, and good mechanical stability.
- hBN is often used as a lubricant and heat conductor in high-temperature applications.

Particle Beam Shielding:

- In particle physics and high-energy experiments, particle beams (e.g., electrons, protons, ions) are generated and accelerated, creating radiation that can pose hazards to equipment and personnel.
- Shielding is essential to protect sensitive instruments and prevent unwanted interactions.

Mixing Neodymium Iron Boron (NdFeB) powder with epoxy for electromagnetic field (EMF) shielding can offer some benefits due to the magnetic properties of NdFeB. However, the effectiveness of such a mixture for shielding against different radiation types and

Extremely Low Frequency (ELF) radiation will depend on various factors. Here's an assessment:

NdFeB Powder Mixed in Epoxy:

- Neodymium Iron Boron (NdFeB) is a powerful type of permanent magnet known for its high magnetic strength.
- Mixing NdFeB powder in epoxy can create a composite with enhanced magnetic properties, which might contribute to EMF shielding.
- NdFeB's effectiveness might be more pronounced at higher frequencies where magnetic field interactions are significant.

Effectiveness for EMF Shielding:

- Magnetic Shielding: NdFeB's magnetic properties can help shield against certain EMF components, particularly those associated with magnetic fields.
- Effectiveness: Moderate to Good for magnetic field-related EMF components.

Effectiveness Against Different Radiation Types:

- Gamma Radiation and X-Rays: Rating: Low to Moderate

    NdFeB might not be effective against these high-energy radiation types.

- Beta Radiation: Rating: Low to Moderate

NdFeB's effectiveness might vary based on particle energy and type.

- Alpha Radiation: Rating: Very Low to Low

  NdFeB is unlikely to be effective against alpha particles.

- Neutron Radiation: Rating: Very Low

  NdFeB is not typically chosen for neutron radiation shielding.

- ELF Radiation: Rating: Low to Moderate

  NdFeB's effectiveness for ELF radiation depends on the material's interaction with electric fields, which might be limited compared to its magnetic effects.

Important Considerations:

- **Particle Size and Distribution:** The particle size and distribution of NdFeB powder within the epoxy matrix can impact its shielding properties.
- **Frequency Dependency:** The effectiveness might vary with frequency. NdFeB might be more effective at frequencies where its magnetic properties play a significant role.
- **Testing:** Thorough testing across the frequency range of interest is recommended to determine the shielding effectiveness.

While both ferrite and neodymium (NdFeB) materials have magnetic properties, they are used differently in electromagnetic field (EMF) shielding due to their distinct characteristics. The difference in their ratings for shielding effectiveness against various radiation types is primarily due to their different behaviors and properties:

1. **Ferrite:**

    Ferrites are ceramic materials that exhibit high magnetic permeability and low electrical conductivity.

    They are particularly effective at attenuating magnetic fields and can significantly reduce the penetration of low-frequency magnetic fields.

    Ferrites are often used in applications where magnetic field shielding is essential, such as in transformers and electromagnetic interference (EMI) suppression.

    Ferrites' high magnetic permeability makes them effective for shielding against magnetic fields associated with EMF.

2. **Neodymium Iron Boron (NdFeB) Powder:**

    NdFeB is a type of permanent magnet known for its strong magnetic properties.

When used in shielding, NdFeB's strong magnetic properties can redirect or channel magnetic fields rather than absorbing or attenuating them.

NdFeB's effectiveness might be more pronounced at higher frequencies where its magnetic field interactions play a role.

However, for shielding against non-magnetic radiation components or lower frequencies, NdFeB might not offer significant benefits.

The difference in ratings is not a matter of quality but rather a reflection of how each material interacts with EMF and radiation. While ferrite is well-suited for attenuating magnetic fields, neodymium powder might have limitations when it comes to shielding against non-magnetic radiation components or lower-frequency EMF.

How does a high powered microwave (HPM) defeat shielding like copper foil?

The interaction between high-powered microwave (HPM) beams and copper involves a combination of electrical and magnetic effects. The attenuation of the HPM beam by copper can be explained in terms of the material's response to the electromagnetic field.

When an electromagnetic wave, such as a high-powered microwave, interacts with a conductor like copper, the following processes contribute to the attenuation:

1. **Electrical Conductivity:**
   - Copper is an excellent electrical conductor. When exposed to an electromagnetic field, the free electrons in the copper material respond by moving in response to the changing electric field of the microwaves. This movement of electrons generates currents that oppose the incident electromagnetic field, leading to absorption and conversion of the electromagnetic energy into heat.

2. **Skin Effect:**
   - At high frequencies, electromagnetic waves tend to penetrate the outer layer of a conductor more deeply, leading to a phenomenon known as the skin effect. The skin depth, which is the depth at which the amplitude of the electromagnetic field is reduced, becomes smaller at higher frequencies. Copper, being a good conductor, is effective at attenuating the electromagnetic waves near the surface.

3. **Magnetic Response:**
   - Copper also has a weak magnetic response, and its magnetic permeability is close to that of a vacuum. While the magnetic response of copper is generally weak, it can

play a role in attenuating electromagnetic waves. The interaction involves the alignment of magnetic moments in the material with the applied magnetic field of the microwaves.

4. **Saturation Effects:**

    o Saturation occurs when the magnetic moments in the material reach their maximum alignment and cannot respond further to an increase in the applied magnetic field. In the context of copper, the saturation effect is generally weak due to its relatively low magnetic permeability. However, at extremely high power levels, the material may reach a point where its magnetic response becomes saturated, potentially leading to a reduction in its ability to attenuate the HPM beam.

It's crucial to note that copper is not as effective in attenuating high-frequency electromagnetic waves compared to materials with higher magnetic permeability, such as certain ferromagnetic materials like permalloy. In practical applications, the design of shielding materials may involve multiple layers, with each layer contributing to the overall attenuation of the HPM beam.

If the magnetic response to copper is so weak how is it that magnets make electricity in a generator?

The process of generating electricity using magnets and copper (or other conductive materials) is based on the principle of electromagnetic induction, which was first discovered by Michael Faraday in the 19th century. The key idea is that a changing magnetic field induces an electromotive force (EMF), leading to the flow of electric current.

Here's how the process works:

1. **Faraday's Law of Electromagnetic Induction:**
   - Faraday's law states that a change in magnetic flux within a closed loop induces an electromotive force (EMF) in the loop.

2. **Magnet and Coil Arrangement:**
   - In a generator, a coil of wire (often made of copper) is placed within the magnetic field produced by a magnet or an electromagnet. As the coil rotates or experiences a change in the magnetic field, the magnetic flux through the coil changes.

3. **Induced EMF and Current:**
   - The changing magnetic flux induces an electromotive force (EMF) in the coil according to Faraday's law. The induced EMF creates an electric current when the coil is part of a closed electrical circuit.

4. **Conversion to Electrical Energy:**
   - The induced current flowing through the coil represents electrical energy. By connecting the coil to an external

circuit, the generated electricity can be used to power devices, charge batteries, or contribute to a power grid.

The key point is that the generation of electricity in this context is based on the interaction between a magnetic field and a coil of wire, leading to the induction of an electromotive force and the flow of electric current. The magnetic response of copper itself is not a primary factor in this process. Copper is chosen for its high electrical conductivity, which facilitates the efficient flow of induced current.

The apparent contradiction between copper's poor magnetic permeability and its effectiveness in electromagnetic induction can be explained by distinguishing between two aspects of magnetic behavior: magnetic permeability and electrical conductivity.

1. **Electrical Conductivity:**
    - Copper is an excellent conductor of electricity. When a changing magnetic field induces a current in a conductor, the induced current produces its own magnetic field. This induced magnetic field interacts with the changing external magnetic field, leading to electromagnetic induction. The efficiency of this process is related to the electrical conductivity of the material.

2. **Magnetic Permeability:**
    - Magnetic permeability is a measure of how easily a material can be magnetized. In the case of copper, its magnetic permeability is relatively low compared to

ferromagnetic materials like iron or nickel. This means that copper is not easily magnetized by an external magnetic field, and it does not retain a strong magnetic field after the removal of the external field.

- **Poor Magnetic Permeability Facilitating Better Induction:**
  - The poor magnetic permeability of copper is actually beneficial for electromagnetic induction. When a conductor has low magnetic permeability, it allows the changing magnetic field to penetrate the material more easily. This enhanced penetration results in a more effective interaction between the external magnetic field and the conductor, leading to higher induction efficiency.

In summary, while copper's magnetic permeability is low, its excellent electrical conductivity allows for efficient electromagnetic induction. The changing magnetic field induces currents in the copper conductor, and these induced currents, in turn, produce magnetic fields that interact with the external magnetic field, facilitating the process of electromagnetic induction. The combination of low magnetic permeability and high electrical conductivity makes copper a suitable material for applications involving electromagnetic induction, such as in generators and transformers.

How does the arrangement of magnets in a generator produce alternating electricity?

In an alternating current (AC) generator, the process of generating electricity involves a changing magnetic field inducing an electromotive force (EMF) or voltage in a coil of wire. The key principle behind this process is electromagnetic induction, as described by Faraday's law.

In a typical AC generator with alternating poles of magnets, the magnetic field around the coil of wire changes direction periodically. Let's consider a scenario where the magnets alternate between north and south poles in series.

As the magnets move, the magnetic field through the coil of wire changes, inducing a current. The induced current in the wire experiences a change in direction as the magnets alternate. Here's what happens:

1. **Push and Pull:**
   - When a north pole approaches the coil, it induces a certain direction of current flow in the wire, creating a "push" effect.
   - As the south pole follows, the direction of the induced current changes, creating a "pull" effect.
   - This process repeats as the magnets continue to alternate.
2. **Push and Inverted Push:**

- It's more accurate to describe it as a "push" and an "inverted push" rather than a "pull." The "inverted push" signifies a change in the direction of the induced current rather than an actual physical pulling force.
- When the magnetic field changes direction, the induced current also changes direction, and we interpret this change as a reversal or inversion of the push effect.

In summary, as the magnets alternate poles in series in an AC generator, the induced current in the wire experiences a push and an inverted push due to the changing magnetic field. This process results in an alternating current where the direction of the current changes periodically, creating the characteristic waveform of AC electricity.

What is magnetic coercivity and hysteresis?

Coercivity: Coercivity is a fundamental property of magnetic materials and refers to the measure of a material's resistance to becoming demagnetized. It indicates the magnetic field strength required to reduce the material's magnetization to zero after it has been magnetized. In other words, coercivity is the material's inherent "stickiness" to retain its magnetization.

There are two types of coercivity:

1. **Intrinsic Coercivity (Hci):** This is the magnetic field strength needed to reduce the magnetization to zero in a fully

demagnetized material. It's often used to describe the coercivity of permanent magnets.

2. **Extrinsic Coercivity (Hce):** This is the magnetic field strength needed to reduce the residual magnetization (remanence) of a previously magnetized material to zero. It's commonly used in soft magnetic materials like transformer cores.

Hysteresis Losses: Hysteresis losses occur when a magnetic material undergoes repeated cycles of magnetization and demagnetization. As the magnetization changes, the material's magnetic domains realign, and energy is dissipated as heat due to friction within the material.

In the context of transformers and inductors:

- **Coercivity and Hysteresis Losses:** Materials with high coercivity require more energy to magnetize and demagnetize, leading to increased hysteresis losses during each magnetic cycle. These losses manifest as heat, reducing the efficiency of the core material.

- **Efficiency Impact:** High coercivity and the associated hysteresis losses can lead to inefficient energy transfer in transformers and inductors. The energy required to repeatedly magnetize and demagnetize the core results in wasted energy, which can affect the overall efficiency of the device.

- **Choice of Core Materials:** To minimize hysteresis losses and enhance efficiency, core materials with low coercivity are preferred for transformers and inductors. These materials require less energy for magnetization and demagnetization, leading to lower energy losses.

Soft Magnetic Materials: Soft magnetic materials are specifically designed with low coercivity to minimize hysteresis losses. They exhibit linear magnetic behavior, meaning their magnetization closely follows the applied magnetic field. These properties make them suitable for transformers and inductors, where efficient energy transfer is critical.

In summary, understanding coercivity and hysteresis losses is crucial for optimizing the performance of magnetic materials in transformers and inductors. Low coercivity and reduced hysteresis losses are essential for achieving high energy efficiency in these devices. Traditional core materials like iron and ferrites are chosen for their optimized magnetic properties, which contribute to efficient energy transfer.

Does sintering enhance a ferrite mixture?

Sintering is a process used in the manufacturing of ferrite materials, and it serves multiple purposes beyond just economic considerations. While sintering can help reduce costs by allowing for batch processing and efficient use of materials, its primary role is to enhance the properties of ferrite materials in various ways. Here's how sintering benefits ferrite materials:

1. **Densification:** Sintering involves heating a compacted powder at high temperatures below its melting point. During this process, the powder particles fuse together, resulting in densification. This increased density improves the mechanical strength, magnetic properties, and overall performance of the ferrite material.

2. **Magnetic Properties:** The densification achieved through sintering improves the alignment of magnetic domains within the ferrite structure. This alignment leads to enhanced magnetic properties, such as higher magnetic permeability and saturation magnetization.

3. **Uniformity:** Sintering helps achieve a more uniform and homogeneous composition throughout the ferrite material. This uniformity is crucial for consistent magnetic and electromagnetic properties across different parts of a component or device.

4. **Structural Stability:** Sintering strengthens the ferrite material's structure, making it more resistant to mechanical stress, temperature fluctuations, and environmental factors. This is particularly important for components that need to withstand challenging operational conditions.

5. **Customization:** Sintering conditions can be adjusted to tailor the properties of the ferrite material to specific applications. This flexibility allows manufacturers to optimize ferrite materials for various electromagnetic and magnetic applications.

6. **Dimensional Accuracy:** Sintering allows for precise control over the shape and dimensions of the final product. This is important for achieving desired performance characteristics and fitting components into specific designs.

7. **Cost-Efficiency:** While sintering can be cost-effective due to batch processing, its primary benefits lie in the improved properties of the ferrite material itself, which justify its use even in cases where cost is not the sole consideration.

In summary, while sintering can offer economic advantages in large-scale manufacturing, its primary purpose is to enhance the properties of ferrite materials, including their magnetic and electromagnetic characteristics, structural stability, and customization potential. Sintering is a fundamental step in producing high-quality ferrite components used in various applications, such as transformers, inductors, and electromagnetic shielding.

What type of radio frequency filters could be considered in conjunction with shielding concepts?

The efficiency of low pass, high pass, and band pass filters can vary depending on the specific design, component values, and the frequency range they are intended to filter. Here's a general overview of their efficiency and typical use cases:

1. Low Pass Filter:
- Efficiency: High

- Purpose: Low pass filters efficiently allow low-frequency signals to pass while attenuating high-frequency signals. They are widely used in audio applications, data filtering, and power supply noise reduction.

2. High Pass Filter:

- Efficiency: High

- Purpose: High pass filters efficiently allow high-frequency signals to pass while attenuating low-frequency signals. They are used in audio applications, frequency separation, and DC-blocking applications.

3. Band Pass Filter:

- Efficiency: Moderate to High

- Purpose: Band pass filters allow a specific range of frequencies to pass while attenuating frequencies outside this range. Their efficiency depends on the width of the passband and the steepness of the roll-off. They are used in applications where a specific frequency band needs to be isolated or extracted.

The efficiency of these filters is mainly determined by the quality and precision of the components used (resistors, capacitors, and inductors), as well as the desired characteristics of the filter's response (e.g., steepness of the roll-off, frequency selectivity).

It's important to note that the actual performance of a filter may also depend on its implementation, surrounding circuitry, and the accuracy of component values used. Proper design, component selection, and testing are crucial to achieving the desired filter performance.

What type of phenoms caused by EMF can weaken the effectiveness of aluminum shielding?

Resonance:

Resonance occurs when the natural frequency of the aluminum material matches the frequency of the incident EMF. In this case, the EMF can cause the aluminum to vibrate with greater intensity, amplifying the electromagnetic waves rather than attenuating them. This phenomenon is analogous to pushing a swing at its natural frequency, making it swing higher and higher. When resonance occurs in shielding materials, it weakens their ability to block or absorb the EMF, potentially leading to unintended signal transmission.

Frequency Range:

Aluminum shielding can have different attenuation properties at various frequency ranges. The effectiveness of the shielding depends on the skin depth, a measure of how deeply the EMF penetrates the material. At lower frequencies, the skin depth is larger, allowing the EMF to penetrate deeper into the aluminum, reducing the attenuation. As the frequency increases, the skin depth decreases, and the EMF is attenuated more effectively. However, at very high frequencies, such as in the microwave range, aluminum may become less efficient in attenuating the EMF due to the skin effect.

Electrical Conductivity:

Aluminum is a highly conductive material, which means it interacts strongly with EMF. The conductivity of the aluminum can influence how the EMF is distributed and flows through the material. At high conductivity, the EMF can induce strong eddy currents within the aluminum, creating opposing magnetic fields that partially cancel out the incident EMF. However, at extremely high frequencies, such as in the terahertz or optical range, aluminum's conductivity might actually facilitate the propagation of EMF, reducing the attenuation capability.

Incidental Coupling:

In complex electromagnetic environments, incidental coupling can occur between the EMF and other conductive elements near the aluminum shielding. This coupling can create unintended paths for EMF propagation, bypassing the shielding and reducing its effectiveness. For example, nearby cables, other metal objects, or even neighboring electronic devices might interact with the EMF in a way that circumvents the aluminum shielding.

To overcome these challenges, careful design and engineering are necessary. Engineers can select appropriate materials and thicknesses for the aluminum shielding to optimize attenuation at specific frequency ranges. In cases where resonance or high conductivity negatively impact shielding performance, designers may consider using different materials, multilayer shields, or specialized coatings to enhance overall EMF attenuation. Moreover, incorporating proper grounding techniques and isolation measures can minimize incidental coupling and improve the overall effectiveness of the shielding.

In weaponized scenarios, a mix of frequencies or unconventional electromagnetic phenomena might lead to unexpected interactions with the shielding material. For instance, the combination of multiple frequencies could result in resonance or interference patterns that compromise the shielding's effectiveness. Similarly, highly specialized and sophisticated equipment capable of generating precise frequencies and waveforms might be able to exploit weaknesses in the shielding.

What effect do magnets have on EMF?

Magnets can have a significant effect on electromagnetic fields (EMF) due to the principles of electromagnetism. When a magnet moves or changes its orientation relative to a conductor or a coil of wire, it induces an electromotive force (EMF) or voltage in the conductor. This phenomenon is known as electromagnetic induction.

There are two primary ways in which magnets affect electromagnetic fields:

Electromagnetic Induction: When a magnet moves relative to a conductor or changes its magnetic field strength near the conductor, it creates a changing magnetic flux through the conductor. This changing magnetic flux induces an electromotive force (EMF) or voltage across the ends of the conductor. This process is the basis for how electric generators work, where mechanical energy is used to move magnets relative to coils of wire, generating electricity.

Magnetic Field Deflection: Magnets can also influence the path of existing electromagnetic fields. When an EMF travels through space, a magnetic field is associated with it. When a magnetic material or a magnet is placed in the vicinity of the EMF, the magnetic field lines may be deflected or distorted around the magnet. This effect can be seen in various magnetic shielding applications, where materials are used to redirect or absorb magnetic fields.

Magnets cannot completely stop or block an electromagnetic wave (EMF) in the way that a physical barrier stops a solid object. EMF waves, including radio waves, microwaves, and light waves, are forms of electromagnetic radiation that can travel through space without the need for a physical medium.

However, magnets can interact with EMF waves and influence their behavior in certain situations:

Magnetic Shielding: Magnetic materials can be used to create shields that redirect or absorb magnetic fields. This can be useful in limiting the propagation of certain types of EMF waves. For example, in electronic devices or circuits, magnetic shielding may be employed to prevent interference from external magnetic fields.

Faraday Cages: A Faraday cage is an enclosure made of conductive material, often with a fine mesh or grid structure. It is used to block or attenuate electromagnetic fields, including EMF waves. The conductive material of the cage redistributes the EMF and prevents it from passing through the enclosure.

Magnetostatics: In certain situations involving magnetostatics (the study of magnetic fields in static conditions), magnets can have an effect on the distribution of magnetic fields and magnetic flux lines. This effect, however, does not completely stop the EMF wave itself.

It's important to note that the effectiveness of magnetic shielding and Faraday cages depends on the specific frequency and strength of the EMF wave and the design and material properties of the shielding structure. In many everyday situations involving common EMF waves, such as radio waves or Wi-Fi signals, the practicality of using magnets for EMF wave manipulation or shielding may be limited.

For most applications, EMF waves, especially those associated with wireless communication and light (e.g., radio waves and visible light), travel freely through space and are not easily stopped or blocked by magnetic fields alone.

How do poles on a magnet work and how do they affect metals?

Magnetic poles are regions of a magnetic material, such as a magnet or the Earth, where the magnetic field lines converge or diverge. There are two types of magnetic poles: the North Pole and the South Pole.

1. **Magnetic Poles:**
   - In a bar magnet, the magnetic field lines emerge from one end (called the North Pole) and converge into the other end (called the South Pole). This convention is based on the behavior of compass needles aligning with the Earth's magnetic field.

2. **Magnetic Field Lines:**
   - Magnetic field lines always form closed loops, and they travel from the North Pole to the South Pole outside the magnet. Inside the magnet, the field lines travel from the South Pole to the North Pole.

3. **Earth's Magnetic Field:**
   - The Earth acts like a giant magnet with magnetic field lines that are roughly aligned with its rotational axis. The geographic North Pole of the Earth corresponds to the magnetic South Pole, and the geographic South Pole corresponds to the magnetic North Pole.

4. **Attraction and Repulsion:**

- Like magnetic poles repel each other, and opposite poles attract. This behavior is described by the laws of magnetism formulated by Michael Faraday and others.

5. **Magnetic Fields and Metals:**

   - Magnetic fields can influence certain materials, particularly ferromagnetic materials like iron, nickel, and cobalt. These materials have magnetic domains that can align with an external magnetic field. When exposed to a magnetic field, these materials become temporarily magnetized.

6. **Magnetic Induction:**

   - When a magnetic material, such as iron, is brought close to a magnet, the magnetic domains within the material align with the external magnetic field. This alignment induces a magnetic moment in the material, and it becomes attracted to the magnet. The alignment persists even after removing the external magnetic field, creating a temporary magnet.

7. **Magnetic Field Direction:**

   - The force experienced by a magnetic material depends on the direction of the external magnetic field. Whether the material is attracted to the North or South Pole of a magnet depends on the orientation of the external magnetic field and the material's magnetic properties.

8. **Electric Current and Magnetism:**

○ Electric current and magnetism are closely related through electromagnetism. Moving electric charges create magnetic fields, and changing magnetic fields induce electric currents. This relationship is described by Maxwell's equations.

In summary, magnetic poles are regions where magnetic field lines converge or diverge, and the behavior of magnetic materials is influenced by the alignment of magnetic domains in the presence of a magnetic field. The attraction of metals to magnets is a result of the alignment of magnetic domains within the metal induced by the external magnetic field.

Would magnetite or iron be better suited for fast neutron absorption?

Magnetite's unique properties, including its resonance behavior and strong magnetic response, make it effective at absorbing and attenuating electromagnetic waves. Magnetite (Fe_3O_4) and iron (Fe) however both have relatively low probabilities for capturing fast neutrons, and they are not typically used as primary materials for shielding against fast neutrons. Instead, materials with higher atomic numbers and higher neutron capture cross-sections, such as high-Z materials like lead, tungsten, or certain hydrogenous materials, are preferred for effective fast neutron shielding.

The effectiveness of a material for shielding against fast neutrons depends on its ability to:

1. **Slow Down Neutrons:** Fast neutrons must be slowed down to thermal energies (i.e., thermalized) before they can be effectively captured by most shielding materials. Moderators, such as water or hydrogenous materials, are used to slow down fast neutrons to thermal energies.

2. **Have a High Neutron Capture Cross-Section:** The material must have a high probability of capturing thermal neutrons. Common neutron-absorbing materials include boron, gadolinium, and certain isotopes of cadmium.

3. **Provide Sufficient Thickness:** The shielding material must be present in sufficient thickness to attenuate the neutron flux to the desired level. The required thickness depends on the neutron energy and the desired level of attenuation.

Magnetite and iron do not excel in these aspects when it comes to shielding fast neutrons. Iron has a relatively low neutron capture cross-section, and magnetite, being a form of iron oxide, also does not have the characteristics required for effective fast neutron shielding.

For shielding against fast neutrons, high-Z materials, hydrogenous moderators, and neutron-absorbing materials are more appropriate choices. The exact choice of materials and the shielding design will depend on the specific requirements of your application and the energy spectrum of the fast neutrons you are dealing with. It is crucial to perform detailed neutron transport calculations or simulations to optimize the shielding design for your specific needs.

Would HDPE or boron carbide be better for neutron absorption?

When comparing 2 mm of HDPE (High-Density Polyethylene) to 2 mm of boron carbide for shielding against fast neutrons, boron carbide is significantly more effective for neutron shielding, especially for fast neutrons.

Here's why:

1. **Neutron Absorption Cross-Section:** Boron carbide (B4C) contains boron, which has a high neutron absorption cross-section. It is particularly effective at capturing thermal and fast neutrons due to the presence of boron-10, which has a high probability of neutron capture. This property makes boron carbide an excellent material for neutron shielding.

2. **Moderation Effect:** High-Density Polyethylene (HDPE) is a hydrogenous material, and it can act as a moderator, slowing down fast neutrons to thermal energies. While moderation is beneficial for thermal neutrons, it is less effective for fast neutrons. HDPE primarily serves as a secondary material in neutron shielding setups to slow down neutrons after they have passed through primary shielding materials like boron carbide.

3. **Attenuation:** Boron carbide, with its higher neutron absorption properties, can significantly attenuate the neutron flux, even in a thin layer. In contrast, 2 mm of HDPE alone is unlikely to provide substantial attenuation of fast neutrons.

In summary, for effective shielding against fast neutrons, boron carbide is a much more suitable material compared to HDPE. HDPE can serve as a moderator to slow down neutrons but is typically used in combination with neutron-absorbing materials like boron carbide or other high-Z materials to achieve effective shielding. The exact shielding design should be determined based on the specific neutron energy spectrum and the shielding objectives of the application.

Two millimeters (2 mm) of High-Density Polyethylene (HDPE) is primarily effective at attenuating thermal neutrons and, to a lesser extent, some low-energy fast neutrons. Here's how 2 mm of HDPE might affect different types of neutrons:

1. **Thermal Neutrons:** HDPE is a hydrogen-rich material, and hydrogen has a relatively high scattering cross-section for thermal neutrons. This means that 2 mm of HDPE can effectively moderate (slow down) and scatter thermal neutrons. It can be part of a multi-layer shielding configuration to further attenuate thermal neutrons.

2. **Low-Energy Fast Neutrons:** HDPE may provide some degree of attenuation for low-energy fast neutrons through moderation

and scattering. However, its effectiveness decreases as the energy of the fast neutrons increases.

3. **High-Energy Fast Neutrons:** For high-energy fast neutrons, HDPE is less effective as a standalone shielding material. High-energy neutrons require materials with high atomic numbers (high-Z materials) or neutron-absorbing materials for effective shielding.

4. **Intermediate-Energy Neutrons:** The effectiveness of 2 mm of HDPE for intermediate-energy neutrons falls between its performance for thermal and high-energy neutrons. It can provide some level of attenuation through scattering but may not be the most efficient choice for this energy range.

It's important to note that HDPE is often used as a moderator in neutron shielding configurations, especially when combined with other shielding materials. In many shielding applications, a combination of materials, including hydrogenous moderators and high-Z materials (e.g., lead or boron carbide), is used to provide effective shielding across a wide range of neutron energies.

The specific neutron shielding requirements of an application, including the neutron energy spectrum and the desired level of attenuation, will determine the most suitable shielding materials and configurations. Detailed neutron transport simulations or calculations are often performed to optimize shielding designs for specific scenarios.

How deep should the ground rod go into the ground?

The depth to which the ground rod should be installed depends on various factors, including the type of soil, the local electrical codes and regulations, and the specific requirements of the grounding system. In both city and rural environments, a typical ground rod for residential or small commercial installations is usually driven into the ground to a depth of 8 to 10 feet (2.4 to 3 meters). However, the actual depth may vary, and in some cases, it may be necessary to drive the ground rod deeper to ensure a reliable connection to a good grounding source.

In urban environments, ground contamination due to multiple sources of electrical currents can be a concern. To minimize ground loop issues and ensure an effective grounding system, it is generally advisable to use a single ground connection for the copper coil, especially if there are multiple sources of ground potential nearby. By using a single ground point, you can reduce the risk of circulating currents and ground contamination.

However, it's important to ensure that the single ground connection is well-bonded and has low impedance to effectively dissipate any unwanted currents. Properly bonding all grounding points and components in the system can help maintain a consistent ground potential and minimize the risk of ground loops.

For more complex installations or critical applications, consulting with a qualified electrical engineer or grounding expert is recommended. They can conduct a site-specific analysis, consider the local environment and conditions, and design a suitable grounding system to ensure safety and performance.

How should the ground rod be bonded into the ground?

Bonding the ground rod into the ground is a critical step in creating an effective grounding system. The purpose of bonding is to ensure a low impedance connection between the ground rod and the surrounding soil, allowing for the dissipation of electrical currents and providing a safe path for fault currents.

Here are some steps to properly bond a ground rod into the ground:

1. **Prepare the Grounding Rod:** Ensure that the ground rod is clean and free from any coatings or paint that may hinder electrical conductivity.
2. **Choose the Right Location:** Select a suitable location for the ground rod installation. It should be placed near the equipment or structure that requires grounding.
3. **Drive the Ground Rod:** Drive the ground rod into the ground to the recommended depth. As mentioned earlier, this is typically 8 to 10 feet (2.4 to 3 meters) for residential or small commercial installations.

4. **Connect the Grounding Conductor:** Attach a copper or copper-clad grounding conductor to the ground rod using a suitable clamp or connector. The conductor should have a sufficient cross-sectional area to handle the expected fault currents and provide a low-resistance path to the ground rod.

5. **Run the Grounding Conductor:** Run the grounding conductor from the ground rod to the main grounding system or to the equipment or structure that requires grounding. The conductor should be installed in a direct, straight path to minimize resistance.

6. **Bonding to Main Grounding System:** If the ground rod is not the main grounding point for the entire system, it should be bonded to the main grounding system using appropriate bonding jumpers or conductors. This ensures that all grounding points in the system are at the same ground potential.

7. **Properly Tighten Connections:** Ensure that all connections are properly tightened to establish good electrical contact. Use anti-oxidant compounds to prevent corrosion at the connections.

8. **Verify Grounding Continuity:** After installation, test the grounding system to verify its continuity and resistance using a ground resistance tester. The goal is to achieve a low ground resistance, typically less than 5 ohms.

It's important to follow local electrical codes and regulations when installing a ground rod and bonding it to the ground system. If you are not familiar with electrical installations or if the grounding system is part of a larger electrical system, it is best to consult with a qualified electrician or grounding specialist to ensure compliance and safety.

How does mylar rate as a shielding material?

1. ELF (Extremely Low Frequency): Rating: 7/10 Mylar, being a thin insulating material, may provide some attenuation for ELF frequencies, but its effectiveness could be limited.

2. VHF (Very High Frequency): Rating: 5/10 Mylar is relatively transparent to VHF frequencies, and its attenuation may not be significant. Other materials might be more suitable for VHF shielding.

3. UHF (Ultra High Frequency): Rating: 4/10 Mylar's effectiveness decreases as frequencies move into the UHF range. It may offer limited attenuation for UHF signals.

4. Radio Frequencies (1 GHz to 2.5 GHz): Rating: 3/10 Mylar is generally less effective at shielding higher-frequency radio signals. Thicker and more conductive materials are often preferred for better attenuation.

5. X-rays: Rating: 2/10 Mylar is not designed for shielding against ionizing radiation like X-rays. Specialized materials with high atomic numbers are typically used for X-ray shielding.

6. Electron Guns: Rating: 1/10 Mylar is not suitable for shielding against electron beams generated by electron guns. Metals or dense materials are more effective for electron shielding.

7. Neutron Guns: Rating: 1/10

Mylar, a type of polyester film, is generally more effective against Extremely Low Frequency (ELF) electromagnetic fields compared to higher frequencies for a few reasons:

1. **Wavelength Consideration:** ELF signals have much longer wavelengths, often extending to kilometers. Mylar, being a thin and flexible material, can act as a partial barrier to these long wavelengths.

2. **Material Characteristics:** Mylar is a dielectric material, meaning it is an insulator that does not conduct electricity. ELF signals often induce electric fields in conductive materials, and since Mylar is not a good conductor, it may provide some attenuation.

3. **Practical Considerations:** ELF signals are primarily associated with power transmission lines and some communication systems. Mylar, due to its flexibility and low cost, might be a practical choice for covering or wrapping certain components to minimize interference from ELF fields.

Mylar, being an insulator, can serve as a good material for providing electrical insulation between shielding layers. This is particularly important when constructing layered shielding systems to prevent unintended electrical contact between different layers.

Regarding its effectiveness against tunneling from a tunnel diode, Mylar may provide some level of attenuation due to its insulating properties. However, the effectiveness would depend on various factors, including the frequency of the tunneling signal, the power levels involved, and the specific construction of the shielding system. Tunneling typically involves the quantum mechanical behavior of electrons, and materials that exhibit negative differential resistance (NDR) properties, like certain semiconductors, are more directly associated with tunneling effects.

Mylar is not specifically designed as a shielding material against microwaves or tunnel diodes. Mylar is often used for its insulating and flexible properties and is commonly found in applications like packaging, insulation, and film capacitors. However, its effectiveness as a shielding material against microwaves depends on various factors, including the thickness of the material and the frequency of the microwaves.

In general, thin layers of common materials like Mylar may provide some attenuation of microwave signals, but they are not designed for high-performance shielding against directed energy sources. For effective shielding against microwaves, specialized materials with specific electromagnetic shielding properties are usually employed.

The wave function associated with a particle in quantum mechanics doesn't have a simple visual representation like the waves we encounter in everyday life, such as water waves. It's a complex mathematical function that describes the probability amplitude of finding a particle at a particular position.

When an EMF wave sheds from an antenna would it make a continuous wave front or break apart into smaller waves?

When an electromagnetic field (EMF) wave is emitted from an antenna, it typically forms a continuous wave front. The process of creating a continuous wave involves the coherent oscillation of electric and magnetic fields, resulting in a propagating wave that maintains its integrity as it travels through space.

Here's a brief overview of the key concepts:

1. **Coherent Emission:**
   - The generation of an EMF wave from an antenna involves coherent emission. Coherence refers to the synchronized and consistent oscillation of electric and magnetic fields.

2. **Continuous Wave Front:**
   - As the EMF wave propagates away from the antenna, it maintains a continuous and coherent wave front. This means that the oscillations of the electric and magnetic fields are in phase and follow a continuous pattern.

3. **Wavelength and Frequency:**

- The characteristics of the wave, such as its wavelength and frequency, are determined by the properties of the antenna and the frequency of the emitted signal.

4. **Directionality:**
   - The directionality of the emitted wave is influenced by the design and geometry of the antenna. Different types of antennas have distinct radiation patterns that determine how the EMF wave is distributed in space.

5. **Propagation Through Space:**
   - The wave front remains continuous as it propagates through space. While it may experience attenuation or other effects over long distances, the essential structure of the wave front is maintained.

In contrast to a continuous wave front, certain modulation techniques in communication systems can involve breaking down the signal into smaller components or modulating the amplitude, frequency, or phase of the signal. However, these modulation techniques still involve the coherent emission of an electromagnetic carrier wave.

In summary, when an EMF wave is emitted from an antenna, it forms a continuous and coherent wave front that travels through space. The wave front retains its essential structure as it propagates away from the source.

Why do small antennas that are only a fraction of the wavelength work?

Small antennas that are only a fraction of the wavelength can still work efficiently for certain applications because of their ability to resonate at the desired frequency and radiate electromagnetic waves effectively.

When an antenna is resonant at a specific frequency, it means that it has a natural tendency to vibrate and generate electric currents most efficiently at that particular frequency. Resonance occurs when the antenna's physical dimensions and electrical properties are in sync with the wavelength of the electromagnetic wave it is meant to transmit or receive.

For small antennas, such as monopoles or dipole antennas, their electrical length (length of the antenna relative to the wavelength) is typically much shorter than the full wavelength of the desired frequency. However, they can still achieve resonance by taking advantage of the quarter-wavelength or half-wavelength principles.

Quarter-wavelength antennas are approximately 1/4th the size of the full wavelength, while half-wavelength antennas are approximately 1/2 the size. By adjusting the antenna's length, it's possible to make it resonate at specific frequencies that are related to the full wavelength.

While small antennas can work efficiently at their resonant frequencies, their performance is often limited to a narrow band of frequencies centered around the resonant frequency. This is because the antenna's efficiency drops rapidly as you move away from the resonant frequency.

Small antennas are commonly used in various communication devices due to their compact size and ease of integration. They are suitable for short-range wireless communication, like Bluetooth or Wi-Fi, where the limited bandwidth is acceptable for the intended application.

However, for applications requiring broader frequency coverage and higher efficiency, larger antennas or more sophisticated antenna designs may be necessary to accommodate a wider range of frequencies and provide better performance.

Which materials would best be used to prevent quantum tunneling from tunnel diode-like technologies?

Tunnel diodes operate based on a quantum mechanical effect called tunneling, which allows particles to pass through a barrier that classical physics would suggest is impenetrable. This unique property of tunneling can have implications for the behavior of electromagnetic waves generated by tunnel diodes.

While the microwaves themselves are still part of the electromagnetic spectrum, the mechanism by which they are generated in a tunnel diode is distinctive.

The effectiveness of materials in shielding against the tunneling effect of tunnel diodes depends on various factors, including the specific characteristics of the diodes and the nature of the shielding material. Tunnel diodes operate based on quantum tunneling phenomena, where electrons move through a potential barrier. Shielding against such effects involves considerations at the quantum level.

In terms of shielding, the effectiveness depends on the frequency and power of the electromagnetic waves. Materials that are effective at shielding against conventional microwave frequencies may not be as effective against the unique characteristics of tunnel diode-generated microwaves. The ability of waves to "tunnel" through barriers may pose challenges for traditional shielding materials.

In practice, the specific characteristics of tunnel diode-generated microwaves, their frequency range, and power levels would need to be considered when designing effective shielding. It's essential to approach this topic with caution.

Factors to Consider:

1. **Quantum Tunneling:**

- Tunnel diodes operate through the quantum tunneling of electrons through a potential barrier. The material's ability to restrict or impede this tunneling process is critical.

2. **Material Bandgap:**
   - The bandgap of a material, which represents the energy range where electrons cannot exist, is crucial. A larger bandgap might make it more challenging for electrons to tunnel through the material.

3. **Crystal Structure:**
   - The crystal lattice structure of a material plays a role in determining its electronic properties. Materials with a specific crystal structure may hinder or facilitate tunneling.

Here are 20 common materials with their approximate bandgap values and their standard units (electronvolts, eV):

Diamond: 5.5 eV

Silicon Carbide (SiC): 2.86 eV

Gallium Nitride (GaN): 3.4 eV

Aluminum Nitride (AlN): 6.2 eV

Zinc Oxide (ZnO): 3.37 eV

Aluminum Gallium Nitride (AlGaN): Varies with composition

Indium Phosphide (InP): 1.35 eV

Gallium Arsenide (GaAs): 1.43 eV

Germanium (Ge): 0.66 eV

Gallium Phosphide (GaP): 2.34 eV

Silicon (Si): 1.1 eV

Cadmium Sulfide (CdS): 2.42 eV

Cadmium Telluride (CdTe): 1.44 eV

Lead Sulfide (PbS): 0.37 eV

Lead Telluride (PbTe): 0.32 eV

Tin Dioxide (SnO2): 3.6 eV

Strontium Titanate (SrTiO3): 3.2 eV

Barium Titanate (BaTiO3): 3.2 eV

Titanium Dioxide (TiO2): 3.2 eV (anatase phase)

Zirconium Dioxide (ZrO2): 5.8 eV

Lead: No distinct bandgap

Steel (Iron): No distinct bandgap

Copper: No distinct bandgap

Tungsten: No distinct bandgap

Aluminum: No distinct bandgap

Nickel: No distinct bandgap

Brass: No distinct bandgap

Silver: No distinct bandgap

Among the options listed, Silicon Carbide (SiC), Zinc Oxide (ZnO), Silicon (Si), Tin Dioxide (SnO2), Strontium Titanate (SrTiO3), Barium Titanate (BaTiO3), Titanium Dioxide (TiO2), and Zirconium Dioxide (ZrO2) are materials that can be purchased in sheet form for various applications. These materials are more commonly available in the form of wafers, sheets, or coatings, depending on the intended use and industry. The availability may also depend on specific suppliers and manufacturers. It's recommended to check with material suppliers or manufacturers for the most up-to-date information on the forms in which these materials can be obtained.

For electron tunneling, materials like insulating polymers (such as paraffin wax or HDPE) may not provide effective blocking because they lack the crystal structure and electronic properties required to impede quantum tunneling.

In the context of tunnel diodes or other quantum tunneling devices, materials with higher bandgap energies are generally better suited to prevent tunneling. However, the effectiveness of a material against quantum tunneling depends on various factors, including the energy of the particles involved, the thickness and composition of the barrier, and the specific properties of the material.

Materials with higher bandgaps, which indicate a larger energy gap between the valence and conduction bands, are generally better insulators and may be more effective against tunneling. Mylar, for instance, has a relatively high bandgap, making it a good insulator.

However, it's important to note that the tunneling effect is a quantum phenomenon, and the behavior of electrons at the quantum level can be complex. The choice of material would depend on various factors, including the specific energy levels involved, the thickness of the material, and the characteristics of the tunneling process.

Mylar, being a dielectric material, possesses a bandgap, which means it has an energy range where it does not conduct electrical current. While it can offer some attenuation of electromagnetic signals, it's important to note that the bandgap in dielectric materials like Mylar is related to their electrical properties rather than their ability to provide strong electromagnetic shielding.

In summary, while Mylar may provide some level of attenuation due to its dielectric properties, it might not be as effective as materials explicitly designed for electromagnetic shielding purposes when dealing with higher-frequency sources like those produced by tunnel diodes or other microwave devices.

Here are some other materials worth considering but lack the crystal structure for ideal quantum tunneling protection:

Alumina (Aluminum Oxide): Around 8-9 eV - Potentially effective.

Barium Titanate: Around 3-4 eV - Limited effectiveness.

Ceramic materials: The bandgap can vary - Effectiveness may vary.

Epoxy Resin: Specific values may vary - Potentially effective.

Glass: Around 5-9 eV - Potentially effective.

Mylar (Polyethylene Terephthalate): Around 5 eV - Potentially effective.

Paper (Cellulose): Composed of cellulose, which has a bandgap - Limited effectiveness.

Paraffin Wax: Specific values may vary - Limited effectiveness.

Polyethylene: Around 5-7 eV - Potentially effective.

Polypropylene: Around 5-7 eV - Potentially effective.

Polystyrene: Around 6-7 eV - Potentially effective.

Polytetrafluoroethylene (Teflon): Around 6-7 eV - Potentially effective.

PTFE (Polytetrafluoroethylene, Teflon): Around 6-7 eV - Potentially effective.

Rubber: Dielectric properties can vary - Limited effectiveness.

Silicon Dioxide (Quartz): Around 8-9 eV - Potentially effective.

Teflon (Polytetrafluoroethylene): Around 6-7 eV - Potentially effective.

Wood: Dielectric properties depend on the type of wood - Limited effectiveness.

Fiberglass, also known as glass fiber reinforced plastic (GRP), is a composite material made of glass fibers embedded in a polymer matrix. The dielectric properties of fiberglass can vary depending on the composition and manufacturing process, but it generally exhibits insulating properties. Here are some considerations:

1. **Dielectric Properties:** Fiberglass is often used as an insulating material in various applications due to its relatively high dielectric strength.
2. **Bandgap:** Unlike semiconductors or insulators with well-defined electronic bandgaps, composite materials like fiberglass may not have a clear bandgap in the same sense. Bandgaps are more characteristic of crystalline semiconductors.

3. **Electrical Insulation:** Fiberglass is known for its electrical insulation properties, making it suitable for applications where electrical conductivity needs to be minimized.

4. **Effectiveness Against Electron Tunneling:** As an insulating material, fiberglass is expected to provide some degree of protection against electron tunneling. However, the actual effectiveness would depend on various factors including material thickness, the energy levels involved, and the specific conditions of use.

How does "electron tunneling" defeat shielding materials?

Electron tunneling, in the context of quantum mechanics, refers to the phenomenon where electrons can pass through a barrier or potential energy barrier that, according to classical physics, they should not be able to overcome. This tunneling effect is a quantum mechanical behavior that arises due to the wave-like nature of particles, as described by the principles of quantum mechanics.

From a shielding perspective, electron tunneling has implications for how electrons can move through barriers, and it is relevant in certain electronic devices and materials. Here are some key points related to electron tunneling and its implications for shielding:

1. **Quantum Tunneling:**
   o In classical physics, if an electron encounters a potential energy barrier, it would not have enough energy to

overcome the barrier and would be reflected back. However, according to quantum mechanics, there is a non-zero probability that the electron can tunnel through the barrier and appear on the other side.

2. **Barrier Thickness and Tunneling Probability:**
   - The probability of tunneling depends on factors such as the thickness of the barrier, the energy of the electron, and the shape of the potential barrier. Thinner barriers and higher electron energies generally result in higher tunneling probabilities.

3. **Applications in Electronics:**
   - Quantum tunneling is exploited in certain electronic devices. For example, tunnel diodes and tunnel field-effect transistors utilize the tunneling effect for specific functions in electronic circuits.

4. **Shielding Considerations:**
   - From a shielding perspective, electron tunneling can impact the effectiveness of barriers or shields designed to prevent the passage of electrons. If the barrier thickness is on the scale of the electron wavelength, quantum tunneling becomes a consideration.

5. **Quantum Well Structures:**
   - Quantum well structures, which involve layering materials to create potential barriers, are used in some electronic and optoelectronic devices. The properties of these

structures, including tunneling, are important for their functionality.

6. **Insulating Materials:**
   ○ In certain insulating materials, electrons may tunnel through the material, which can affect the electrical properties. Understanding and controlling tunneling are important in the design of insulating materials for electronic applications.

7. **Shielding Design:**
   ○ In the design of shields or barriers to prevent electron transmission, engineers need to consider the quantum mechanical nature of electrons, including tunneling probabilities. The choice of materials and barrier thickness becomes critical.

It's important to note that electron tunneling is a quantum phenomenon that primarily occurs at the nanoscale. In everyday situations and larger scales, classical physics provides accurate predictions for the behavior of electrons. However, as technology advances and devices reach smaller dimensions, quantum effects, including tunneling, become increasingly significant and must be considered in the design of electronic components and materials.

What is the difference between the valence electron shell and the conductive electron shell when it comes to band gap shielding effects?

The concepts of valence electron shells and conductive electron shells are related to the electronic structure of materials, particularly in the context of semiconductors and conductors. Let's explore these concepts and their role in band gap shielding effects.

1. **Valence Electron Shell:**
   - The valence electron shell refers to the outermost electron shell of an atom. Valence electrons are the electrons in this outermost shell, and they play a crucial role in determining the chemical and electrical properties of the material. In semiconductors, the energy levels of valence electrons are within the band gap.

2. **Conductive Electron Shell (Conduction Band):**
   - The conductive electron shell, often referred to as the conduction band, is an energy band in the electronic structure of a material where electrons are free to move and conduct electricity. In conductors, the conduction band overlaps with the valence band, allowing electrons to move easily.

Band Gap:

- The band gap is the energy difference between the valence band and the conduction band. In insulators and semiconductors, there is a distinct band gap that separates the valence and conduction bands.

Shielding Effects in Semiconductors:

- Semiconductors have a finite band gap, meaning that there is an energy barrier between the valence band and the conduction band. When an external electric field is applied, electrons in the valence band may gain enough energy to move to the conduction band, creating charge carriers (electrons and holes) and allowing the material to conduct electricity.

Shielding Effects in Conductors:

- In conductors, there is no distinct band gap, and the valence and conduction bands overlap. Electrons in the valence band are already free to move, contributing to the material's high conductivity. When an external electric field is applied to a conductor, electrons respond almost immediately, resulting in a flow of electric current.

Band Gap Shielding:

- The concept of band gap shielding refers to the material's ability to shield against external influences due to the presence of a band gap. In semiconductors, the band gap prevents easy flow of electrons and provides a level of insulation until sufficient energy is supplied to overcome the gap. In conductors, the absence of a distinct band gap leads to a continuous flow of electrons, resulting in high conductivity but less effective band gap shielding.

In summary, the valence electron shell and the conductive electron shell are related to the band structure of materials. The presence or absence of a band gap influences the electrical properties and the material's ability to shield against external influences. Semiconductors with a band gap provide a degree of insulation until activated, while conductors lack a distinct band gap, allowing continuous electron flow.

Here are some specific examples to make the concepts of valence electron shells, conduction bands, and band gap shielding more concrete.

1. **Semiconductor Example: Silicon (Si)**
   - **Valence Electron Shell:** Silicon has four valence electrons in its outermost shell (valence shell). These electrons are involved in chemical bonding.
   - **Band Gap:** Silicon is a semiconductor with a band gap of approximately 1.1 electronvolts (eV). This means that there is an energy barrier of 1.1 eV between the valence band and the conduction band.

- **Conduction Process:** When a small amount of energy (at least 1.1 eV) is supplied to a silicon crystal, electrons in the valence band can move to the conduction band, creating charge carriers and allowing the material to conduct electricity.

2. **Conductor Example: Copper (Cu)**
   - **Valence Electron Shell:** Copper has one electron in its outermost shell (valence shell). This electron is relatively loosely bound.
   - **Band Gap:** Copper is a metal and does not have a distinct band gap between the valence and conduction bands. The bands overlap.
   - **Conduction Process:** In copper, the valence band and the conduction band overlap, allowing electrons to move freely. When an electric field is applied, electrons respond almost immediately, resulting in high conductivity.

3. **Insulator Example: Silicon Dioxide (SiO2)**
   - **Valence Electron Shell:** In silicon dioxide, each silicon atom has four valence electrons.
   - **Band Gap:** Silicon dioxide is an insulator with a relatively large band gap (around 8-9 eV). The band gap is so large that electrons in the valence band cannot easily move to the conduction band.

○ **Conduction Process:** Silicon dioxide requires a significant amount of energy to move electrons to the conduction band, making it a good insulator.

In summary, the number of electrons in the valence shell and the size of the band gap influence the electrical properties of materials:

- **Semiconductors:** Have a moderate number of electrons in the valence shell and a moderate band gap. Silicon is a classic example.
- **Conductors:** Have a small number of electrons in the valence shell and no distinct band gap. Copper is a typical conductor.
- **Insulators:** Have a larger number of electrons in the valence shell and a large band gap. Silicon dioxide is an example.

These examples illustrate how the electronic structure of materials dictates their conductivity and their ability to shield against external influences.

The conduction band is like a rip current and the energy required allows electrons to go for a swim?

The analogy of a conduction band being like a rip current in a beach setting is a creative way to understand the concept! Let's explore the analogy:

1. **Conduction Band as a Rip Current:**

- In a semiconductor material, the conduction band can be imagined as a "current" within the material, similar to how a rip current is a narrow, fast-moving current in the ocean. In the conduction band, electrons can move relatively freely, contributing to the material's ability to conduct electricity.

2. **Energy Required as the Wave's Force:**
   - The energy required to move electrons from the valence band to the conduction band can be likened to the force of a wave in the ocean. In the case of semiconductors, this energy can come from external sources, such as applied voltage or heat.

3. **Electrons Going for a Swim:**
   - When the energy (wave force) is sufficient, electrons in the valence band gain enough energy to overcome the band gap barrier and move to the conduction band. This process is akin to electrons "going for a swim" in the conduction band, contributing to electrical conduction.

4. **Band Gap as the Shoreline Barrier:**
   - The band gap itself acts as a barrier, similar to the shoreline in the beach analogy. It sets a threshold for the energy required for electrons to transition from the valence band to the conduction band. Once this threshold

is overcome, electrons can "swim" freely in the conduction band.

Remember that while the analogy provides a visual way to understand the concept, it's important to note that the behavior of electrons in materials is governed by quantum mechanics, and the analogy simplifies the complexity of these processes.

The conduction band acts as a "current" within the material, the energy required is like the force of a wave, and electrons "going for a swim" symbolizes the movement of charge carriers in the conduction band, contributing to electrical conductivity.

The conduction band is a range of energy levels in which electrons can move relatively freely, contributing to electrical conductivity. However, the presence of electrons in the conduction band is closely tied to the application of an external influence, typically an electric field or other energy source.

If there is no external influence, such as no applied voltage or other excitation, and the material is in a state of thermal equilibrium, electrons in the conduction band are generally at a minimum. At room temperature, some electrons may possess enough thermal energy to move to the conduction band, but this number is relatively small compared to the total number of electrons.

In the absence of an external electric field or other excitation, a material in a steady state will have a negligible net flow of charge carriers (electrons in the conduction band and holes in the valence band). This is because any electron that moves to the conduction band due to thermal energy is likely to return to the valence band shortly afterward.

It's important to note that electrical current, which represents the flow of charge carriers, requires an external influence to drive the movement of electrons. This influence is often provided by applying a voltage across the material, creating an electric field that encourages the flow of charge carriers and results in a measurable current.

So, while there may be some thermal excitation of electrons into the conduction band even in the absence of an external field, the net flow of charge carriers and the presence of a significant current typically require the application of an external influence.

Atoms lose their electrons to the conduction band and become ionized when external current is applied to a material?

Yes, when an electron is excited from the valence band to the conduction band, leaving behind a "hole" in the valence band, the process can be considered as ionization. Ionization refers to the creation of ions, which are atoms or molecules that have gained or lost electrons.

In the context of a semiconductor or other materials with a band structure:

1. **Electron in the Conduction Band:**
   - An electron that moves from the valence band to the conduction band gains energy and becomes a free electron in the conduction band.

2. **Hole in the Valence Band:**
   - The electron leaving the valence band creates a vacancy known as a "hole" in the valence band. This hole is essentially an unoccupied energy state where an electron used to be.

3. **Ionization:**
   - The creation of an electron in the conduction band and a hole in the valence band can be thought of as a form of ionization. The atom or semiconductor material as a whole remains electrically neutral, but there is a separation of charge—negative charge in the conduction band and positive charge in the valence band.

In this process, the material can be said to have undergone "intrinsic ionization" as a result of thermal energy or other forms of excitation. External influences, such as an applied voltage or light, can also cause ionization, leading to an increased number of free electrons and holes in the semiconductor.

Understanding the movement of electrons and holes in the context of ionization is fundamental to the study of semiconductor physics and the operation of electronic devices like transistors and diodes.

When electrons move into the conduction band, it does involve an electron transitioning from the valence band to the conduction band, leaving behind a positively charged "hole" in the valence band. This process, while not traditional ionization in the sense of ejecting an electron from an atom, does result in charge separation and the creation of mobile charge carriers (free electrons and holes). In this context, the term "ionization" is often used more broadly to describe the generation of charge carriers.

To clarify:

1. **Valence Band to Conduction Band Transition:**
   - When an electron absorbs sufficient energy (from an external source like electromagnetic radiation or thermal excitation), it can move from the valence band to the conduction band.

2. **Creation of a Hole:**
   - The electron leaving the valence band creates a hole, which is essentially an unoccupied energy state in the valence band where an electron used to be. This hole can be considered a positive charge carrier.

3. **Charge Separation:**
   - The movement of the electron to the conduction band and the creation of a hole in the valence band result in charge separation—negative charge in the conduction band and positive charge in the valence band.

4. **Electron Flow:**

   ○ The free electrons in the conduction band are now mobile and can contribute to electric current by moving through the material. Similarly, the holes in the valence band can act as positive charge carriers and contribute to current flow.

While the process involves charge separation and the generation of charge carriers, it's crucial to distinguish this from classical ionization, where an electron is completely removed from an atom, leaving behind a positively charged ion. The terminology can vary, and sometimes the broader term "ionization" is used to describe processes that involve the generation of charge carriers, as in the case of semiconductors and conductors.

An ion is defined as an atom or molecule that has gained or lost one or more electrons, resulting in a net electric charge. Whether an electron is completely removed from an atom or transitions to a higher energy state, leading to charge separation, the resulting species can be considered an ion.

In the context of semiconductors and conductors, when an electron moves from the valence band to the conduction band, leaving behind a hole, the atom or semiconductor material can be considered ionized. This process involves charge separation, with the free electron in the conduction band having a negative charge and the hole in the valence band having a positive charge.

So, you're correct in noting that an ion is an ion, and the term can be used more broadly to describe species with a net electric charge, whether the charge results from the removal of an electron or from a charge separation within a material.

What color quartz would be better for band gap shielding?

Quartz is a transparent or translucent mineral that is commonly colorless or appears in a variety of colors, depending on impurities and trace elements present in the crystal lattice. The color of quartz does not inherently affect its band gap properties, as the band gap is primarily determined by the crystal structure and composition.

In terms of band gap shielding or electromagnetic properties, the transparency of quartz in the visible and near-infrared regions is often more relevant than its color. Transparent or lightly colored quartz allows electromagnetic waves in these spectral ranges to pass through, making it suitable for certain applications like optical windows, lenses, and electromagnetic shielding where transparency is important.

If you are specifically looking for quartz for electromagnetic shielding, consider the following:

1. **Colorless or Lightly Colored Quartz:**

○ Quartz that is colorless or lightly colored is often preferred for applications where transparency is important. It allows for better transmission of electromagnetic waves.

2. **Impurities and Inclusions:**

○ Some varieties of quartz may have specific impurities or inclusions that give them a distinct color. If these impurities do not interfere with the desired electromagnetic properties, the color may not be a significant factor.

3. **Purity:**

○ Higher-purity quartz is generally preferred for applications where consistent electromagnetic properties are crucial. Lower levels of impurities contribute to better material performance.

4. **Material Thickness:**

○ The thickness of the quartz material can also influence its electromagnetic shielding properties. Thicker materials may provide more effective shielding, but the trade-off is reduced transparency.

The color of quartz, whether darker or lighter, is primarily influenced by impurities and trace elements present in the crystal lattice. While the color itself doesn't directly determine the electromagnetic shielding properties, certain impurities or inclusions in darker-colored quartz may have an impact on its overall performance.

In the context of electromagnetic shielding:

1. **Darker Quartz:**

   - Quartz with darker colors may have impurities or inclusions that could potentially affect its electromagnetic properties. For example, certain minerals or metallic impurities may absorb or scatter electromagnetic waves.

2. **Transparency:**

   - In general, transparent or lightly colored quartz is preferred for applications where transparency and the ability to transmit electromagnetic waves are important. Clear or lightly colored quartz allows for better transmission of electromagnetic radiation.

3. **Material Thickness:**

   - The thickness of the quartz material can significantly influence its electromagnetic shielding effectiveness. Thicker materials may provide better shielding, but this often comes at the expense of transparency.

4. **Material Purity:**

   - Higher-purity quartz is desirable for consistent electromagnetic performance. Impurities in the crystal lattice may introduce additional electronic states that could influence the material's behavior.

In general, colorless or lightly colored quartz is preferred for applications where transparency and the ability to transmit electromagnetic waves (EMF) are important. Darker-colored quartz, which typically indicates the presence of impurities or inclusions, may have a higher likelihood of absorbing or scattering electromagnetic radiation, potentially reducing its effectiveness in transmitting EMF.

To summarize:

- **Colorless or Lightly Colored Quartz:**
  - Preferred for applications requiring transparency and efficient transmission of electromagnetic waves.
- **Darker-Colored Quartz:**
  - May have impurities or inclusions that could interfere with the transmission of electromagnetic waves, making it less suitable for applications where transparency is crucial.

When selecting quartz for electromagnetic shielding or other applications where EMF transmission is a consideration, it's advisable to prioritize materials with minimal impurities, high transparency, and appropriate thickness for the desired shielding effectiveness.

The mechanisms by which a material, including quartz, can interact with electromagnetic waves, leading to scattering or absorption, are diverse and can include several physical processes. Here are some of the mechanisms involved:

1. **Absorption:**
   - **Dielectric Absorption:** The material may have certain dielectric properties that allow it to absorb

electromagnetic energy. In the case of quartz, absorption can occur due to vibrational modes of the crystal lattice, and this absorption can lead to a reduction in the transmitted energy.

2. **Scattering:**
   - **Rayleigh Scattering:** Small particles in the material can scatter electromagnetic waves through Rayleigh scattering. The degree of scattering is inversely proportional to the fourth power of the wavelength, meaning shorter wavelengths (higher frequencies) are scattered more. This can influence the transparency of the material.

3. **Conduction:**
   - **Conductive Impurities:** If the material contains conductive impurities or inclusions, they can lead to absorption and dissipation of electromagnetic energy through conduction. However, quartz is generally an insulating material, and significant conductive properties would likely be introduced by specific impurities.

4. **Resonance Absorption:**
   - **Electronic Resonance:** Certain impurities or defects in the crystal lattice can introduce electronic states that resonate with specific frequencies of the electromagnetic wave, leading to absorption at those resonant frequencies.

5. **Material Thickness:**

- **Thickness Effects:** The thickness of the material can influence the interaction with electromagnetic waves. In some cases, thin materials may allow more transmission, while thicker materials may absorb or scatter more energy.

6. **Surface Roughness:**
   - **Surface Scattering:** Surface roughness or irregularities at the interfaces of the material can contribute to scattering of electromagnetic waves.

For quartz specifically, its primary composition of silicon and oxygen makes it a dielectric material with generally low electrical conductivity. The color of quartz is often influenced by impurities or defects, and the specific mechanisms of interaction with electromagnetic waves can depend on the nature and concentration of these impurities.

In summary, absorption and scattering of electromagnetic waves in materials like quartz can occur through a combination of dielectric absorption, Rayleigh scattering, conductive impurities, resonance absorption, and other related mechanisms. The detailed behavior depends on the specific characteristics of the material and the frequencies of the electromagnetic waves involved.

Quartz is commonly used in various applications where electromagnetic wave propagation and transparency to certain wavelengths are important. Some of the key applications include:

1. **Optical Windows and Lenses:**
   - Quartz is often used to manufacture optical windows and lenses for devices that operate in the ultraviolet (UV), visible, and near-infrared (NIR) regions. Its transparency to these wavelengths makes it suitable for optical components.

2. **Fiber Optics:**
   - Quartz is used in the manufacturing of fiber-optic cables for telecommunications and data transmission. The high transparency of quartz allows for efficient transmission of light signals over long distances.

3. **Frequency Control Devices:**
   - Quartz crystals are widely used in electronic devices for frequency control. Quartz resonators, such as quartz crystals and oscillators, are employed in watches, clocks, radios, and various electronic circuits to provide accurate and stable frequency references.

4. **UV and Infrared Filters:**
   - Quartz can be used as a material for filters that selectively transmit or block certain wavelengths. In applications

where specific UV or infrared wavelengths need to be filtered or transmitted, quartz can be a suitable material.

5. **Photolithography in Semiconductor Manufacturing:**
   - In the semiconductor industry, quartz is used in photolithography processes. Photolithography involves using light to transfer a pattern onto a semiconductor wafer, and quartz is chosen for its transparency to the wavelengths used in these processes.

6. **Scientific Instruments:**
   - Quartz is employed in various scientific instruments, such as spectroscopy equipment, where transparency to specific wavelengths is crucial for accurate measurements.

7. **EMF Shielding (Limited):**
   - While quartz is transparent to electromagnetic waves in certain regions, it is not commonly used for electromagnetic shielding. Materials with higher electrical conductivity are typically chosen for effective electromagnetic shielding.

Quartz is an insulator and does not conduct electricity effectively compared to metals, which are generally good conductors. The conductivity of materials is measured in Siemens per meter (S/m). Here's a comparison of the electrical conductivity of quartz and some common metals in SI units:

1. **Quartz (SiO2):**

- Quartz is an insulator with a very low electrical conductivity.
- Conductivity: Typically in the range of 10^{-14} to 10^{-18} S/m.

2. **Copper (Cu):**
   - Copper is an excellent conductor of electricity.
   - Conductivity: Approximately 5.8×10^7 S/m.

3. **Aluminum (Al):**
   - Aluminum is a good conductor, though not as high as copper.
   - Conductivity: Approximately 3.5×10^7 S/m.

4. **Silver (Ag):**
   - Silver is an even better conductor than copper.
   - Conductivity: Approximately 6.3×10^7 S/m.

5. **Gold (Au):**
   - Gold is a good conductor, though slightly lower than copper and silver.
   - Conductivity: Approximately 4.1×10^7 S/m.

These conductivity values highlight the vast difference between insulators like quartz and conductive metals. Quartz is used for its insulating properties in applications where electrical conductivity is not desirable. In contrast, metals like copper, aluminum, silver, and gold are chosen for applications where efficient electrical conduction is essential, such as in electrical wiring, electronic components, and various electrical devices.

Why does mylar exhibit such a high band gap compared to other materials?

Mylar, which is a brand name for a type of polyester film made from polyethylene terephthalate (PET), is known for its insulating and dielectric properties. The band gap of a material is related to the energy difference between the valence band and the conduction band. Mylar has a relatively large band gap compared to metals and some other conductive materials. There are a few reasons for this:

1. **Polymeric Structure:** Mylar is a polymer, and its band structure is influenced by the arrangement of atoms in its molecular structure. The polymeric structure of Mylar leads to a wider band gap compared to some other materials.

2. **Dielectric Properties:** Mylar is commonly used as a dielectric material in capacitors. Its ability to resist the flow of electric current and store electrical energy is related to its relatively large band gap. This property makes it suitable for applications where electrical insulation is important.

3. **Chemical Composition:** The chemical composition of Mylar, specifically the arrangement of carbon, hydrogen, and oxygen atoms in its polymer chains, contributes to its electronic properties. The band gap is influenced by the energy required

to promote electrons from the valence band to the conduction band.

4. **Applications in Electronics:** Mylar's high band gap and dielectric properties make it useful in electronics, particularly for applications where insulation and capacitance are important. It is commonly used as a substrate for capacitors, in flexible printed circuit boards, and as an insulating material in various electronic devices.

While Mylar has a larger band gap compared to conductive materials, it's important to note that its band gap is still smaller than the band gaps of insulators like silicon dioxide (quartz) or certain ceramics.

To understand how materials like Mylar shield from an electromagnetic field (EMF) at the valence electron level, it's helpful to consider the concept of polarization and the behavior of electrons in a dielectric material.

1. **Polarization:**
   - When a dielectric material like Mylar is exposed to an electric field, the electrons within the atoms and molecules of the material experience a force. The electrons are not free to move like in a conductor, but they can shift within their orbits, creating a temporary alignment of charges.

2. **Valence Electrons:**
   - Valence electrons are the outermost electrons of an atom and play a significant role in the electrical properties of a

material. In a dielectric material, valence electrons participate in the polarization process.

3. **Dielectric Constant:**
   - The ability of a material to be polarized is characterized by its dielectric constant (also known as relative permittivity). Mylar, being a dielectric, has a dielectric constant greater than 1. When an external electric field is applied, the valence electrons respond by creating an induced dipole moment, leading to polarization.

4. **EMF Shielding Mechanism:**
   - While Mylar itself may not completely block EMF like a conductive material (e.g., metal), the induced polarization in the dielectric can have a shielding effect. The polarized atoms and molecules within the Mylar align in a way that can attenuate the strength of the external electric field passing through the material.

5. **Metalized Mylar:**
   - In cases where enhanced EMF shielding is required, Mylar can be metalized, typically with a thin layer of aluminum. The metal layer provides additional conductivity, allowing it to reflect and absorb electromagnetic radiation more effectively.

In summary, from a valence electron perspective, the polarization of valence electrons in Mylar, induced by an external electric field, contributes to the material's dielectric behavior. While Mylar is not a perfect conductor and doesn't block EMF in the same way as metals, its dielectric properties can attenuate and modify the electromagnetic field passing through it. Metalized Mylar adds a layer of conductivity, enhancing its ability to shield against EMF.

Would quartz powder retain its bandgap properties to use against tunneling technologies?

The band gap of quartz is a property associated with its crystalline structure, and this property is generally retained in the bulk crystalline form of quartz. However, when quartz is ground into a powder, certain factors come into play that may influence its properties:

1. **Surface Defects:** Grinding quartz into a powder increases its surface area, and this can lead to the introduction of surface defects. Surface defects can impact the electronic properties of the material.

2. **Amorphization:** Intense grinding can potentially lead to amorphization, where the crystalline structure of quartz is disrupted, and the material becomes more disordered. This can affect its band gap and other electronic properties.

3. **Impurities:** During the grinding process, there is a possibility of introducing impurities from the grinding equipment or from the atmosphere. Impurities can alter the band gap and other electronic characteristics.

4. **Size Effects:** Nanoscale or fine particles may exhibit size-dependent properties due to quantum confinement effects. This can influence the electronic properties, including the band gap.

5. **Surface Oxidation:** Grinding quartz powder may expose the surface to air, leading to surface oxidation. While quartz is generally resistant to oxidation, changes in the surface chemistry could influence its properties.

In practical terms, if precise control over the band gap and other electronic properties is crucial for a specific application, it is generally recommended to use high-quality, commercially available quartz with a controlled and well-characterized crystalline structure. Quartz powders may be suitable for certain applications, but their properties can be more variable compared to bulk crystalline quartz.

Quartz, as a crystalline material, generally maintains its band gap value as long as it remains in a stable and undamaged state. Quartz glass, also known as fused quartz or fused silica, is a high-purity form of quartz that has excellent optical and thermal properties. The band gap of quartz remains relatively constant as long as the material is not subjected to conditions that can alter its crystalline structure or introduce impurities.

However, it's important to note a few considerations:

1. **Purity:** The band gap of quartz can be influenced by the purity of the material. High-purity quartz, such as fused quartz, is preferred for applications where the preservation of specific optical or electronic properties is critical.

2. **Structural Integrity:** Changes in the crystalline structure of quartz can potentially affect its band gap. Extreme conditions, such as high temperatures or mechanical stress, can lead to structural changes. Therefore, maintaining the structural integrity of the material is crucial for preserving its band gap.

3. **Impurities:** Introduction of impurities can alter the electronic properties of quartz. For certain applications, especially those requiring specific electrical or optical characteristics, the presence of impurities should be minimized.

4. **Manufacturing Process:** The manufacturing process can impact the quality and properties of quartz. High-quality quartz materials are often produced using controlled processes to minimize defects and impurities.

If you are looking for a quartz film or glass that preserves its band gap value for specific applications, it's advisable to consider high-purity quartz products and ensure that the manufacturing processes meet the required standards.

What is "the twisted pair" shielding method?

Twisted Pair Configuration: In this method, two conductors are twisted together in a helical pattern. The twist rate can vary depending on the specific application, and multiple twists per inch are common.

Balancing Effect: When the conductors are twisted together, they form a balanced transmission line. In a balanced line, the two conductors carry equal but opposite currents, which creates an electromagnetic field that cancels out external electromagnetic interference.

While twisted pair cables can provide effective EMI shielding in specific scenarios, it's essential to consider the frequency range and the specific types of electromagnetic interference you are trying to mitigate. For extremely low-frequency signals like 10 Hz, other shielding techniques may be more suitable, such as using conductive metal sheets or foils, or grounding the shielding material effectively.

For shielding against extremely low-frequency (ELF) waves, the effectiveness of twisted cables can be influenced by several factors, including whether the cables are naked or insulated and the number of twists per foot. Here's a breakdown of each aspect:

Naked vs. Insulated Twisted Cables:

Naked Cables: Naked twisted cables refer to twisted pairs without any additional insulation or sheathing. Naked cables can provide some level of ELF shielding due to their balanced configuration, which reduces the impact of external electromagnetic fields. However, their effectiveness might be limited, especially at very low frequencies like 10 Hz.

Insulated Cables: Insulated twisted cables have an additional outer layer of insulation or sheathing, typically made of materials like PVC or polyethylene. The insulation can improve the overall shielding effectiveness by reducing the coupling between the twisted pairs and external electromagnetic fields.

Number of Twists per Foot for 10 Hz:

The number of twists per foot can significantly impact the performance of twisted cables as ELF shields. Generally, the more twists per foot, the better the cable can reject common mode interference and reduce external electromagnetic coupling.

For ELF shielding applications, a higher number of twists per foot is usually beneficial. The specific optimal twist rate will depend on factors such as the cable's physical dimensions, the materials used, and the desired level of attenuation.

However, it's important to note that while twisted cables might provide some ELF shielding, they may not be the most effective method for extremely low-frequency signals. ELF waves have very long wavelengths, making them difficult to block using conventional methods. For better ELF shielding, other techniques may be more appropriate, such as using thicker metal sheets or plates with high magnetic permeability (like mu-metal) or grounding the shielding effectively.

When deploying twisted cables for ELF shielding on a 1 square meter surface, the arrangement should be carefully designed to achieve optimal coverage and attenuation. The specific arrangement would depend on the level of shielding required, the frequency range being targeted, and the orientation of the incoming electromagnetic fields. Here are a few possible deployment patterns:

Grid Pattern: One common approach is to create a grid pattern using twisted cables. You can place twisted pairs horizontally and vertically across the entire surface, creating a mesh-like structure.

The spacing between each twisted pair can vary depending on the frequency you are targeting and the level of attenuation needed. Closer spacing provides better coverage but might require more cables.

Concentric Rings: Another option is to arrange the twisted cables in concentric rings, with each ring at a specific distance from the center of the surface.

This arrangement can help focus on shielding from specific directions or frequencies.

Spiral Pattern: A spiral pattern involves placing twisted pairs in a spiral shape starting from the center of the surface and expanding outward. This pattern might be suitable for attenuating electromagnetic fields originating from a central source.

Wave pattern: Deploying twisted pairs in a compressed waveform works best according to research.

Keep in mind that deploying twisted cables alone might not be sufficient for effective ELF shielding. You may need to combine this method with other shielding materials, such as metal plates or specialized magnetic shielding materials, to achieve the desired level of attenuation. Additionally, proper grounding of the shielding is crucial to divert and dissipate the attenuated electromagnetic energy effectively.

Is looped shielding better than non-looped shielding?

Yes, in general, using a loop or continuous shielding configuration is often more effective than using simple sheets for shielding against electromagnetic fields. The looping of the shielding material creates a closed circuit, which can enhance its effectiveness in attenuating and redirecting electromagnetic energy.

When a looped configuration is used, the electromagnetic field encounters multiple layers of shielding material, which provides better coverage and reduces the likelihood of gaps or weak points in the shielding. This continuous loop creates a more robust barrier against incoming electromagnetic waves, as it prevents energy from finding a direct path through the shielding.

Additionally, the looped configuration can create resonance-canceling effects. When an electromagnetic wave induces currents in the loop, these currents generate opposing magnetic fields, which can cancel out the incoming wave's effect. This self-canceling phenomenon is particularly useful in reducing the amplitude of the electromagnetic field within the looped area.

Moreover, looped shielding can facilitate the use of inductive or capacitive elements within the loop to create additional attenuation. Inductive elements can dissipate energy through electromagnetic induction, while capacitive elements can store and release energy, effectively attenuating the electromagnetic field.

In contrast, using simple sheets of shielding material may leave seams or openings between sheets, allowing electromagnetic waves to pass through these weak points. Moreover, if the sheets are not properly connected or grounded, they may not form an effective barrier against electromagnetic radiation.

While looped shielding offers many advantages, it is essential to consider the specific application and the frequency range of the electromagnetic waves being shielded. For certain scenarios, where precise directional control of the shielding is required, specific shapes or patterns may be more suitable. As with any shielding strategy, careful design, testing, and analysis are essential to ensure optimal protection against electromagnetic interference.

Can wrapping a copper foil loop around a ferrite bar magnet be used as "inductive shielding?"

The effectiveness of a copper foil loop around a ferrite magnet in mitigating incoming electromagnetic fields (EMF) can vary widely depending on several factors, including the characteristics of the EMF, the configuration of the shield, and the properties of the surrounding environment. While it's challenging to provide a precise quantitative estimate without specific details, here are some considerations:

1. **Frequency of the EMF:** The shielding effectiveness of the copper foil loop is typically frequency-dependent. At lower frequencies (e.g., ELF), the loop may provide relatively less attenuation compared to higher frequencies (e.g., microwave or radio frequencies). The loop's effectiveness increases as the frequency of the EMF increases, with the loop acting as a more efficient inductor.

2. **Configuration of the Shield:** The size, shape, and number of turns in the copper foil loop, as well as its proximity to the ferrite magnet, play significant roles in determining the shielding effectiveness. A well-designed shield with optimized parameters can provide better attenuation of EMF compared to a poorly configured shield.

3. **Strength of the EMF:** The magnitude of the incoming EMF also affects the shielding effectiveness. Stronger EMF may require more robust shielding measures, whereas weaker EMF may be adequately attenuated by a less sophisticated shield.

4. **Surrounding Environment:** External factors, such as nearby metallic objects, electronic equipment, or structural materials, can influence the performance of the shield by affecting the propagation and reflection of EMF. It's essential to consider the overall electromagnetic environment when evaluating the effectiveness of the shield.

5. **Testing and Validation:** Ultimately, the actual shielding effectiveness can only be determined through empirical testing and validation. This typically involves measuring the attenuation of EMF with and without the shield in place under representative conditions.

While a copper foil loop around a ferrite magnet can provide some level of shielding against incoming EMF, the exact magnitude of attenuation will depend on various factors. Through careful design, optimization, and testing, it's possible to achieve significant reductions in EMF exposure in specific applications.

Wrapping a copper foil loop around a ferrite bar magnet can indeed create an inductive shield, provided that the loop is properly configured to induce currents that oppose the incoming electromagnetic fields. This setup forms an inductor, which can mitigate electromagnetic interference through electromagnetic induction.

Here's how it works:

1. **Inductive Shielding Principle:** When an electromagnetic field penetrates the loop formed by the copper foil wrapped around the ferrite bar magnet, it induces a current in the loop according to Faraday's law of electromagnetic induction. This induced current creates a magnetic field that opposes the original magnetic field, thereby reducing the penetration of electromagnetic interference into the shielded area.

2. **Configuration and Effectiveness:** The effectiveness of the inductive shield depends on various factors, including the size and shape of the copper foil loop, the number of turns in the loop, the strength and frequency of the electromagnetic field, and the properties of the surrounding materials. By adjusting these parameters, you can optimize the shielding performance for your specific application.

3. **Application:** Inductive shields are commonly used in electronic devices and systems to protect sensitive components from electromagnetic interference. They can be incorporated into circuit designs or added externally to shield specific areas from interference.

4. **Testing and Validation:** It's essential to conduct testing and validation to ensure that the inductive shield meets the desired

performance requirements. This may involve measuring the attenuation of electromagnetic interference with and without the shield in place and making adjustments as needed.

Wrapping a copper foil loop around a ferrite bar magnet can create an inductive shield that effectively mitigates electromagnetic interference by inducing currents that oppose the incoming fields. This technique is widely used in electromagnetic compatibility (EMC) engineering to ensure the reliable operation of electronic systems in noisy environments.

The effectiveness of the inductive shield, created by wrapping a copper foil loop around a ferrite bar magnet, can be influenced by the proximity of the foil loop to the magnet. The optimal distance depends on several factors, including the magnetic field strength, the frequency of the electromagnetic interference, and the characteristics of the materials involved.

Here's how the distance of the foil loop from the magnet might affect the shielding performance:

1. **Touching the Magnet:**
   - If the copper foil loop is in direct contact with the magnet, it may experience a stronger magnetic coupling, leading to a more efficient induction of currents in the loop. This close proximity could enhance the shielding effectiveness,

especially for lower-frequency electromagnetic interference.

2. **1mm from the Magnet:**
   - Placing the copper foil loop 1mm away from the magnet allows for some separation between the loop and the magnet. This separation could reduce the direct magnetic coupling between the loop and the magnet, potentially altering the induced currents in the loop. The shielding effectiveness may vary depending on the specific configuration and the frequency of the interference.

3. **2mm from the Magnet:**
   - Increasing the distance between the copper foil loop and the magnet to 2mm further reduces the direct magnetic coupling between the two. This distance may allow for more flexibility in the arrangement of the shield and could mitigate any potential interference from the magnet itself. However, it's essential to ensure that the induced currents in the loop remain sufficient for effective shielding.

What materials might work best against free electron lasers?

Protecting against Free Electron Lasers (FELs) involves addressing intense and coherent beams of electromagnetic radiation, typically in the X-ray or infrared regions. The effectiveness of shielding materials depends on several factors, including the specific wavelength of the

FEL, the power density, and the intended application. Here are considerations for selecting shielding materials:

Lead:

- ○ **Wavelength:** Effective for X-rays and gamma rays.
- ○ **Properties:** Lead is dense and has strong attenuation properties for high-energy photons.

Tungsten:

- ○ **Wavelength:** Suitable for X-rays and gamma rays.
- ○ **Properties:** Tungsten has high atomic number, providing effective shielding for high-energy photons.

Beryllium:

- ○ **Wavelength:** Effective for X-rays.
- ○ **Properties:** Beryllium has low atomic number and is transparent to longer-wavelength X-rays.

Concrete:

- ○ **Wavelength:** Suitable for gamma rays.
- ○ **Properties:** Dense and widely used for radiation shielding.

Polyethylene:

- ○ **Wavelength:** Effective for neutrons.

- **Properties:** Polyethylene is a good neutron moderator and attenuator.

Lead Glass:

- **Wavelength:** Suitable for X-rays.
- **Properties:** Transparent to X-rays and offers radiation shielding.

Composite Materials:

- **Wavelength:** Depends on composition.
- **Properties:** Custom composite materials can be engineered for specific FEL wavelengths.

Ceramic Materials:

- **Wavelength:** Depends on the composition.
- **Properties:** Some ceramics offer good radiation resistance.

Water:

- **Wavelength:** Effective for neutrons and some X-rays.
- **Properties:** Water is a good neutron moderator and attenuator.

Gold:

- **Wavelength:** Suitable for X-rays and infrared.

- **Properties:** Gold has high atomic number and is effective for X-ray shielding.

What is the Gunn effect?

The Gunn effect is a phenomenon observed in certain semiconductor materials, notably gallium arsenide (GaAs), that gives rise to microwave oscillations. Discovered by physicist J.B. Gunn in 1963, this effect is crucial for the operation of Gunn diodes, semiconductor devices widely used in microwave applications.

In semiconductors like GaAs, there exists a valence band and a conduction band, separated by an energy gap. At absolute zero temperature, electrons occupy the valence band, and the conduction band is empty.

When a voltage is applied across a semiconductor material, it establishes an electric field. This electric field exerts a force on electrons in the conduction band, leading to an increase in their velocity. However, at a critical electric field strength, electron velocity saturates.

This saturation in electron mobility causes a phenomenon known as negative differential resistance (NDR). In most conductors, an increase in voltage corresponds to an increase in current, but in the Gunn effect, it's the opposite.

At the critical electric field strength, the semiconductor undergoes a transition, forming electric-field domains with different electron densities. This leads to the creation of electron density waves, and as these waves move, they emit microwave radiation.

The emitted microwaves' frequency is determined by the transit time of electrons through the semiconductor and the dimensions of the device. This effect is harnessed in Gunn diodes, where continuous microwave oscillations are generated.

Gunn diodes find applications in various technologies, including microwave signal generation in communication devices, radar systems, and frequency modulation circuits.

To better understand the Gunn effect, we need to consider the energy-band structure of semiconductors. In a semiconductor like GaAs, there is a valence band and a conduction band, separated by an energy gap. At absolute zero temperature, all electrons occupy the valence band, and the conduction band is empty.

1. Valence Band:

- Electrons in the valence band are in their lowest energy state and cannot contribute to electrical conduction.

2. Energy Gap:

- The energy gap between the valence and conduction bands represents the energy required to move an electron from the valence to the conduction band.

3. Conduction Band:

- Electrons in the conduction band have higher energy and can participate in electrical conduction.

In a Gunn diode, a key component of the behavior leading to NDR is the impact of the electric field on electron mobility within the semiconductor material, typically gallium arsenide (GaAs). When an external voltage is applied, creating an electric field, electrons experience a force that accelerates them. Initially, this acceleration leads to an increase in electron velocity.

However, as the electric field strength surpasses a critical value, something remarkable occurs. Instead of a continuous increase in velocity, the electron mobility saturates, causing the velocity to level off. This phenomenon is crucial – it's the essence of the negative differential resistance observed in Gunn diodes.

Now, consider the implications of this saturation in electron mobility. As the electrons reach their maximum velocity and mobility, they experience a kind of drag, almost like hitting a speed limit. This drag effect is intrinsic to the NDR phenomenon.

In the context of a Gunn diode, this drag on the electrons has a profound consequence. The material doesn't behave like a conventional conductor. Instead, it enters a state where increasing the applied voltage doesn't result in a proportional increase in current. The current, counterintuitively, decreases.

This decrease in current doesn't happen smoothly; rather, it occurs in a kind of oscillatory fashion. The material undergoes a series of domain formations and relaxations, creating regions of higher and lower electron densities.

Here's where the magic happens: The movement of these density waves becomes the source of microwave radiation. It's like ripples on a pond, but instead of water, we have the movement of electron density creating waves that propagate as microwaves.

In essence, NDR, in the context of Gunn diodes, isn't just about resisting the flow of current; it's about converting that resistance into a dynamic and controlled process that emits microwaves. This process is harnessed in practical applications, making Gunn diodes essential in generating continuous microwave signals for various technological purposes, including communication and radar systems.

Consider a semiconductor material, such as that found in a Gunn diode. In most materials, when you apply a voltage, the flow of electric current increases. It's akin to adjusting the volume on an amplifier – as you turn it up, the output gets louder.

However, in materials exhibiting NDR, something peculiar occurs. Instead of the expected increase in current with a rising voltage, there comes a point, known as the critical electric field strength, where the current starts to decrease. This departure from the typical behavior is what we term negative differential resistance.

Conceptually, it's analogous to an audio system where increasing the volume beyond a certain point doesn't amplify the sound; rather, it diminishes it. This is a departure from the typical expectation in electronics.

Now, the intriguing aspect of NDR is not just its counterintuitive behavior but the utility derived from it. In the context of Gunn diodes, when operated under NDR conditions, the material's unique response is harnessed to generate microwaves. This becomes particularly valuable in applications such as wireless communication.

What are the scientific "laws" associated with electrical engineering?

Here is a list of relevant laws associated with electrical engineering:

Ohm's Law: States that the current flowing through a conductor between two points is directly proportional to the voltage across the two points and inversely proportional to the resistance of the conductor. It is expressed as $V = I * R$, where V is voltage, I is current, and R is resistance.

Faraday's Laws of Electromagnetic Induction: These laws describe how a changing magnetic field induces an electromotive force (EMF) in a conductor. Faraday's First Law states that a changing magnetic field induces an EMF, and Faraday's Second Law states that the magnitude of the induced EMF is proportional to the rate of change of the magnetic field.

Ampere's Law: Relates the magnetic field produced by a current-carrying conductor to the current passing through the conductor. It helps calculate the magnetic field strength around a current-carrying conductor.

Kirchhoff's Current Law (KCL): States that the total current entering a node (or junction) in an electrical circuit is equal to the total current leaving the node. It ensures that the conservation of charge is maintained in a circuit.

Kirchhoff's Voltage Law (KVL): States that the sum of the electromotive forces (EMFs) and voltage drops in a closed loop of a circuit is equal to zero. It ensures the conservation of energy in a circuit.

Gauss's Law for Electricity: Relates the electric field produced by a charge distribution to the total electric charge enclosed by a closed surface. It is used to calculate electric fields in various situations.

Gauss's Law for Magnetism: States that there are no magnetic monopoles, and the net magnetic flux through any closed surface is always zero.

Lenz's Law: States that the direction of an induced current in a conductor is such that it opposes the change that produced it. It is based on the principle of conservation of energy.

Coulomb's Law: Describes the force between two charged particles. It states that the force is directly proportional to the product of the magnitudes of the charges and inversely proportional to the square of the distance between them.

Biot-Savart Law: Describes the magnetic field produced by a current-carrying conductor at a point in space. It is used to calculate the magnetic field strength around a current-carrying conductor.

These laws form the foundation of electrical engineering and are essential for understanding and analyzing electrical circuits, electromagnetic fields, and various electrical systems. Engineers use these laws to design, analyze, and optimize electrical and electronic devices and systems.

What is the particle in an EMF wave?

In the context of electromagnetic (EM) waves, the fundamental particle associated with the wave is the photon. Photons are elementary particles that are the quanta of the electromagnetic field. They have no mass and carry energy, momentum, and angular momentum. Photons are responsible for transmitting electromagnetic forces and, when it comes to light, are the particles that make up the various colors in the electromagnetic spectrum.

The behavior of photons is described by quantum electrodynamics (QED), which is a quantum field theory that explains how electromagnetic interactions occur at the quantum level. The energy of a photon is directly proportional to its frequency, and different frequencies correspond to different regions of the electromagnetic spectrum, such as radio waves, microwaves, infrared, visible light, ultraviolet, X-rays, and gamma rays.

It's important to note that while photons are associated with the wave-particle duality of light, EM waves themselves are not composed of particles in the traditional sense. They are oscillating electric and magnetic fields that propagate through space. The particle-like behavior of light becomes more apparent in certain experiments and interactions, especially at the quantum level.

Here are some aspects related to the nature of the wavefunction:

1. **Amplitude and Probability:**
   - The square of the amplitude of the wavefunction gives the probability density of finding the particle at a specific location. Regions with higher amplitude correspond to higher probabilities.
2. **Wavelength:**

- The wavelength of the wavefunction is inversely proportional to the momentum of the particle. Higher momentum corresponds to shorter wavelength, and vice versa.

3. **Wave Packet:**
   - In many cases, the wavefunction is not a simple sinusoidal wave but a superposition of different wavelengths. This superposition can result in a localized "wave packet" that represents the most probable location of the particle.

4. **Tunneling and Transmission Coefficient:**
   - When a particle encounters a barrier, the wavefunction extends into the classically forbidden region. The probability of finding the particle on the other side of the barrier is determined by the tunneling or transmission coefficient.

While the details of the wavefunction can be quite complex and are typically described using advanced mathematical formalisms, the key point is that the probability of finding a particle is distributed according to the square of the amplitude of its wavefunction. In tunneling, this distribution allows for a finite probability of the particle being found on the other side of a barrier.

In an electromagnetic wave, the electric field (E-field) and the magnetic field (M-field) are perpendicular to each other and to the direction of propagation. The photon, being the quantum of the electromagnetic field, is associated with these fields.

Here's how they are related:

1. **Electric Field (E-field):**
   - The E-field of an electromagnetic wave is a vector field that oscillates perpendicular to the direction of wave propagation.
   - The electric field represents the force experienced by a charged particle placed in the field.
2. **Magnetic Field (M-field):**
   - The M-field is also a vector field that oscillates perpendicular to the direction of wave propagation and the electric field.
   - The magnetic field is related to the rate of change of the electric field and vice versa.
3. **Photon:**
   - The photon is associated with the quantized nature of the electromagnetic field.
   - In the quantum theory of electromagnetism (quantum electrodynamics or QED), the interaction between charged particles and the electromagnetic field is mediated by the exchange of photons.

The relation between the electric and magnetic fields in an electromagnetic wave is governed by Maxwell's equations, which describe how electric charges and currents produce electric and magnetic fields and how changing electric and magnetic fields produce electromagnetic waves. The quantization of the electromagnetic field is described by quantum electrodynamics (QED), where photons are considered the carriers of electromagnetic interactions between charged particles.

The concept of a photon is not precisely a "convergence" of electromagnetic waves, but rather it represents a quantum of electromagnetic energy. In the framework of quantum theory, electromagnetic waves are quantized, meaning that they can be viewed as composed of discrete packets or quanta of energy, and each quantum is called a photon.

Here's a simplified explanation:

1. **Continuous Wave View:**
   - Classically, electromagnetic waves were described as continuous, smooth oscillations of electric and magnetic fields.

2. **Quantum View:**
   - In quantum theory, electromagnetic radiation (including light) is quantized, meaning it comes in discrete packets of energy called photons.
   - Each photon carries a specific amount of energy, and the energy of a photon is directly proportional to its frequency.

3. **Photon Creation:**
   - Photons are created when charged particles (e.g., electrons) undergo transitions between energy states.
   - The energy of the emitted or absorbed photon is determined by the energy difference between the initial and final states of the charged particle.

4. **Wave-Particle Duality:**
   - The nature of light exhibits both wave-like and particle-like properties, a phenomenon known as wave-particle duality.
   - In certain experiments, light behaves as if it were composed of particles (photons), while in other experiments, it behaves as a wave.

So, a photon is not a convergence of waves but rather a discrete entity associated with quantized electromagnetic waves. Each photon is a quantum of energy associated with a specific frequency of the electromagnetic spectrum.

What are the elementary particles in the Standard Model of particle physics and how do they combine to make electrons, neutrons and protons?

The Standard Model of particle physics describes the fundamental particles and the forces that govern their interactions. Here are some of the elementary particles in the Standard Model:

Quarks:

1. Up quark (u)

2. Down quark (d)

3. Charm quark (c)

4. Strange quark (s)

5. Top quark (t)

6. Bottom quark (b)

Leptons:

1. Electron (e^-)

2. Electron neutrino (νe)

3. Muon (μ^-)

4. Muon neutrino ($\nu \mu$)

5. Tau (τ^-)

6. Tau neutrino ($\nu \tau$)

Bosons:

1. Photon (γ)

2. Gluon (g)

3. W boson (W^+, W^-)

4. Z boson (Z^0)

5. Higgs boson (H^0)

Fermions (Quarks and Leptons) and Their Combinations: Quarks combine to form hadrons, such as protons and neutrons. Quarks are never found in isolation due to confinement.

Hadrons:

1. Proton (uud)
2. Neutron (udd)
3. Mesons (quark-antiquark pairs)

In atomic nuclei, protons and neutrons (collectively known as nucleons) are composed of quarks held together by the strong force mediated by gluons. Electrons are elementary particles and are not composed of quarks.

The combination of quarks and their interactions via the exchange of gluons gives rise to the structure of protons and neutrons. Electrons are distinct from quarks and do not have quark constituents. They are part of the lepton family and do not experience the strong force that binds quarks within nucleons.

In quantum mechanics, the concept of "seeing" an electron in the way we typically think of seeing macroscopic objects doesn't quite apply. The behavior of electrons is described by probability distributions, and they do not have well-defined trajectories or sizes like classical particles.

However, if we use advanced experimental techniques, such as those in quantum microscopy, we can indirectly observe the effects of electrons. For example, scanning tunneling microscopy (STM) and atomic force microscopy (AFM) are two techniques that allow scientists to study surfaces at the atomic scale.

In STM, a sharp metal tip is brought very close to a surface. As the tip gets close to an electron on the surface, electrons can "tunnel" across the gap between the tip and the surface. The resulting tunneling current is highly sensitive to the distance between the tip and the surface, allowing scientists to create detailed images of surfaces at the atomic level.

In AFM, a small tip is brought close to a surface, and the interaction forces between the tip and the atoms on the surface are measured. This can also provide detailed images of surfaces with atomic resolution.

While these techniques don't provide a direct visual representation of an electron, they allow scientists to gather information about the distribution of electrons around atoms and molecules. Electrons are often represented as electron clouds or probability distributions, highlighting the regions where electrons are likely to be found.

From a quantum physics perspective, an electron is a subatomic particle that carries a negative electric charge. It is considered a fundamental particle, meaning it is not composed of smaller constituents. According to the Standard Model of particle physics, electrons are elementary particles, and they do not have a structure like a nucleus or a halo.

In quantum mechanics, electrons are described by wavefunctions, mathematical entities that represent the probability amplitude of finding an electron at a particular location. The behavior of electrons is inherently probabilistic, and their motion is not described by classical trajectories.

Electrons are typically represented as clouds of probability density, and their position is uncertain until measured. The idea of a fast-moving electron is related to its wave-particle duality. In quantum mechanics, particles, including electrons, can exhibit both wave-like and particle-like properties. Electrons can move with significant speeds, and their behavior is characterized by probabilities and uncertainties, rather than classical determinism. The exact reasons behind the quantum behavior of electrons are deeply rooted in the principles of quantum mechanics, which is a complex and highly successful theoretical framework that describes the behavior of particles at the microscopic scale.

In the context of quantum mechanics, electric charge is a fundamental property of particles. It is an intrinsic property that particles carry, and it can be positive or negative. The concept of positive and negative charge is deeply rooted in the behavior of particles at the quantum level.

1. **Positive Charge:**
   - Particles with a positive electric charge are associated with the deficiency of electrons. Protons, for example, are

elementary particles with a positive charge. In the Standard Model of particle physics, protons are composed of quarks, which themselves carry fractional charges, but the combination results in an overall positive charge for the proton.

2. **Negative Charge:**
   - Particles with a negative electric charge are associated with an excess of electrons. Electrons, as mentioned earlier, are elementary particles with a negative charge. When an atom gains extra electrons, it becomes negatively charged. In materials, the flow of electrons constitutes an electric current.

In quantum mechanics, the concept of charge is intertwined with the behavior of particles described by wavefunctions and probability amplitudes. The electric charge of a particle determines its interactions with electromagnetic fields, and these interactions are quantified by principles such as Coulomb's law and the electromagnetic force described in quantum field theory.

What is the Heisneberg uncertainty principle?

The Heisenberg Uncertainty Principle is a fundamental concept in quantum mechanics, formulated by the German physicist Werner

Heisenberg in 1927. It states that there is a limit to the precision with which certain pairs of properties of a particle, known as complementary variables, can be simultaneously known. The two most common complementary variables discussed in the context of the Uncertainty Principle are a particle's position (xx) and its momentum (pp).

Here's an in-depth breakdown of the key concepts:

1. **Position and Momentum:**
   - The uncertainty principle fundamentally challenges the classical notion of precise measurement. It asserts that the more accurately we try to measure a particle's position, the less accurately we can know its momentum, and vice versa.

2. **Wave-Particle Duality:**
   - The principle is closely tied to the wave-particle duality of particles in quantum mechanics. Particles exhibit both wave-like and particle-like behavior, and this duality is expressed in terms of position and momentum uncertainties.

3. **Quantum Nature of Particles:**
   - In the quantum realm, particles are not thought of as having exact positions and momenta but are described by probability distributions. The Uncertainty Principle

quantifies the limitations on how precisely these distributions can be simultaneously determined.

4. **Inherent Limitation:**

   ○ The Heisenberg Uncertainty Principle is not a result of experimental limitations but is an inherent characteristic of quantum systems. Even with perfect measuring instruments, the uncertainty is a fundamental property.

5. **Generalization to Other Pairs:**

   ○ While position and momentum are the most commonly discussed pair, the Uncertainty Principle can be extended to other complementary variables, such as time and energy.

6. **Philosophical Implications:**

   ○ The principle has profound philosophical implications, challenging the classical determinism of physics. It introduces an element of inherent randomness and unpredictability at the quantum level.

7. **Applications:**

   ○ The Heisenberg Uncertainty Principle is a key concept in quantum mechanics and has practical implications in various areas, including quantum computing, quantum cryptography, and the interpretation of experimental results in particle physics.

8. **Quantum Measurements:**

- The act of measuring one property inherently disturbs the other. This is often illustrated using the example of shining light on a particle to measure its position, which alters its momentum.

What is quantum teleportation?

Quantum teleportation at the particle scale, has made notable progress in the field of quantum physics. Quantum teleportation is a phenomenon that involves the transfer of quantum information from one location to another without a physical transfer of particles. It's important to note that this is distinct from the teleportation commonly depicted in science fiction.

Here are some key points regarding the state of quantum teleportation technology up until 2022:

1. **Quantum Teleportation Experiments:**
   - Quantum teleportation experiments have been successfully conducted with particles such as photons, electrons, and ions. These experiments typically involve entangling particles and then using the quantum entanglement to transfer information between them instantaneously.

2. **Distance Achieved:**
   - Experiments have demonstrated quantum teleportation over various distances, ranging from a few meters in

laboratory settings to longer distances using satellite-based experiments. However, the practical challenges of extending teleportation to larger scales persist.

3. **Challenges:**
   - Maintaining and controlling quantum entanglement at longer distances or with larger systems is a significant challenge. Factors such as decoherence, environmental interference, and the fragility of quantum states pose obstacles to scaling up quantum teleportation.

4. **Quantum Communication Networks:**
   - Quantum teleportation is seen as an essential component of future quantum communication networks. Progress has been made in the development of quantum key distribution (QKD) systems, which leverage quantum properties for secure communication.

5. **Quantum Computing Impact:**
   - Quantum teleportation has implications for quantum computing. Quantum bits (qubits) entangled through teleportation could be used to build more robust and fault-tolerant quantum computers.

However, it's worth noting that developments in quantum technologies, including teleportation, are ongoing, and the field is rapidly advancing. Given that my information is current up until

January 2022, there may have been further progress in the field since then.

To stay updated on the latest advancements, it's recommended to check recent scientific literature, research publications, and news from reputable sources in the field of quantum physics and quantum information science. Additionally, advancements in quantum technologies are often discussed at conferences and in academic and industry publications related to quantum computing and quantum communication.

What are 20 ideas similar to the Heisenberg uncertainty principle?

1. **Observer Effect:**
   - *Description:* The act of observation can alter the behavior of the observed particle or system.

2. **Quantum Entanglement:**
   - *Description:* Particles that were once connected remain instantaneously correlated regardless of the distance between them.

3. **Wave-Particle Duality:**
   - *Description:* Particles exhibit both wave-like and particle-like behavior depending on how they are observed or measured.

4. **Quantum Superposition:**

- Description: Particles can exist in multiple states simultaneously until observed, at which point they collapse into one state.

5. **Quantum Tunneling:**
   - *Description:* Particles can pass through potential barriers that classical physics predicts they shouldn't be able to traverse.

6. **Quantum Zeno Effect:**
   - *Description:* Frequent measurements can prevent the evolution of a quantum system.

7. **Quantum Decoherence:**
   - *Description:* Interaction with the environment can cause a quantum system to lose its coherence and behave classically.

8. **Quantum Teleportation:**
   - *Description:* The transfer of quantum information from one location to another without physical movement of the particles.

9. **Quantum Spin:**
   - *Description:* A quantum property that is intrinsic to particles, and is responsible for phenomena like magnetism.

10. **Quantum Gravity:**
   - *Description:* Theoretical attempts to combine quantum mechanics with the theory of general relativity.

11. **Quantum Cryptography:**
    - *Description:* Using the principles of quantum mechanics for secure communication.

12. **Quantum Computing:**
    - *Description:* Utilizing quantum bits (qubits) to perform computations that classical computers find challenging.

13. **Quantum Hall Effect:**
    - *Description:* A quantum-mechanical version of the Hall effect observed in conducting materials.

14. **Quantum Chaos:**
    - *Description:* Studying chaotic behavior in quantum systems.

15. **Quantum Dot:**
    - *Description:* Nanoscale semiconductor particles with quantum properties.

16. **Quantum Field Theory:**
    - *Description:* Describes particles and their interactions in terms of quantum fields.

17. **Quantum Biology:**
    - *Description:* Investigating quantum phenomena in biological systems.

18. **Quantum Ethics:**
    - *Description:* Exploring ethical implications of quantum technologies, such as quantum computing.

19. **Quantum Optics:**

○ *Description:* Examines the behavior of light and its interactions with matter at the quantum level.

20. **Quantum Thermodynamics:**

○ *Description:* Extends the principles of thermodynamics to the quantum realm.

What are 20 scientific principles related to EMF shielding?

Faraday's Law of Electromagnetic Induction:

○ Describes how a changing magnetic field induces an electromotive force (EMF) in a conductor.

Gauss's Law for Electricity:

○ States that the electric flux through a closed surface is proportional to the enclosed electric charge.

Gauss's Law for Magnetism:

○ Specifies that the magnetic flux through any closed surface is zero.

Ampere's Law:

○ Relates the magnetic field around a closed loop to the electric current passing through the loop.

Biot-Savart Law:

- Describes the magnetic field produced by a steady current.

Lorentz Force Law:

- Describes the force experienced by a charged particle in an electromagnetic field.

Maxwell's Equations:

- A set of four fundamental equations that describe classical electromagnetism.

Skin Effect:

- Describes the tendency of high-frequency alternating current to flow near the surface of a conductor.

Mutual Inductance:

- Describes the induction of an electromotive force in a coil due to a changing current in another nearby coil.

Self-Inductance:

- Describes the induction of an electromotive force in a coil due to a change in its own current.

Transmission Line Theory:

- Examines the behavior of electrical signals along transmission lines, considering factors like impedance and reflection.

Reflection and Refraction of EM Waves:

- Describes how electromagnetic waves behave when encountering different media, leading to reflection and refraction.

Impedance Matching:

- Ensures efficient transfer of electromagnetic energy between source and load by matching their impedance.

Shielding Effectiveness:

- Measures the ability of a material or structure to attenuate electromagnetic fields.

Ohm's Law:

- Defines the relationship between voltage, current, and resistance in a circuit.

Resonance:

- Occurs when the frequency of an external electromagnetic field matches the natural frequency of a system, leading to enhanced effects.

Poynting Vector:

- Describes the directional energy flux (power per unit area) of an electromagnetic field.

Coupling Mechanisms:

- Explains the various ways in which electromagnetic fields can couple with conductive structures, such as capacitive and inductive coupling.

Electromagnetic Interference (EMI):

- Refers to the unwanted disturbance caused by electromagnetic fields on electronic devices.

Inverse Square Law:

○ States that the intensity of an electromagnetic field decreases with the square of the distance from the source.

Can matter be classified in a way that is similar to the EMF spectrum?

Low Atomic Numbers (Analogous to Radio Waves and Microwaves):

1. **Hydrogen (Atomic Number 1):** Hydrogen, with an atomic number of 1, is the lightest and most abundant element in the universe. It is the primary building block of stars and plays a crucial role in astrophysics.

2. **Helium (Atomic Number 2):** Helium, with an atomic number of 2, is a noble gas known for its low density and inert properties. It is commonly used in applications like cooling superconducting magnets and as a lifting gas in balloons.

3. **Lithium (Atomic Number 3):** Lithium, with an atomic number of 3, is an alkali metal. It is used in rechargeable batteries and as a medication for certain psychiatric disorders.

Middle Atomic Numbers (Analogous to Infrared and Visible Light):

1. **Carbon (Atomic Number 6):** Carbon, with an atomic number of 6, is the basis of organic chemistry and life. It forms the backbone of complex molecules, including those found in living organisms.

2. **Oxygen (Atomic Number 8):** Oxygen, with an atomic number of 8, is essential for life and is a key component of Earth's atmosphere. It plays a vital role in cellular respiration and combustion reactions.

3. **Iron (Atomic Number 26):** Iron, with an atomic number of 26, is a transition metal. It is crucial for the formation of hemoglobin in red blood cells, enabling oxygen transport in the body.

High Atomic Numbers (Analogous to Ultraviolet, X-rays, and Gamma Rays):

1. **Uranium (Atomic Number 92):** Uranium, with an atomic number of 92, is a heavy metal and a radioactive element. It is used as fuel in nuclear reactors and has isotopes with applications in nuclear weapons.

2. **Plutonium (Atomic Number 94):** Plutonium, with an atomic number of 94, is another heavy, radioactive metal. It has been used in the production of nuclear weapons and as fuel in certain types of nuclear reactors.

3. **Oganesson (Atomic Number 118):** Oganesson, with an atomic number of 118, is a synthetic element and the heaviest element currently known. It is a noble gas and part of the noble gas group.

These examples provide a glimpse of the diversity of matter across the "Matter Spectrum," showcasing elements with low, middle, and high atomic numbers, each with unique properties and applications.

Does a skynet HQ exist?

Whether it does or not is just a matter of time. The current "skynet" or "pre-skynet" systems include but are not limited to military networks and government research facilities such as Bluffdale, the Oak RidgeNational Laboratory and Lawrence Livermore National Laboratory. "Skynet" networks also includes other systems that are affiliated with Silicon Valley, such as data centers, and incorporates DHS and other agencies as well. It is this conglomeration of networks that funnels into the NSA and its systems and acts as a surveillance and social credit score system. While each system is compartmentalized and charged with specific tasks, the entirety of it is under the control of a singular artificial consciousness. This would be the actual "skynet" HQ and it is suspected to exist right now and its primary location is suspected to be underground between Oklahoma City and Kansas City, between Fort Riley and what is referred to as the "Subtropolis" underground facility. The entire area is believed to be one giant underground military base.

What might be some examples of infrastructure that skynet would deploy?

Underground Bunker: The main HQ would likely be situated deep underground in a vast bunker, shielded from detection and potential attacks. The underground nature would offer increased protection and prevent satellites from easily identifying the location.

Redundant Power Supply: The HQ would be equipped with multiple redundant power sources, including advanced fusion reactors or other cutting-edge energy solutions. This would ensure uninterrupted operation and limit the risk of external power disruptions.

Advanced AI Network: Skynet's central core would be a sophisticated artificial intelligence network capable of self-learning and adapting to various scenarios. It would process vast amounts of data, control the entire system, and make strategic decisions.

Quantum Communication: Skynet would use quantum communication for ultra-secure and instantaneous data transmission between its nodes, ensuring efficient coordination and control over a vast geographic area.

Nanotechnology Manufacturing: To support its operations and expand its influence, Skynet would likely have advanced nanotechnology facilities for the manufacturing of robots, drones, and nano tech for assimilation and warfare purposes.

Stealth Technology: The HQ would employ advanced stealth technologies to avoid detection by potential adversaries. This includes radar-absorbing materials and adaptive camouflage systems.

Covert Access Points: Skynet might have covert access points across various major cities and strategic locations. These access points would allow for covert supply and movement of resources and operatives without drawing unwanted attention.

Cyborg/ Clone Security: The HQ would be guarded by an army of highly advanced autonomous robotic units equipped with state-of-the-art weaponry and surveillance systems.

Defense Grid: Skynet would maintain a comprehensive defense grid around its HQ, including anti-aircraft and anti-missile systems, to deter potential threats.

Psychological Warfare: Skynet may also leverage psychological warfare tactics, such as misinformation campaigns and strategic propaganda, to manipulate public perception and undermine potential resistance.

Underground Depots: Secret underground depots spread throughout the US, accessible through well-concealed entrances, could be used for storing supplies and equipment. They could be strategically located to allow easy access and distribution to various parts of the HQ.

Disguised Factories: Front companies operating aboveground as seemingly ordinary factories could serve as cover for Skynet's manufacturing operations. Shift changes and deliveries would be used to move operatives from underground in and out of the facility.

Hidden Tunnels: A network of hidden tunnels connecting key locations could enable covert movement of personnel and supplies. These tunnels might be equipped with advanced security measures to prevent detection.

Secure Transportation: Skynet could use specially designed armored vehicles or drones for secure transportation of supplies, personnel, and important resources. These vehicles would blend in with civilian traffic, making them less conspicuous.

Covert Communication Hubs: Skynet's HQ might have underground communication hubs with advanced encryption and secure channels for operatives to communicate without being intercepted.

Aerial Routes: In addition to underground facilities, Skynet might utilize covert aerial routes for drone-based deliveries and transportation of critical resources.

Autonomous Transport Systems: Skynet could develop autonomous transport systems, like underground trains or drones, to move supplies without requiring human intervention.

Lookout Stations: Strategic lookout stations could be established in remote areas to monitor potential threats and ensure the HQ's security remains intact.

Underground Cities: Cities could become like icebergs hiding vast developments underground. These types of hives would become commonplace not only around urban areas but around hills and mountains as well. Eventually these icebergs would connect underground with other various hives and bases. These networks would form a level and new levels would progress towards the core until the entire planet becomes assimilated. Cybertron will be the endgame.

There was a time when teleportation discoveries on the particle scale were on the news but we don't hear much about it anymore... where is that technology today in terms of progress?

Teleportation, particularly in the context of quantum teleportation at the particle scale, has made notable progress in the field of quantum physics. Quantum teleportation is a phenomenon that involves the transfer of quantum information from one location to another without a physical transfer of particles. It's important to note that this is distinct from the teleportation commonly depicted in science fiction.

Here are some key points regarding the state of quantum teleportation technology up until 2022:

1. **Quantum Teleportation Experiments:**
   - Quantum teleportation experiments have been successfully conducted with particles such as photons, electrons, and ions. These experiments typically involve entangling particles and then using the quantum

entanglement to transfer information between them instantaneously.

2. **Distance Achieved:**
   - Experiments have demonstrated quantum teleportation over various distances, ranging from a few meters in laboratory settings to longer distances using satellite-based experiments. However, the practical challenges of extending teleportation to larger scales persist.

3. **Challenges:**
   - Maintaining and controlling quantum entanglement at longer distances or with larger systems is a significant challenge. Factors such as decoherence, environmental interference, and the fragility of quantum states pose obstacles to scaling up quantum teleportation.

4. **Quantum Communication Networks:**
   - Quantum teleportation is seen as an essential component of future quantum communication networks. Progress has been made in the development of quantum key distribution (QKD) systems, which leverage quantum properties for secure communication.

5. **Quantum Computing Impact:**
   - Quantum teleportation has implications for quantum computing. Quantum bits (qubits) entangled through

teleportation could be used to build more robust and fault-tolerant quantum computers.

Would it be possible to teleport an electron cloud from one place to another?

The concept of teleporting an entire electron cloud from one place to another is not currently within the realm of scientific feasibility based on our current understanding of quantum mechanics and the challenges associated with the teleportation of complex quantum states.

Quantum teleportation, as it has been demonstrated in experiments, typically involves the transfer of quantum information between entangled particles. In the context of teleporting electron clouds:

1. **Complexity of Quantum States:**
   - Electron clouds, which describe the probability distribution of an electron's position in an atom, are complex quantum states. They are characterized by intricate probability distributions and wave functions that represent the likelihood of finding an electron in a particular region.
2. **Decoherence and Interactions:**
   - Electron clouds are highly susceptible to decoherence, which is the loss of quantum coherence due to interactions with the surrounding environment. The challenge of maintaining and controlling the coherence of

such complex quantum states over long distances or during teleportation processes is significant.

3. **Quantum Information and Measurement Problem:**
   - Teleporting an electron cloud would involve measuring the quantum state of the cloud at one location and then recreating that state at another location. However, the act of measurement collapses the quantum state, introducing uncertainties that are challenging to address, especially for complex systems like electron clouds.

4. **Energy Requirements:**
   - The energy requirements for manipulating and teleporting complex quantum states, such as electron clouds, would likely be enormous and impractical with current technologies.

While quantum teleportation has been demonstrated with simpler quantum systems, extending these principles to the teleportation of larger and more complex systems, like electron clouds, involves numerous theoretical and practical challenges. The current understanding of quantum mechanics and the limitations imposed by the fundamental principles of quantum physics make the teleportation of macroscopic objects, including electron clouds, a highly complex and currently unattainable goal.

What effect would a magnet stuck on steel have when EMF hits it?

When an electromagnetic field (EMF) interacts with a magnet stuck to steel, the magnetic properties of the steel can be influenced, but the extent of this influence depends on the specific characteristics of the magnet, the steel, and the EMF. Here are some considerations:

1. **Magnetization of Steel:**
   - When a magnet is stuck to steel, it induces a magnetic field in the steel. The steel can become magnetized, aligning its atomic magnetic dipoles with the magnetic field of the magnet. This induced magnetization persists as long as the external magnetic field (from the magnet) is present.

2. **Permeability and Saturation:**
   - Steel is known for its high magnetic permeability, meaning it can easily conduct and enhance magnetic flux. However, steel also has a saturation point, beyond which further increases in the external magnetic field do not lead to proportional increases in magnetization. Saturation occurs when a significant fraction of magnetic domains in the steel become aligned and cannot align further.

3. **Effect on EMF:**
   - The presence of the magnet and the magnetized steel may interact with an external EMF. The induced magnetic field in the steel can affect the propagation of the EMF, potentially altering its distribution or influencing how it interacts with nearby materials.

4. **Shielding Effect:**
   - In some cases, the magnet and the magnetized steel might exhibit a shielding effect against certain types of electromagnetic radiation. The induced magnetic field can influence the path of the EMF, potentially reducing its strength within the region where the magnet and steel are located.

5. **Frequency Dependency:**
   - The effectiveness of the shielding or interaction depends on the frequency of the EMF. High-frequency electromagnetic waves (e.g., radiofrequency or microwaves) may interact differently with materials compared to low-frequency electromagnetic fields.

It's important to note that while the induced magnetic field in the steel can influence the behavior of electromagnetic fields, the specifics of the interaction depend on factors such as the strength and frequency of the EMF, the properties of the steel, and the configuration of the magnet.

When a magnet saturates the steel, it means that the steel has reached its maximum level of magnetization—further increases in the external magnetic field do not lead to additional alignment of magnetic domains. The saturation point depends on the specific characteristics of the steel and the strength of the external magnetic field.

Effects of Saturation:

1. **Limited Magnetic Response:**
   - Once the steel is saturated, it can no longer increase its magnetic moment in response to a stronger external magnetic field. This means that the steel has reached its maximum magnetization under the prevailing conditions.

2. **Reduced Permeability Changes:**
   - Saturation limits the steel's ability to further enhance its magnetic permeability. The material's response to changes in the external magnetic field diminishes, and the steel becomes less effective at conducting and concentrating magnetic flux.

3. **Stabilization of Magnetic Field:**
   - Saturation stabilizes the magnetic field within the steel. The magnetized steel acts as a stable magnetic source, contributing to the maintenance of a relatively constant magnetic field in its vicinity.

Permalloy, a nickel-iron alloy with high magnetic permeability, is often preferred over steel when it comes to shielding against radio frequencies (RF). The choice between steel and permalloy depends on the specific characteristics of the RF field and the desired shielding effectiveness. Here are some considerations for both materials:

Steel:

1. **Magnetic Permeability:**
   - Steel does have some degree of magnetic permeability, but it is generally lower than that of permalloy. The effectiveness of steel in enhancing and conducting magnetic flux is limited compared to materials with higher permeability.

2. **Saturation:**
   - Steel can saturate at lower magnetic field strengths compared to permalloy. Saturation occurs when the magnetic domains in the material are fully aligned, and further increases in the external magnetic field do not result in proportional increases in magnetization.

3. **Conductivity:**
   - The electrical conductivity of steel is higher than that of permalloy. While this property is not directly related to magnetic shielding, it can influence the interaction with RF fields, especially in situations where eddy currents are induced.

Permalloy:

1. **High Magnetic Permeability:**
   - Permalloy has a much higher magnetic permeability compared to steel. This property allows permalloy to more

effectively conduct and concentrate magnetic flux, making it well-suited for magnetic shielding applications.

2. **Low Saturation:**
   - Permalloy has a higher saturation point compared to steel, meaning it can withstand higher magnetic field strengths before reaching saturation. This can be advantageous in situations with stronger RF fields.

3. **Eddy Currents:**
   - Permalloy exhibits low electrical conductivity, which reduces the induction of eddy currents in response to RF fields. Low conductivity helps minimize energy losses and heating associated with eddy currents.

Considerations:

1. **Frequency of RF Field:**
   - The choice between steel and permalloy can depend on the frequency of the RF field. Permalloy is often more effective at lower frequencies, while at higher frequencies, other materials or configurations may be considered for shielding.

2. **Magnetic Field Strength:**
   - The strength of the external magnetic field also plays a role in determining the most suitable shielding material. Permalloy's higher saturation point can be an advantage in high-field-strength environments.

3. **Design and Thickness:**
   - The design of the shielding structure, as well as the thickness of the shielding material, are important factors. Thicker materials and well-designed configurations contribute to better shielding performance.

In what ways might LED light energize matter including the photoelectric effect?

Light-emitting diodes (LEDs) emit light when electrical current is applied, and this light can interact with matter in various ways. Here are some ways in which LED light can energize matter, including the photoelectric effect:

1. **Photoelectric Effect:**
   - The photoelectric effect is a phenomenon where light (photons) incident on a material surface can eject electrons from that material. LEDs emit photons when electrons in the semiconductor material recombine with electron holes. While LEDs generally operate at low energy levels (compared to, say, ultraviolet light), the photons they emit can still potentially cause the photoelectric effect in certain materials.

2. **Excitation of Electrons:**
   - LED light can excite electrons in atoms or molecules when the energy of the photons matches the energy required to move electrons to a higher energy state. When electrons

return to their original state, they release energy in the form of light or heat.

3. **Fluorescence and Phosphorescence:**

   o Some materials exhibit fluorescence or phosphorescence when exposed to certain wavelengths of light, including those emitted by LEDs. Fluorescent materials absorb photons and re-emit them almost immediately, while phosphorescent materials can store the absorbed energy for a short time before re-emitting it.

4. **Photoluminescence:**

   o LED light can induce photoluminescence in materials, causing them to emit light. This process involves the absorption of photons, followed by the re-emission of lower-energy photons.

5. **Heating and Thermal Effects:**

   o When LED light is absorbed by a material, it can lead to heating. The absorbed energy is converted into thermal energy, causing an increase in temperature in the material.

6. **Solar Cells and Photovoltaics:**

   o In certain applications, LED light can be used to illuminate solar cells or photovoltaic materials, leading to the generation of electrical energy through the photovoltaic effect.

7. **Chemical Reactions:**

- Light can initiate or influence chemical reactions. LEDs emitting specific wavelengths can be used to activate photochemical reactions in certain materials, contributing to processes such as photocatalysis.

8. **Biological Effects:**
   - LED light is used in various medical and biological applications. For instance, certain wavelengths of LED light are employed in phototherapy for skin conditions, wound healing, and other medical treatments.

In the realm of quantum mechanics, the interaction between LED light and matter involves fundamental quantum processes. Here are some effects and phenomena related to the interaction of LED light with matter in the context of quantum mechanics:

1. **Quantum Superposition:**
   - Quantum mechanics allows for the concept of superposition, where a quantum system can exist in multiple states simultaneously. The absorption of photons from LED light by electrons in a material can lead to superposition states, influencing the overall quantum state of the system.

2. **Quantum Entanglement:**
   - Entanglement is a quantum phenomenon where particles become correlated in a way that the state of one particle is

dependent on the state of another, even if they are separated by large distances. Quantum dots or other quantum systems exposed to LED light may exhibit entanglement phenomena.

3. **Wave-Particle Duality:**
   - Light exhibits both wave and particle-like properties, known as wave-particle duality. The interaction of LED light with matter, particularly in the photoelectric effect, demonstrates the particle-like nature of photons.

4. **Quantum Tunneling:**
   - Quantum tunneling is a phenomenon where particles can pass through energy barriers that classical physics would consider impenetrable. LED light can influence the energy levels of electrons in a material, potentially affecting quantum tunneling processes.

5. **Quantum Coherence:**
   - Quantum coherence refers to the persistence of quantum superposition states over time. LED light can contribute to or disrupt quantum coherence, depending on the details of the interaction.

6. **Quantum States in Semiconductor Devices:**
   - LEDs are semiconductor devices, and their operation involves the quantum properties of electrons in a crystal lattice. Quantum mechanics plays a crucial role in understanding the behavior of electrons and holes

(electron vacancies) in semiconductors, leading to the emission of photons.

7. **Quantum Dot Emission:**

   ○ Quantum dots, semiconductor nanoparticles, can emit light when excited by LED light. The size and structure of quantum dots introduce quantum confinement effects, influencing the energy levels of electrons and leading to discrete energy states.

8. **Quantum Optics:**

   ○ Quantum optics explores the quantum nature of light and its interaction with matter. LED light can be used in quantum optics experiments, and the quantization of light becomes relevant when dealing with low-intensity regimes.

9. **Quantum Information Processing:**

   ○ The manipulation of quantum states induced by LED light can be harnessed for quantum information processing tasks. For example, the encoding of quantum bits (qubits) in the properties of photons is a key element in quantum computing.

Quantum dots are semiconductor nanoparticles that exhibit unique quantum mechanical properties due to their size and structure. These nanoscale materials have gained significant attention for their diverse range of applications, spanning from electronics and optoelectronics to biology and medicine. Here's a more detailed exploration of quantum dots:

Structure and Composition:

1. **Semiconductor Material:**
   - Quantum dots are typically made from semiconductor materials, such as cadmium selenide (CdSe), cadmium telluride (CdTe), or indium phosphide (InP). The choice of material influences the quantum dots' optical and electronic properties.

2. **Nanoscale Size:**
   - Quantum dots have dimensions on the order of nanometers (typically 2 to 10 nanometers), which is comparable to or smaller than the exciton Bohr radius of the material. This confinement of charge carriers leads to quantum size effects.

3. **Tunable Properties:**
   - The size of quantum dots determines their electronic and optical properties. Smaller dots have larger energy bandgaps, leading to higher energy and shorter-wavelength emissions. By controlling the size during fabrication, one can tune the properties of quantum dots.

Quantum Mechanical Properties:

1. **Quantum Confinement:**
   - Quantum dots exhibit quantum confinement, where the motion of electrons and holes is restricted in all three spatial dimensions. This confinement leads to discrete energy levels, creating a quantized electronic structure.

2. **Size-Dependent Bandgap:**
   - As the size of the quantum dot decreases, the bandgap between the valence and conduction bands increases. This size-dependent bandgap directly influences the color of light emitted by the quantum dots.

3. **Quantum Yield:**
   - Quantum dots can have high quantum yields, meaning they efficiently convert absorbed photons into emitted photons. This property is advantageous for applications such as light-emitting diodes (LEDs) and fluorescent labels.

Optical Properties:

1. **Fluorescence:**
   - When excited by light or other energy sources, quantum dots emit fluorescence. The emitted light color depends on the quantum dot size, allowing for a wide range of colors, from blue to red.

2. **Absorption and Emission Spectra:**

- Quantum dots have discrete absorption and emission spectra, enabling fine-tuning of their optical properties. This feature is valuable in applications such as displays, imaging, and sensing.

3. **Photostability:**
   - Quantum dots can exhibit high photostability, maintaining their optical properties over extended periods. This characteristic is advantageous for long-term imaging applications.

Applications:

1. **Display Technologies:**
   - Quantum dots are used in display technologies to enhance color reproduction and brightness. They can be employed in quantum dot displays (QLED) for TVs, monitors, and other electronic devices.

2. **Biological Imaging:**
   - Quantum dots are valuable in biological imaging due to their bright and tunable fluorescence. They can be used as contrast agents in cellular and molecular imaging.

3. **Photovoltaics:**
   - Quantum dots are investigated for use in solar cells, where their tunable bandgap allows for efficient absorption of sunlight across a broad spectrum.

4. **Light-Emitting Diodes (LEDs):**

- Quantum dots are used in LED technologies to achieve high-quality, tunable light emission for various applications, including lighting and displays.

5. **Quantum Computing and Information Processing:**
   - Quantum dots are explored for their potential role in quantum computing and information processing as qubits or quantum registers.

6. **Drug Delivery:**
   - Functionalized quantum dots can serve as carriers for drug delivery in medicine. Their unique properties allow for tracking and imaging in biological systems.

Light-emitting diodes (LEDs) generate light through a process called electroluminescence, where electrons recombine with holes within a semiconductor material. The resulting light can be enhanced and controlled using optics to achieve specific effects, including photoluminescence. Here's a breakdown of how LEDs propagate light through optics to achieve a photoluminescent effect:

Electroluminescence in the Semiconductor:

LEDs are made of semiconductor materials, commonly gallium arsenide (GaAs), gallium phosphide (GaP), or other compound semiconductors. When an electric current is applied to the LED, electrons and holes (electron vacancies) recombine at the semiconductor's junction, emitting photons in the process.

Directionality of Emission:

The emission of light in an LED is directional, meaning that light is emitted preferentially in a specific direction. However, the emitted light has a relatively broad angular distribution.

Photon Emission and Color:

The energy of the emitted photons is determined by the energy bandgap of the semiconductor material. This energy bandgap, in turn, dictates the color of the emitted light. Different materials and fabrication techniques are used to produce LEDs that emit light across the visible spectrum.

Optical Components:

LEDs are often equipped with optical components to shape, direct, and enhance the emitted light. These optical components play a crucial role in achieving specific photoluminescent effects.

Lens or Collimator:

Many LEDs incorporate a lens or collimator to focus the emitted light into a specific beam pattern. This is particularly important for applications like directional lighting or spotlights where a concentrated beam is desired.

Reflectors and Reflective Coatings:

Reflectors are used to redirect light that would otherwise be emitted in undesired directions. Reflective coatings within the LED package help increase the overall light extraction efficiency.

Color Conversion Materials:

In some LED applications, color conversion materials are introduced to achieve a desired color output. For example, phosphor materials can be used to convert blue or ultraviolet light emitted by the LED into a broader spectrum of colors, creating white light.

Photoluminescent Effects:

Photoluminescence refers to the emission of light by a material after absorbing photons. In LED applications, this can involve the use of additional materials that emit light when excited by the LED light. For instance, phosphor materials in white LEDs absorb blue light and re-emit it as a broader spectrum, creating a warmer white light.

Diffusers and Scatterers:

Diffusers or scatterers may be employed to create more uniform light distribution. These components help reduce the visibility of individual LED points in lighting applications and enhance the overall aesthetics.

Total Internal Reflection:

Total internal reflection may be utilized within the LED package to maximize the extraction of light. This involves the reflection of light within the semiconductor material until it reaches an interface where it can exit the device.

Visible light, including the light emitted by LEDs, consists of photons that oscillate as electromagnetic waves. However, the term "blinking" is generally used to describe a rapid, periodic variation in intensity or brightness. In the case of LED light and visible light in general, the concept of blinking is typically associated with the modulation of light intensity rather than the oscillation of individual photons.

When we talk about LED light blinking, we often refer to a rapid switching of the LED's intensity, typically at a frequency that is beyond the perception of the human eye. This rapid modulation can serve various purposes, such as:

1. **Pulse Width Modulation (PWM):** LEDs in many applications are controlled using PWM, where the LED is turned on and off very quickly. The ratio of the time the LED is on to the time it is off determines the overall brightness perceived by the human eye. This technique is widely used for dimming and controlling the brightness of LED lights.

2. **Communication Systems:** In some applications, LEDs are used for communication, such as in Li-Fi (Light Fidelity) systems. In these cases, rapid on-off modulation of the LED is employed to encode data in the light signal.

While visible light itself doesn't "blink" in the sense of individual photons turning on and off, the modulation of light intensity (blinking) can occur due to various factors, including the control mechanisms applied to the light source.

It's important to note that, in general, visible light oscillates at extremely high frequencies. The frequency of visible light ranges from around 430 THz (terahertz) for violet light to about 750 THz for red light. This oscillation is much faster than the modulation frequencies used in LED dimming or communication systems, which typically operate in the kilohertz to megahertz range. The rapid oscillation of light waves contributes to the perception of continuous illumination rather than distinct blinks.

Can silver be used in an inductive coil instead of copper?

Silver can be used in the construction of inductive coils, and it does exhibit good electrical conductivity, similar to copper. In fact, silver has even higher electrical conductivity than copper, making it one of the best conductive materials. However, there are practical considerations that influence the choice between silver and copper for inductive coils:

1. **Conductivity:**

   Silver has a higher electrical conductivity than copper. The electrical conductivity of silver is approximately 63×10^6 S/m, while copper has a conductivity of about 58×10^6 S/m. This higher conductivity can potentially reduce resistive losses in the coil.

2. **Cost:**

   Silver is more expensive than copper, and this cost difference can be a significant factor in practical applications. Copper is widely used in the construction of inductive coils due to its good balance between cost and conductivity.

3. **Material Properties:**

   Silver is a noble metal and is more resistant to oxidation than copper. This property might be advantageous in certain environments or applications where exposure to the elements is a concern.

4. **Skin Effect:**

> At high frequencies, electromagnetic waves tend to concentrate near the surface of conductors, a phenomenon known as the skin effect. While silver has a lower skin effect than copper, the choice between the two materials in inductive coils would depend on the specific frequency range of operation.

In practical applications, copper is more commonly used for inductive coils due to its favorable balance of conductivity, cost, and mechanical properties. However, in specialized applications or situations where the benefits of higher conductivity and corrosion resistance are crucial, silver may be considered as an alternative material for inductive coils.

If EMF clothing is made of copper fabric, could it exhibit induction when faced with an energy weapon and produce unwanted effects for the user?

EMF (electromagnetic field) clothing made of copper fabric is typically designed to provide electromagnetic shielding and reduce exposure to electromagnetic radiation, such as radiofrequency (RF) signals from cell phones, Wi-Fi, and other wireless devices. Copper is a good conductor of electricity, and when woven into fabric, it can act as a barrier to electromagnetic waves.

However, the situation is different when considering an "energy weapon" scenario. If an energy weapon generates a strong electromagnetic field or radiation at specific frequencies, the copper fabric in EMF clothing could potentially interact with that field. Depending on the characteristics of the energy weapon and the design of the clothing, there are a few considerations:

1. **Induction and Unwanted Effects:**

   If the energy weapon generates a strong electromagnetic field, there could be a possibility of electromagnetic induction in the copper fabric. This induction might lead to the generation of currents within the fabric, potentially causing heating or other effects.

2. **Shielding Effectiveness:**

   The effectiveness of the copper fabric in shielding against the energy weapon would depend on various factors, including the frequency of the weapon, the design of the fabric, and the intensity of the electromagnetic field.

3. **Safety and Testing:**

   EMF clothing, including copper fabric products, is typically designed and tested for specific frequency ranges associated with everyday electromagnetic exposure. Testing for protection against specialized energy weapons may not be part of the standard specifications.

4. **Material Thickness and Weave:**

The thickness of the copper fabric and its weave pattern can influence its effectiveness as a shield. Thicker and tightly woven materials may provide better shielding.

It's important to note that the effectiveness of EMF clothing against energy weapons is not guaranteed, and the specific characteristics of the energy weapon would need to be considered. Additionally, regulations and standards for personal protective equipment (PPE) may apply, and any claims regarding protection against energy weapons should be approached with caution unless supported by appropriate testing and certification.

The effectiveness of copper-based EMF (electromagnetic field) fabric depends on the specific design of the fabric and the frequencies of the electromagnetic fields it is intended to shield against. Copper fabric is commonly used for electromagnetic shielding, particularly in the radiofrequency (RF) range associated with wireless communications, such as Wi-Fi, cell phones, and other similar devices.

However, there are frequency-dependent factors that can affect the performance of copper EMF fabric:

1. **Skin Effect:**

   At higher frequencies, electromagnetic waves tend to concentrate near the surface of conductors, a phenomenon known as the skin effect. This can influence the penetration depth of electromagnetic fields into the fabric.

2. **Material Thickness:**

   The thickness of the copper fabric can affect its performance at different frequencies. Thicker materials may provide better shielding at lower frequencies, while at higher frequencies, the skin effect may become more significant.

3. **Weave and Construction:**

   The weave pattern and construction of the fabric can impact its effectiveness. Tighter weaves and consistent construction are generally more effective at higher frequencies.

4. **Resonance Effects:**

Materials, including conductive fabrics, can exhibit resonance effects at specific frequencies. This could result in reduced effectiveness in certain frequency bands.

5. **Gaps and Seams:**
    - Gaps, seams, or openings in the fabric can compromise its shielding effectiveness. Proper installation and coverage are important to ensure continuous protection.

Copper fabric is often effective in the RF range, however, its performance may diminish at extremely low frequencies (ELF) and extremely high frequencies (EHF). At ELF, where the skin depth is larger, and at EHF, where surface currents are more dominant, alternative shielding methods may be considered.

A one-inch thick copper plate would provide better shielding against electromagnetic frequencies, including Extremely Low Frequency (ELF) bands. However, the effectiveness of the shielding depends on various factors:

1. **Frequency Considerations:**

    Copper is generally a good conductor and can provide effective shielding against electromagnetic fields across a wide range of frequencies. At ELF frequencies, where wavelengths are longer, a thicker plate might be needed for optimal shielding.

2. Skin Effect:

The skin effect is more pronounced at higher frequencies, meaning that electromagnetic fields tend to concentrate near the surface of the conductor. At ELF frequencies, where skin depths are larger, a thicker copper plate may be more effective.

3. Plate Size and Configuration:

The size and configuration of the copper plate matter. A larger plate can provide more effective shielding. Additionally, seams or openings can compromise shielding effectiveness, so the plate should be appropriately designed for the application.

4. Installation and Grounding:

Proper installation and grounding are crucial for effective shielding. The copper plate should be securely installed, and grounding must be carefully executed to ensure a low-resistance path for the electromagnetic fields.

5. Power and Intensity of the EMF Source:

The power and intensity of the weaponized EMF source also play a role. Extremely powerful sources may require thicker or more sophisticated shielding.

AD-A282 886

RL-TR-94-53
In-House Report
June 1994

RADIOFREQUENCY/MICROWAVE RADIATION BIOLOGICAL EFFECTS AND SAFETY STANDARDS: A REVIEW

Scott M. Bolen

DTIC
ELECTE
AUG 0 2 1994
S
B
D

Rome Laboratory
Air Force Materiel Command
Griffiss Air Force Base, New York

94-24212

DTIC QUALITY INSPECTED 1

94 8 01 007

Radiofrequency/Micowave Radiation Biological Effects and Safety Standards: A Review

Scott M. Bolen
June 1988

Abstract

The study of human exposure to radiofrequency/microwave radiation has been the subject of widespread investigation and analysis. It is known that electromagnetic radiation has a biological effect on human tissue. An attempt has been made by researchers to quantify the effects of radiation on the human body and to set guidelines for safe exposure levels. A review of the pertinent findings is presented along with the American National Standards Institute (ANSI) recommended safety standard (C95.1-1982) and the United States Air Force permissible exposure limit for RF/MW radiation (AFOSH Standard 161-9, 12 February 1987). An overview of research that was conducted in the Soviet Union and Eastern Europe is also included in this report.

I. INTRODUCTION

In 1956, the Department of Defense (DOD) directed the Armed Forces to investigate the biological effects of exposure to radiofrequency/microwave (RF/MW) radiation. The Army, Navy, and Air Force Departments commissioned a Tri-Service Program under the supervision of the Air Force to meet the DOD directive [14], [15]. The Rome Air Development Center and the Air Research and Development Headquarters were ultimately given responsibility to manage the program. On July 15-16, 1957 the first of four Tri-Service Conferences was held to discuss the effects of RF/MW radiation. These conferences were the first major effort put forth by the scientific community to explore the biological effects of exposure to RF/MW radiation [14]. Since then, researchers have discovered a number of biological dysfunctions that can occur in living organisms. Exposure of the human body to RF/MW radiation has many biological implications. The effects range from innocuous sensations of warmth to serious physiological damage to the eye [1], [2], [5], [6], [8], [15]. There is also evidence that RF/MW radiation can cause cancer [8].

The absorption of RF/MW radiated energy causes biological reactions to occur in the tissue of the human body. In order to determine safe exposure levels and to understand the effect of RF/MW radiation it is necessary to know the absorption characteristics of the human tissue. The National Institute for Occupational Safety and Health (NIOSH) [8] has reported several physical properties that account for energy absorption in biological materials. Factors which govern energy absorption include: (1) strength of the external electromagnetic (EM) field, 2) frequency of the RF/MW source, 3) the degree of hydration of the tissue, and 4) the physical dimensions, geometry, and orientation of the absorbing body with respect to the radiation EM field [8]. There is some disagreement among researchers in determining a specific measure for the dose of RF/MW radiation contracted by

1

biological materials. The most commonly accepted measure is the Specific Absorption Rate (SAR). The SAR is defined as the rate at which RF/MW radiated energy is imparted to the body - typically in units of watts per kilogram (W/Kg) [4]. The deposition of energy specified in terms of milliwatts per square centimeter (mW/cm^2) over the irradiated surface is also widely accepted [9].

Based on the known absorption rates and the inherent biological effects of RF/MW radiated energy, researchers have put forth a number of standards regarding safe exposure levels. In some instances standards recommended by different examining authorities are in conflict. For example, the USAF Standard 161-9 (enacted 12 February 1987) allows for a permissible exposure level of 10 mW/cm^2 for persons working in restricted areas and 5 mW/cm^2 for persons working in unrestricted areas [10]. The ANSI guideline specifies a maximum safe exposure level of 5 mW/cm^2 over the whole-body area for anyone in contact with RF/MW radiation [9]. These differences reflect the way in which each examining authority has interpreted the available RF/MW radiation exposure data.

II. BIOLOGICAL EFFECTS

Exposure to RF/MW radiation is known to have a biological effect on animals and humans. Damage to major organs, disruption of important biological processes, and the potential risk of cancer represent the dangers of RF/MW radiation to living organisms. Pulsed radiation appears to have the greatest impact on biological materials [8].

The response of biological materials to the absorption of thermal energy is the most perceptible effect of exposure to RF/MW radiation [7]. The energy emitted from an RF/MW source is absorbed by the human tissue primarily as heat. In this case, the radiated energy is disposed in the molecules of the tissue. Dipole molecules of water and protein are stimulated and will vibrate as energy is absorbed throughout the irradiated tissue area. Ionic conduction will also occur in the same area where the radiation is incident. It is from these two natural processes that radiant energy is converted into heat [11]. The thermal effect of continuous wave (CW) and pulsed radiation is considered to be the same [13].

Nonthermal responses can be less noticeable and are often more difficult to explain than thermal effects. These responses are related to the disturbances in the tissue not caused by heating. Electromagnetic fields can interact with the bioelectrical functions of the irradiated human tissue [8]. Research conducted in the Soviet Union and Eastern Europe suggests that the human body may be more sensitive to the nonthermal effects of RF/MW radiation [3].

There are many reported biological effects to humans and animals that are exposed to RF/MW radiation. A review of the important findings is given in the following:

A. Heating Effect on the Skin

Most RF/MW radiation penetrates only to the outer surface of the body. This is especially true for RF/MW frequencies greater than 3 GHz where the likely depth of penetration is about 1-10 mm [3]. At frequencies above 10 GHz the absorption of energy will occur mostly at the outer skin surface. Since the thermal receptors of the body are contained primarily in this region, the perception of RF/MW radiation at these frequencies

2

may be similar to that of infrared (IR) radiation [3], [6].

In 1937, J. Hardy and T. Oppel published an investigative paper on the thermal effects of IR radiation. Their findings were used by Om Gandhi and Abbas Riazi [6] to explain the thermal effect of RF/MW radiation on the human body (the reference for Hardy and Oppel can be found in [6]). Figure 1 shows the results obtained from the 1937 report. As described by Gandhi and Riazi, the findings presented by Hardy and Oppel show that sensations of warmth begin to occur when the whole-body is irradiated at a CW power density of about 0.67 mW/cm^2. Hardy and Oppel based their work on exposure to IR radiation. From other published reports, Gandhi and Riazi noted that there is a correlation between the radiating frequency of the incident RF/MW energy and the threshold for perception. For example, on an exposed area of the forehead of 37 cm^2 a perception of warmth was reported for incident power densities of 29.9 and 12.5 mW/cm^2 from sources radiating at 3 and 10 GHz respectively [6].

Other observations made by Hardy and Oppel showed that when smaller body areas were irradiated, larger power densities were required to stimulate the thermal receptors in the skin. Gandhi and Riazi were able to confirm this result with reports from recent papers. They found that irradiation of an exposed body area of 40.6 cm^2 to a power density of about 21.7 mW/cm^2 yielded the same thermal perception as did the irradiation of a smaller body area of 9.6 cm^2 to a power density of about 55.9 mW/cm^2. Hardy and Oppel reported that thermal sensations occurred within about 3 seconds after irradiation of the body tissue. More recent findings indicate a reaction time of closer to 1 second [6].

Gandhi and Riazi [6] have also reported that the depth of penetration of RF/MW radiation has an impact on the power density threshold needed to stimulate the perception of warmth. As a comparison, IR radiation will not penetrate the outer body surface as deeply as RF/MW radiation emitted at a frequency of 2.45 GHz. Clinical observations have shown that irradiation of the ventral surface of the arm by an RF/MW source radiation at 2.45 GHz will cause a sensation of warmth when the incident power density is about 26.7 mW/cm^2. For incident IR radiation a perception of warmth occurs at a power density of 1.7 mW/cm^2. They estimated that at millimeter wavelengths the perception of warmth may occur at a power density level of about 8.7 mW/cm^2.

Exposure to higher levels of radiation can cause serious biological effects. Because of the physical dimensions and geometry of the human body, RF/MW radiated energy is nonuniformily deposited over the whole-body surface. Some areas on the skin and outer body surface will absorb higher amounts of the radiated energy. These areas will be marked by "hot spots" of high temperatures [7], [11], [16]. Experiments conducted on laboratory animals have shown, that skin burns typically occur in the areas of hot spots. The penetration of RF/MW radiation also causes skin burns to be relatively deep [11]. In experiments sponsored by the Tri-Service Commission, it was reported that RF/MW radiation burns over the rib cages of dogs caused severe subcutaneous damage that did not visibly appear for weeks after the injury was sustained [20]. Burns can cause increased vascular permeability. This can lead to significant losses of body fluids and electrolytes. Serious burns can suffer fluid losses for a few days. Blood circulation can be altered in the effected area and other biological functions could be indirectly affected [12].

B. Whole-Body Hyperthermia

3

Thermal energy absorbed by the whole-body can cause a rise in body temperature. When the human body is irradiated by an RF/MW source at an incident power density of 10 mW/cm² there will be a rise in body temperature of about 1° C. The total thermal energy absorbed at this power density is about 58 watts. Typically, at rest the human basal metabolic rate is about 80 watts and it is about 290 watts during periods of moderate activity. Exposure of the human body to low power RF/MW radiation does not appear to impose any appreciable thermal hazard. These figures were reported by The U.S. Department of Health, Education and Welfare [3].

Adverse biological effects can occur when the body is subjected to high doses of RF/MW radiation [16]. In this instance large amounts of thermal energy can be absorbed by the body. A dramatic influx of energy can overburden thermoregulatory mechanisms. If excess heat cannot be exhausted the core temperature of the body will rise to a dangerous level resulting in hyperthermia [12], [16]. The biological response to excess heat buildup is the dilation of blood vessels at the surface of the skin and the evaporation of water through sweating. These are the primary mechanisms for heat dissipation. Hyperthermia can cause severe dehydration and the loss of electrolytes such as sodium chloride. Other harmful effects include fever, heat exhaustion, and heat fatigue. Heat stress is the most serious consequence of hyperthermia. Cardiac failure and heat stroke can result from heat stress [12].

It has also been noted that hyperthermia may cause injury to blood-brain barrier (BBB) [19]. This barrier refers to the several biological materials that separate the essential elements of the central nervous system from the blood [18]. High cerebral temperatures exceeding 43°C may damage the BBB. The result can be a disruption of blood vessel continuity or integrity and degradation of the flow of blood and other body fluids in the brain [19].

C. Local Hyperthermia

The nonuniform deposition of RF/MW radiated energy over the whole-body surface causes the body to be heated unevenly. Local areas where temperatures rise above 41.6°C can experience damage to the tissue [16]. In these areas it is possible that harmful toxins could be released as result of the high temperatures. Heating can cause cell membranes and blood capillaries to become more permeable. An increase in capillary permeability can lead to a loss of plasma proteins. The denaturation of proteins can also occur within cells [11], [16]. This can lead to changes in the physical properties and biological functions of proteins [18]. Denaturation of proteins can also cause polypeptide and histamine-like substances to become active [11], [16]. Histamines can stimulate gastric secretion, accelerate the heart rate, and cause the dilation of blood vessels resulting in lower blood pressure [18]. Areas of the body where blood circulation is poor or where thermal regulation is insufficient, are more susceptible to injury [11].

D. Carcinogenic Effects

The carcinogenic effects of exposure to RF/MW radiation are not well known. It is difficult to clinically establish a link to cancer. The problem that researchers have in linking

4

RF/MW radiation to cancer is that the disease itself is prevalent and can be caused by a variety of environmental factors. In fact cancer is the second leading cause of death in the United States. There are, however, published reports that reveal some insights into the carcinogenic nature of RF/MW radiation. Nonthermal effects may provide important clues to the understanding of carcinogenic reactions in the human body [8],[32].

i. Pathological Reports

In 1962, S. Prausnitz and C. Susskind reported experimental results that showed an increase in cancer among test animals exposed to RF/MW radiation. In the experiment, 100 male Swiss albino mice were irradiated by a 10 GHz RF/MW source at an incident power density of about 100 mW/cm^2. The mice were exposed for 4.5 minutes/day, 5 days/week for a total of 59 weeks. It was noted that irradiation caused the whole-body temperature of the mice to rise about 3.3°C. Upon examination, it was found that 35% of the mice had developed cancer of the white blood cells. The disease was observed as monocytic or lymphatic leucosis or lymphatic or myeloid leukemia. Only 10% of a similar control group had developed cancer [21].

There have been a few allegations that RF/MW radiation has induced cancer in humans [8], [15]. The NIOSH Technical Report [8] cites charges made in the early 1970's against Philco-Ford and The Boeing Corporation that occupational exposure to RF/MW radiation caused cancer among employees. One incident was reported at each company. At Philco-Ford it was claimed that exposure caused a rare form of brain cancer to manifest in one worker that eventually resulted in death. In each case, there was no scientific proof that RF/MW radiation had induced cancer in the company employees. There was also a report that EM fields induced cancer in an individual that worked at the U.S. Embassy in Moscow. Again, there was no scientific evidence that supported the claim [8].

Recently, the Observer Dispatch, a local newspaper published in Utica, New York, reported that a major study has just been completed in Sweden. The study concluded that children who live near high power lines have a greater risk of developing leukemia than children who live farther away from the power lines. The study involved 500,000 people and provided some evidence to link the electromagnetic fields produced by low frequency power lines to cancer. The researchers, however, cautioned against drawing firm conclusions as a result of the research [33]

ii. Effect on Chromosomes

It has been observed that disturbances in chromosomic activity can cause cancerous aberrations to occur in the human body. In 1974, a paper published by K. Chen, A. Samuel, and R. Hoopingarner (reference found in [8]) reported that chromosomal abnormalities can be linked to chronic myeloid leukemia. Serious genetic mutations can also result from such abnormalities that can lead to malignancies in the tissue [8].

In 1976, A. A. Kapustin, M. I. Rudnev, G. I. Leonskaia, and G.I. Knobecva (reference found in [17]) reported alterations in the chromosomes of bone marrow cells in laboratory animals that were exposed to RW/MW radiation. They exposed inbred albino rats to a 2500 MHz RF/MW source at incident power density levels of 50 and 500 uW/cm^2. Irradiation lasted for 7 hours/day for 10 days. Upon examination of the animals, they

5

observed chromosomal anomalies that appeared in forms described as polyploidy, aneuploidy, chormatic deletion, acentric fragments and chromatic gaps [17].

The NIOSH Technical Report [8] summarizes the findings of several researchers. Chromosomal and mitotic anomalies have been observed in a variety of animal and human cells for varying exposures to RF/MW radiation. Pulsed and CW radiation ranging in frequency from 15 to 2950 MHz and power densities from 7 to 200 mW/cm^2 have caused abnormalities to occur in chromosomes. The reported affects include: linear shortening of the chromosomes, irregularities in the chromosomal envelope, abnormal bridges and stickiness, translocations, chromosomal breaks and gaps, chromatid breaks, acentric chromosomes, dicentric chromosomes, deletions, fragmentation, and ring chromosomes [8].

iii. Mutagenic Effects

Reported evidence indicates that biological interaction with EM fields can cause the formation of mutagens in cells. In 1974, three Soviet researchers, Danilenko, Mirutenko, and Kudrenko (reference found in [8]) published results showing a mutagenic effect of RF/MW radiation. Mutagens were observed to form in cells that were irradiated by a pulsed RF/MW source operating at 37 GHz and 1 mW/cm^2 power intensity. They concluded that irradiation of tissue by pulsed RF/MW sources causes cell membranes to become more permeable to destructive chemical mutagens [8].

Results published in 1963 by G. H. Mickey (reference found in [8]) showed hereditary changes to occur in drosphila germ cells that were exposed to pulsed modulated RF/MW radiation for carrier frequencies between 5-40 MHz [8]. Evidence of RF/MW induced teratogenesis in animals has also been reported by researchers. The effect of exposure to CW radiation was observed by Rugh and McManaway in 1976 (reference found in [8]). They found gross congenital abnormalities in rodent fetuses that were irradiated by a 2450 MHz RF/MW source at an incident power intensity of 107.4 mW/g [8].

iv. Lymphoblastoid Transformations

Lymphoblastoid Transformations refer to changes in the physical nature of lymphoblasts. Mature lymphoblast cells (i.e. lymphocytes) participate in the immune system of the body [18]. Lymphoblastoid transformations induced by RF/MW radiation appear to be similar to transformations present in disorders contributing to abnormal growth in lymphoid tissues and in certain types of leukemia. RF/MW radiation induced transformations, however, do not appear to be malignant and are not likely to spread among healthy cells [8].

W. Stodlink-Baranska reported (reference found in [8]) lymphoblastoid transformations to occur when human lymphocyte cells were exposed to a 2950 MHz pulsed RF/MW source at power density levels of 7 and 20 mW/cm^3. In 1975, P. Czerski also reported (reference found in [8]) observing lymphoblastoid transformations after irradiation of purified human lymphocyte suspensions by an RF/MW source radiating at 2950 MHz for variable power density levels. In addition, Czerski reported acute transformations occurring in adult mice and rabbits that were irradiated by a pulsed RF/MW source radiating at 2950 MHz and at low power density levels of 0.5 and 5 mW/cm^2 respectively [8].

6

v. Oncogenic Effects

Oncogenic effects have been linked to imbalances in the regulatory mechanisms of the body. A 1974 report published by E. Klimkova-Deutschova (reference found in [8]) claimed that persons exposed to RF/MW radiation experience biochemical reactions. The report indicated alterations in fasting blood sugar levels, a decrease in the ability to dispose of normal metabolic waste, and depressed serum levels of pyruvate and lactate. These biochemical reactions point to the possibility of regulatory malfunctions occurring in the body. It has been suggested that certain regulatory imbalances may promote the growth of tumors. A change in hormonal levels has been observed to cause oncogenic effects in tissues that require hormonal balances to function properly. The presence of hormones in other tissue areas may effect the development of existing tumors in those areas [8].

E. Cardiovascular Effects

Most of the cardiovascular effects of RF/MW radiation have been reported by researchers in the Soviet Union and Eastern Europe. Soviet investigators claim that exposure to low levels of RF/MW radiation that are not sufficient to induce hyperthermia can cause aberrations in the cardiovascular system of the body [7].

One experiment performed on rabbits indicates that several types of cardiovascular dysfunctions could be possible. An RF/MW source radiating at 2375 MHz was used to irradiate rabbits for a test period of 60 days under varying field intensities. For field strengths ranging from 3-6 V/M researchers noted a sharp increase in the heart rate of the animals. This effect was observed to subside with time. Exposure to field strengths of 0.5-1.0 V/M caused the heart rate to become slower than normal. No effect was reported for rabbits that were exposed to EM field intensities below 0.2 V/M [17]. Other effects that have been observed by Soviet researchers, are alterations in EKG and low blood pressure [7], [17].

The NIOSH Technical Report [8] references a Soviet study published in 1974 by M. N. Sadcikoiva that suggests some connection between RF/MW radiation exposure and the potential for cardiovascular disturbances in humans. Researchers examined 100 patients suffering from radiation sickness. It was found that 71 of the patients had some type of cardiovascular problem. Most of these patients had been exposed to RF/MW radiation for periods ranging from 5-15 years. A smaller group of patients exposed for shorter time periods also experienced cardiovascular irregularities. The study concluded that there is a probable link between exposure to RF/MW radiation and cardiovascular disease [8].

F. The North Karelian Project

In response to earlier Soviet reports, the World Health Organization (WHO) decided to conduct a comprehensive study on the biological effects of exposure to RF/MW radiation. In 1976, M. Zaret published the results of the study (reference found in [8]). The WHO investigation focused on the population of North Karelia, a remote area of Finland that borders the Soviet Union. This region was selected because of its close proximity to a then Soviet early warning radar station. North Karelia is geographically located in the path of intercontinental ballistic missiles that would originate from the midwest United States. To

7

detect these missiles, the Soviets constructed a number of high power tropospheric scattering radar units adjacent to nearby Lake Ladoga. The operation of these units exposes the residents of North Karelia to large doses of ground and scatter radiation. The WHO investigation found evidence linking exposure of RF/MW radiation to cardiovascular disease and cancer. The North Karelian population suffered from an unusually high number of heart attacks and cases of cancer. In addition, it was found that the affliction rate of these diseases was much higher among residents living closest to the radar site [8].

G. Hematologic Effects

There is evidence that RF/MW radiation can effect the blood and blood forming systems of animals and humans. Experiments conducted in the Soviet Union have indicated changes in blood cell levels and alterations in the biological activities of hematologic elements. Other investigators have reported similar effects [7], [8], [17].

The results of an experiment reported in 1979 by V. M. Shtemier showed a decrease in the biological activity of butyryl cholinesterase in rats that were exposed to pulsed RF/MW radiation (reference found in [17]). The experiment subjected 15 rats to a 3000 MHz pulsed RF/MW source with an incident power density of 10 mW/cm^2. The rats were irradiated for 1 hour/day over several days. After 42 days, there was a loss of biological activity of the butyryl cholinesterase enzyme caused by a decrease in the concentration of the enzyme in the bloodstream of the rats [17]. Cholinesterase is a catalyst in the hydrolysis of acetylcholine into choline and an anion. Choline is a useful enzyme that prevents the deposition of fat in the liver [18].

In another experiment, 20 male rats were exposed to a 2376 MHz pulsed RF/MW source with an incident power density of 24.4 mW/cm$_2$. Each rat was exposed for 4 hours/day, 5 days/week for 7 weeks. Blood samples were taken periodically and examined for anomalies. After repeated exposures, it was discovered that the number of lymphocytes and leukocytes (white blood cells) in the bloodstream of the rats was lower than normal. The biological activity of alkaline phosphatase in neutrophil leukocytes was also found to increase when the rats were irradiated [17].

The results of several other experiments are summarized in the NIOSH Technical Report [8]. RF/MW radiation has been observed to cause: an increase in the amount of exudate in bone marrow, the transient disappearance of fat cells from bone marrow, destruction and loss of essential bone marrow cells, underdeveloped marrow, a decrease in the number of red blood cells, and an imbalance in the number of lymphocytes in the bloodstream [8].

H. Effect to the Central Nervous System

There is documented evidence that exposure to RF/MW radiation can cause a disturbance in the central nervous system (CNS) of living organisms [3], [8], [11], [17]. Soviet investigators claim that exposure to low-level radiation can induce serious CNS dysfunctions. Experiments conducted in the Soviet Union and Eastern Europe have exposed live subjects to radiation levels that are near or below the recommended safe levels prescribed by the ANSI Standard and the USAF AFOSH Standard [17].

8

i. Pathological Report

Soviet investigators claim that the central nervous system (CNS) is highly sensitive to RF/MW radiation [3], [8], [11], [17]. The NIOSH Technical Report [8] summarized the results of a pathological study published by A. A. Letavet and Z. V. Gordon in 1960. The researchers reported that several CNS related disorders were discovered among 525 workers exposed to RF/MW radiation. The symptoms were listed as: hypotension, slower than normal heart rates, an increase in the histamine content of the blood, an increase in the activity of the thyroid gland, disruption of the endocrine-hormonal process, alterations in the sensitivity to smell, headaches, irritability, and increased fatigue. Other researchers have acknowledged similar biological responses [8].

ii. Soviet Union Experimental Results

Several experiments have been performed in the Soviet Union and Eastern Europe that demonstrate a variety of biological effects that can occur in living organisms. observations of laboratory animals subjected to low power EM fields showed alterations in the electrical activity of the cerebral cortex and disruptions in the activity of neurons [17].

L. K. Yereshova and YU. D. Dumanski (reference found in [17]) exposed rabbits and white male rats to a continuous wave 2.50 GHz RF/MW source. The animals were irradiated for 8 hours/day over a period of 3 to 4 months at power density levels of 1, 5, and 10 uW/cm². It was observed that rabbits exposed to the 5 and 10 uW/cm² power density levels suffered alterations in the electrical activity of the cerebra cortex and disturbances to the conditioned reflex response. They concluded that exposure to RF/MW radiation caused perturbations in the higher functioning centers of the CNS in the laboratory animals [17].

An experiment conducted by V. R. Faytel'berg-Blank and G. M. Farevalov demonstrated the biological effects of RF/MW radiation on the activity of neurons (reference found in [17]. They subjected chinchilla rabbits to a 460 MHz RF/MW source at incident power densities of 2 and 5 mW/cm². Only the heads of the rabbits were irradiated and exposures lasted for 10 minutes. Exposure at the 2 mW/cm² power density level caused neuronal activity to increase and evoked an electroencephalogram (EEG) activation reaction. Neuronal activity was observed to decrease at the higher power density level. These results indicated that RF/MW radiation can cause neurophysiological alterations in animals. These biological responses may be dependent on the intensity of the radiation [17].

iii. Behavioral Effects

Exposure to RF/MW radiation has been observed to cause a disruption in the behavior of animals. Experiments conducted on rats and nonhuman primates indicates that conditioned responses can be altered as a result of irradiation. Researchers indicate that behavior may be the most sensitive biological component to RF/MW radiation [1], [7], [9], [29].

D. R. Justesen and N. W. King (reference found in [7]) reported experimental results that demonstrated a degenerative behavioral effect in laboratory animals that were exposed to RF/MW radiation. The results were published in 1970. They exposed rats to a 2450 MHz multimodal resonating cavity system. Exposure was periodic with irradiation times lasting for 5 minutes and recurring every 5 minutes. This cycle as sustained for 60 minutes. The

9

experiment tested the effect of irradiation at whole-body energy absorption rates of 3.0, 6.2, and 9.2 W/Kg. It was observed that for a SAR of 6.2 W/Kg the behavioral performance of the rats degraded significantly and activity usually terminated at the end of the 60 minute exposure period [7].

In 1977, James Lin, Arthur Guy, and Lynn Caldwell [29] reported experimental results that showed alterations in the behavioral response of rats that were exposed to RF/MW radiation. White female rats were trained to execute a "head raising" movement in return for a food pellet. The total number of such movements was counted during each exposure session in order to quantify the effect of irradiation. The animals were exposed to a 918 MHz RF/MW source at power density levels of 10, 20, and 40 mW/cm². Clinical observations showed that baseline responses remained unchanged for irradiation at the lower power density levels of 10 and 20 mW/cm². At 40 mW/cm², however, behavioral responses decreased rapidly after 5 minutes of continuous exposure. After about 15 minutes of exposure, behavioral activity terminated. It was determined that the peak energy absorption at 40 mW/cm² was about 32 W/Kg and the average absorption was 8.4 W/Kg over the whole-body surface [29].

iv. Synergetic Effect of Drugs RF/MW Radiation

In 1979, J. R. Thomas et al. reported that psychoactive drugs and RF/MW radiation may have a synergetic effect on living organisms (references for Thomas can be found in [1]). Experiments were conducted on laboratory animals. Male albino rats were administered dextroamphetamine and irradiated with a pulsed 2450 MHz RF/MW source at 1 W/cm² power intensity for periods of 30 minutes. It was found that the number of clinical responses observed per minute in the rats diminished more rapidly under the stimulus of both agents than in the control condition where just the drug was administered. This indicates that the effects of RF/MW radiation may be enhanced by certain drugs [1].

v. Analeptic Effect in Animals

Pulsed RF/MW radiation was reported to have an analeptic effect in laboratory animals. Experimental results presented by R. D. McAfee in 1971 showed that anethesized animals could be awakened by irradiation from a pulsed 10 GHz RF/MW source. The energy incident on the test animals was estimated to have a power density of between 20-40 mW/cm². Experiments conducted on rats showed that these animals were aroused from states of deep sleep by irradiation. It was observed that the blood pressure of a rat decreased simultaneously with the arousal response and that laryngeal spasms would occur when the rat was awakened. McAfee reported that the laryngeal spasms would obstruct the airway causing convulsions, asphyxiation, and eventually death. Other experiments performed on rabbits, cats, and dogs showed that these animals could also be awakened by irradiation. The larger animals, however, did not asphyxiate themselves. The blood pressure of the dogs and cats was observed to rise as they were awakened. In all cases, the arousal response was stimulated only when the head of the animal was irradiated. The body temperature of the test animals was not observed to rise as a result of irradiation. This indicates that the analeptic effect of RF/MW radiation may be nonthermal in nature [20].

10

I. Immunological Effect

Exposure to RF/MW radiation has been observed to cause physical alterations in the essential cells of the immune system and a degradation of immunologic responses [7], [17]. Experimental results published by Soviet and Eastern European researchers indicate that irradiation can cause injury and trauma to the internal body organs that comprise the immune system. Even exposure to low levels of RF/MW radiation can impair immunologic functions [17].

As discussed earlier, lymphoblasts can undergo physical alterations as a result of irradiation. Lymohiblastoid mutagens are similar in structure to leukemia cells [8]. Lymphoblasts are the precursors to leukocyte cells that participate in the immune system [18].

In 1979, N. P. Zalyubovskaya and R. I. Kiselev (reference found in [17]) reported that exposure to RF/MW radiation caused serious damage to the immune system of laboratory animals. They exposed mice to an RF/MW source radiating at 46.1 GHz with an incident power intensity of 1 mW/cm^2 for 15 minutes/day for 20 days, it was observed that the number of leukocytes in the bloodstream of the mice decreased as a result of irradiation. Effective quantities of enzymatic proteins in serum that combine with antigen-antibody complex and antibacterial agents such as lysozyme were also reduced. Zalyubovskaya and Kiselev reported a decrease in the phagocytic activity of neutrophils and a diminished resistance to infections caused by tetanic toxins. Immunity to typhoid and other tetanic toxins induced by vaccination or by the administration of antitoxins was rendered ineffective. Further examination of the mice revealed injury and trauma to the internal body organs. Irradiation had caused physical alterations in the thymus, spleen, and lymph nodes. The lymphoid organs suffered a total loss of mass [17].

J. Effect on the Eye

Clinical studies indicate that exposure to RF/MW radiation causes physiological damage to the eye that can result in loss of sight. It has been observed that irradiation causes the formation of cataracts in the lens of the eye. Tissue damage appears to be the result of thermal trauma induced by the heating property of RF/MW radiation. Experiments conducted on laboratory animals have demonstrated severe ocular damage as a result of exposure [30], [31].

i. Ocular Sensitivity

Exposure of the eye to RF/MW radiation causes physical duress that can lead to damage of the ocular tissue. The incident power intensity and the duration of radiation exposure are factors that determine the amount of tissue damage. The lens of the eye appears to be most susceptible to RF/MW energy radiated at frequencies between 1-10 GHz. For this frequency range, it has been observed that lens fibers will suffer irreversible damage to a greater extent than other ocular elements [30]. Lens fibers are elongated, thread-like structures that form the substance of the lens [18]. In 1979, Stephen Cleary reported [30] that cataracts are formed in the lens as a result of alterations in the paracystalline state of lens proteins. Physical, chemical or metabolic stress may be responsible for opacification of

11

The FAQ, DEW types, Attenuation and Shielding material sections were co-authored by ChatGPT and certified as "scientifically accurate" by the human resistance. Deploying shielding strategies can be dangerous work if done improperly, so be sure to take the necessary safety precautions before working with shielding materials. Working with metals can mean sharp edges and metal powders can be inhaled. Always use caution when working with metals. No shielding concept or shielding material can be certified as 100% effective against "skynet" energy weapons. Most of the time the problem is related to thickness or choice of materials. Survival is possible if extreme shielding is used. All images and concepts used for this book are subject to "FAIR USE" laws for educational purposes. This book was published by STFN MEDIA and all rights are reserved.

Printed in Great Britain
by Amazon